KINGDOM OF FEATHERS

THE KINGDOM TALES BOOK FOUR

DEBORAH GRACE WHITE

LUMINANT PUBLICATIONS

KINGDOM OF FEATHERS: A RETELLING OF THE WILD SWANS

By Deborah Grace White

For Mel W
For a decade of friendship...and for making this story better.

Oh for the life of a fairy tale royal!

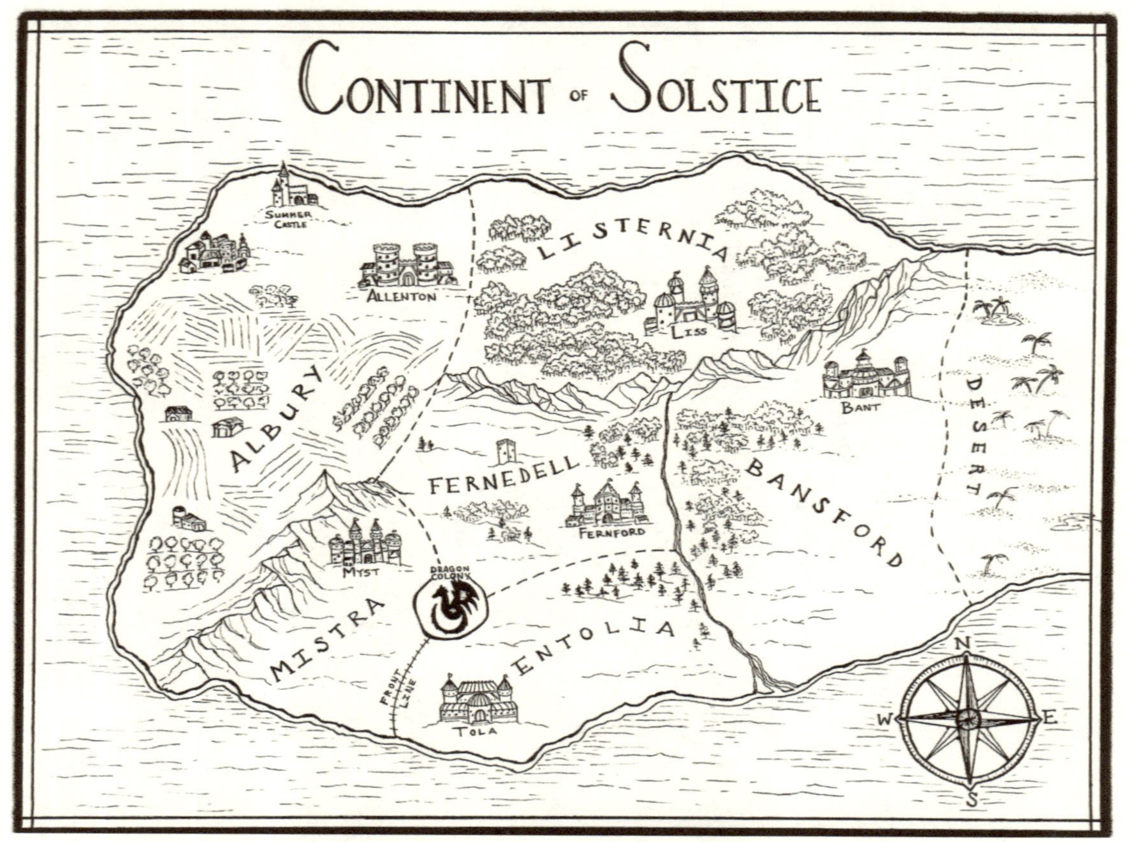

Continent of Solstice
Summer Castle
Allenton
Listernia
Liss
Desert
Bant
Albury
Fernedell
Bansford
Fernford
Myst
Dragon Colony
Mistra
Front Line
Entolia
Tola
N
W
E
S

<u>Royal family of Mistra</u>
King Lloyd – Queen Liana
– Crown Prince Caleb (27)
– Prince Averett (25)
– Prince Bram (23)
– Prince Conan (22)
– Prince Lyall (20)
– Prince Ari (18)
– Princess Wren (17)

<u>Royal family of Entolia</u>

King Thorn – Queen Lucille

- Crown Prince Basil (18)
- Princess Zinnia (17)
- Princess Lilac (16)
- Princess Violet (14)
- Princess Daisy (12)
- Princess Briar (11)
- Princess Jasmine (9)
- Princess Magnolia (9)
- Princess Cassia (7)
- Princess Dahlia (6)
- Princess Holly (4)
- Princess Ivy (4)
- Princess Wisteria (3)

Wren

"Wren, do you *ever* stop talking?"

Wren scowled at her brother's tone, but gave the question her genuine consideration. "I'm not talking when I sleep," she produced at last.

"Are you sure?" muttered another brother, Ari, from next to her. Wren's only answer was to shove him with her shoulder.

"Your Highness," scolded the middle aged woman walking sedately along behind the princess. "Don't make me regret giving you leave to accompany your brothers on this expedition."

"*We* already regret it," Ari said. "Who wants an eleven-year-old *girl* tagging along on a hunt?"

The taunting grin that accompanied his words told Wren he was saying it to rile her up more than anything. He knew that if she retaliated, she would again be reprimanded by her governess. Given he was only twelve himself, he should really have been with his own tutor, but everyone knew the youngest prince had the man wrapped around his finger.

"I don't see why only princes get to go on hunts and things,"

Wren said mutinously. "Why do you all get to run around in the forest while I have to sit inside and embroider?"

Bram, the brother who had complained about her talking, rolled his eyes. At seventeen, he had more restraint than Ari, but hadn't yet developed the patience of his older two brothers. "It's not because you're a girl that we didn't want you to come, Wren," he said, shooting her a look. "It's because you scare off the birds, with your chatter, and your general…" he waved his arm vaguely, "bouncing around."

Wren was indeed bouncing on the balls of her feet as she followed her six older brothers through the small wood that backed onto their castle. It was such a rare treat to be outside with them instead of inside with her governess, she couldn't help herself.

"Yeah," Ari agreed, nodding sagely. "An eleven-year-old is far too young to be on a hunt."

"You're only twelve!" Wren protested. "And I'll be twelve soon."

"By then I'll be thirteen," Ari shot back. But the familiar argument was interrupted by yet another brother.

"Enough." Averett, the second-oldest prince, sounded impatient. "You're both far too young to be on a hunt, and the fact that you think this is a real hunt shows it. As if any quarry would still be hanging around with all the racket you're making. Father just wanted us all out of the castle while he spoke to the envoy from Entolia, so he had Caleb suggest a hunt."

"Averett."

Caleb didn't raise his voice, but everyone fell instantly silent. He'd always had a commanding presence, for as long as Wren could remember. Perhaps it was because he was the oldest, and the heir. Perhaps it was also that, at the age of twenty-one, he was far past any childish rivalries with his younger siblings.

Whatever it was, Wren had always considered Caleb to be

just about the most incredible person in the world. Her heart swelled as he sent a swift frown toward Bram and Ari.

"Leave Wren alone, you two. She has as much right to be here as any of us." His voice turned dry as he glanced at Averett. "And if it's not a *real* hunt, then I see no reason why she can't talk as much as she wants."

Averett shrugged, clearly unrepentant. "I didn't complain about her talking."

Bram—the initial complainer—rolled his eyes for a second time. But Wren didn't care about his scolding now, any more than she cared about Averett's habitual brashness. Caleb had taken her part, and that was all that mattered. When the crown prince flashed a small smile toward his sister, Wren abandoned her place at the back of the group beside Ari, and tripped forward to her oldest brother's side.

"Hey Magpie," he said, in his quiet, friendly way.

She gave him the lightest of shoves at the nickname, but she wasn't really annoyed. It was apt, after all. She did tend to chatter.

Averett gave her a long-suffering look, but Caleb shook his head at his brother.

"She can walk with us, Rett, don't be so sour. She won't carry tales." He followed the words with the hint of a wink in Wren's direction.

Elated, Wren slipped her hand into Caleb's, almost jogging to keep up with his long, steady strides. Ten years older than her, Caleb had treated her with kindness from her earliest memory. And now that he was fully grown, he was an even more awe-inspiring figure.

Eager to show herself worthy of this trust, Wren fell silent, more than happy just to listen to her two oldest brothers' conversation.

"I'm surprised you didn't want to be part of the discussion

with the Entolian envoy," Averett said, his gaze sharp as it rested on Caleb. "If tensions over this border issue are as serious as I thought, I would have expected you to want a say in the negotiations."

"They're more serious," said Caleb curtly, and Wren saw Averett raise an eyebrow. "There was a skirmish yesterday."

"What, actual fighting?" Averett demanded. "Soldiers shed blood?"

"There were no deaths," Caleb said, his voice grim. "But there was fighting."

"Entolia is ready to go to war over a few leagues of land?" Averett said incredulously.

Caleb shot his brother a look. "A few leagues with more iron than the rest of our two kingdoms put together. They're probably shaking their heads, asking whether Mistra is really ready to go to war over a few leagues of land."

"But it's on our side of the border!" Averett insisted.

Caleb sighed. "Well, that depends on who you ask, doesn't it? That border has been in dispute for a hundred years. Did we really expect them to cede our claim just when iron ore has been discovered there?"

Averett fell silent, frowning. "Surely we won't actually go to war over this." He cast his brother a look full of meaning. "Will we?"

Wren felt a flicker of surprise at the alarm in her usually over-confident brother's voice. What did Averett have to worry about? She knew, in a vague way, that war was bad. But nothing bad was going to happen to Mistra. Caleb wouldn't allow it. He was the strongest and bravest person she knew. It was impossible not to feel safe with him looking after things.

"No one wants it to come to that," Caleb assured Averett, his calm voice reinforcing Wren's confidence. "That's why Father wanted today's discussions to be as non-threatening as possible.

It will just be him and the chief advisor meeting with the envoy."

"Your Highness." Unnoticed by Wren, the castle's head huntsman had come up on Averett's other side. He spoke in a hushed voice, and the two princes fell silent. "I've been scouting ahead, and there's a bevy of swans at the lake."

Bram appeared behind them, the next brother down—Conan—at his side. "Excellent. Maybe we'll get some sport this morning after all."

"Oh, don't shoot the swans," protested Wren, forgetting her intention to remain admirably silent. "They're so beautiful—I love them!"

"Do you, girly?"

The cackle made them all start. Caleb, Averett, Bram, and Conan all reached instinctively for the hilts of their swords, and Wren understood why. The aged woman who emerged from the trees up ahead looked neither strong nor skilled. Yet there was something sinister about her. Wren could only be glad when Caleb pushed her behind him.

"Who are you?" demanded Mistra's crown prince. "How do you come to be in the castle woods?"

But the old woman ignored him. Her eyes remained on Wren, and she was still cackling, as though the princess's defense of the swans had been especially humorous. "Don't worry, girl, your brothers won't be able to kill the swans once I've killed them first. Not that you'll be alive to appreciate it, either. They'll never find so much as a piece of any of you when I'm done."

Her words acted like a trigger. The scream let loose by Wren's governess was lost in the scuffle, as the various guards and huntsmen in their group sprang into action. Caleb's sword was out of its sheath before Wren could blink, but he hung back, allowing his guards to do their job.

Only they couldn't. Their sudden activity just made the old woman cackle more loudly. Not one of the guards had reached her when she raised her hands and shrieked something inaudible. At once, everyone dropped like stones, with the exception of the seven royal siblings. Wren screamed, sure for a horrible moment that her governess, and all the others in their group, were dead.

But as she stared, eyes wide and horrified, at the closest felled guard, she saw the man's chest rising and falling. She didn't know what kind of magic could incapacitate a dozen people all at once, but there was no doubt left in her mind that this woman was an enchantress.

All the magic-users Wren had so far met had been as well-intentioned as they were impressive, usually attending the castle to perform a service for the crown. Never before had she seen magic used for evil, and she felt paralyzed with terror as the realization of her own powerlessness washed over her. Caleb raised his sword, and a measure of security returned to Wren's panicked mind. Her eldest brother would protect her. He would protect all of them.

"How dare you?" Caleb demanded, and authority seemed to radiate from him.

But apparently, the enchantress didn't feel it. Laughing in his face, she lifted her hands before her.

"Your father thought he could toss me aside, but I'll have the last laugh." Her eyes slid to Wren, still cowering behind Caleb. The old woman's gaze was unfocused, and she looked thoroughly mad. "Time to save your swans, girl." And she thrust out a hand toward Caleb.

The crown prince took a half step forward, then fell to his knees with a cry of pain. Wren heard the shocked, angry shouts of her five other brothers, but she couldn't pull her eyes from Caleb. The sight of her strong, steady brother in a posture of defeat sent fire racing through her veins. With a scream of horror, she threw herself forward, draping her small body over his strong frame. Her hair, fanning around her in the usual frizzy mane that was the despair of her maids, hid the enchantress from her sight, but she could feel the woman's magic. It reached into every inch of her body, pain flowing with it, and a scream was ripped from her throat.

"Wren, no!"

Caleb's yell was accompanied by a gesture Wren could make no sense of. Her hand was seized, and she felt something small and hard slipped over her finger. Her mind was too consumed by fear to grasp what Caleb was doing, but at once the pain stopped. She found herself on her knees, coughing and gagging as feeling returned to her limbs.

A grunt of pain brought her head snapping up, and she stared with horror at the sight of all six of her brothers writhing on the ground.

"Stop!" she screamed, stumbling to her feet and throwing herself at the enchantress. "Stop!"

The woman faltered for a moment, her eyes confused as she took in Wren's clearly unaffected form. "No matter," she hissed, spit flying from her mouth. "You'll have your turn in a minute." She turned back to the princes, letting out a guttural grunt that showed just how much energy she was pouring into her curse.

With a scream, Wren flew at her, scrabbling desperately at the woman's upraised hands. The enchantress let out an ear-splitting shriek.

"Don't interfere, swan-girl!"

Wren had no magic in her blood, and therefore couldn't sense power the way an enchantress could. But even she could feel the force that burst out from the woman, throwing Wren backward and washing over the still-writhing princes. Facedown on the ground, Wren lifted her head from the dirt, terrified of what she would see. But instead of lifeless forms, her eyes fell on a sight more bizarre than anything she'd ever imagined.

All six of her brothers were shrinking, their bodies changing before her eyes. Caleb, nearest to her, reached out a protective hand, as if to pull her to safety. But even as Wren stretched her own arm toward him, his smooth brown skin transformed into white feathers, and instead of an arm, it was a wing lying across the forest floor.

As unbelievable as it seemed, there was no denying the evidence of her eyes. Not just Caleb, but all six of them had been turned into—

"Swans?!" shrieked the old woman. She turned to Wren with murder in her eyes. "Swans! This is your fault! Do you have any idea how powerful that magic was? How rare? It was supposed to kill you all, not turn them into swans!"

The enchantress made as if to advance, but clearly her strength was spent. With a grunt of pain, she fell to the forest floor, her eyes still fixed on Wren.

"Nothing...left..." she muttered. "All that extra power... gone...for nothing..."

"Turn them back!" Wren screamed, falling to her knees and shaking the enchantress. "Turn them back!"

A thin cackle arose from the woman before her. "Can't... none left...all that power they offered me..." A violent coughing fit interrupted her speech, and Wren's panic rose.

"What power? Who offered it to you?" she demanded desperately.

But she could see the madness in the woman's eyes, and was unsurprised to receive a nonsensical answer. "In a dream," the enchantress said, her voice singsong. "But it's all gone now." Suddenly the woman gasped, her eyes flying open. "The counterforce!" she cried. "I haven't crafted the counterforce yet. That won't take extra power. I can still do that!"

"Yes!" Wren said eagerly, struggling to remember what she'd been taught about enchantments.

She knew it was normal practice to build a counterforce into an enchantment, providing some way to break it. Some kind of natural counterforce always existed, and by building in a remedy, the enchanter could control that counterforce. An enchanter who didn't do so ran the risk of the subject of the curse discovering the natural counterforce and using it to break the enchantment entirely.

Wren knew that in the case of malicious curses, such as whatever this enchantress had done, a built-in counterforce was likely to be something horrible, such as a requirement that she exchange her life for that of her brothers. But she didn't care. Whatever it was, she would do it. The idea of being left in the dark, with no way to change her brothers back to their true forms, was much worse. She doubted she would have success figuring out the natural counterforce—most likely even the enchantress wouldn't be able to do so, since turning the princes into swans wasn't even what she'd intended to do.

"You should've...stayed out of...it..." The enchantress's brief moment of excitement had passed, and she was once again flagging. "But you're in it now." She waved a hand feebly, but with purpose. "You're bound up in the curse, and you can't escape it."

"What's the counterforce?" Wren cried, impatient of the woman's ramblings.

All around her, those who were supposed to protect and guide her lay unconscious on the ground. And her brothers, even the seemingly invincible Caleb, were nothing but a bevy of birds, stirring feebly and flapping awkward wings as they struggled to rise from the ground. There was no one but her, and she *had* to get answers before the enchantress succumbed to the darkness that seemed to be closing in on her.

"The counterforce!" she yelled again, when the woman

didn't respond. "What is it? Tell me! Tell me what I have to do! Tell me how to change them back! Say something! Tell me—"

"Silence!" snapped the woman. "Stop shouting and let me die in peace!"

"But—"

"Not a word!" shrieked the enchantress. Her eyes flew open, and the madness was back in them. It made Wren's blood run cold, but she forced herself to lean in, hoping desperately to hear something she could use. "That's it," cackled the old woman. "Not a word. You're bound up in the curse now, and so is your voice. You mustn't say a word, you mustn't tell anyone," she gestured vaguely at the swans, one of whom had found its webbed feet and was now advancing menacingly, "or they'll die. All of them, one by one!"

Wren gasped in horror, and the woman's laugh was cut off by another cough. "Yes, that's good," she muttered feverishly. "It's the counterforce, so it costs me nothing extra. The others can't even be angry with me—they'll still get their war. Because you can't possibly succeed, so in the end I'll win." She glanced up at Wren, and seemed to see the blazing determination in the princess's eyes. "Think you can do it, girly? By all means, try. Six years I've suffered—if you can stay silent for six years, the magic's hold will break. They'll probably return to their human forms then." She shrugged a careless shoulder. "Who can say? I didn't intend to turn them into swans, so I can't be sure."

She coughed again, and there was malice in her eyes. "But you'll never last six years. And when you fail, you'll kill them."

Before Wren could do a thing, the enchantress fell back limply, the feverish light fading from her eyes.

"No!" Wren cried, unthinkingly.

At once, the swan who had waddled closest—Caleb, she was pretty sure—let out an agonized honking sound and fell onto its side. Restraining her scream of horror with every ounce of willpower she possessed, Wren raced to the bird's side. The creature was lying on the forest floor, its eyes unnervingly familiar as it stared up at her. It was breathing hard, and when it tried to right itself, one wing seemed to be bent and painful. The other five swans were waddling over now, surrounding the one who had fallen.

A groan drew Wren's attention to one of the guards, and she realized with a leap of her heart that the rest of the group were coming around. She stumbled to the man's side, tugging at his arm until he regained full consciousness.

"Your Highness," he said, sounding dazed. "What..." He glanced around, his brow furrowed. As he looked, others stirred as well. The guard's gaze settled on the enchantress's body, and his eyes widened. But before he could speak, another groan sounded from alongside him.

"What in the blazes is going on?" It was the huntsman who had approached Caleb earlier, and he scowled disapprovingly at the birds milling around the clearing. "So much for hunting the swans," he muttered. "No sport in pursuing such tame birds." He flapped a hand. "Be off with you."

"Where are the princes?" The sharp voice brought Wren's attention back to the guard. He was raking the area frantically with his gaze, and Wren could see her own panic growing behind his eyes.

She opened her mouth to tell him exactly where her brothers were, and only just remembered in time. Clamping it shut, she curled her fists in frustration. What could she do? How could she tell them? And even if she could tell them, how would they fix this?

Her parents. They were the ones she needed to find. She had to get back to the castle.

Pushing herself to her feet, she ran. She could hear chaos erupting behind her, as everyone in the group tried to understand what was happening. She could imagine what they were all thinking—the last thing they'd heard was the mad enchantress announcing her intention to kill all seven of the royals. Then they'd been knocked out, and awoken to find only her.

No one would be pleased with the identity of the survivor.

Pounding feet told Wren she was being pursued, and she even thought she heard the flapping of wings. But she didn't turn. Within minutes she was hurtling through the door of the castle, two guards at her heels. She knew where her father would be meeting with the Entolian envoy, and she directed her steps straight there. Ignoring the startled protests of the guards outside the door, she threw herself into the room.

"Wren!" King Lloyd gasped, his expression shocked.

Wren came to a halt, panting hard. She realized how foolish she must look, racing into the room with such frantic haste, only to stand there silently.

"Wren, what is going on?" the king demanded. His eyes flicked to the guards behind her.

"Your Majesty," one of the guards gasped. He wiped a hand across his sweaty forehead, and Wren could see in his eyes how reluctant he was to be the one to bring this message. "We were attacked, in the castle woods."

"What?" King Lloyd stepped toward them. Movement behind the king drew Wren's eyes, and she frowned at the sight of the Entolian envoy shifting nervously.

"An enchantress, Your Majesty," the guard went on. "She... she said she would kill the princes, and the princess, and then she did something...I don't know what happened. We were all knocked unconscious, and when we awoke...when we awoke..."

"Well?" King Lloyd demanded, his furious impatience unsuccessfully concealing the terror beneath it.

"The enchantress was dead. It looked as though she'd used

more power than her body could survive. And...and the princess was the only one left."

The guard's words seemed to ring in the silence that followed. Wren saw her father's gaze move slowly to her face, and she shook her head frantically.

"What is it, Wren?" he asked. "Do you know where your brothers are?"

As he asked the question, a different sound reached Wren's ears. Everyone in the room looked over at the rattle of the window, and Wren blinked in amazement as she saw two swans flapping their wings against the glass. They'd followed her. That was encouraging—hopefully it meant they still retained their right minds. She hadn't liked the idea of trying to identify them among the rest of the swans at the lake.

"Those swans are still all excited," muttered the other guard, and the king sent an inquiring look toward him.

"We were hunting swans when the woman attacked, Your Majesty," he explained. "But they were a little too tame for sport."

Wren stamped her foot, frustration eating at her. She gestured wildly toward the swans, but her father just blinked in confusion.

"Wren? Why don't you speak! Where are your brothers? What happened?"

Again Wren gestured at the window, but she could see from everyone's blank faces that her message wasn't getting through. Casting her eyes around the room, she brightened at the sight of a writing desk. Hurrying toward it, she pulled a piece of blank parchment onto the flat surface and seized a quill. She wasn't allowed to talk, but surely she was allowed to write.

The woman attacked us. She said you'd cast her aside, and she was going to kill us all as revenge. But it didn't work, at least not fully. They're

The scratching of her quill ceased abruptly at the loud honk. Wren froze, terrified. It was the same sound she'd heard from one of the swans when she spoke that one illicit word back in the forest, and it was unmistakably an expression of pain.

She dropped the quill as though it had burned her. What had she done? Surely writing was allowed. Two whole sentences she'd managed, with no repercussions. She'd been about to write, *They're not dead*, but apparently doing so had breached the conditions of the curse.

What had the enchantress said?

You mustn't say a word, you mustn't tell anyone, or they'll die.

Clearly the prohibition against saying a word was absolute. No talking, no exceptions. But perhaps the second part, forbidding her to tell anyone, meant that she couldn't communicate her brothers' fate even by means other than speaking. Wren trembled with fear. Had the swan survived her mistake? And how would she get the help her brothers needed now?

She felt her father's gaze on her, and looked back at him.

"Wren?" he demanded. "Did she put some kind of silencing curse on you?"

Wren paused, fearful of telling him more details. Who knew which aspects of the incident would be captured by the curse? Besides, the enchantress hadn't cursed her. She shook her head slowly, and was relieved when no further squawk of pain came through the window.

Her father placed a hand on her shoulder. He was clearly trying to be gentle, but she could feel the way his whole body quivered with tension.

"What happened, Wren? Tell me."

She just shook her head, tears of frustration welling in her eyes. Looking over her shoulder, her father scanned her half-finished message, and she saw a shudder go over him.

"They can't be dead," he whispered, his voice coming out nothing like its usual commanding tones.

Wren looked back at him miserably, desperate to reassure him, terrified of killing Caleb and the others if she did so.

If she hadn't killed Caleb already.

Tears once again filled her eyes, as she realized how paralyzed she truly was. The look on her father's face was torture to behold, but it was better that he temporarily think his sons were dead than that they actually died as a result of her telling him the truth.

Her father again scanned her message. "It didn't work fully," he read quietly. His eyes returned to her. "I see that." He was barely holding himself together. Wren gripped his arm, whether giving or seeking comfort, she didn't know. "But how did you survive, Wren?" the king whispered.

Even as he said the words, his eyes seemed drawn to her hand, where it rested on his arm. He frowned and, following his gaze, Wren saw what was on her own finger. Caleb's signet ring. That was what he'd slid onto her finger when she tried to throw herself between him and the curse. She remembered clutching her fist in an unconscious instinct to keep it on as she ran back to the palace, but she hadn't actually stopped to look at it until now. The familiar Mistran crest decorated it, formed out of a dull red stone.

"So that's how..." Her father trailed off, and his eyes flew to hers. "Caleb gave it to you? When he saw you were in danger?"

Wren nodded. She was confused by her father's tone, and even more confused when he suddenly buried his face in his hands. Desperate frustration arose in her when he didn't explain himself. It was infuriating not to be able to just ask him. She tugged on his sleeve insistently, and after a moment he lowered his hands.

"That ring carries a powerful protective enchantment," he said hollowly, his voice a hoarse whisper she could barely hear. "Incredibly powerful. It is rare and valuable magic, or I would have had one made for all of my children. As it was, I could only provide one for my heir…"

His voice trailed off, and something icy seemed to drop into Wren's stomach. Her father didn't need to finish the thought. She understood perfectly. Caleb was the heir, the future of Mistra. If only one of the seven of them could survive, it should be him. She didn't blame her father for what she read on his face—that he would have chosen for Caleb, not her, to be the one wearing the ring when the curse hit them all. She didn't even disagree. She'd much rather be stuck as a swan while Caleb found a way to fix everything than be charged with the responsibility of rescuing all her brothers alone.

But still, the anguish on her father's face as he stared at the ring stung a little. She couldn't help it.

"But I don't understand," the king burst out, clearly still not ready to accept it. "Magic that powerful—to fell so many with one blow. There's no way one enchantress could—"

Spinning around, Wren grabbed hold of the parchment again. Tentatively, trying not to be too specific, she added to her message.

She said she had help. She talked about others, and extra power. She said "they'll still get their war".

No further sound came from outside, and she let out a breath of relief, laying down the quill with finality. It seemed important to impart that information, but that was it. She wasn't going to tempt fate by testing the boundaries any further.

"War? Extra power?" The king's voice took on an ominous note. "Whose power?"

Wren shook her head helplessly. She had no more idea than he did. But as the king's gaze slid, with growing fury, to the Entolian envoy standing horror struck by the window, Wren suddenly understood. Dimly, she remembered Caleb telling Averett about the conflict with Entolia. Averett had said that the Entolians surely wouldn't go to war, but Caleb hadn't seemed so sure. He must have suspected their neighbors were willing to fight. But surely they wouldn't stoop to such depths as this?

"Get her out."

It took Wren a moment to realize that the king was speaking of her. By the time she understood, the guards were already dragging her gently backward.

"And one of you, take two squadrons and return to the castle woods. Scour every inch of it for the princes, and bring back the body of this enchantress."

"Yes, Your Majesty."

Wren didn't even protest. She was desperate to get to the swans, to check that all six were still alive. Almost at the door, she heard her father's quiet voice, something in its tones more terrifying than the maniacal screams of the enchantress.

"You."

"Your Majesty, I assure you that—"

The guards slammed the door shut on the Entolian envoy's words, but even from the other side, Wren heard her father's scream of fury.

"SILENCE!"

Clearly now that his eleven-year-old daughter was no longer before him, he was allowing the dam of his grief and fury to burst. He continued to shout, but Wren couldn't make out the words. Her governess appeared at her side, visibly shaken and showing unmistakable signs of tears.

"Come along, Your Highness," she said. "Come with me, now."

Wren clutched Caleb's signet ring in her fist, barely able to make sense of the emotions coursing through her. In spite of her governess's presence, she'd never felt so alone, or so terrified. How could she sustain this crippling, isolating silence? She stood frozen, with no idea what she should do next.

She wasn't given the opportunity to decide. She was shepherded firmly to her rooms, although not quickly enough to avoid glimpsing the body of the enchantress as it was carried into the castle by a pair of guards. Wren shuddered, and made no further protest about being herded into her suite.

The rest of the day passed in a horrifying blur that Wren knew she would never forget. Her mother's explosion of emotions was even worse than her father's, and Wren thought she would lose her mind with the horror of knowing her brothers were alive and not being able to tell her parents. The castle was in complete uproar within the hour, and from her window, Wren saw the Entolian envoy mount his horse in the castle courtyard, and ride hard out of the southern gate.

By mid-afternoon, the servants were whispering about murder and war.

Wren, of course, didn't whisper. She didn't mutter so much

as a single word. Everyone was understandably unnerved by her silence, and she was watched every minute. Accordingly, she had no opportunity to seek out her brothers until night fell. The maid who was keeping watch in her room soon fell asleep, exhausted by the day's excitement, and apparently convinced by Wren's own feigned slumber.

The princess slipped out of bed, wondering how she was going to get past the six guards currently stationed outside her door.

But she didn't need to. As she was padding across the room, she heard a tap on the window. Glancing over, she stifled a gasp at the sight of a swan, hovering in mid-air and—unless she was much mistaken—glaring at her through the glass.

She raced to the window and opened the catchment. Awkwardly, the swan glided in. She searched its figure hopelessly. Which one was it? Impossible to tell.

The swan dropped to the floor and folded its wings inexpertly. When Wren stood motionless, at a loss for what to do next, it reached out and tweaked her nightdress with its beak. It still seemed irritated, judging by the way it was ruffling its feathers.

She knelt down, reaching a tentative hand toward it. The moment she touched the swan's glossy feathers, a familiar—and rather abrasive—voice filled her mind.

Now how do I get you to understand?

She jumped, her mouth falling open in a silent gasp. Focusing hard, she pressed her hand against the bird's surprisingly warm side, and just *thought* the words.

Averett? Is that you?

The swan stilled, staring up at her from small, beady eyes.

Yes, it's me. How are you doing that?

I don't know, Wren thought, exasperated. *Do you think I have any idea what's going on? You're the one who's a sort-of talking swan.*

The swan-Averett flapped his wings in agitation, and Wren glanced nervously toward the sleeping maid. Pressing her hand back against his side, she added, *Where are the others?*

The swan jerked its head toward the window. *Down in the gardens.*

Wren swallowed, afraid to ask. *Caleb?*

Somehow, Averett's gruff tone came through perfectly, even inside her mind. *He's in a state. Something happened to him back in the clearing, and again when we approached the castle.*

Blinking back tears, Wren rocked back on her heels. Averett didn't yet realize it had been her fault. She hardly knew what to say. Pushing herself to her feet, she padded quietly to the window. Her suite was on the castle's second level. Looking down, she could see five swans huddled on the ground below, their very avian heads raised to her window. One of them—noticeably the largest—had one wing folded at an awkward angle.

Without giving herself time to think too hard about it, Wren clambered onto the window sill. She'd never done this before, but she knew both Bram and Conan, her third and fourth brothers, had climbed out their windows many times.

One of the swans—most likely Caleb—made an admonitory trumpeting sound at her risky behavior, but she ignored it. Lowering herself slowly, she searched with her bare toes for a foothold on the stone. She managed to get halfway down the first level before she tumbled, with a total lack of royal dignity, into the bush positioned directly below her window.

Ow, she thought ruefully, only just remembering in time not to speak the word aloud. Before she could scramble to her feet, she was surrounded by trumpeting, flapping swans. Averett glided down from her window sill to join them, with only marginally more dignity than Wren's descent.

The largest swan flapped its wings in agitation as Wren

crawled out of the bush. The action caused it to let out a honk of pain as its injured wing was jostled.

Reaching out, Wren laid a hand against the bird's heaving side.

Caleb? Can you…I don't know what this is. Hear my thoughts?

The swan bugled, but while Wren's ears heard the absurd sound, her mind heard Caleb's voice, just as she'd heard Averett's.

Yes, I can hear you. I don't understand what's happening.

Wren shook her head. She doubted anyone had those answers. Even if the enchantress wasn't lying dead inside the castle, even she had clearly been taken by surprise by the effect of her own magic. Casting her mind back over those terrifying minutes when—but for the swans—she'd been alone in the clearing with the dying enchantress, Wren pressed her fingers against the swan-Caleb's feathers.

All I can think of is that she said I'm bound up in the curse some-how, even though it didn't actually get me. She turned reproachful eyes to Caleb. *You shouldn't have given me your protective ring, Caleb.*

He shook out his good wing, his long swan's neck snaking from side to side.

Of course I should, he trumpeted. *You're my little sister. I'm supposed to protect you.*

Wren's eyes filled with tears as his words reminded her of how she'd failed to protect him. *Are you all right?* she thought at him. *It's my fault you're injured, Caleb. I'm not allowed to speak, or the curse will kill you. And I don't think I'm allowed to write about what happened either. I'm so sorry.*

I know, Caleb bugled, obviously catching on more quickly than Averett had. *I heard what the enchantress said.* His words became stern in her mind, although his birdlike noises communicated nothing in particular. *And don't apologize. This isn't your fault. I won't let you carry our burden.*

Wren didn't answer. She had a horrible feeling that she had no choice but to carry the burden, but she wasn't ready to face that reality yet.

One by one, she laid a tentative hand against each of the swans, identifying them in turn. She could hear them in her mind, but only when she was physically touching them. She took momentary comfort from confirming that they were all there, and all in possession of their senses.

The blind panic had subsided slightly since discovering she could communicate with her brothers, but when she reached twelve-year-old Ari, the relief melted away. The smallest of the swans filled her mind with a barrage of terrified questions, none of which she could answer, and she once again felt panic rising within her.

Apparently sensing her distress, the Caleb-swan waddled forward. He gave a sharp honk, and Ari subsided. Since she wasn't touching him at the time, Wren couldn't understand Caleb's words. But it seemed as though her other brothers could. Certainly these weren't ordinary swans, and she could only be grateful for it.

The Caleb-swan lifted his good wing and placed it reassuringly on Wren's arm. Instead of being comforted, Wren felt unnerved at seeing such a human gesture from a bird.

It's going to be all right, Wren. We'll fix it.

Wren looked at her brother out of wide, terrified eyes, and she knew, for the first time in her life, that he was wrong. Yesterday, she would have accepted Caleb's certainty without question, trusting him to fix everything. This was Caleb. Strong, unshakable, always in control.

But her world had dramatically changed since yesterday. In the long hours in her room, as she searched her mind for a way around the curse's restrictions, she'd slowly given in to the horrible reality. Caleb had no more control over their situation than she did. Her big brother was no longer invincible—he'd been beaten by a madwoman, and now he couldn't protect anyone anymore, least of all Wren. On the contrary, his very life was in her hands, his safety dependent on her ability to curb her chattering tongue.

For six years.

Royal or not, with six older brothers, Wren had never really had responsibility for anything. And now, she carried the future of the kingdom. Already she'd maimed the heir to the throne, and in his current form, they had no way of knowing how serious the damage was, or whether it would heal. And if she spoke another word, it might be enough to kill him.

The horror of that thought washed over her, and for a moment all she wanted to do was curl up on amid the bushes and cry. The crazed enchantress was right—there was no way she could do it. She'd slip up, and her brothers would pay the price.

But as the six swans gathered around her, trumpeting softly and brushing their wings against her nightdress, Wren felt determination spreading through her. She ran her fingers over the soft feathers of their wings, giving them a silent promise. She wouldn't let either them or Mistra pay the price for that evil woman's madness. She would just have to be stronger than she thought she was. There was nothing else to it. At least she wouldn't be totally alone, not if she could speak to her brothers through the strange connection the curse had forged.

She couldn't find a way around the curse, so she would have to achieve the impossible challenge set her by the one who'd cast it. It wasn't as if she had to be clever, or perform some complex task. She just had to swallow her words for six years, and at the end of them, her brothers would be restored to her, and the kingdom would once again have its heir.

She could do it.

She had to do it.

It was only six years. She'd lived almost twice that already. How hard could it be?

FIVE YEARS, NINE MONTHS, AND TWELVE DAYS LATER...

CHAPTER ONE

Basil

"Enough of this posturing!"

Basil sighed at the familiar anger in his father's voice. Life in Entolia's royal castle held two certainties. The sun would rise over the eastern cliffs, and the king would lose his temper within the first five minutes of any council regarding the war with Mistra.

Basil made little attempt to hide his impatience as his eyes scanned the assembled advisors. If they shared his sentiments, they didn't show it. Too well-trained, perhaps. But Basil had never been reluctant to let his father know his opinions.

"Almost six years they've been violating our borders!" King Thorn raged. "And still we let them walk all over us?! Someone explain to me why we haven't finished this!"

Basil's eyes fell on his mother, who happened to be present for this particular council. She gave him a small frown, silently reproving him for his open displeasure. Heroically resisting the urge to roll his eyes, he gave her a long-suffering look. He knew what she would say if they were alone. She would remind him that his father's injury, and the ongoing pain he experienced from it, made him short-tempered.

Basil wasn't convinced.

It wasn't as though he had no sympathy for his father. There was no doubt the king was often in considerable pain, including right now, if Basil was any judge of his father's body language. But Basil had been twelve when the Mistrans had launched the attack that turned their little border skirmish into full scale hostilities. He was plenty old enough to remember a time before the war. And to remember that King Thorn had always been short-tempered.

The queen's frown made it seem as though she could read his thoughts. Basil allowed himself a small smile. She just about could, most likely. He'd said it all before, and he knew neither of his parents had much appreciation for his bluntness. But he didn't believe in swallowing his words, or dancing around unpleasant truths. A king was more in need of plain speaking than anyone, the way Basil saw it.

The trouble was, most of the counselors in the room were too wary of the irritable king to tell him what he didn't want to hear. Fortunately, Basil's position wasn't one that could be stripped away if he offended his sovereign.

Or unfortunately, depending how you looked at it.

Basil sighed again, shifting so that his elbows rested on the table before him. "We haven't 'finished' it, Father, because our forces are no stronger than theirs. And because an attempt to push an offensive past the disputed territory and storm their capital could just as easily end up with Mistran troops storming ours. And no one wants that."

King Thorn scowled at his only son. "I didn't realize you were such a military expert, Basil."

Basil met his father look for look. "I don't need to be an expert to know it would benefit no one for the war to consume our whole kingdom, or theirs."

"Have you forgotten," the king demanded, his voice again

rising angrily, "that *they* started this? They are the ones who sent highly-trained guards to ambush our commander, attacking *me* in the process!"

"Well, they didn't know it was you," said Basil fairly. "They just got lucky that the king happened to be paying an unannounced visit to the army's commander."

"LUCKY?!" roared his father. But predictably, the exertion ignited the old wound to the king's lung, and he broke off, violent coughs rocking his once-strong frame.

Basil winced in sympathy as his father bent over, gripping one side of his chest as he continued to cough and wheeze. The prince felt a little chastened for his impatience with his father. That one powerful thrust from a spear shaft—or rather, the collapsed lung that had resulted from it—really had stolen the king's strength, and probably many years from his life. It was enough to make even a milder man short of temper.

"Forgive me, Father, I meant lucky from their perspective," Basil amended hastily. "Although I'm not sure even they would think it lucky now."

"Of course they would," the king managed between coughs. "They were determined to destroy us, all over an ore deposit."

Basil waited, but as usual, no one else contradicted his father's blatantly false words.

"You know that isn't, true, Father," he said, speaking as patiently as he could. The king's wheezes were gradually subsiding now, but he'd been forced to resume his seat. "They attacked us because they believe we were behind the magic attack that killed all six of their princes. Can you really say you wouldn't do the same in their position?"

"Couldn't," grunted King Thorn. "I don't have six sons to lose."

Fortunately for the progress of the council, the queen caught her only son's eye at that moment, her expression forbidding.

Basil swallowed his exasperated retort, and the king blustered on.

"Besides, we all know that allegation is nonsense. They don't really think we had anything to do with what happened to the Mistran princes. It was just a convenient excuse for King Lloyd to declare open war without any of the other kingdoms chastising him for it."

"With all due respect, Father," Basil said quietly, "I suspect that the murder of six of his children seemed about as *convenient* to him as your injury seems *lucky* to you."

King Thorn scowled at his son. "You know what I mean." He turned his gaze upon the rest of his council. "Winter is almost past. I want to see a serious proposal for a spring offensive. They're much too secure up in Myst, with their capital so far from the front lines. They need reminding that as long as our borders are being violated, there will be no peace. It's time to push the fight to where they'll feel it."

Basil sat up straight, horrified by the determination in his father's eyes. Surely the king wasn't going to push them into full scale war, after all this time! But again, Queen Lucille caught her son's eye, and Basil leaned back, frowning. She was right—this wasn't the time.

It took almost fifteen minutes for the discussion to die down, and the last of the advisors to file from the room. Basil remained in his seat, his eyes fixed on his father's face as he rolled a small paperweight back and forth in his hand.

At last no one remained but the king's steward, along with the queen, and the crown prince. King Thorn stood, and the steward hurried forward to gather the monarch's parchments. When Basil's father turned toward the door, however, Basil cleared his throat.

"Father," he said mildly. "Could I have a word?"

King Thorn scowled at his son. "Seems you had enough words to say at the council," he snapped.

Basil shrugged. "I thought I was expected to attend now that I'm eighteen. I assumed that meant I was entitled to speak, like any other member of the council."

"Just because you're entitled to speak, doesn't mean you need to speak every word that passes through your fool head," the king shot out, then winced as he rubbed a hand along one side of his chest. "And you're not any other member of the council. You're my son, and you should give me your full support."

Fully aware that his father was in the grip of a particularly painful attack, Basil disregarded the insult. "You have my full support, Father," he said patiently. "My purpose is the same as yours—to serve Entolia's interests. How can I show you true support if I don't give you my honest opinion?"

"Prettily said," grunted the king. "But what do you know of war?"

"I know it's not good for our people," said Basil frankly. "The fighting at the border is bad enough. Pushing the conflict further into either kingdom would be immeasurably worse. It's been almost six years. Has either side even tried to propose a compromise?"

Before his father could respond, Basil flipped the parchment before him, exposing its underside. The king and queen both blinked down at the crude map.

"It's only a rough calculation," Basil pressed on, "but you'll see here that my proposed re-alignment of the border gives each kingdom—"

"Cede land to the Mistrans?" roared the king. He coughed again, but waved off his wife's approach with an impatient hand. "Never would I consider such a thing!" he wheezed. "What possible reason could we have for handing them a victory when our forces haven't begun to be depleted?"

"Haven't begun to—" Basil drew a deep breath, his own temper starting to stir. "If you don't like my map, Father, maybe you'd be more interested in this." He slammed another parchment onto the table, glaring at his father's furious face.

The king glanced down at the list of names, his brow creasing. "And what is it I'm supposed to be interested in?"

"This list," said Basil acidly, "represents all Entolian casualties since the war began almost six years ago." He lifted the paper, revealing a small stack of several more beneath it. "Six hundred names, Father. Six hundred lives lost, six hundred families torn apart. And that's only half!"

"Nonsense," the king contradicted, his voice a little gruff. "Last count I heard was in the five hundreds. It can't have more than doubled since then."

"I was referring to the Mistran lives lost," said Basil curtly. "Although when it comes to that figure, I'm only speculating, of course."

The king made a scornful noise in his throat. "The Mistrans aren't my responsibility."

"But the Entolians are," Basil said, jumping instantly on this opening. "And too many of them have already suffered for this pointless war. We must end it, Father."

"You heard what I said to the council," the king said grimly. "I intend to end it."

Basil ran his hands over his face in frustration. "Father, my proposal would give us access to almost half the ore. That would enable us to—"

"Almost half!" the king demanded, once again rising to his feet. "You're suggesting we give away the greater portion to Mistra?"

"Better to mine half of it than none," insisted Basil. "Which is how much we can access while a battleground remains in place above it."

"It's not about the ore," snapped King Thorn. "It's about ceding our sovereignty to a ragtag bunch of—"

"I'm glad we agree, Father," said Basil tartly, pushing himself to his feet as well. "It's *not* about the ore. It's never been about the ore. It's about what you've suffered. And I imagine that for the Mistrans it's about the death of their princes. And no amount of fighting, no amount of territory, will redeem either of those losses. All we can do now is prevent further death and destruction!"

"THEY are in the wrong!" The king slammed one hand down against the polished tabletop, causing an inkwell to rattle.

Basil steadied it absentmindedly, inured to his father's explosions of temper.

"Them, Basil!" the king raged on. "Not us! We will not yield to them! I don't want to hear any more of this traitorous proposal. And if you wish to attend future councils, you will show me more respect!"

King Thorn's burst of emotion had taken the inevitable toll. He was wheezing as he glared at Basil, his eyes daring the prince to argue further. But for all his bluntness, Basil knew when to refrain. He met his father's look steadily, but said no more.

Apparently satisfied, the king turned on his heel and strode from the room, the steward bobbing along anxiously in his wake.

Basil let out a breath, lowering himself back into his seat with a rueful glance at his mother.

"That went well."

"What were you thinking, Basil?" the queen chastised him, without heat. "The weather's been so cold this last week, he's hardly slept. I thought you knew better than to distress him when his pleurisy is troubling him so much."

"I was thinking that unless someone *distresses* him, pleurisy or no, we'll find ourselves in the midst of open war," said Basil dryly. He frowned at his mother. "Surely you don't think it's a good idea to mount a proper invasion?"

Queen Lucille sighed. "It probably won't come to that. He only asked for a proposal."

"You heard him, Mother," Basil protested. "Winter is almost past. He thinks himself safe for another year, and he's ready to march on Myst."

"Well, he's not safe," said the queen sharply. "Infections can take root at any time, and it's not good for him to be excited. I would expect you to have more sympathy, Basil."

Basil ran another hand over his face, then tugged his fingers through the light brown waves that fell just above his ears. "I do have sympathy, Mother, you know I do."

He was silent for a moment, dwelling with discomfort on his many memories of the illnesses that too often gripped his father in the colder months. The damage to the king's lung had never fully healed. Not only was he prone to catching every illness that passed through the castle, but he always took infections extremely hard. Too many times Basil had sat by his father's bed, wondering if he'd be an underage king by dawn. For all his father's bad humors, Basil didn't want to lose him any more than he wanted to claim the king's throne. But there was no denying that one day—and perhaps sooner than they all hoped—he would have to claim it. And the less of a mess he inherited that day, the better.

"I don't want to distress him," he said, his voice more moderated. "Of course I don't. But we can't indulge his whims to the point of war, Mother."

"We're already at war," the queen said simply. "And if you think you can convince your father to walk away from the conflict, you don't know him."

Basil sighed. "I do know him." He met his mother's eyes. "It's not like I expected him to give in easily, but he could have at least listened to my proposal."

"He did," said the queen. "You proposed to realign the border."

Basil shook his head. "There was more to it than that. I want to go to Myst, to negotiate a ceasefire on Father's behalf."

"What?" The utter horror on the queen's face made it unnecessary for her to put her opinion into words, but of course she did so anyway. "You want to travel into the heart of our enemy's territory, and make yourself vulnerable to their malice?" She shuddered. "Thank goodness you didn't say that in front of your father. Send his only son into Mistra? You must be mad to think he'd countenance such a thing!"

Basil grimaced. "If that's your reaction, I don't think I have much chance of convincing Father."

"You have none at all," said the queen firmly. "My advice is not to even bring it up. Why would you wish to go yourself? If we were going to send someone to negotiate—which I highly doubt your father will agree to do—it wouldn't be you. Have you forgotten that our last envoy barely escaped with his life?"

"That was almost six years ago," Basil said impatiently. "And the princes had just been killed. I just don't believe the Mistran king is as aggressive as Father always claims. Otherwise he would have attempted a true invasion long before now. If I went, it would be a show of goodwill, to demonstrate how serious we are."

"Basil, your life is too important." There was an edge of genuine fear to his mother's words. "You are our only son."

"Yes," said Basil dryly, thinking of his twelve younger sisters. "I'm aware of that."

"Then you should know we would never risk your life like that! Isn't what happened to Mistra's princes evidence enough of the need to be careful?"

"Actually," said Basil, meeting her look, "what happened to Mistra's princes is evidence that no matter how careful you are, you can't guarantee nothing terrible will happen. They were walking in their own castle grounds when they were attacked and murdered by an enchantress whom we can only assume was legitimately mad. What's to stop such a thing happening here?"

"The dragons might help protect you if you were attacked." There was a hopeful edge to the queen's voice that made Basil roll his eyes.

"Zinnia and I might be friendly with some of the dragons," he said, naming the oldest of his younger sisters, "but they don't exactly follow us around, ready to protect us against enchantments." He narrowed his eyes slightly at the thoughtful look on his mother's face. "And if you think the dragons would ever take sides when it came to war between two human kingdoms, you must be out of your mind."

His mother frowned at his habitual lack of tact, but she was so used to it, she didn't bother speaking the chastisement aloud. "Of course I don't think that."

"Good," said Basil briskly. "Now about this trip of mine to Myst—"

"There will be no trip to Myst," said Queen Lucille firmly. "Don't waste your energy on something that won't happen. Your father will never send his heir to treat with his enemies."

"All this nonsense about me being irreplaceable," Basil said impatiently. "You have *twelve* other children, Mother! I don't see why Zinnia couldn't just take the throne if anything happened to me. Father's obsession with having another son makes no sense. I know the deaths of the Mistran princes only made him more determined, but I don't understand why. I mean, they were all killed. It didn't help that there were six of them, did it?"

The queen sighed. "I'm not saying I disagree with you." Her

usually serene face betrayed a hint of weariness, and Basil suspected, not for the first time, that she would be glad to stop having children. "But your father wants to pass his crown to his son, as his father passed it to him."

"The Listernian king doesn't seem to mind having a daughter as an heir," Basil pointed out.

His mother gave him a look. "I'm not sure that example would do much to convince your father. Have you forgotten the furor over a princess being named as heir was such that someone cursed the entire kingdom, and sent her into an enchanted sleep?"

"Yes, but that's all resolved now," said Basil impatiently.

His mother ignored him, pushing on relentlessly. "And the only other princess to be the heir is Mistra's, who—"

"Who by all accounts is addled in her mind," Basil finished, unruffled. "Yes, it's not an excellent promotion for crown princesses. But Zinnia would be all right."

"What would I be all right at?" The suspicious question made both Basil and the queen turn, but before they could greet the oldest princess, an insistent voice cut across the adult conversation, as a small shape hurtled toward the prince.

"Basil, look! Look what I made! I did it perfect!"

Basil blinked down at the offering being held out to him. "I see that," he informed the still-bobbing three-year-old seriously. "It's most definitely the most perfect flower crown I've ever seen." He shot a cheeky look at his mother. "Just what I need to proclaim my unassailable status of crown prince and sole heir. I'll wear it at once."

He made to take the crown of daisies, but his youngest sister shrieked and clutched it out of his reach. "No, I was just *showing* you!" she protested. "You can't *have* it!"

"I'm terribly sorry, Wisteria," said Basil, his lips twitching as he met Zinnia's eyes. "My mistake."

"You can have *my* flower crown, Basil," said a sweet little voice, and another of Basil's sisters sidled up to him, holding out her own creation.

"Thanks, Holly," he grinned, taking the crown. "But I think you should wear it." He placed it meticulously on her head. "There, like I thought. You look just like a princess!"

The four-year-old giggled, but the queen's voice interrupted this promising conversation.

"If princesses normally had bare feet." She shot a pained look at Zinnia. "Why aren't they wearing shoes?"

The oldest princess shrugged. "We were at the beach. These two raced back ahead, because they were determined to show Basil their crowns. I could barely keep up with them. I think the maids are still carrying their shoes back up."

"We found a real crab, Mama!" Wisteria interjected, her face alight with excitement. "And it nipped Ivy!" She was positively glowing with delight at the pronouncement, and Basil and Zinnia again exchanged glances, grinning appreciatively.

"I *told* her not to put her hand in there," said Holly, looking faintly distressed at this mention of her twin's misfortune.

"Never mind Ivy's self-inflicted mishap," said Zinnia, pinning her mother with a searching look. "What were you two saying about me? What would I supposedly be all right with? If you're talking about a political marriage—"

"Oh, enough of that," said Basil, rolling his eyes. "Let it go— no one is trying to marry you off."

"You say that now," Zinnia said darkly. "But I haven't forgotten, even if you have, that Father tried to arrange my marriage with the Bansfordian prince. And I was only fifteen!"

"No one was suggesting that you marry immediately," said the queen calmly. "It was just a betrothal discussion."

"And since both the Bansfordian princes have been married for a year now, I think you're safe," said Basil impatiently.

"Yes," mused Zinnia. "I'm still sore we couldn't go to the wedding in Bant. I mean, Penny—Princess Penny, I should say—is a friend of ours, after all."

"We met her *once*," Basil laughed.

"And you know we would have attended if we could have," the queen cut in. Her quiet words sobered her two oldest children at once, reminding them of how ill their father had been in the lead up to the wedding in question.

A giggle drew Basil's eyes to the trail of sand leading under one of the council tables, where Holly and Wisteria had disappeared, presumably to compare rival merits of their flower crowns. He remembered a time when he and Zinnia had been as carefree as that. Back when there was no war, when his father hadn't been constantly at death's door. The child of those memories felt like an entirely different Basil, one who lived in an almost-forgotten world.

"Well," said Zinnia roundly, returning his mind to the conversation, "Bansford might have no unmarried princes left, but I know for a *fact* that Father has been corresponding with the Fernedellian king. And even if Prince Amell wasn't as foolhardy as he is irritating, I'd never leave this," she gestured out the window at the rocky stretch of shore that sat just below the council room, "for the only kingdom in Solstice that doesn't even have a coastline!"

"No one is talking about a political marriage between you and Prince Amell," said the queen patiently.

Basil gave a snort which made his mother sigh and his young sisters poke their heads out from under the table with another giggle. "Fernedell is not going to ally themselves with a kingdom at war," he said. "All you overheard was me saying you'd be all right as the future monarch if I got myself killed."

The theatrical gasps from the two small children were nothing to the horror on Zinnia's face. "Bas, you wouldn't!" she cried. "You couldn't be so beastly as to get yourself killed! I don't want to be queen!"

Basil grinned at her. "You wouldn't have a choice. Maybe you'd best come on my dangerous quest with me, so if it comes to it, we both get killed. Lilac can inherit the throne."

"Basil," said the queen sharply.

Basil raised his hands in surrender. "I'm joking. Of course I wouldn't do anything to put any of my sisters in danger." He glanced at Wisteria's and Holly's wide eyes, and tried to make his voice reassuring. "And I'm not really going on a dangerous quest."

"No," agreed his mother tartly. "You most certainly are not."

"Because it wouldn't be that dangerous," Basil explained.

"Because," corrected the queen, "you're not going anywhere."

"We'll see," muttered the prince mutinously. His mother's reaction wasn't promising, but that didn't mean he was ready to give up. King Thorn might be as stubborn as a cantankerous goat, but Basil was his father's son through and through. He would wear him down if it took a month.

As it turned out, Basil didn't have the opportunity to wear his father down, and King Thorn didn't have a month. The prince hadn't yet raised the matter of his projected trip when he found himself walking down the corridor with Zinnia, two days later. Their conversation ceased abruptly at the accustomed sight of the castle's physician bustling past, led by an anxious-looking maid.

The familiar sick dread settled in Basil's stomach. He and Zinnia came to a halt, exchanging tense glances. The weather had turned, and sunlight was filtering in through windows that now revealed gently lapping waves instead of the storm-lashed beach of a week before.

"Winter's almost passed," said Zinnia tightly. "Surely he can't have caught anything too nasty." But she spoke without conviction. They both knew that, as their mother had said, King Thorn was never really out of danger. Winter was often the worst time for the infirm king, but infections could run through the castle at any time, and try as they might to be cautious, the king was almost certain to catch them.

They made no attempt to follow the physician, knowing how their father disliked fuss. But for the rest of the afternoon, Basil held himself tensely, hardly taking in his little sisters' chatter. He didn't need the message delivered by a frightened-looking page to know that the council he was to attend that afternoon was postponed. The whole castle always held its breath when the king was ill, and the level of hush that pervaded the halls—not to mention his mother's continued absence—told Basil that this time it was serious.

He therefore wasn't surprised when he was called to his father's bedchamber just as he was rising from the evening meal. Zinnia sent him a charged look, and he responded with a reassuring nod. Entolia's monarch had never been good at communicating with his children, but Basil's position as heir gave him a certain level of information. Sympathetic to his sister's frustration, he'd long ago made a habit of passing on to Zinnia anything that was personal rather than diplomatic in nature.

The king's room was dark, and almost oppressively warm. The fire roaring in the hearth was suited to the dead of winter, not the milder weather now upon them. Queen Lucille sat by her husband's bed, her expression strained as she watched her son enter.

"Mother," he said softly, laying a hand on her shoulder. She swallowed, but said nothing, just rising so that he could take her seat.

He did so, turning his gaze to his father's wan face. The king's eyes searched the room restlessly, struggling to settle on his son.

"Basil?" His voice was impatient. "Are you there?"

"Yes, Father," said Basil calmly, taking his father's hand. "I'm here."

"Good, good. I need to speak with you, Basil. This one has done for me."

"We've thought that before, Father, and you've always rallied," said Basil firmly.

The king shook his head, more impatient than ever, and Basil glanced back at his mother. The look on her face made him clench his jaw. Clearly he'd be foolish to dismiss his father's fears. He'd seen the king worse than this, but that was no guarantee of recovery. The illness had certainly come on quickly this time.

"The Mistrans did this to me, Basil," King Thorn said, drawing the prince's attention back to him. "Don't forget that, once I'm gone."

Basil said nothing.

"Promise me," the king rasped, the words sounding painful to utter, "promise me that you'll win this war."

Basil took a moment before he answered. His heart wrenched with pain on his father's behalf, but his mind was quite clear. It helped that he'd been called on to make such deathbed promises multiple times over the last few years. He'd learned not to let the emotion overwhelm him, and he knew better than to make promises he didn't intend to keep.

"I promise I will seek an outcome that is favorable for Entolia," he said at last. "In all things, not just the war. I will serve our people and the interests of our kingdom."

The king's hand twitched irritably within Basil's, and the

prince could tell his father wasn't satisfied. But mercifully, he didn't push the matter.

"And Zinnia," King Thorn pressed on instead, "she is much too independent. I wish her to marry a prince, and the Fernedellian heir is the only one left. You must promise that—"

"I will do all in my power to ensure that *all* of my sisters are provided for," Basil interrupted firmly. "I will encourage Zinnia to marry someone with whom she will thrive."

His father let out a frustrated noise, again recognizing that Basil hadn't given the requested promise.

"Trust me, Father," Basil said gently, pressing the older man's hand. "I have sworn to serve Entolia, and I won't fail my vows."

King Thorn's response was lost in a paroxysm of coughing, and Basil winced as he watched pain lance across his father's features. When the fit had passed, the king lay back against his pillows, for a moment too spent to speak.

He turned his eyes toward his son, his expression softened. "I'm sorry for all that will fall on you, Basil," he said, his voice barely recognizable in its gentleness. "You're too young for this burden."

Basil opened his mouth, but nothing came out. For once he had no words. The uncharacteristic vulnerability in his father's eyes unsettled him. More than all the king's words, it made Basil wonder whether this time really would be the last. But as another cough rocked King Thorn's frame, the familiar irritability returned to his features.

"They're the ones to blame for the position you're in— they're the ones who've done this to me. And they should be punished. It will be up to you to punish them now."

"Don't distress yourself, Father," Basil said quickly, unable to bear the impotent fury and desperation on his father's face. He once again pressed the king's hand. "Focus on resting. I will see to anything that needs taking care of."

He didn't tell his father he would recover. Perhaps he would, but Basil could hardly promise as much. And he didn't think he would do his father any favors by pretending the situation was less serious than it was. The king knew the truth, after all.

With a nod, the king laid his head back again, closing his eyes as if it was too much effort to hold them open. Gently, Basil released his father's hand and rose. He gestured with his head, and the queen stepped with him into her husband's receiving room.

"What does the physician say?" Basil asked, without preamble.

His mother made a hopeless gesture. "What he always says. The old injury has made him more susceptible, and the infection has taken root in his lungs. Nothing can be known for certain."

Basil nodded slowly. "He certainly seems bad. But we've seen him worse."

The queen said nothing, and Basil laid a hand on her shoulder. Looking into her eyes, he made no more attempt to offer her empty promises than he had with his father.

"Whatever happens, Mother, I'll be here to help you. And so will Zinnia, and the rest of the girls."

The queen gave a watery sniff. When Basil squeezed her shoulder, she shifted into him, laying her head against his shoulder for a moment. The rare gesture sent fear spiking through Basil's heart. Whether she was right, he couldn't say, but it was clear to him that she believed this time was different.

She pulled back quickly, standing upright and blinking rapidly in an attempt to cover her moment of raw emotion.

"Couldn't you have promised him, Basil?" she reproached, meeting his eyes. "It would set him at ease to know you were going to carry on his efforts once he's gone."

Basil frowned, trying to make his tone gentle. "But I'm not going to carry on his efforts, Mother. Not all of them, anyway."

"But he doesn't need to know that," said the queen impatiently.

Basil was silent for a moment, trying hard to exercise a restraint that didn't come naturally to him, and to choose his words with care. "I don't believe in placating people with the lies they want to hear, Mother."

"Not even on their deathbed?" The queen's voice broke slightly on the last word, and Basil gave her shoulder another squeeze.

"Especially not then. If anything, promises matter more at such times. And we don't know it's his deathbed, Mother. He's pulled through worse before. He's strong."

His mother made no answer, and Basil deemed it best not to push the point. "Shall I stay with him? You could get some sleep now, while the servants are all still up. I know you'll be sitting with him through the night, say what I will to dissuade you."

She shook her head. "I couldn't sleep if I tried. You go, get some rest. You'll need to take on his commitments tomorrow, so it will be a big day. You can check in at first light, and I'll tell you how the night has passed."

Basil hesitated, reluctant to leave her. But her expression was determined, and he knew how jealously his mother guarded her place at her husband's sickbed. He had no desire to take that comfort from her.

"Very well," he said. "I'll be back at dawn."

Pausing only to give Zinnia a brief report, which he could trust her to pass on to those of their younger sisters she thought ready to hear it, Basil went to his own chamber. He knew his mother was right, and he should rest. But it was many hours before he was able to still his mind enough to approach sleep.

He told himself, as he drifted uneasily, that there was every like-lihood his father would pull through, as he so often had.

Basil only knew he'd fallen into a shallow slumber when he was awoken by an insistent rapping. Judging by the gray smudge he could see through his open curtains, dawn had almost arrived. But Basil had no attention for the normally impressive view. Before he'd fully pulled himself from his bed, the room seemed to be full of people, and he knew from the look on his mother's face what was coming.

Still emerging from the fog of sleep, Basil's eyes found the king's steward, who was lowering himself to his knees.

"King Thorn is dead," the man said solemnly.

Even over the ringing in his ears, Basil heard the rustle of movement as everyone in the room, including the queen, knelt before him. His mind in a daze, he returned his eyes to the steward, who spoke again.

"Long live King Basil."

CHAPTER TWO

Wren

Drawing her cloak around her, Wren settled her shoulders into a more comfortable position against the back of the bench. If a hard stone seat could ever be considered comfortable, which she highly doubted.

The sky was just starting to lighten. Wren glanced up and paused her work, captivated for a moment by the sight of three winged figures passing overhead, far, far above. The dragons were too high to make out their colors, but the rising sun still glinted off their scales. They were heading south west, so they must be returning to their colony from some draconic errand.

A familiar weight brought Wren's attention back down to see a sleek white head resting on her knee, regarding her with disapproval out of beady little eyes.

You don't have to sit out here, you know. You can't possibly be comfortable. And it's freezing.

Wren smiled, returning her eyes to her work. *I know it is,* she replied, her lips not moving. *Do you think I'm doing this for fun?*

The swan clicked its beak, but Bram made no further comment. Wren's needles moved fluidly through the wool, something strangely satisfying about the clacking sound they made as they connected. It was a shame, she reflected absently, that her mother didn't consider knitting to be as desirable an accomplishment for a princess as embroidering. It was much more practical. No embroidered material, however daintily done, would keep the boys warm like this wool would.

Of course, her mother might have been more inclined to encourage Wren's interest in knitting if she'd been making something a little more conventional than garments for waterfowl.

She held up her current project, silently inviting Bram to admire it.

Instead, her brother lifted his head, stretching his long neck back in the direction of the pond. With their contact broken, he could no longer communicate his words directly into Wren's mind, but she made no attempt to ask him what he was looking for. She'd acquired a level of patience in the last several years that her younger self would never have believed possible.

Bram had learned a thing or two as well, she reflected with a secret smile. Every detail of that awful day was engraved into her memory, including Bram's criticism. The Bram who had complained about her chattering was almost unrecognizable in the brother who now hovered protectively near her, urging her to return to the warmth of her fire rather than suffer the morning's chill out by the pond.

A soft trumpet of greeting drew Wren's attention from her task at last. An orange beak was protruding from the reeds at the edge of the castle garden's enormous pond, and she had no difficulty recognizing it. Putting her knitting aside, she hurried over to the water's edge, a slight frown marring her forehead. Spring had almost arrived, but the mornings were still very cold. She wished Caleb would let her sneak him into her suite at night—she'd learned the hard way years ago that openly bringing her swans into her rooms was more than her parents would tolerate

—but he wouldn't hear of it. He claimed it was a matter of her privacy, but she suspected it was more that he didn't want to be sheltered in the warm castle while his brothers had to sleep on the frigid waters of the pond.

She sighed as she knelt beside the water. That was Caleb. Always the responsible, selfless leader, even when he had no one to lead but a bevy of swans.

She reached out both hands and helped guide the large bird over the rocks at the water's edge. He was heavy enough that she didn't just lift him straight over, but she tried to take enough weight to ease his awkward clamber to flat ground.

Thanks, Sis.

Caleb's voice in her mind was as warm as always, showing neither frustration nor embarrassment at his limitation. But the familiar stab of guilt raced through Wren as she watched him steady himself, his ruined wing bent painfully. She no longer had any hope that the injury would heal with time. In over five years, there had been no improvement to the damage done by her one careless word, and by her solitary attempt to write out the truth of her brothers' state. What the impact of the injuries would be once he resumed his human form was impossible to tell.

What are you doing out here in the cold? Caleb scolded, honking aloud with the words.

Bram waddled up, honking as well. Wren could only assume he was telling his brother that he'd already tried to convince her to go inside. She ignored their noise, her gaze fixed on the other four swans who were now gliding across the surface of the lake.

With the exception of the lopsided Caleb, her swan brothers were incredibly graceful. Even Ari moved with an elegance that was almost comical, given the madcap boy she knew to be underneath. Not boy, she reminded herself. Ari was a man now, like the rest of them. Strange thought.

Once all the swans had emerged from the pond, trumpeting and flapping their wings, Wren returned to her bench. She pulled a completed jacket from underneath, and turned to the birds now gathering around her. Kneeling down, she laid her hand on the neck of an uninjured swan about the same size as Caleb.

This one's for you, Averett, she informed him cheerfully.

The swan said nothing, merely sending her a look that was far more human than any bird should be capable of. Wren grinned, wrestling the garment over the swan's head in defiance of his unhappily clicking beak. She pulled it down around him, patting the wool into place to provide an extra layer of protection against the chill air. Averett let out a disgruntled trumpet, which somehow translated to a groan in Wren's mind.

It scratches my feathers, and it looks ridiculous. Why do you waste your time on this nonsense?

"Your Highness."

The clear disapproval in the new voice made all six swans gather around Wren. Even Averett abandoned his complaints as he joined the others in flapping their wings aggressively and jostling one another in their attempts to get between the princess and her approaching governess. They all disliked the older woman even more than Wren did.

With a rueful smile, Wren lifted her eyes from the identically defensive posture of the birds. Their newfound grace wasn't the only thing her brothers had gained during their time as swans.

"Your Highness, *what* are you doing out here at this hour of the morning, and all alone?"

Angry honks sounded around Wren, and she shook her head in amusement at her brothers' offense over being disregarded.

The governess sent them a nasty look, but otherwise ignored

them as she began on a familiar lecture about the proper conduct for a princess.

Tuning out the words, Wren touched her hand to the top of Caleb's head, where he'd hustled up next to her. *She's not going to eat me, you know. You can all stop trying to fight her off.*

We're your brothers, Wren, Caleb reminded her firmly. *We're supposed to be protective of you.*

Wren clucked her tongue, unconvinced. Of course Caleb said that—he'd always been that way. But it wasn't just him now. All of them, from the brazen Averett to the heedless Ari, suffered from an overactive sense of protectiveness toward their sister.

Is protectiveness a swan instinct, maybe? she mused, projecting the thoughts into Caleb's mind simply because she could. *Or is it just that I'm the only one you can all communicate with? Talk about forging a sibling bond.*

What do you mean a swan instinct? Caleb's voice was unusually sharp in her mind. *Surely you know why we all want to look out for you?*

Wren glanced down at the large bird, whose neck was craned gracefully back to allow Caleb to look at her face. For a moment she was at a loss, then the answer washed over her, leaving a chill more pervasive than the frosty morning air.

Of course. Her quiet thoughts were the equivalent of a whisper, but she knew Caleb would be able to make them out. *Your very survival depends on me. Of course you want to keep me safe.* She shivered, hating the reminder that one heedless word from her might be enough to end Caleb's life. But it was a reminder she needed constantly, to make sure she didn't get careless.

Caleb clicked his beak in a sound that clearly betokened distress. But there was no time for further exchanges. The governess had reached the end of her patience.

"Princess Wren!" she snapped. "Did you listen to a word I said?"

Wren hadn't, of course. But there was no need to admit that. Feigning a look of concentration, she pulled her slate from the pocket that hung from her waist and leaned over it as if to write.

"Oh, never mind explanations," said the governess impatiently. "Just come inside now."

Wren hid a smile at the predictable response. Her governess had never had much patience with Wren's silent communication, a fact the princess had often used to her advantage.

Why do you even still have a governess? Caleb demanded, brushing his good wing against Wren's leg so she could hear his words. *You're almost eighteen. I'd moved beyond my tutor's training years before that.*

Yes, because you were already a very satisfactory crown prince, Wren responded, trying not to let the bitterness creep into her thoughts. *I'm so far behind the level of training required from an heir, no one quite knows what to do with me.*

You're more than capable of filling the role of Mistra's heir, Wren. Caleb's voice was a perfect blend of sternness and encouragement, and Wren could picture the slight crease that would appear between his brows if he was wearing his own face.

Whatever that face would look like, now he'd aged six years.

You just need to have confidence in yourself, and stop being afraid to put yourself forward.

Wren scowled. Put herself forward? Yes, right into Caleb's place. *I won't usurp your position, Caleb,* she projected. *Not even temporarily.*

She stepped away from her brother's feathery form, to cut off any further protests he might try to make. The governess was still waiting for Wren to obey her command, one arm wrapped around her own narrow torso in an expression of clear discomfort as she watched her eccentric charge fraternizing with a flock of waterfowl.

"Well, come inside then, Your Highness," she repeated at last, beckoning imperiously.

With a frown, Wren gestured at her half finished knitting project. The older woman made a disapproving noise.

"It's not good for the birds to domesticate them so, Princess Wren. And it's certainly not good for you. Swans aren't supposed to wear clothes."

Scowling, Wren pulled out her slate and scribbled a message. She thrust it into her governess's face this time, demanding to be heard.

Have you felt the temperature?

"They should have migrated for the winter, like the rest of their kind," said the older woman. "You've made them too tame, that's why they've stayed with you. To their detriment as well as yours," she added, her eyes lingering distastefully on Caleb's damaged wing, and Averett's admittedly ridiculous knitted garment. "Now come."

Scrubbing her slate clean, Wren scribbled again.

I still have time before the council meeting.

"I already told you," huffed her governess, after reluctantly reading the words. "Their Majesties are waiting for you now."

Wren blinked. Her parents had summoned her? Perhaps she should have been listening after all. Stowing her slate back in its pocket, she stepped between her avian brothers to collect her knitting.

The boys waddled after her as she followed her governess

toward the castle. The garden in which her brothers lived formed an enormous central courtyard, around which the four main wings of the castle marched. Their pond—almost big enough to be considered a small lake—sat in the middle of the garden, and teemed with fish and bird life. Even before it had become her brothers' sanctuary, Wren had always loved stepping from the solid stone corridors of Myst's castle into the tranquil beauty of the gardens, with their splashes of color, tantalizing fragrances, and gentle bird calls.

Now, she spent as much time there as she could get away with. Caleb never left the gardens, and Wren would have preferred the rest of her brothers to remain safely there as well. But, given the inconvenient fact that they had wings, she couldn't exactly stop them from exploring further. And if she was honest, she couldn't blame them for wanting a change in scenery. The gardens, while lovely, were a small kingdom for six grown princes to occupy every minute of every day.

Most of the swans slowed as they approached the open double doors, but Ari, Lyall, and Bram waddled forward confidently. The fact that the birds were always rebuffed didn't stop Wren's brothers from routinely trying to gain entry to the castle to accompany her about her daily activities. She understood it to be a show of support for her, and she appreciated it.

When the guards at the door opening from the gardens into the castle fended the three swans off with the shafts of their spears—gently, as no one would dare to actually injure the princess's pet swans—Wren sent her brothers a casual wave. She couldn't help grinning at the sight of Averett. He looked none too pleased to have been left with the jacket on.

"Making clothes for her feathered dolls again?"

Wren kept her expression blank, not even bothering to look around to identify who had made the sniggering remark. She knew most of the court thought she'd lost her mind years ago, and it wasn't as though she could correct them. It wasn't news to Wren that her determination to knit jackets for her swans was considered one of her most embarrassing eccentricities.

Her governess was right, of course—all the true swans had left many weeks ago, to spend the colder months elsewhere on the continent of Solstice. But Wren would never have allowed her brothers to leave, even if they wanted to, which of course they didn't. She shuddered to think how anxious she would be if all six of her brothers had been far away somewhere, where she couldn't take care of them, make sure they weren't shot by hunters, or brought down by foul weather.

It had been stressful enough two years before when she'd been forced to travel into Albury in a completely futile attempt to explore an alliance with the then-cursed crown prince. Wren couldn't have said what was more painful, the battle it had taken to be allowed to take Caleb—whom she would have been terrified to leave alone and vulnerable—or the worry she felt regarding the other five, who *had* been left behind.

She'd been grateful that rumor had proven wrong, and the missing prince hadn't yet been found. They said his marriage had softened him, but at the time Prince—now King—Justin had been known as a hard, cold man. She shuddered to imagine what he would have thought of her, traveling with a half-lame swan all but attached to her side.

Wren's steps slowed as they approached the council chamber. She really had no idea why her father forced her to attend these meetings.

Actually, that wasn't true. She knew exactly why he forced her to attend, and it made her more determined than ever not to take part. When they reached the door, Wren's governess held out her hands imperiously, and Wren gladly surrendered her knitting. The council already thought her enough of a fool without her bringing a hobby to the meetings.

To her surprise, however, there was no gathered council when she entered the room. Only her parents, with ominously identical expressions of determination on their faces. Wren's heart sank. This couldn't be good.

"Wren," said Queen Liana, her voice full of a warmth that didn't fool her daughter. "Sit down."

Wren sank into the indicated seat, across from her mother. She barely held in her sigh. Not because she had to—she'd learned long ago that sighs were allowable under the curse—but because it would be impolite.

"I assume you're aware of the topic of the council meeting that will commence shortly?" King Lloyd said, and Wren nodded. "Good." He pinned her with a look. "I trust you've read the materials provided to you yesterday?"

This time Wren did sigh. She nodded again, hardly noticing as her fingers drummed impatiently on the table.

"Wren." Her mother's reproachful voice drew the princess's attention to the unladylike conduct, and Wren stilled her hand.

Turning her face back to her father, she waited for him to continue. She *had* read the materials, and a tedious waste of time it had been.

"Do you have any questions you wish to ask me before the council commences?" the king pressed.

Wren pulled out her slate.

Do I have to attend?

Her father scowled as he read the words upside down. "I meant, do you have any questions about the materials? Or any other questions that we haven't already exhaustively discussed?"

Wren rubbed the slate clean and wrote again.

Not really.

A familiar look of impatience crossed her father's features. He opened his mouth to speak, then closed it again. To the casual eye, it looked like he had just changed his mind. But Wren knew better. She'd become very observant during her years of silence, and very much alive to all the subtle cues of body language. She hadn't missed the speaking look her mother had shot at the king, and she understood perfectly that her father restrained his true feelings only under protest.

"Wren," said the queen, in a soothing tone, "I know it's not the most exciting topic, but it's important to understand the reports from the Blacksmiths' Guild. They have a unique insight into the conflict with Entolia, since they best understand the nature of the deposit located in the contested land."

With the ease of long practice, Wren kept herself still, even while inside she was seething with frustration. Did her mother really think the problem was boredom? Compared to the embroidery and other such skills she'd been expected to spend her time on back before the curse, reading guild reports was downright fascinating.

"Wren, you need to apply yourself," burst out the king, evidently unable to hold it in anymore. When all this was over, Wren reflected, she could give him lessons in keeping his thoughts inside. She was a master by now. "You need to understand matters of state, and how to communicate with such groups as the guilds. You can't sit unresponsive through every council meeting—one day you'll be queen, and you'll have to *lead* the council!"

Wren felt her face set into unyielding stoniness. She shook her head once, her mouth clamped in a thin line. Unconsciously, she reached up a hand to play with the signet ring suspended around her neck on a thick chain. She'd grown considerably in the years since Caleb had slipped it over her eleven-year-old finger, but it was still much too large for her to wear on her hand. Thankfully.

"Wren," her mother cut in, in a voice much gentler than her husband's, "we all miss them, but denying your position won't bring your brothers back."

A flash of pain crossed the king's features, and Wren felt the familiar stab in her gut. There were times she wished she was less adept at reading body language. Even after six years —*almost* six years, she reminded herself...she'd know when it was six years—her father still couldn't hide his reaction to the loss of his six sons. *And the unfortunate survival of his one daughter*, Wren added in her mind. But she knew the thought was unjust, and she tried to banish it.

She dropped her hand from the ring quickly. Once again clearing her slate, she wrote the closest explanation she could without risking further harm to Caleb.

I will not train to be queen.

The desperate longing to tell them why, to explain everything, had long since settled to a dull ache. She didn't even fidget as she watched frustration cross her parents' faces.

"Wren, you *must* train to become queen," her mother said. Before she could say more, an insistent tapping drew all of their attention to the window.

Lyall! Disregarding her father's grunt of disapproval, Wren hurried to the window and unlatched it. The swan soared gracefully into the room, its dark feet making a slapping sound as it landed on the council table. Wren laid her hand against the swan's side, a question forming in her mind.

Is everyone all right, Lyall?

The swan gave a soft trumpet, but Wren was focusing with her mind rather than her ears.

Yes, we're all fine. I just wanted to make sure Mother and Father aren't giving you a hard time.

"Wren, you may recall that we're in the middle of a discussion."

Her father's irritated voice called Wren's attention back to her audible conversation. She turned, bracing herself for the usual recriminations. Her swans made the king even more uncomfortable than her silence.

Thanks, she told Lyall, tossing him a look. *But I'm fine.*

Are you sure? Lyall sounded doubtful. He shifted on his webbed feet as his small, beady eyes locked on to his oblivious parents.

Wren didn't know whether to smile or roll her eyes. What in the world her brother thought he could do to help her in his current form, she couldn't imagine.

Before she could say as much, the door opened, and several men walked in. Wren didn't miss the momentary wince that crossed her father's face before the king smoothed out his expression. Her father's discomfort over Wren's interaction with her bevy of swans always escalated to true embarrassment when others were present to witness it.

"Your Majesty," said one of the courtiers, in a pained voice. His emotions took no skill to read. "Should we really have water-fowl *inside* the castle?"

CHAPTER THREE

Wren

"My Lords," the king greeted the newcomers with stiff formality. "Thank you for your presence."

The nobleman who had spoken bowed respectfully, but Wren heard him mutter to his neighbor at the snub the king had delivered by ignoring his question. She paid him no heed. Lord Kinley had always been one of her greatest critics. Her brother, however, ruffled his feathers indignantly.

Puffed up little pond worm, Lyall said, bunching up his long neck so that his head sat almost against his feathered chest. *What does he have against waterfowl?*

Wren resisted the urge to laugh. *Are there worms in your pond?* she asked sympathetically.

"It's an embarrassment." Lord Kinley had settled into a seat not far from where Wren still stood near the window, and he threw her and the swan-Lyall a disgruntled look as he continued complaining to his companion. "You know they've had her thoroughly checked by the top physicians from three kingdoms? *And* by Sir Gelding, who's an enchanter. There's nothing medically wrong with her, and there's no curse on her. She could speak if she wanted to. She just chooses not to. And don't get me started on the swans."

Wren frowned slightly. Who was Sir Gelding again? Why did the name tickle her memory?

Lyall's mind was clearly fixated on other things, however, as he flapped his wings aggressively toward the mutterer. With her hand still on his flank, Wren could hear his angry thoughts.

Is he an unmannered boor, or just an imbecile? Doesn't he realize you're standing right here and can hear every word he says?

Wren gave a bitter smile. *It's hardly the first time,* she informed her brother. *Plenty of people seem to think that since I don't speak, I can't hear either. You'd be amazed what people say in front of me.*

It was often quite useful, actually.

Casting a glance at the offended nobleman, Wren sighed. *It's not that I don't appreciate the support, Lyall, but I think it will be easier for me if you leave.*

With a doleful honk, Lyall nipped her sleeve, then waddled to the edge of the table. Spreading his wings, he flapped his way back through the window, just as two more men walked into the room. Their astonished eyes passed from the bird to the princess, their mouths hanging open.

Wren didn't recognize them, so she doubted they were part of her father's court. Unable to easily ask anyone their identity, she cast an eye over their attire, looking for clues as to why they were at the council meeting. One of them clutched a leather binder with a small anvil sketched into one corner. Guild members, she realized suddenly. They were the representatives from the Blacksmiths' Guild.

The realization triggered her memory—she'd recognized Sir Gelding's name from the report. He was a baronet from Mistra's south who had oversight of the Blacksmiths' Guild. He also happened to be an enchanter. She remembered him only dimly from the early days of the curse. He'd been summoned to the capital to look her over. Wren couldn't even picture him across the intervening years. All she remembered was feeling embarrassed at his scrutiny.

Closing the window behind Lyall, Wren made her way back to her original seat. King Lloyd sent her an exasperated look, but didn't publicly call her out on her refusal to take the seat to his right, the one reserved for his heir.

Caleb's seat.

Nothing would prevail on Wren to sit in Caleb's place. Half the time she wished someone would understand her subtle communication, and realize that the true heir to Mistra's throne was still alive to claim his position. The other half, she was afraid that if someone did figure it out from her behavior, it would activate the curse and kill all six of her brothers, one by one.

It was a difficult balance to walk. And with no way to test the limits of the curse without endangering Caleb, she had long ago decided to err on the side of caution.

The king was calling the council to order, and although his voice was even, Wren knew him well enough to read the turmoil beneath. He was embarrassed by the odd behavior of his daughter and supposed heir, and frustrated with her for her continued lack of interest in the training required for a future monarch.

"Well then." The king turned to the guild members. "What is the view of the guild? Could we mine the ore from underneath the battleground? Perhaps if we concentrate our troops closer to the front line, could we access the deposit from behind them?"

A gray-bearded man in military uniform cleared his throat. Wren's eyes flicked to him. She'd been surprised to see the general of her father's army enter the room. He wasn't often to be found in Myst, spending most of his time at the military base situated near the front lines.

"Your Majesty, I would caution against such an approach," the general said. "We would risk cutting our fighters off from base, and trapping them on the front line."

"Thank you, General," said King Lloyd gravely. "I understand that there are risks, and I would not make such a decision without seeking military advice. I merely wish to know if the Blacksmiths' Guild considers it possible."

The general bowed his head in acknowledgment, and everyone turned back to the guild member. The man spread a map over the table, angling it to give the king the best view.

"Your Majesty, our best reports are that the greatest deposits lie in this region."

The members of the council all leaned forward for a better look. In spite of herself, Wren copied them. She frowned. The ore in question was on the Entolian edge of the disputed territory. Not much hope of getting access to that.

"The area currently occupied by our troops is not conducive to exploration," the blacksmith went on. "The guild would not recommend any attempt to mine while the fighting continues. A more detailed analysis is provided in the guild's report."

The king sighed, and inclined his head slightly. The blacksmith resumed his seat, and King Lloyd cast his eyes around the table.

"For the benefit of the council, let me add that the guild's report also states that we have a kingdom-wide shortage of iron."

"Yes, Your Majesty," affirmed the second blacksmith. "The demand from the military has depleted our reserves."

Wren fought the urge to snort. How ironic. The war they were fighting over iron ore was draining them of the iron they did have. The general was speaking again, defending his army's need for the supplies they'd ordered, but Wren's thoughts were elsewhere. She didn't want to wrestle with the complex dynamics between the guilds, the military, the court, and the crown. That was her father's job, and Caleb's, and they were both good at it. She had to work so hard just to keep up, and it was wasted effort, since she'd never have responsibility for such decisions. Her time would be much better spent continuing her clandestine research into enchantments. That was an area of knowledge she had practical use for.

Her eyes passed around the room, taking note of who was listening closely and who, like her, was distracted by other things. The guild members looked ill at ease, and Wren's gaze lingered on them. It was hard to put her finger on what gave her that impression, but she definitely thought they were uncomfortable. Perhaps they felt out of their depth, debating with a general.

"Wren."

Her father's calm voice pulled her from her reverie. She looked at him, alarmed at the question in his eyes. She'd become so good at keeping her thoughts hidden, she wasn't sure he realized she hadn't been listening. What was he asking her?

"Do you have an opinion on the matter?" he pressed.

Stalling, Wren took a moment to glance again around the assembled council members. The general merely looked impatient with the interruption, and the blacksmiths were awkwardly avoiding looking at their mute princess. But several of the noblemen wore openly disdainful expressions. Wren felt a flash of anger. How could they all expect her to be as good at these things as Caleb had been? Her brother had been trained for his position from infancy, whereas no one had ever bothered to explain matters of import to Wren until they had no other options.

Returning her gaze to her father, Wren shook her head.

"You don't have any thoughts on how our people might receive a new tax to fund the import of iron from Albury?"

The grim expectancy in her father's eyes told Wren he wasn't going to let her get away with melting into the background. With an expression that betrayed none of her frustration, Wren retrieved her slate from its pocket and bent to write on it.

A pointedly cleared throat made her pause.

"Your Majesty," said Lord Kinley, the same nobleman who had commented scathingly on the swan-Lyall's presence. He had a look of determination on his face, and Wren felt her heart sink. "If Her Highness wishes her opinion to be heard by the council, should she not state it aloud, as the rest of us do?"

"It is not your place to set limits on the conduct of the princess, My Lord," responded the king icily.

His voice was as hard as stone, but Wren could see the embarrassment beneath, and she cringed internally.

"Your Majesty," said another of the nobles, rising to join his fellow, "I must agree with Lord Kinley." This man's face was also set in resolute lines, and it was clear to Wren that they had agreed ahead of time to speak. She'd been expecting something like this, but it didn't make it any easier to hear.

"It was one thing when the princess was a child, and was recovering from the distress of..." the man's courage seemed to fail him in light of the thunderous look on the king's face, and he didn't actually mention the princes' murders, "of what occurred." He inclined his head stiffly toward Wren, not meeting her eye. "A distress that was, of course, understandable. But she is a child no longer. Her refusal to speak—"

"Not to mention the swans," muttered Lord Kinley, and the speaker inclined his head.

"—and indeed her other eccentric behavior, surely ought not to be tolerated any longer."

Wren felt many pairs of eyes on her, as various of the other council members made noises of assent. She kept her face impassive, but her insides writhed with her humiliation. She knew she was no one's choice of heir. She knew her "eccentric behavior" was a national embarrassment. But to have it stated so baldly, and to her face...

Only three more months, she chanted to herself. *Less than three months. Then the nightmare will be over.*

She could feel indignation radiating out from the queen, but she couldn't bear to meet her mother's eyes. Even less could she bring herself to look at her father, whose anger once again poorly concealed his chagrin.

"You forget yourselves, My Lords," he said bitingly. "It is not your place to sit in judgment over my heir."

He stumbled over the last two words, and Wren knew the rest of the room had heard it, too. It took all her control not to bury her face wearily in her hands. She knew why the lords were worked up. She'd been braced for it. They were right about one thing—she wasn't a child anymore. In a few short months, she would turn eighteen, at which time everyone expected her to be anointed as crown princess. Not that the ceremony really changed anything—according to everyone else, she was already the crown princess. But it was a public declaration of her status that she knew made many in the castle uncomfortable, given her undesirability as their future monarch. She also suspected that formalizing it would make things complicated on Caleb's return.

Not that it mattered. The six years of the curse would run out shortly before she turned eighteen. Her father's true heir— anointed almost a decade ago—would be back by then. He'd be able to assume his position and end the farce they'd all been trapped in for far too long.

"We mean no disrespect to you, Your Majesty," said Lord Kinley, squaring his shoulders. "We seek only the good of

Mistra. And we fear that our kingdom cannot afford the loss in standing that will result from the public anointing of an heir who is—"

"Choose your next words with great care."

The king's voice was so forbidding, even Wren felt a chill pass over her. She sat straighter in her seat, gratified to see that for once the king's anger allowed no hint of discomfort to show through, even to her sharp eyes. Reminding herself that she was the king's daughter, after all, she frowned at Lord Kinley. A sharp retort rose to her tongue, but of course she didn't utter it. And a moment's reflection made her glad of the forced restraint —scathing comments from her would help nothing. Instead she watched him with dignity, daring him to finish his sentence.

But he was given no opportunity to do so. At that moment, the door to the council room was flung open, and a messenger hurried inside.

Along with everyone else, Wren stared at the young man, who wore a military uniform. After a quick bow to his sovereign, the messenger scurried to the general's side, murmuring into the older man's inclined ear.

Wren could tell from the sudden stillness of the general's frame that the news was something big. The grizzled soldier turned to his king, his expression hard to read.

"General?" asked King Lloyd, tension in every line of his face. His eyes flicked to Wren. Was he regretting insisting on her presence? Or just remembering the last time he'd been brought portentous news, and reassuring himself that his one remaining child was accounted for?

"A report from our scouts, Your Majesty," said the general curtly. "They say King Thorn died early this morning. Prince Basil is to be crowned immediately."

There was a moment of shocked silence, then the room

erupted in speculation. Wren sat frozen, turning the information over in her mind. So the Entolian king had died at last.

"What caused his death?" A nobleman shot the question at the messenger.

The man cleared his throat. "The report is that he succumbed to an infection, My Lord."

Wren saw many faces reflecting her own wry thoughts. They all knew what had really killed King Thorn. He'd been felled by the old injury, inflicted by Mistran soldiers years before.

She chewed on her lip. What would this development mean for them? For the war? What would the new king do with his suddenly acquired power?

"Your Majesty," said Lord Kinley, apparently forgetting that he had been midway through being chastised by the sovereign, "this matter calls for serious consideration."

"Indeed," said King Lloyd, his expression thoughtful. "This may change everything." He turned to the general. "Is there more to the message?"

The older man shook his head. "Very little, Your Majesty. Just that there is to be a state burial in three days' time."

"Three days," mused Wren's father. "And at that time the prince will be crowned?"

"If not before," interjected one of the noblemen. Wren recognized him as her father's chief advisor on foreign affairs. "They conduct all matters of state very promptly in Entolia, Your Majesty, with a minimum of ceremony."

The king nodded slowly, his brows still furrowed in thought. The general hubbub was growing, as everyone discussed the dramatic news with those seated around them. As usual everyone ignored Wren completely, and she again scanned the group, taking note of the demeanor of the various advisors. People's unguarded first reactions to news were often most telling, and Wren had discovered that when she wasn't trying to make her own voice heard, she could turn all her faculties to measuring others' responses.

The general, she noticed, showed no sign of the fear that lurked in the faces of many of the nobles. If anything, his demeanor suggested a faint excitement, and Wren wasn't at all surprised when he was the first to speak.

"Your Majesty." The general's clear voice cut across the chatter. "May I remind you of our previous conversations regarding this eventuality? Our force is the strongest it's ever been, and Tola isn't situated far from the front lines. I could leave within the hour, and I truly believe our forces could reach their capital before the burial."

Wren blinked into the sudden silence that followed this pronouncement. For a moment she struggled to comprehend the general's meaning. Then his words clicked into place, and she gave a sharp gasp.

The sound was lost in the renewed clamor. The king raised his hands for silence, but the arguments continued. Everywhere the nobles were getting heated, arguing their points to their neighbors, while the blacksmiths from the guild watched on with wide eyes.

Wren shook her head, surprising herself by the strength of the anger that rose within her. All out war? The general wanted to invade Entolia in earnest?

"It makes sense, Your Majesty," Lord Kinley called above the many voices. "This is the time to strike. They'll be at their weakest."

Wren clenched her fist under the table, watching with disbelief as her father considered the idea.

"I take it that is your advice, General?" The king turned to the military commander, who stood.

"Your Majesty, you already know that I have planned for this event. My advice remains the same as during our previous discussion. I believe this is the opportune moment to strike, and end this war once and for all."

With what intent? Wren shouted in her head. *Will we annex Entolia?*

She noticed that no one seemed interested any longer in the ore that sat below the battlefield. It was, as they all knew, merely an excuse. The hostilities that had simmered for nearly six years had nothing to do with iron, and everything to do with the attack on Wren's brothers. And now that the Entolians had finally suffered the loss which Mistra had attempted to inflict in retaliation all those years ago, the general was ready to drive the hammer home.

"The new king is barely of age," the general continued, not a flicker of emotion showing in face or voice. "He will be completely out of his depth, not to mention distressed from the loss of his father. He will be in no position to defend his capital. And from what we understand, King Thorn's resentment over-ruled his reason more often than not. I do not believe he will have set up proper contingencies to cover his kingdom's vulnera-bility on his death. Now is assuredly the time to strike."

Wren found herself on her feet, not quite sure how she'd gotten there. *No.* She opened her mouth, only just clamping it shut in time. It had been a very long time since she'd come close to slipping up, and she hardly knew why she felt so strongly about this matter. She just knew, deep within herself, that if Mistra did this thing, it would be a terrible stain on their history.

NO.

She pulled out her slate, but it was clear that no one was paying her attention. In growing frustration, she actually waved her hand above her head, like a child asking permission to speak. Still no one even glanced at her. When rapping the polished table sharply with her knuckles failed to cut through the general hubbub, she clapped. Nothing. Her mother was watching her father with anxious eyes, and the king was listening seriously to the general, who was continuing to argue his case over the top of the heated voices of the council.

Irritation swelled within Wren. Her father was determined to make her give an opinion about the report of the blacksmiths, on which topic she could offer nothing of value. But when she had something she desperately wanted to say, he forgot her existence entirely.

Lifting her slate, Wren set her fingertips against it. Dragging them slowly and with all the pressure she could muster, she scraped her nails along the whole length of the slate. The horrible screeching cut through all the noise, and even the stalwart general winced slightly. Some of the lords actually covered their ears as they turned to look indignantly toward the princess.

"Wren!" chastised the king, who looked like it had cost him all his kingly control not to cringe at the sound.

Wren ignored the admonishment, snatching up the slate to write one clear word, the two letters sprawled in such large script that they took up the entire surface.

NO

"No what?" King Lloyd demanded, when she held the slate aloft.

One of the lords cleared his throat. "Your Majesty, I believe the princess intends by her message to give an opinion on the proposed invasion."

Wren nodded emphatically. To her great annoyance, she saw many of those present exchange amused glances.

"Well," said King Lloyd, clearly a little taken aback. "You are of course welcome to express an opinion, Wren. However, in military matters, it is the advice of my general which—"

The king stopped speaking as Wren pushed her way out from her chair, moving with agitated strides to her father's side. She rubbed the slate clean with her sleeve and scribbled hurriedly on it again, this message intended for the king alone.

For years you've been pressing me to become involved in matters of state. Are you going to dismiss me when I do, because you don't like what I'm saying?

The whole room had paused while she wrote, and she could feel her father's impatience, as well as the habitual embarrassment that always leaked out when he was forced to communicate with her in this way in public. Wren disregarded both the council members and her father, determined to say her piece for once. When she finally finished, the king let out a frustrated breath.

"Of course I'm not going to dismiss your opinions, Wren," he said quietly. "I'm pleased to know you *have* them."

Wren was aware of the avid interest of the watching council members, but she ignored them once again, focusing all her attention on her father. She usually avoided writing multi-sentence messages. It was too tedious. But this occasion warranted it.

Is this who we are? A kingdom who invades its neighbors when they're burying their monarch?

"Wren," sighed the king, barely patient enough to wait for

her to finish scratching out the words. "We're speaking of Entolia."

Scowling, Wren bent back over her slate. She wrote furiously, but it still seemed to take an age for the words to get from her mind onto the surface.

> *I haven't forgotten what they've done. I haven't forgiven them, and I'm not asking you to, either. But the prince is barely older than I am. He was a child at the time. Will you exploit his grief over losing his father?*

She looked up and met her father's eye before adding a final question.

> *Have you forgotten your own state six years ago —my state?*

King Lloyd had stilled as she wrote, for once showing no impatience, even though it was such a long message, it filled the entire slate. When he'd read it all, his gaze passed from the words to his daughter's face, and a familiar shadow of pain flitted across his features before he could suppress it.

"I will never forget it," he said quietly.

"Perhaps the princess forgets," the general interjected gruffly, "that it was the Entolians who inflicted the losses to which I assume she refers."

Wren started at the unexpectedly close voice. Clearly the general hadn't read the whole message. She sent him a hard look. She wasn't likely to forget any detail of that day's events. It was only thanks to her recollection that they'd had any inkling of the Entolians' involvement in the attack on her brothers.

"This is no time for sentiment and compassion," barked Lord Kinley. "This may be our only opportunity to—"

"I, for one, am not in the habit of seeing a death as an opportunity," interrupted Queen Liana, speaking for the first time. Her voice was cool, and she stood, placing herself alongside her daughter. "Nor do I generally hear compassion spoken of as a failing."

The nobleman fell silent, although he looked slightly resentful.

King Lloyd didn't answer for a long, thoughtful moment, but when he spoke, his voice was decisive. "This is not a time for rash action, military or otherwise. We will send our condolences to the royal family, and consider how best to open negotiations with the new king."

Wren let out a long breath. She wasn't sure what astonished her more—that she'd spoken up in a council meeting, or that her father had actually listened to her. Over the general! She snuck a look at the military commander and saw that he looked less than pleased.

"Your Majesty," the general said, clearly trying to speak delicately. "Are you sure you don't wish to capitalize on this situation?"

"It's all very well to speak of negotiating with the new king," Lord Kinley agreed, "but we'd be foolish to assume he'll be reasonable. We all know King Thorn was an enraged old battle-ax, and he will have filled his son's head with his hatred of Mistra. The prince will probably take up the cause with even more fervor in light of his father's early death."

Wren frowned, once again clearing her slate to scratch a new message.

Haven't our intelligence reports consistently
suggested that the prince is difficult to lead, and
not inclined to blindly follow his father's
decisions?

The conversation had long since moved on around her by the time she finished, but her father looked over her shoulder at her words.

"An excellent point," he said briskly.

Everyone in the vicinity leaned forward to read what she'd written, then stared up at her in evident surprise. Wren wanted to roll her eyes. She'd attended every council for the last two years. Did they really think she never read the reports?

Her father gave her a nod before turning back to the council. "There is much to discuss. We will need to carefully consider our approach to the border conflict in light of this new, younger king."

A strange glow in her chest, Wren sank into her chair and let the conversation flow around her. She was more than satisfied with the result of her intervention, and had no desire to contribute to the heated discussions that followed.

It wasn't until the council had ended that she realized the seat into which she'd so unthinkingly settled was directly to her father's right.

CHAPTER FOUR

Basil

B asil stood in front of the marble tomb, feet planted firmly against the wind, and arms clasped behind his back. Beyond the simply designed structure, the ground fell sharply away, and he could hear the waves pounding against the base of the cliff, far below.

In accordance with tradition, no one stood beside the new king as he watched the tomb being sealed on the final resting place of his predecessor.

The new king. Basil had thought he was prepared for this moment for many years, but it was still hard to take in. He could hear his mother's quiet sobs behind him, but he didn't turn. Zinnia would be supporting the queen, he knew. Basil's eyes drifted out over the ocean. The stretch of cliff faced southwest, and away and to the right the sun was descending below the waterline, in a glorious display of color.

The sun was setting on King Thorn's reign. At dawn, Basil would be crowned in a simple ceremony, and the sun would rise on a new king.

Basil sighed. Symbolism had never been of much interest to him. Once again catching the sound of his mother's grief, he wondered fleetingly if he was heartless to be so little affected by his father's funeral. It wasn't that he didn't care. There was certainly a heaviness weighing on him every time he thought of his father. But his thoughts were much more consumed with the duties he'd inherited, particularly the war with Mistra. That was a mess, no question. And it had fallen to him to sort it out, as he'd always known it would.

The golden disc slipped fully below the horizon, and the clear call of conch shells sounded from all around him. Basil could hear the crowd beginning to disperse, but still he didn't turn, keeping his eyes on the horizon. He suspected his father would have preferred more ceremony, but Basil liked the simplicity of Entolian rites.

His father would probably have been pleased to see the half dozen dragons who circled low to watch the funeral procession. Basil hadn't recognized any of them, so he wasn't surprised they hadn't stopped to speak. But it would have been unusual to hold a ceremony as momentous as a monarch's burial without at least a few dragons coming by for a curious look.

"Bas." His sister's voice made him turn at last.

Basil smiled tightly down at Zinnia. "You're allowed to approach my royal person, you know."

Zinnia, who'd stopped a good three feet away, returned the smile, although her face was pale. "I was being respectful for the sake of the crowd. You're not one of us anymore, you know."

Basil sighed softly. He did know it, and the thought brought him no joy. He glanced behind him, to where his other eleven sisters stood. Lilac and Violet, the oldest but for Zinnia, flanked the queen, each with one arm wrapped comfortingly around her. Even Wisteria, the usually precocious three-year-old, was silent and subdued, apparently grasping the solemnity of the occasion.

"What will you do now?"

Zinnia's question brought Basil's attention back to her.

"I'll attend the formal supper, of course."

The princess gave him the royal equivalent of an eye roll. "I meant afterward. I meant," she gestured to her right, where the cliffs gave way to a gentler slope, across which the city of Tola sprawled, "with everything."

Basil's eyes followed her arm, and for a moment he was silent. His gaze rested on the castle, sitting proudly at the top of a low section of cliffs, commanding an excellent view of the buildings on the flatter ground below.

"I'm going to make some changes," he said frankly. "For one thing, I'm going to get rid of anyone who just tells me what I want to hear."

"Executing advisors as your first move," said Zinnia lightly. "Bold beginning."

Basil went to elbow her in the ribs, and remembered just in time that a king probably couldn't do that in public.

"Not that kind of *get rid of*," he said. "You know what I mean. I want a council of advisors who will tell me the truth, and say what they really think."

"And if they do, will you follow their advice?"

For a moment a genuine grin lit Basil's face. "I didn't say that." The smile faded immediately as his eyes returned to Tola marble structure that stood between him and the open ocean below. "I hope I'll always listen to others' advice, but I'm not going to let anyone talk me out of doing what I know needs to be done."

"That sounds ominous," said Zinnia, frowning.

Basil said nothing, and before his sister could further interrogate him, a soft call from their mother made them both turn. The mourners had almost all departed, leaving only the royal family. Of course, since there were fourteen of them, along with their attendants and a host of royal guards, the clifftop still seemed fairly crowded.

Responding to the semblance of privacy provided by the much smaller audience, six-year-old Dahlia detached herself from the bevy of princesses and hurtled toward Basil and Zinnia. She buried her face in her brother's leg, and watery sobs emanated from the spot. The queen started to chide her ninth daughter, but Basil shook his head. Detaching Dahlia from his leg, he hoisted her up so their faces were level.

"When did you get so heavy, Dahlia?" he asked, with an exaggerated grimace.

"I'm not!" Dahlia hiccuped. She hovered uncertainly, evidently torn between expressing her outrage at the slight and burrowing into Basil's comforting solidity.

"I'm only teasing, Dee," said Basil lightly. With a quick squeeze, he set her back on her feet. "Come on, Father wouldn't want us to miss his memorial feast."

"It's not a feast, Basil," corrected Briar, sounding scandalized. "It's a funeral supper. You make it sound like a festival."

"My mistake," said Basil gravely. He caught Zinnia's eye, and saw the ghost of a smile on her face as well.

"You wanted to surround yourself with people who say what they're really thinking," she reminded him in a mutter.

Basil couldn't help smiling. Briar had always been meticulous about the facts. When she was an adult, it would probably fit her for a very useful role. In an eleven-year-old, it was usually either annoying or entertaining. But Zinnia was right—at least she wasn't afraid to tell him he was wrong, king or not.

"Your Majesty."

Queen Lucille turned reflexively, and Basil didn't. But it was the new king whom the messenger was watching, and Basil nodded for the man to continue.

"A courier has just arrived from Mistra, bearing a message for you. Apparently he wasn't told to wait for a response, but the steward wasn't sure whether to let the courier just leave, or whether to remand the man in custody. I was sent to bring you the message immediately."

An angry hiss from the queen told Basil exactly what his mother thought of the Mistrans interrupting his father's funeral with any kind of message. But he was intrigued more than anything. Holding out his hand, he received the sealed billet, and pulled it open, fracturing the Mistran royal crest that was pressed into the wax.

"Well?" prompted Queen Lucille tensely, as he ran his eyes over the short message.

Basil looked up at her. "It's a simple message of condolence from King Lloyd," he said, unable to keep a hint of satisfaction from his voice. "With a carefully worded comment about hoping for constructive communication in the new reign."

"That's outrageous," said Daisy, the sister between Violet and Briar. "They're the ones who killed Father! Now they want constructive communication with you?"

"Would you prefer them to declare open war and march on Tola?" Basil asked her dryly.

His mother shot him a sharp look that suggested that she, like him, had recognized the possibility of such a response from Mistra to King Thorn's death.

"More like we should march on them," muttered Daisy.

"We are not going to do that," said Basil. He spoke calmly, but even he could feel the authority that came with the words. The conversation stilled at once. Basil looked between the heavy eyed faces, struggling to pull his mind from strategic considerations. He was bolstered by the message—it confirmed him in the course he already intended to take. But this wasn't the time.

"Come on, everyone," he said gently. Putting his plans for the future momentarily aside, Basil led the way back toward the castle, the family of which he was now the head following in his wake.

"Let me stop you there." Basil raised a hand, calmly stopping the relentless flow of words pouring forth from the nobleman across the table. "It won't be necessary to detail the report."

"But, Your High—I mean, Your Majesty," protested the man. "A great deal of time has gone into this report. Surely you recall our instructions to put together a proposal for a spring offensive. The plans before you constitute the preferred strategy of our army's most senior commanders. They—"

"I must interrupt you again, My Lord," said Basil, his tone still calm but his voice now raised in order to be heard. "I remember your instructions perfectly, and no doubt *you* remember that it was not I who issued them."

Silence fell around the council table, and several of the lords shifted uncomfortably.

"Of course, Your Majesty," said the first nobleman. "And please allow me to offer my condolences again on the great loss you've suffered—the loss we've all suffered."

"I appreciate your condolences," said Basil steadily. "But I wasn't speaking out of sentiment. I don't wish to discuss any proposal for a march on Myst. We will not be invading Mistra. I intend to negotiate a ceasefire with our neighbors."

There was another moment of silence as a dozen pairs of eyes blinked at him.

"Your Majesty," said the speaker cautiously. "I think it highly unlikely that the Mistrans will be brought to simply concede their claim and withdraw from the contested land."

"Yes, thank you, My Lord," said Basil, with what patience he could muster. "I naturally don't expect to reach an armistice by way of total concession by our adversaries. That's why I used the word negotiate."

"But Your Majesty!" gasped a mid-level military commander who was seated two chairs down from Basil. "Surely you're not suggesting *we* cede our claim? King Thorn would never have countenanced such a thing! Almost his last orders were to win the war!"

"I believe he said *end* the war, which is precisely what I intend to do," said Basil dryly. "But in any event, it is immaterial." He paused, taking a deep breath and once again reminding himself that he needed to think carefully before speaking. It was a tiresome aspect of being royal. "While I have the greatest respect for my father's memory, I would not be fulfilling the oath I took if I were to just blindly continue on whatever course he set before I was crowned. It is my duty and my privilege to take whatever action I believe is best for our kingdom. And I want it understood from the start, My Lords, that my first priority is disentangling us from this ill-advised war with Mistra."

In spite of the weight of the moment, Basil couldn't help but find the looks on the lords' faces humorous. The military commander in particular looked like Basil had slapped him across the face with a limp fish.

"Now," said Basil, his voice turning businesslike. But he wasn't given the opportunity to continue.

"Your Highness," cut in the slightly oily voice of one of the council's oldest members. "You have come very suddenly into your position. It is natural that you would still be finding your way. Inheriting a crown at your age, and when the kingdom is in the grip of an invasion, would be daunting for anyone. Naturally, you will wish to be led by those who have the experience you lack. We are here to guide and assist you, and you can trust our judgment where your own is as yet...undeveloped."

Basil didn't know if the lord's failure to use his new title was intentional or not, but he honestly didn't care. And he was entirely unimpressed by the solicitous speech.

"Let me speak plainly, My Lord," he said in crisp tones. "First, my ascension to the throne was anything but sudden. My father's final illness may have been brief, but we all know I've been expecting to be thrust into this role at any time since I was twelve years old." His voice turned wry. "However insufficient you feel my experience to be, at least we can all be thankful the situation isn't as drastic as that."

"Your Majesty," said the nobleman quickly, getting the title right this time. "I didn't mean to suggest an insufficiency in your—"

"No, don't ruin it now by trying to take it back," Basil cut him off impatiently. "I want you to say what you mean, and stand by it. Otherwise what use can your counsel be to me? I understand your concerns. I know I'm young, and I know I have a great deal to learn." He leaned forward in his chair. "But there are some other things I know. One is that we are *not* in the grip of an invasion. In six years of fighting, Mistra has made no attempt to claim territory beyond the disputed ore fields. And, in spite of their claim that we murdered all six of their princes, they have made no further attempt to retaliate."

"That claim is a blatant fabrication," said the military officer dismissively. "There's no evidence to support it, and they don't truly believe it."

"Perhaps," said Basil. "That's a matter I intend to clear up as part of my negotiations." His eyes scanned the room at large. "I've formed the intention of traveling to Myst myself, to open negotiations with King Lloyd. I anticipate leaving within the week, and I wanted to give any council member the chance to volunteer for a place on the delegation."

Predictably, his words produced an uproar. Half the people in the room were suddenly on their feet, and everyone seemed to be talking at full volume. Basil remained in his seat, waiting patiently for one voice to rise above the others, which it inevitably did.

"Prince—I mean King Basil! You cannot be serious!"

The speaker was once again the oldest nobleman in the room, the one with the oily manner. Interesting. Basil didn't remember him being so outspoken when King Thorn was running the council. Apparently he was emerging as a new figure of dominance now that the young king had taken charge. Basil locked the information away for later. He knew the dynamics of the court would change dramatically with his ascension, and he would have to pay close attention to make sure he had a handle on what was happening. It didn't help that as yet he had no sense of whom—if anyone—he could trust to keep an ear to the ground and provide him with insights free of their own agendas.

Slowly, Basil rose to his feet. Every face remained turned to him, with expressions ranging from fury to horror, and the room quietened enough for him to be heard without shouting. He faced the nobleman who had exclaimed.

"I have my faults, My Lord, but I don't believe I've often been accused of failing to take my duties seriously." The silence was suddenly absolute. "I assure you, I am very serious. As I said, ending the war is my first priority. I intend to send a message to King Lloyd this afternoon, proposing a state visit to discuss the conflict."

"Prince Basil!" cut in another nobleman, slipping back into Basil's old title in his outrage. "Your father is barely sealed in his tomb, and your first act is to go against all he worked for all these years? His own son—he would be horrified!"

An image of a dying man's face rose before the young king's eyes—his father's familiar features strained in anger and bitterness as he demanded that Basil win the war to avenge him. For the first time during the council meeting, Basil's calm deserted him, and he felt a surge of hot anger. Who were these men to cast his father's resentment-fueled expectations in his face? What did they know of their former king's bitterness, and its impact not only on his kingdom, but on his family?

His eyes kindled as he turned to the one who had spoken. "Do not presume to tell me what my father expected of me." His voice was even enough, but he couldn't quite keep the anger from his eyes. A little rattled by the absoluteness of the hush that had fallen over the room, Basil pulled himself together, adding more mildly, "Or to tell me what I expect of myself."

"King Basil," said the older nobleman, his voice resolute, and his expression forbidding. "I'm afraid we simply cannot allow you to walk willingly into the den of our enemies."

Basil fought the desire to laugh, wishing momentarily that Zinnia was in the room to appreciate the absurdity of it all. Not that he would ever really wish this mess on her, despite what he'd said to his mother.

"Den?" he repeated humorously. "I know none of us have a high opinion of the Mistrans, but are we referring to them as animals now?"

"Your Majesty, I meant—"

"I know what you meant," Basil cut the nobleman off mercilessly. "And I wasn't seeking your permission, My Lord." He once again glanced around the group. "Do I take it, then, that no one wishes to volunteer for the delegation?"

A cleared throat made Basil turn toward the far end of the table, where a nobleman no more than fifteen years his senior sat. The man hadn't spoken before now, and Basil struggled for a moment to remember his name.

"Lord Baldwin, Your Majesty," the nobleman said, the upward tilt to his lips suggesting he took no offense at Basil's failure to recognize him. "And if you are truly determined to venture into Mistra yourself, I would like to accompany you."

"It's preposterous," muttered a middle aged courtier next to Lord Baldwin, but no one else spoke loudly enough for the room to hear.

"Thank you, Lord Baldwin," said Basil gravely. "I will be glad to have a representative of the Lords' Council with me," he nodded slightly to the military officer, "in addition to the small military escort I expect to claim."

The officer didn't look happy, but he made no comment.

"If you'll excuse me, My Lords," Basil pushed his chair back, "I have a great deal to attend to, as you can imagine. And given that the original purpose of this meeting is no longer of relevance, I propose that any further matters be discussed at a later time."

Inclining his head, Basil strode from the room without a backward glance. He knew how quickly information would spread from the council to the rest of the castle, and he wanted to tell his mother his intentions before she heard it from a gossiping servant.

He found both Zinnia and Lilac in their mother's suite. Basil frowned at the sight of the queen. It was strange to see her idle. He didn't know much about such things, but it seemed to him that it would be better for her to be active, to engage herself in something that reminded her what life still held for her, rather than to spend yet another day isolated in her rooms, grieving the life that was gone.

"Mother," he said, once he'd greeted her and his sisters. "I've just met with the council, and I wanted you to know what we discussed."

"That's thoughtful of you, Basil," said Queen Lucille, a little absently. "But I'm sure you have it in hand."

"I do," said Basil flatly. "And in order to *keep* it in hand, I'm going to need your assistance."

She blinked up at him, and Lilac made a protesting noise in her throat.

"Can't Mama have a little peace, Basil?"

Shaking his head, Basil forced his voice into as gentle a tone as he possessed. Which wasn't saying a great deal. "Not really, Lilac. I don't think we should expect to enjoy peace even in the castle while our kingdom remains at war."

Heartened by Zinnia's approving nod, Basil met his mother's suddenly suspicious gaze.

"Why are we talking about the war, Basil?" the queen demanded, her uncharacteristic languor falling away for a moment. "What exactly did you discuss in the council?"

Basil pulled up a chair, seating himself so that his face was on a level with his mother's. "Nothing I haven't discussed with you before, Mother. I told the council of my intention to travel into Myst, hopefully within the week, to attempt to negotiate an armistice."

"Basil!" All traces of lethargy were gone from the queen's face. So were all signs of color, but Basil still felt it was an improvement. "We certainly have discussed this before, and I thought I made it clear that it was out of the question!"

"You made your opinion clear," Basil agreed. "But you must recognize that the situation has changed now."

"Yes, now it's even more important that you remain here, where you're safe!"

Basil shook his head. "I don't want to be safe at the cost of our soldiers dying needlessly, Mama. And you know I disagree about my supposed irreplaceability." He glanced at Zinnia. She was frowning, but she didn't once again voice her desire to avoid becoming queen.

"You wouldn't really go if you thought your life was in danger, would you?" she asked instead.

"Of course not," Basil said staunchly. "Naturally I won't be going unless the Mistran king agrees to receive me. I recognize there's always risk, and nothing can be certain. But I don't for a moment believe the Mistrans would agree to meet with me, and then assassinate me upon arrival."

"Why not?" protested the queen.

Basil shrugged. "Because I'm the king of Entolia," he said simply. "It's not such a small matter to murder me, Mother. They couldn't expect to do so without the direst of consequences. I've never seen evidence to make me think the Mistran king is either that bloodthirsty or that foolish."

"These supposed scruples didn't stop them attacking your father!" insisted the queen. "The king of Entolia!"

"They didn't know he was the king, Mother," said Basil quietly.

She made an impatient noise in her throat. "Of course they did. They wanted to cripple us by removing our monarch, and leaving a child in charge."

Basil was silent for a moment, watching his mother's face. "I don't think that's true, actually. Have you ever heard a firsthand report of what happened that day?"

"Of course I did!" the queen said. "Your father described it to me more times than I—"

But Basil was shaking his head. "That's not what I meant. Did you hear any account other than Father's?"

She didn't answer, but her frown told him she hadn't.

"I did," he said simply. "When I was fifteen, I realized it would be wise of me to seek a more unbiased report about the incident. I spoke to all three of the commander's aides who were present in the tent that day. Even though by then it had been three years, they all gave a consistent account. All were agreed that the Mistran soldiers seemed shocked at the realization of who they'd attacked. Father was prone and injured. They could have finished him off then, but they withdrew. No doubt to seek instructions in light of the drastic turn their mission had taken."

Lilac frowned at him. "Whose side are you on, Basil?"

"Ours," said Basil promptly, and with feeling. "Entolia's, until the final beat of my heart." His eyes sought his mother's face again. "I bitterly regret what happened that day, and I always will. I don't condone the Mistrans' attack. But they were soldiers, Mother, on a battlefield. We can't assign them the blame of murderers."

His mother wouldn't meet his eye, but he could see from her discomfort that she recognized the truth in his words. Satisfied, he said no more.

"How did it go with the council?" Zinnia asked curiously. "When you told them that Your Royal Majesty plans to trot along into Mistra yourself?"

Basil shot her a wry look. "Apparently the council's habit of only telling their monarch what he wants to hear has not transferred with the crown."

She grinned. "Tried to tie you to the council table, did they?"

Basil grunted. "Literally, no. But in essence, yes. Although I hardly think my safety was their true concern. Most of them find the idea of negotiating peace via compromise as hard to swallow as Father did. I offered them the opportunity to accompany me and see that I come to no harm. Strangely, they were mostly uninterested in taking up that offer."

To his surprise, Zinnia didn't laugh. Instead, she looked troubled.

"But you can't just leave, Basil," the queen tried again. "You're needed here more than ever! You've just been crowned—there's so much to take care of!"

"I know," Basil acknowledged. "And I wouldn't leave at such

a time for anything less important than stopping a war. But to be frank, I don't think there's a single member of the council whom I would trust to undertake the task on my behalf. They don't believe in my cause, and they're not yet accustomed to following my direction whether they agree or not." He frowned slightly at his mother. "And of course you'll have regency while I'm gone. I have no doubt you'll handle things as well as I would, if not better."

"What?" The queen looked aghast. "Basil, I've never been trained to be a reigning monarch like you have. I can't take on that role."

"Of course you can," said Basil, with a touch of impatience. "What nonsense is this about not being trained? What do you call twenty years of being married to the king? Mother, I'm eighteen years old. My training can't possibly equal the experience you have. You're more than capable of running the kingdom without my presence."

And, he added in his head, *unless I'm very much mistaken, it will be an excellent thing for you.* Much better than sitting around in her rooms, with nothing to do but be swallowed by her grief.

As if reading his thoughts, the queen went on, her voice not quite steady. "Your father never expected me to take on responsibility in matters of state."

Basil sighed. "That's because Father held the belief that a strong monarch is one who rules alone and unchallenged. But I don't share that view." He passed a hand through his hair, disarranging it. "Unless I'm much mistaken, I'm going to need all the help I can get."

True to his word, Basil dispatched a courier that very afternoon. He watched from the battlements of the castle as the man rode away toward the border. How would King Lloyd receive his request? For all his confident words, Basil wasn't at all sure the

Mistran monarchs would take well to the idea of hosting Entolia's new king.

Once the courier was out of sight, Basil turned his gaze southward, toward the ocean. He felt his tension leak out, calmed by the sight of the waves pounding relentlessly, uncaringly, predictably against the cliffs. Whether he succeeded or failed, whatever his populace thought of his rule...whatever his *father* would have thought of it...the tide would continue to ebb and flow, and the waves would beat against the rocks. He didn't need to be a spectacular king—in fact, it was better if he wasn't. What Entolia needed from its throne was less ego and more quiet stability. If he could pull them out of war and make the wheels turn smoothly for the kingdom's basic function, he would be well satisfied. He suspected even that would take every bit of his effort, for the many decades likely still to come in his rule.

Letting out a sigh, Basil strode back into the castle. It would take time for his message to reach the Mistran capital, and for King Lloyd's reply to reach Tola, even if all went well. The courier was unlikely to return in much less than a week.

With a great effort of will, Basil put Mistra and the war from his mind, and turned his thoughts to the thousand other things requiring his urgent attention.

CHAPTER FIVE

Wren

Wren knelt down at the water's edge, dipping her fingers into the pond.

That's freezing! she protested, turning to the large swan leaning against her leg. *How can you sleep in that?*

Caleb's trumpet sounded like a chuckle in Wren's mind. *You get used to it.*

A shrieking honk drew both of their eyes toward the middle of the pond. Wren sighed at the sight of Bram and Conan, engaged in their favorite occupation.

"Your Highness. Do you mind if I join you?"

The gentle voice made both Wren and Caleb start. Turning, Wren smiled warmly at the young woman before her. Feeling Caleb fidget at her side, she heroically refrained from smirking at him.

"I didn't mean to interrupt..." Lady Anneliese trailed off uncertainly, and Wren hastened to stand, brushing her hands off on her skirt. She gave the young noblewoman another smile, and gestured toward a nearby bench.

The two women lowered themselves onto the seat, Caleb making his slower way over with his lopsided waddle.

"I hope you're well."

Wren nodded, tilting her head in an inquiry. She'd always thought highly of the older girl, and doubly so since the curse. Lady Anneliese was one of the few people in the castle who didn't seem uncomfortable in the princess's presence.

Lady Anneliese smiled again. "Yes, I'm well." Another honk drew her eyes across the pond, a slight frown marring her pleasant features. "Are...are they all right?"

Wren followed her gaze, and chuckled internally. It was no surprise that Lady Anneliese looked alarmed. If she hadn't been so used to it, Wren would also have been taken aback by the sight of the two swans fighting. It was a bizarre spectacle, their necks wrapped around one another's as they wrestled, and their wings flapping violently.

She nodded in response to Lady Anneliese's question.

"They look angry," the noblewoman pressed. "They won't... hurt each other?"

Wren shook her head, smiling openly now. She knew it looked that way, but Bram and Conan weren't genuinely angry with each other.

"I didn't realize it was normal for swans to play fight," the noblewoman added doubtfully.

Responding to the gentle brush of a wing, Wren leaned down and helped Caleb up onto the bench beside her.

She's not wrong, he reflected, as he settled against her side.

I know they say they want to stay in fighting shape, Wren commented skeptically, *but do you really think any of their swan fighting skills will transfer to their human forms?*

Caleb gave a non-committal trumpet. *Who knows? But I don't begrudge them the sport. There isn't a great deal to do as a human in a swan's body, to be honest.*

Wren grimaced sympathetically. *Where did they even learn to do that?* she asked, watching in fascination as Conan's head snaked all the way around Bram's neck, pulling the other bird's head almost down to the water.

Instinct, bugled Caleb. *Same way we know how to fly, and what's safe to eat. Our minds are an absolute jumbled mess of human thoughts and swan instincts. I can't even describe to you how strange it is.*

Ari's tried, Wren informed him. *Repeatedly. He says it's like his body is playing tug of war with his mind every second of every day.*

Before Caleb could respond, Lady Anneliese's soft voice broke into their silent conversation. She hadn't seemed bothered by Wren's distraction, but she looked a little uncomfortable as she spoke.

"I hope it's not impertinent of me to say, but I heard about your intervention at the council." Lady Anneliese met Wren's eye, something most people avoided doing. "I'm glad we're not going to invade Entolia."

Wren blinked at her, surprised. Not surprised that Lady Anneliese knew what had happened at the meeting. The noblewoman's father was on the council, and even if he wasn't, Wren putting herself forward was such a rarity, she assumed it would have spread throughout the whole castle in a day.

No, what surprised her was that Lady Anneliese had sought her out to express support. The sweet-tempered young woman was usually almost as quiet as Wren.

By way of acknowledgment, Wren gave what she hoped was a graceful nod. It was all the response she could offer. With Caleb pressed against her, she couldn't easily reach her slate. Plus she tried to avoid using it much with anyone but her parents and her governess. She no longer cared—much—what people thought of her silence, but that didn't mean she enjoyed making a spectacle of herself.

What's she talking about? Who said anything about invading Entolia?

Caleb's sharp voice cut into Wren's thoughts, and she hid a wince. She hadn't told her brothers about what had passed at the council meeting. She especially didn't want to explain to Caleb how she'd done what she'd always promised herself she wouldn't, and used her usurped position as heir to influence matters of state.

With a sigh, Wren turned to look at him. *That was the general's advice. He had discussed it with Father before, that whenever King Thorn died would be the ideal time to invade, because the kingdom would be weakened, and the new king floundering.*

Caleb's graceful head swiveled toward the pond, where Conan had just bested Bram. *It makes sense. That's a strategically sensible option.*

Wren started visibly, and she saw Lady Anneliese watching her out of the corner of her eye. She ignored the other woman.

Caleb! You mean you would have supported it? She wasn't sure what distressed her more—the idea that she'd used Caleb's position to give advice opposite to what he would have said, or the idea that Caleb would approve the general's plan.

No, Caleb responded calmly. *Because I don't think an invasion is either justified or wise. We've avoided full scale war all this time, and I think we'd be foolish to court it now.* He paused. *Plus I don't like the idea of exploiting the new king's grief.* He turned his head back to Wren, his voice serious in her mind. *But that doesn't mean it's not a strategically sensible plan. If the general believes war is advisable, it makes sense for him to suggest this timing.*

Wren felt her frame relax, but she shook her head slightly. This was why Caleb was fitted for the role, not her. She struggled to remove emotion and think strategically.

And you intervened against that proposal? Caleb added suddenly.

Wren squirmed. She could have spoken directly into Caleb's mind, but she didn't want to. She just gave a reluctant nod.

Caleb was silent for a moment, and guilt swirled through Wren. He always told her to put herself forward, but surely the reality of it would make him as uncomfortable as it made her.

I'm proud of you, Wren.

The words surprised Wren so much she could hardly keep her face straight. Tears prickled at her eyes, but she could feel Lady Anneliese's gaze on her, and she forced herself not to surrender to them. Turning instead to her companion, she summoned a smile.

But Lady Anneliese's answering smile seemed forced, and she looked away quickly. Frowning a little, Wren studied her profile. The noblewoman had said she was well, but she didn't look it. Her usually pleasant face had a strained quality about it, and her eyes were troubled.

Hesitatingly, Wren reached out and touched the other woman's arm. Lady Anneliese started slightly, and whipped her head back around to face the princess. Reading the question in Wren's eyes, she gave an unconvincing laugh.

"I'm all right. Sorry, I was lost in my thoughts."

Wren tilted her head, raising her eyebrows encouragingly.

Lady Anneliese let out a long breath. "I don't wish to burden you with my troubles."

A hasty disclaimer was on the tip of Wren's tongue, but with long practice, she didn't even have to remind herself not to utter it. Instead she waited, silent and patient.

"I just thought that you..." Lady Anneliese burst out, then trailed off. "That is, no one feels the loss more keenly than you, and..." Her words faded once again, color rising up her cheeks.

Wren paused, taken aback by the reserved woman's outburst. She was glad she hadn't been able to utter the polite reassurance that had been in her mind. Most likely the proper courtesy would have caused Lady Anneliese to retain her usual formal manner. It wasn't the first time Wren had observed that prolonged silence had an intensity to it that could conversely unlock people's tongues.

Sensing, however, that the other woman needed some encouragement to continue, she gave Lady Anneliese's arm a gentle squeeze. She had suspected before now that their shared grief might be the reason the other woman sought out her company sometimes, but it had never been articulated between them before.

"Father wishes me to marry," Lady Anneliese said in a rush. "He's received an offer from a suitor, and he's pressing me to accept."

Caleb's feathery form had become utterly still, and Wren had to force herself not to look at him.

No, she thought. *Don't do it, Lady Anneliese! Not after all this time. Not when we're so close.*

She is free to do as she wishes, Wren. Caleb's soft voice in her mind made Wren wince. She hadn't realized she'd shared her thoughts. She was obviously distracted.

She's not really free—not while she doesn't have all the facts, Wren shot back stubbornly.

She has always been free. Nothing was ever formalized.

Wren didn't bother arguing. Caleb's words might be true, but they were beside the point. He knew as well as she did that the entire court had been living in daily expectation of the announcement of the crown prince's betrothal to Lady Anneliese when the curse hit.

Lady Anneliese was watching the princess for her reaction, and Wren hardly knew what to do with her face. She was terrified of accidentally communicating Caleb's presence—and survival—and therefore dooming him. But it would be unthinkably horrible if Lady Anneliese, after defying all expectation and remaining unwed for almost six years in memory of her lost sweetheart, married someone else mere months before Caleb was finally free.

Some of her anguish must have shown in her eyes, because Lady Anneliese grimaced.

"I hope you don't think less of me for considering it," she said. "I find it difficult even to contemplate it myself. And I don't want you to feel...well, betrayed."

Wren stared at her. Lady Anneliese was hesitating out of consideration for *her*? She'd never even imagined the reserved noblewoman to be feeling such a thing. She wished she could reassure her, could tell her how much her undemanding companionship meant to Wren. But she didn't want her to be so reassured she married someone other than Caleb, just to satisfy her father.

After a moment's hesitation, Wren pushed Caleb away enough to reach into her pocket for her slate. It was worth both the effort and the spectacle on this occasion.

The other woman watched her curiously, leaning forward with interest when Wren was finished writing.

What do you want?

Lady Anneliese sat back with a sigh. "What I want isn't possible," she said softly, looking out at the now-calm pond.

Wren's heart leaped. Caleb still held the noblewoman's heart, it seemed. But Lady Anneliese wasn't finished.

"If I'm honest," she went on, her eyes still on the water, "I am weary of feeling sad and alone."

Wren could feel Caleb's tension beside her, and she realized she was holding her own breath.

"But I don't want to leave my home, and go far away from my

family and my friends," Lady Anneliese added. "And Sir Gelding lives a long way south."

Sir Gelding? Who oversaw the Blacksmiths' Guild? Wren hardly noticed Caleb's start, lost in her own surprise. Her eyes flew to Lady Anneliese's, and the other woman gave her a wry look.

"You're surprised? So was I, a little. I had thought he was older than he is, though. He's only about forty, I believe."

Wren wasn't quite able to hide her distaste, and she could feel a similar reaction from Caleb. Forty might not be as old as Lady Anneliese had expected, but in Wren's opinion, a fifteen year age gap was still too much.

"Or are you thinking of his station?" Lady Anneliese asked delicately. "I hadn't expected Father to countenance a baronet, not when he once thought I would be...well." She cleared her throat. "I thought the reason he'd let me be for so long was because he was hoping for someone of higher standing." She was fiddling with the embroidered cuff of her sleeve. "Those things matter more to Father than they do to me. But Sir Gelding is an enchanter, you know. And I suppose that gives his bloodline a different kind of strength."

Caleb fidgeted beside Wren at the word *bloodline*, and she couldn't help but feel for him. At least it was encouraging that Lady Anneliese didn't seem to find the possibility of having children with magic—which didn't always pass down the generations, after all—especially alluring.

Still unsure of what would be safe to say, Wren just shrugged. But on the inside, her voice wasn't silent.

She can't marry a man she doesn't know or like, fifteen years older than her, only months *before you're free.*

Of course she can, said Caleb. He spoke evenly, but his swan body didn't have the iron control his human form had done, and a soft bugle of distress escaped him with the silent words. A pang went through Wren at the sound. *I would never have asked her to wait six years for me, even if I could have,* Caleb added.

But she's done it anyway! Wren said. *She'd be devastated to marry someone else only to have you return to your human form immediately afterward.*

We don't know that's even going to happen, Wren, Caleb reminded her in a tight voice.

An icy shot of horror passed over Wren, as it always did when one of the boys reminded her of this argument. She refused to hear it.

You're going to go back to your true form, she told Caleb firmly. *The enchantress said so.*

I was there, Wren, Caleb said, a bitter edge to his voice that wasn't usually present. Lady Anneliese's revelation was obviously weighing on him more than he wanted to let on. *She said we would* probably *return to our human forms after six years of your silence. But she was completely mad, and she also said she didn't intend any of this.*

Wren ignored him, mashing her lips together into a thin line. Pushing her wayward hair back from her eyes, she leaned once again over the slate, adding a second line below the first.

What are you going to do?

Lady Anneliese bit her lip, giving the tiniest of shrugs with one slender shoulder. "I don't know. I barely know Sir Gelding, but apparently he's coming to Myst for a while. I'll reserve judgment until I see what he's like. I suppose I should at least give him a chance."

Wren frowned slightly. It wasn't the answer she wanted, but it wasn't a completely closed door, either.

"There's another matter I wanted to ask you about," said

Lady Anneliese, with the air of one eager to change the topic. In fact, she looked like she'd been holding the question in for some time, whatever it was.

Wren lifted an eyebrow inquiringly.

"I saw a courier arrive about an hour ago," Lady Anneliese said quickly. "He was in a military uniform, so I suppose he must have come from the border." She looked sideways at the princess. "I'm probably not supposed to ask, but do you know if there have been any casualties? My brother..."

She trailed off, and understanding blazed in Wren's mind. She'd completely forgotten that Lady Anneliese's younger brother was eager to pursue a military career, and had joined the border force a short time before. No wonder the noble-woman was pleased they weren't going to mount an invasion!

Wren shrugged, an apologetic look on her face, and Lady Anneliese deflated. For a moment they sat in silence. It was normal for military couriers to bring updates from the border to the capital, but Lady Anneliese's information still seemed ominous for some reason. With a decisive nod, Wren stood. Catching Lady Anneliese's eye, she jutted her chin toward the castle.

The noblewoman stood hurriedly, and dipped into a curtsy. It was unclear whether she understood that the princess intended to follow up on the news, but Wren didn't stay to explain. With only a nod to Caleb—whom she still hadn't entirely forgiven for daring to suggest that he might not be returning to his true position—she hurried into the building.

When she reached her father's study, she knew from the four guards stationed outside that she would find the king within. They hesitated, seeming unsure about granting her entry. In an apparently casual gesture, Wren twitched the chain around her neck into place, drawing attention to the signet ring—that of Mistra's heir—dangling from it. Exchanging a quick look, the guards opened the door for her. Pushing down her guilt at once again using Caleb's position to gain influence, Wren hurried inside.

King Lloyd was deep in conversation with his general, and neither looked terribly excited to see the princess.

"Wren," said the king, trying to smile in greeting, and not quite managing it. "What brings you—"

Wren gestured impatiently toward the billet in her father's hand, and the king sighed.

"You heard about the courier, did you? I daresay most of the castle has by now." For a moment he was silent, seeming to weigh the parchment in his hand as he frowned thoughtfully at his daughter. Then he passed it to her.

Ignoring the disapproving way the general cleared his throat, Wren scanned the letter quickly. Her eyes widened as she grasped the meaning of King Basil's message. He wanted to come to Myst? She applauded his desire to negotiate an armistice, but in person?

Her eyes passed up to her father's, and the king raised an eyebrow.

"You seem keen to have input on this matter, Wren," he said. "What do you think?"

Wren frowned. What *did* she think? She scanned the letter again, and her indignation grew. She pictured Caleb's distress as Lady Anneliese talked about how weary she was of being sad and alone, and his resignation as he reminded her that they couldn't be sure her silence would be enough to end the curse. Entolia had done this. Maybe it hadn't been King Basil's decision, but he still had to bear the consequences.

Her frown turning into a full scowl, Wren tossed the parchment onto the desk in a gesture of disapproval.

The general looked heartened. "Much my own thoughts," he said gruffly, although he still couldn't bring himself to look

Wren in the eye. "He'd be mad to suggest coming himself in earnest. It must be a trick. I wouldn't be surprised if he's looking for an excuse to declare full scale war. Or perhaps to spy on us."

King Lloyd frowned at the letter, then looked up at his daughter. "Yes, I'm afraid of the same thing," he confessed. "Looking for an excuse for war, that is. If espionage was his aim, he'd be foolish to conduct it by way of an open state visit. Surely it would be easier to infiltrate us more subtly."

"Not necessarily," said the general. "He might think we'd be less likely to suspect him if he moved in the open."

"He'd be foolish if he thought that," said King Lloyd dryly.

The general gave an impatient grunt. "Of course he's foolish, Your Majesty! He's an eighteen-year-old monarch."

King Lloyd rubbed his face wearily. "Either way, he's put us in a bind. If we refuse to treat with him, we give him his excuse for open war without him even having to work for it."

Wren frowned. Her father had a point, but she still didn't like the idea of the Entolian king coming to Myst.

"We can treat with him without it being on his terms," the general pointed out.

King Lloyd gave a humorless laugh. "How much less *on his terms* could it be than in our own capital? I'm not willing to do the reverse, if that's what you're suggesting. I have no intention of setting foot in Tola while the border is still in contest."

"Of course not, Your Majesty," frowned the general. "But perhaps you could meet him at the border."

"Truth be told, I'm reluctant even to do that," said King Lloyd. His eyes rested on his daughter. "As King Thorn has so clearly demonstrated, even kings can be injured and die."

Wren felt her cheeks heat as she filled in the rest of her father's unspoken thought. Unlike King Thorn, he had no son to step in and take control if he were to die. He didn't want to risk leaving the kingdom in her inept hands, and could she really blame him?

"You don't like the idea, Wren?" King Lloyd raised an eyebrow. "I thought you were inclined to sympathize with Entolia's new king."

Wren shook her head emphatically, Caleb's quiet anguish fueling her anger. Being reluctant to mount an invasion against King Basil while he buried his father was one thing. Hosting him in their own castle was taking it much too far.

"Well, be that as it may, I think we have little choice but to accept his request," said King Lloyd, sighing.

"It's preposterous, Your Majesty," blustered the general. "He's little more than a boy, and he expects you to sit down and treat with him like an equal? After his kingdom's aggression toward ours?"

Wren frowned, not liking the older man's tone. She didn't like the proposed visit either, but in fairness, she had to acknowledge King Basil's right to communicate with her father as an equal. He was the king of Entolia, after all. His age had nothing to do with it.

"Yes, I don't relish being made a fool of," King Lloyd acknowledged. "But inviting him here doesn't mean I have to give him full access."

"True," said the general, brightening. "I could assign a military officer to liaise with him. Someone who'll hear what he has to say, but won't have the authority to make any promises that will bind you."

The king shook his head. "I don't wish to offend the new king. I don't know enough of King Basil to predict his response for certain," his voice turned dry, "but his father would have been angered enough by such treatment that he probably would declare full war and invade immediately."

The general frowned. "I suppose a nobleman of high

standing could perform a similar office. But if I can speak freely, Your Majesty, I don't like it. They wouldn't have the training my men do. If King Basil's intent is to ferret out information about us, some well-intentioned but untrained earl from your council would be an absolute windfall for him."

King Lloyd nodded slowly, and although he spoke to the general, his eyes rested on Wren. "You make good points, General. But there may be another solution entirely. King Basil is, as you say, not of my generation. Perhaps he would prefer to meet not with his father's counterpart, but with his own."

Wren's eyes widened as her father's meaning settled over her.

"An interesting idea, Your Majesty," mused the general, looking at Wren as though she was a military proposal instead of a sentient person. "He'd have no cause to be offended."

Anger rushed over Wren at the hypocritical words. The general could barely hide his disdain any time he was in Wren's presence. But she understood perfectly what the gray-haired man meant. If King Basil was offended to be pushed off on her —as he surely would be—he would be unable to express that offense without causing even greater offense. Everyone might think it, but no one dared to put into words their total lack of respect for Mistra's damaged crown princess.

She understood also what her father was thinking. Wren's status would keep the Entolian king from having cause for complaint, but her muteness would make it unlikely he'd be able to weasel any information of value out of her.

"It's decided then," said the king, sounding pleased. He smiled at Wren, as if he was giving her a boon, instead of exposing her to the ridicule of yet another kingdom. "An excellent opportunity for you to be more active in an important matter of state, Wren. I'll meet with King Basil when he arrives, of course. But if he wishes to stay for extensive negotiations, you can act as his guide and minder. With the protective presence of your guards, of course. What do you say?"

Wren stared at him. He was truly going to pass the Entolian king off on her? Hands shaking in her anger, she pulled her slate from her pocket. But before she could write a word, her eyes were drawn to the scribblings still there from her earlier conversation with Lady Anneliese.

What do you want?

What are you going to do?

Wren stared at the two messages. She couldn't remember the last time the answer to those two questions had been the same. All at once, her defiance leaked out of her. It didn't matter that she didn't want to be polite, and play hostess to the representative of the kingdom that had ruined her life. It was the duty required of her.

Stowing her slate back in her pocket, she nodded. She took no pleasure from her father's satisfied tone as he called for a page to prepare his response to the Entolians.

Wren didn't stay to hear the details, moving back into the corridor with heavy steps. Why couldn't King Thorn have held on for a few more months, so that all of this would be Caleb's problem? Her brother would treat with the young king gladly and capably. He would secure a favorable outcome for Mistra, and there would be no question of offense.

Instead, Wren was once again shouldering a burden she was completely incapable of carrying. She sighed, trying to lift her thoughts as she made her way through the castle. Perhaps she'd get lucky. Perhaps King Basil would get cold feet about the whole idea, and stay far away in his own kingdom.

CHAPTER SIX

Basil

Basil didn't bother looking up from his desk as the door to his study crashed unceremoniously open. Only one person was still willing to be so casual with the young king's privacy.

"For the last time, Zinnia, I *am* leaving in the morning, and you are *not* coming."

"Hey!"

Basil turned at last, smiling slightly at the outraged look on his sister's face.

"I wasn't going to say any of that," Zinnia huffed.

"Then why did you come charging in here like you're on a life-saving mission?" Basil asked calmly, as she rushed over to his desk.

"Well, I am on a mission, and I hope it's not as drastic as that, but I do want to keep you alive," Zinnia said in a rush.

Basil blinked at this flow of words. "You...what?"

"Come on, Bas," said Zinnia impatiently, tugging at his arm. "I don't know how long they'll stick around."

"Who?" Basil demanded, perplexed.

"I'll explain on the way!" Zinnia said, still pulling fruitlessly on him. Basil remained seated, untroubled. "Don't you have ten minutes to listen to your sister?" she scolded him.

"If I'm honest—" Basil started.

"When are you anything else?" Zinnia muttered.

"If I'm honest," Basil repeated, ignoring her, "I *don't* have ten minutes. I'm due to meet with the head of my military escort in five, and I have a great deal to take care of before I leave for Mistra. Besides, I seriously doubt you'll confine yourself to ten minutes."

"Your military escort will wait on their king's convenience," said Zinnia impatiently. "The dragons won't."

"Dragons?" Basil shot to his feet at last. "If there are dragons here to see me, you should really open with that, Zinnia."

In a surprisingly canny move, Zinnia didn't respond until they had already hurried from the castle's entrance.

"They're not here to see you, precisely," she said, no apology in her voice. "It's just Dannsair, and she's down at the shore."

"Zinnia!" Basil protested, pulling up. "You interrupted something important for this! If Dannsair is at the shore, she wants to be left alone. She'd come to the castle if she wanted to speak with me."

"She won't mind," said Zinnia, prodding him back into motion. "I've been checking the beach every day since you sent that message to King Lloyd, hoping she'd come before your departure. And she finally did!"

Basil frowned, glancing back at the castle's entrance, and the two stone dragons that flanked it. He really did have about a hundred other things he should be doing with this time. With a sigh, he surrendered, following his eager sister through the castle's open gates and down the short path that led from their low cliff to the ocean below. Two guards went ahead of them, and four trailed behind. Basil had left the castle so rarely since his coronation, he still wasn't entirely used to the honor guard such outings required.

As his sister had promised, once the familiar shoreline came into sight, it was impossible to miss the enormous reptilian figure draped over a rock a short distance out to sea.

Well, enormous compared to a human. Basil knew that, at three times his own height, Dannsair was on the small side for a dragon. It was due to her relative youth—she was probably only several decades older than him. Not that he would ever be impolite enough to ask. The brightness of her purple scales also proclaimed her youth. Basil had heard that the oldest of the dragon elders were so darkened by time their scales were almost black.

He wasn't likely ever to confirm that information for himself, however. The elders rarely left their colony, even to meet with human royalty. They certainly didn't wander past Entolia's seaside capital every month or so to indulge a love of sun-baking the way Dannsair did. Inasmuch as dragons and humans could be friends, Basil and Zinnia had considered her a friend since their childhood. She'd told them the love of the ocean was in the bones of every dragon, but most preferred to commune with the vast expanse of water in less populated areas. Basil had indeed caught sight of unfamiliar dragons from time to time, brooding on top of the wave-lashed cliffs far to the east, staring out over the sea like landlocked sailors.

Dannsair, however, didn't seem to mind being near people. In dragon terms, she was downright friendly.

"Greetings, Dannsair!" Zinnia called brightly, once they'd reached the shoreline.

The dragon raised her head in an unhurried gesture, swinging her long neck around to take stock of her visitors.

"Greetings, Dannsair," Basil echoed his sister, bowing to the majestic creature.

"Greetings, Princess Zinnia," said Dannsair. Her yellow orb-like eyes lingered unblinkingly on Basil. "And to you, King Basil, Entolia's new monarch."

Basil inclined his head again, fighting the urge to smile at the dragon's solemn words. Dannsair was sprawled on her back, stomach exposed to the sky, and tail dangling into the water in a posture of total relaxation. Nothing in her dignified tone suggested any awareness of the ridiculousness of the posture.

Straightening again, Basil glanced from the wicked talons, as long as his forearm, which tipped Dannsair's feet, to the sharp triangular plates that ran along the back of her neck, all the way down to the tip of her tail.

He wasn't a fool. Dannsair had so far shown herself inclined to be friendly, but he would be wise to remember that she, and the rest of her kind, were more powerful than he was, crown or none.

"I'm so glad you're here!" Zinnia said brightly. "I've been waiting for you for a week, and I thought you wouldn't come in time."

Basil frowned slightly at his sister. She'd always lacked the appropriate fear of the dragons. He worried that one day Zinnia would go too far, and get herself into trouble with the unpredictable beasts.

"Is that so?" Thankfully, Dannsair's voice held curiosity rather than offense. "Why were you waiting for me?"

"I wanted to ask for your help," said Zinnia. As she spoke, she hiked up her skirts and removed her slippers. Basil saw one of the princess's guards shift uncomfortably as she stepped into the water, toward the dragon. He didn't envy them the task of keeping her safe. "My brother is leaving for Mistra in the morning, to put himself at the mercy of our enemies." She flashed the dragon a grin that was far too cheeky for Basil's liking. "Into the dragon's mouth, so to speak."

Dannsair made a gurgling sound that Basil knew to be laughter. "The Mistrans may be your enemies," she said indulgently, "but they are hardly as dangerous as dragons. Do you mean to suggest you fear for his safety?"

Zinnia nodded. "We all do."

"Zinnia," Basil started impatiently, but she waved him off.

"I have my own interests at heart," she told him sternly. "You think I want you to be knocked off, and to find myself queen at seventeen?"

"What is it you wish me to do for your new king?" Dannsair asked, mercifully cutting off the rising sibling squabble.

"Well," said Zinnia, then trailed off. For all her apparent confidence around the dragon, it sounded to Basil like she was finding it hard to put her request into words after all. "We count you a friend..." She paused, perhaps waiting for the dragon to reciprocate.

Dannsair remained serenely silent. With an unhurried movement, she flipped herself over, catching at the rocks with her talons, and pulling herself back onto the mostly flat shelf on which she had been reclining. She gave herself one shake, a rippling motion that started in her tail, and passed all the way up to her reptilian head. Then she settled onto her belly, resting her chin on her folded front feet, for all the world like a dog waiting for a treat.

Clearing her throat, Zinnia tried again. "I wondered if you would go with him," she said in a rush. "Just to sort of...keep him company."

"Zinnia!" Basil scolded, aghast. He turned to the dragon. "Dannsair, I apologize on my sister's behalf. I would never ask you to join me on a state visit to another crown."

The dragon didn't look angry, but there was no compromise in her voice as she replied. "I am glad to hear it. I have no intention of accompanying you. Dragons do not involve themselves in the politics of human kingdoms."

Zinnia visibly deflated. "Sure you do," she wheedled, although Basil could tell she didn't have much hope of actually changing the dragon's mind. "I know for a fact that you paid a state visit to Princess Penny and Prince Rian after their wedding last year. She wrote to me and told me that you descended right into the castle's central courtyard, and presented her with a wedding gift in front of the king and queen."

Dannsair's mouth stretched into a slightly unnerving smile, her thin lips pulled all the way back past her eyes. "That was not a state visit. That was a little reminder to the Bansfordian monarchs." She paused. "And I am very fond of little Penny, of course."

"A reminder of what?" Basil asked, in spite of himself.

The dragon's voice was suddenly steely, and there was a dangerous glint in her eyes. "That while we may have chosen to forgive the Bansfordians for their audacity in banning magic from their kingdom for fourteen years, we haven't forgotten."

Before either human could respond, something enormous broke the surface of the water just behind Dannsair. Basil and Zinnia both jumped, and threw up their arms to shield their faces from the sudden spray, and Basil heard alarmed cries from the guards just behind them. Dannsair, of course, had no reaction whatsoever.

Lowering his arms, Basil saw that another dragon had appeared behind Dannsair, bobbing in the water like an over-sized—and excessively scaly—duck. This dragon was of a similar size to Dannsair, but he had only a hint of purple edging his bright yellow scales.

"Greetings, Rekavidur," said Basil, bowing once again.

"Greetings, King Basil," said the dragon, regarding him fixedly.

"Reka!" Zinnia smiled at the newcomer. "Where did you come from?"

The dragon blinked in surprise. "Did you not see? I came from under the water."

Zinnia looked like she was trying not to laugh, but to Basil's relief, she didn't comment on the dragon trait of taking everything literally.

"Can you breathe under there?" she asked instead, her head tilted curiously.

"Of course not," said Rekavidur, sounding amused.

"Find anything?" Dannsair asked her fellow dragon, disregarding the two humans.

Rekavidur shook his head. "Not so much as a hint."

"What were you looking for?" Zinnia asked.

"That is my own affair," said Rekavidur unencouragingly. "You never know what, or whom, you might find if you look." He cast his orb-like eyes over the king and princess. "What brings you here?"

"It is our own kingdom," Zinnia pointed out, sounding slightly offended. "Basil's even the king now."

"I am aware of that," said Rekavidur calmly. His gaze rested consideringly on Basil. "Are you here in your official capacity?"

"No," said Basil quickly. "I'm here as an unwilling brother."

"Traitor!" gasped Zinnia. She turned to Rekavidur. "Reka, you're not from Solstice. I *know* you don't always follow the rules of the dragon colony here. Will you go with Basil to Mistra, to make sure they don't kill him off? All you'd have to do would be to show your face. They wouldn't dare pick a fight with him if he had a dragon on his side."

"But I'm not on his side," Rekavidur pointed out reasonably.

Dannsair nodded sagely. "We are fond of you, Zinnia. But we owe no allegiance to Entolia." She inclined her head to Basil.

"Much as we already think better of your reign than we did of your father's."

"Aha!" Zinnia cried, cutting off Basil's opportunity to respond to the unexpected compliment. "It seems you *do* take some interest in human politics. Otherwise what would you know of Basil's reign?"

"Not involving ourselves is not the same as not knowing what's happening," said Dannsair, in an aloof tone that didn't altogether erase the impression that she had indeed been caught out.

"Either way," said Basil firmly. "I don't have any expectation —or, if I'm honest, desire—to have either one of you accompany me to Mistra."

"Honesty in humans is so refreshing," commented Rekavidur, spreading his wings so as to shake water from them. "It almost makes me want to accompany you."

"Why don't you wish it?" Dannsair asked curiously.

Basil shrugged. "My aim is to reach a peaceful solution. If I wanted to overwhelm with force, I would mount a military attack. I want to negotiate, and I suspect that in order to do that, I'll need to earn enough of a measure of trust to find out what's really behind this conflict. Somehow I suspect that showing up with dragons in tow would destroy any chance of that."

"We do tend to intimidate," Dannsair agreed placidly. She reached up one of her front feet, using one long talon to pick a fishbone from between her razor-sharp teeth.

To Basil's dismay, Zinnia snorted. "If you say so." Her gaze passed between the two dragons, her shoulders slumped. "So there's nothing you can do to look out for Basil?"

"Zinnia," said Basil, as patiently as he could. "There's no reason whatsoever they should be looking out for me."

"Isn't the Mistran princess the one who doesn't speak?"

Rekavidur asked Dannsair, disregarding both humans entirely. "Because of a curse?"

"According to our intelligence," Basil cut in, "her silence isn't related to the curse that killed her brothers. It just started at the same time."

The yellow dragon regarded him thoughtfully. "Humans are very bad at recognizing magic, however." His gaze passed to Dannsair. "I believe the Listernian curse involved stopping people's tongues, did it not?"

A look came over the female dragon's face that Basil didn't understand at all. Clearly some form of silent communication was occurring between the pair. A glance at Zinnia showed that she was equally confused.

"Perhaps it is worth having a look," said Dannsair slowly. "No harm in checking."

"You'll go with him?" Zinnia gasped excitedly.

Dannsair shook her head. "I have already told you that we do not involve ourselves in human politics. But although the Mistran capital has no coastline to draw us there, we are perfectly welcome in Myst, I believe." Her eyes passed to Basil. "Perhaps we will pay the city a visit of our own, during your stay there."

"That would be wonderful," said Zinnia, clapping her hands. "Oops."

In her enthusiasm, she'd forgotten that she was holding her skirts up out of the ankle-deep water, and they were now saturated. Basil rolled his eyes.

"I'd feel much more easy knowing you'll be looking in on him," Zinnia went on, beaming at her brother.

Basil sighed. It obviously wasn't for him to approve or disapprove of the dragons visiting another kingdom's capital, but he still felt some response was required of him.

"As always, it would be my honor to see you," he offered. It seemed to be acceptable, as both dragons inclined their heads graciously.

"Until then," nodded Dannsair. Then, without warning, both dragons dove fluidly beneath the water, disappearing instantly into the depths.

Basil blinked. "Since when do dragons favor underwater travel?" He turned to Zinnia, bemused.

But she was clearly uninterested in such details. "Not most dragons," she said impatiently. "Just Reka and Dannsair, I think. But never mind that! Bas, this is great! The Mistrans won't kill you with dragons looking over their shoulders."

Basil frowned. "Zinnia, it was incredibly irresponsible to ask them for that favor. You know the unwritten rule that allows dragons and humans to coexist peacefully. We don't ask for their help, and they don't ask for ours."

Zinnia made an impatient noise as she waded out of the water and picked up her slippers. "You know that's not the rule. They don't use magic on us—to help or hinder—and we don't use it on them. They're not supposed to help us with breaking *enchantments*. It doesn't mean they can't help us in other ways. Besides..." she gave Basil a shifty look, "Dannsair and Reka don't exactly follow the rules."

They'd started climbing back up the cliff path, but Basil paused, frowning back at his sister.

"What does that mean?" he asked. His eyes drifted to the guards, and he thought better of the question, hurrying on before his sister could answer. "You should be careful what you say. If anyone thought they were breaking the agreement for us..." He shook his head. He honestly didn't know what would happen in that event, and it was the last thing he wanted to find out, mere days into his time as king. "And when did you become so very friendly with them?"

Zinnia shrugged, pushing past him. "We're all friendly with

them. The girls and I come down here a lot, and so do they. We don't have the responsibilities you do. Most of the time, everyone's happy to have us out of the castle."

Basil frowned as he followed his sister up the slope. He didn't need a reminder of the depressing separation between him and his sisters. Still, little as he would admit it to her, he was heartened by the idea that the dragons would look in on him in Myst. At least he'd be guaranteed two friendly faces, no matter how sharp-toothed and reptilian they might be.

CHAPTER SEVEN

Basil

Basil pulled his horse up, sensing that the creature would appreciate a rest. His gaze passed measuringly over the city spread out before him. Myst gave a pleasant appearance, at least from a distance. It was settled at the base of the long mountain range that formed Mistra's border with Albury, and its elegant towers and brightly colored pennants stood out cheerfully against the gray rock.

"Are you sure you're ready, Your Majesty?"

Basil turned his head at the now familiar voice. Lord Baldwin had ridden up alongside his king, a slight frown creasing his brow as he followed Basil's gaze toward Myst.

"Of course, My Lord," said Basil calmly. "As you know, I don't share the expectation of the rest of the delegation that I'm going to be eaten on arrival."

Lord Baldwin gave a tight smile. Clearly he found no humor in Basil's joke, but felt he was honor bound to acknowledge it. "We'll be there within the hour, apparently."

Basil nodded. "That would be my estimate as well." He glanced up at the sun. "We're a little behind schedule, so I daresay they'll be well and truly ready for our arrival."

His companion sent him a sharp look. "If you will tolerate me speaking plainly, Your Majesty—"

"You already know that I not only tolerate it, but insist on it," Basil interrupted placidly.

Lord Baldwin inclined his head. "We wouldn't be behind schedule if you hadn't insisted on lingering so long at the front lines. It took only a moment to ascertain that the Mistrans intend to honor the temporary ceasefire during negotiations. If we'd continued straight on, we could have arrived yesterday as intended."

"It was worth the delay," said Basil. "I wished to see the conditions for myself. It will help inform the negotiations, if nothing else."

"Perhaps," said Lord Baldwin, shifting in his saddle. "But was it really necessary to visit all the wounded personally?"

Basil considered his companion silently. The young nobleman had so far struck him as sensible and down-to-earth. He'd been quite surprised by Lord Baldwin's evident discomfort when they spent time among the injured soldiers.

"It was necessary in my view," he said simply. "They were injured fighting in my name. What honor would I show if I passed through their camp and failed even to acknowledge their sacrifice?"

"But you don't even agree with the war," said Lord Baldwin, regarding him curiously. "You never asked them to fight in your name."

Basil smiled ruefully. "That's not how a crown works, My Lord. I inherited all my father's responsibilities along with his title. His decisions are mine now."

Lord Baldwin shook his head slightly. "You are a very unusual eighteen-year-old, Your Majesty."

Basil laughed aloud at that. "That comes with the crown, too."

"With respect, King Basil," Lord Baldwin insisted, "I disagree."

"How old are you, My Lord?" Basil asked bluntly. The nobleman looked surprised, but didn't hesitate to answer. Basil felt a surge of satisfaction. It was nice when his exalted position actually worked in favor of his preference for plain speaking. He could get away with asking questions that would be impertinent in anyone else.

"I'm thirty-five. I also came into my father's position young, although not quite as young as you, Your Majesty. He died almost ten years ago."

"My sympathies," said Basil gravely, and Lord Baldwin gave an awkward nod.

"Are your family's holdings near Tola?" Basil asked, thinking he should have taken the time to familiarize himself with his companion's history before their departure.

Lord Baldwin shook his head. "Further west, Your Majesty. We rode by not far from them on our journey."

"Did we? You should have pointed them out." The young king turned his horse's head toward the city. "Well then, enough of a rest, my friend," he told the creature. "We are, as Lord Baldwin has so accurately pointed out, late. Let's not delay any further."

Without another word, the two men spurred their mounts back into motion, the combination of soldiers and guards fanning out into formation around them, and the few servants and officials who formed part of their delegation riding a short distance behind.

Somewhat to his own embarrassment, Basil found himself surreptitiously searching the sky as they rode. No winged shapes blotted out the sun, and he shook his head at his own folly. The dragons wouldn't come so soon. He just hoped their very non-human perception of time wouldn't cause them to visit Myst in a decade, expecting Basil to still be present. He didn't truly wish for their presence to dominate his first meeting with King Lloyd, anyway.

They had almost reached the city gates when a group of horsemen rode out to meet them. The senior military officer on the Entolian delegation rode up to Basil's side as the riders approached, speaking to the king while they still had privacy from their hosts.

"Soldiers, Your Majesty," he said, jerking his chin toward the oncoming Mistrans.

Basil regarded the riders curiously. "Really? They're not wearing uniforms."

The officer grunted. "I would guess they don't want to proclaim their position. But you can see it in the way they ride, and in their weapons. Soldiers or guards, no question."

Basil nodded his thanks, and the officer fell back slightly just as the two groups converged. Whatever his companions might be, the rider heading the approaching group was clearly a nobleman. He greeted Basil formally, his words of welcome belied by the tension and suspicion in his tone. Basil responded with his usual calm, and didn't hesitate to allow himself to be subsumed into the Mistran group as they turned to ride back toward the capital.

A glance back showed Basil that his own military escort looked far from pleased, but he just sent the ghost of a shrug toward his senior officer. The other man might be suspicious at the deception, but Basil took heart from the fact that King Lloyd had sent non-uniformed soldiers. It suggested that while the other king wished—most understandably—to minimize the threat Basil posed, he also didn't wish to offend his visitor by greeting him with a show of military force.

Either way, Basil couldn't see anything to be gained by refusing to fall in with the soldiers. He had chosen to put his head into the dragon's mouth, as Zinnia would say. If his hosts wished him harm, his own small force would be powerless to protect him. Allowing the Mistrans to escort him to the city put him at no greater risk than he was already facing.

Still, he didn't really blame his officer for not seeing it that way.

Conscious of the hard stares of the guards on the parapet, Basil rode through the city's open gates still ensconced in the Mistran troops. His visit was obviously anticipated by the populace, and the streets were lined with curious onlookers. Most just stared, their expressions ranging from curiosity to fear, but a few called out abuse at the foreign king, and one or two even spat onto the road as Basil rode past.

Some of the members of Basil's delegation made noises of outrage at this treatment of their king, but Basil mainly just felt grieved. It wasn't unexpected—or even unreasonable, he reflected, picturing the hostility many of his own people showed toward the Mistrans. But he'd never been spat at before. It was a painfully personal reminder of how far the two kingdoms had sunk into conflict. They'd never been close allies—there had been tension over the border for a century, long before the armed conflict began—but how had they allowed things to deteriorate this far?

Picturing his inflexible father, Basil reminded himself that he knew exactly how. He set his face in grim lines. That was what he was here to fix.

When they reached the castle, Basil got his first look at the man he knew must be King Lloyd. He was a tall man, his crisp white doublet striking against his dark skin, and his unmoving posture giving him a regal and unyielding air. To his left stood an elegant woman, dressed in a gown as fine as any of Basil's mother's, her ears glinting with understated jewels. This, undoubtedly, was Queen Liana.

To the king's left, another figure stood. Like her parents, her dark skin glowed warmly in the afternoon sun, and she was dressed with great elegance. The soft pink of her gown became her excellently, with open sleeves that trailed all the way to the cobblestones below her feet, and delicate embroidery lining the scooped neckline. Basil reflected irrelevantly that if Lord Baldwin knew with what detail Basil had assessed the gown, he would probably once again proclaim him an unusual eighteen-year-old. This time it had nothing to do with being king, however, and everything to do with having twelve sisters.

In spite of her elegant attire, the young woman was unadorned except for a thick chain that disappeared below her gown, and a tiara, which Basil didn't need in order to identify her. This had to be Princess Wren, King Lloyd's only surviving heir, and Mistra's future ruler.

When Basil dismounted, a groom appeared immediately to lead his horse off, and he saw with approval that the man was speaking soothingly to the animal. Hopefully the Mistrans' suspicion of Entolians wouldn't extend to their steeds. Basil couldn't escape being punished for his father's decisions, but there was no need for his horse to suffer as well. Turning to the Mistran royals, Basil bent his upper body in a swift bow.

"King Basil," said King Lloyd, his voice somber. "Welcome."

Straightening, Basil searched the other king's face. It was hard to tell if the greeting was sincere. He didn't know King Lloyd well enough to read his expression.

"Thank you, Your Majesty," said Basil evenly. "I'm glad to be here."

His eyes passed to the queen and the princess, and he inclined his head. "Queen Liana, Princess Wren."

Neither spoke in reply, although they both inclined their heads slightly. Basil found his eyes lingering on Princess Wren, surprise passing over him. Obviously his preparatory research had been insufficient. Perhaps it was all the talk of her silence and timidity, but he had formed the impression that King Lloyd's heir was still a child. Up close, however, he could see that the princess before him was undoubtedly a young woman.

She looked ill at ease compared to her parents, her hands folded in front of her as if they needed assistance to avoid fidgeting. Her hair was unconfined, erupting around her head in unruly black curls that looked like they would defy any attempt to tame them.

Not that the effect was unpleasant. On the contrary, Basil was a little startled to discover that not only was Princess Wren a young woman, she was a very attractive one.

Furthermore, the hard look she was giving him didn't support what he'd been told about her timidity. He would have expected her eyes to be fixed on her feet, like his shy young sister Magnolia's so often were. But Princess Wren was watching him closely, her searching brown eyes narrowed in suspicion. Clearly she didn't trust him as far as she could throw him. Which, he reflected, looking at her slim form, probably wouldn't be far.

"I daresay you wish to freshen up before partaking of some food," said King Lloyd, still speaking with a slight stiffness. "My steward is waiting to show you and your party to your quarters, but first my daughter will show you where to find the dining hall once you are ready."

Basil blinked in surprise. The silent princess was going to give him a tour? If she felt equally surprised, she showed no sign of it.

"Thank you for your hospitality, Your Majesty," he said, inclining his head toward the king once again. "I will be glad to freshen up and to take some food, but then I look forward to fruitful discussions between us soon."

King Lloyd raised one eyebrow, but Basil didn't regret his

direct speech. He hadn't ridden all the way from Tola—in defiance of the wishes of his family and all of his advisors—to partake in luncheons and diplomatic chitchat. He fully expected to negotiate directly with King Lloyd, and without delay. The sooner he made that clear, the better for all concerned.

Without a word—of course—the princess turned and climbed the shallow steps leading into the castle. With a final respectful nod to the king and queen, Basil followed her, his retinue trailing behind him. Two of his own guards flanked him, but the Entolian soldiers remained outside, ready to be led to the barracks where they were to be accommodated. Basil caught an uneasy look from his senior officer, and gave the man what he hoped was a reassuring nod.

Princess Wren led the small party through a well lit and pleasant entranceway, climbing a flight of stairs and proceeding some way down a broad corridor before stopping. She gestured through an open door, and glancing in, Basil saw a large dining hall, dominated by an immense and highly polished table of mahogany. A lavish spread already covered the surface, and servants stood at the ready around the edge of the room.

Basil hid a smile. Intimately familiar with castle life as he was, he doubted that the royal family of Mistra habitually ate such an extravagant luncheon in the late afternoon. Not that he was complaining. If his hosts were inclined to try to intimidate him with their opulence, he would be well pleased if they did so by means of food.

He nodded to the princess. "Thank you, Your Highness."

She nodded back, but her eyes weren't on him. They were scanning the corridor, apparently looking for someone or something. Basil took the opportunity to further measure her. It was well known that Mistra was embarrassed by its eccentric crown princess, and Basil had therefore expected her silences to be awkward. But now he saw her in person, he didn't find it so at all. In fact, in spite of her evident unease with the whole situation, he was struck primarily with an impression of quiet elegance and grace.

Picturing Zinnia's alarming levity around magical creatures which could kill her with a single swipe, Briar's uncomfortable obsession with accuracy, and Wisteria's generally uncontrolled exuberance, it occurred to Basil that Mistra could do much worse in its heir. At least there was every likelihood that King Lloyd would have a long life, so that Princess Wren wouldn't have to shoulder the burden of ruler until she was well into adulthood, by which time any issues of confidence would surely have disappeared.

The princess turned to him, her brow slightly furrowed. When she saw how closely he was watching her, she stilled. Basil didn't look away, meeting her gaze steadily. When the silence stretched out, he raised one questioning eyebrow, and was amazed to see the princess's cheeks tinge slightly with color.

She cleared her throat, raising one hand to fidget slightly with something suspended around her neck on the chain he'd noticed earlier. A glance showed Basil that it was a heavy gold signet ring, the Mistran royal crest adorning it in some kind of red stone. Princess Wren evidently saw him looking, because she dropped her hand quickly, instead gesturing further down the corridor.

Basil suddenly realized what she must have been looking for —King Lloyd had said that the steward would show the visiting king to his rooms, but no such person was in sight. Gathering that the princess intended to perform this office herself, Basil moved forward as directed. As he walked—Princess Wren beside him, and his delegation behind them—Basil thought about that cleared throat. Had the sound been confirmation of the rumors, that there was nothing physically wrong with the princess's voice?

It wasn't far from the banquet hall to the king's suite. They had just reached the relevant corridor, and Princess Wren was looking uncertainly between several doors, when a middle aged man came hurrying up.

"I beg your pardon Your Highness," he said to Princess Wren, before turning to Basil, "Your Majesty. Allow me to show you and your attendants to your rooms."

"No pardon necessary," said Basil lightly. "Her Highness has looked after us very graciously."

The princess shot him a suspicious look. Surprising himself by how much he wanted to remove the distrust from her eyes, Basil gave her a half-bow.

"Thank you, Princess Wren."

She gave a tight nod, still looking unconvinced, and swept away up the corridor. Basil watched her for a moment too long, and when he turned he found the steward watching him curiously.

"Your Majesty," said the man quickly, bowing again before gesturing to a nearby door. "Your suite."

The two Entolian guards accompanying Basil stepped forward, performing a quick check of what turned out to be a large and well-appointed two room suite. Once they had cleared the space, Basil thanked the steward politely. The man, having pointed the other guests to their nearby accommodation, hurried away.

Basil turned to Lord Baldwin. "I would like to convene in my rooms before we eat," he said, his gaze encompassing everyone. He noticed that several of them were looking around fearfully.

"Your Majesty," said Lord Baldwin quickly, "allow me to offer my rooms for—"

"Mine will be the largest," Basil cut him off. "It's most practical to meet there."

Within minutes, they had all gathered in Basil's enormous

receiving room. As he had predicted, the space was large enough to comfortably accommodate the dozen people now gathered.

"We shouldn't tarry too long," Basil said curtly, thinking of the feast spread out for their benefit. "But I would be interested to hear any first impressions you've formed."

"It's clear they don't trust us," grunted Lord Baldwin.

Basil nodded slowly. He turned to a middle aged couple, merchants from Tola, his eyes settling on the wife. "You had an opportunity to see the princess up close sooner than I expected. What did you find?"

The woman swallowed nervously. "As reported, Your Majesty. I don't think she's under a curse. Unless I'm mistaken, the ring she wears around her neck is some kind of artifact. I'm not versed enough in such matters to detect its purpose."

Basil nodded. "Unlikely it holds a silencing curse," he said dryly.

She ventured a small smile. "Very unlikely, Your Majesty. I didn't detect magic clinging to her in the way I would expect from a curse over her. But I'm no expert," she added hastily.

Basil gave her a tight smile. "Much more of an expert than the rest of us," he said encouragingly. He tapped a finger thoughtfully on his leg. "I would be grateful if you would keep your...extra sense on the alert. I imagine that if the signet ring is an artifact, it's something she acquired from her parents and its function is well known to them, so it's unlikely to be of relevance. But there's no harm in finding out for sure. I want to get to the bottom of her silence if possible. The timing of it makes me suspect it may be more central to the conflict than we've previously supposed."

He thought of Rekavidur's cryptic comments about Princess Wren's silence. The dragon clearly thought it might be more than it seemed. "I think it's worth exploring the possibility that her silence is magical in nature, and you're the only one in a position to do that. Your input could be invaluable to resolving our differences."

"Yes, Your Majesty," said the woman, her curtsy not quite quick enough to hide the flush of pleasure on her face at her skills being so highly regarded.

Basil turned from her, well pleased. He had never doubted it would be worth his while to bring a magic-user along, but he was pleased to have the enchantress's abilities prove useful so quickly.

"Lord Baldwin," he addressed the nobleman. "As the sole representative of the Lords' Council, you are likely in the best position to get a sense of what the Mistran court thinks of our visit. I would be grateful to hear any insights you might have."

Lord Baldwin nodded quickly. "I will see what I can discover, Your Majesty."

Basil frowned into empty space. "The princess herself is a surprise, isn't she?"

"Is...is she?" Lord Baldwin asked.

Basil nodded. "She doesn't strike me as timid at all. And I was expecting a child."

"Were you?" The nobleman's tone suggested his information had been better. "I understand she'll turn eighteen shortly, at which time she'll be formally anointed as King Lloyd's heir."

Basil shook his head slightly. Mistrans and their formalities. She was the king's heir by virtue of her birth. Why did they need a special ceremony when she turned eighteen? Banishing the trivial detail from his mind, Basil cast his eyes over the various servants, standing behind the delegation members. "Any of you have observations to share?"

"Us, Your Majesty?" asked a manservant nervously.

"Of course," said Basil briskly. "I want to hear all perspectives."

The man cleared his throat. "Well, the servants don't seem...afraid."

Basil tilted his head questioningly to the side. "Of us, you mean?"

The manservant shook his head. "No, Your Majesty. Just generally. Of their own masters, I suppose."

Another servant nodded. "It says a lot about a royal family," she piped up timidly, and the other servants made murmurs of assent.

Basil considered this point with interest. "Thank you," he said sincerely. He was glad he'd pushed for their opinions. He would never have thought to assess the mood of the local servants, but he could see how it would give an insight into the Mistran royals.

The servants all looked as pleased as the enchantress had done, and Lord Baldwin was watching Basil with an expression that looked strangely like respect. It was something Basil had never yet experienced from one of his nobles, so he couldn't be sure.

Still, looking around at the small group gathered in his chambers, each one of whom was now watching him with definite expectation, he felt a surge of satisfaction. He'd much rather be backed by this motley collection of guards, servants, and others, with one canny representative of the Lords' Council, than be bogged down by a host of stiff-rumped courtiers, more focused on his dignity than he'd ever be himself.

"Come on," he said to his little crew. "Let's end this war."

CHAPTER EIGHT

Wren

Wren frowned down at her plate, aware that she was fidgeting, but unable to stop herself. The meal had already gone for an eternity, and there was still a dessert course to come. The late afternoon welcome banquet had turned into an early dinner, as had been inevitable given the Entolian party's late arrival.

Rude, she called it.

The worst of it was, in furthering his intention to palm King Basil off on her, Wren's father had arranged for the visiting king to be seated next to her at the long table. Of course she'd made no conversation, and it wouldn't have been so bad if the visiting king had just ignored his silent companion, as most people did. But instead, he'd been uncomfortably focused on her for the entire meal.

Even now, she was acutely aware of his gaze, seeming to weigh her as she ate. Unable to resist any longer, she looked up quickly, hoping to throw him off balance by catching him staring.

She was disappointed. In their short acquaintance, she'd already gotten the sense that the Entolian king wasn't someone who was easily thrown off balance. The trouble was, he wasn't staring at her rudely, such that he would be embarrassed by her sudden attention. He was just...looking at her. When she met his eye, he gave her a polite smile, and suddenly his steady regard seemed like the most natural courtesy, instead of the unnerving spectacle it really was.

Wren tried to remember the last time someone outside her intimate circle had held her gaze like that, and she came up blank. Fleetingly, she wished for her voice, to deliver some witty quip that would discompose him.

It was a foolish thought. Not only was it as impossible as ever for her to use her voice, no witty quips sprang to mind. She was too unsettled by King Basil's bizarre failure to find her unsettling.

At least he hadn't tried to press her into uncomfortably one-sided conversation.

When the meal at last drew to a close, King Lloyd rose to his feet. All the Mistrans present at the dinner mirrored the gesture. After the briefest of pauses, King Basil did the same, and as soon as their king was no longer seated, the rest of the Entolian delegation hastened to their feet as well. Shooting a surreptitious look at King Basil, Wren saw that he stood with his hands clasped behind his back, a look of calm expectancy on his face as he watched the Mistran king.

Instead of listening to her father's carefully worded welcome, Wren found herself watching the young king as avidly as he'd been watching her. She wondered what he was thinking —she was usually good at reading people, but his reactions were so unexpected, she felt all at sea. Unable to make headway on assessing what was happening within, she focused instead on what she could see on the outside.

He was considerably taller than she was, and although his frame still held the litheness of youth, she could see strength in his broad chest, and in the lean muscles of his arms. His skin was much paler than hers, like most Entolians, but its tan showed that he spent a fair amount of time in the sun. His hair, on the lighter end of brown, was cut just above his ears, although its length was still enough to show a tendency to waviness. His unnervingly sharp eyes were hazel, and were at present fixed unblinkingly on Wren's father.

If King Basil felt her gaze, he gave no sign of it. But when a slight frown settled on his forehead, Wren thought she'd better pay a bit less attention to King Basil's muscular frame, and a bit more attention to what was happening.

"I imagine you are all tired after your travels," her father was saying commandingly. "I trust your rest will be comfortable, and I look forward to opening discussions tomorrow."

The frown between King Basil's brows was more pronounced now. He opened his mouth to speak, then clamped it shut, seeming to think better of it. Wren had no doubt he was swallowing what he'd wished to say, and the look of frustration on his face was so familiar, she felt a tiny shoot of fellow feeling. She squashed it immediately. He wasn't like her—for one thing, he was under no true compulsion not to speak his mind. For another, she reminded herself, Entolia was the enemy. And as its head, King Basil represented everything she and her family had suffered. Were still suffering.

The room began to empty—it hadn't been a large group, as King Lloyd had decided that the Entolians' visit didn't merit a full court banquet—but King Basil remained in position. His retinue copied him, and Wren noticed them looking between the two kings a little nervously. Her attention caught, she made no move to leave herself. What were they concerned about?

"Your Majesty," King Basil said calmly, once most of the Mistran diners had left. "I appreciate your consideration, but it's early yet. I'm not especially tired from my journey, and I was hoping to speak with you tonight."

King Lloyd raised his eyebrow in an expression that was coldly polite at best. It was possible King Basil couldn't read it, but Wren recognized the offense on her father's face.

"Your eagerness is admirable, King Basil. But we will have time enough to discuss our intentions."

Wren could see that King Basil wasn't satisfied with this answer, but after a moment of obvious struggle, he held his peace. With a swift bow to King Lloyd, and an inclined head in the queen's and princess's directions, he strode from the room. His companions followed him, several of them looking around them nervously, as if expecting to be attacked. Wren caught one man, a nobleman who looked to be in his thirties, watching her curiously. When he saw that she'd noticed, he colored slightly and dipped his head, clearly eager to avoid locking eyes with her.

Now *that* behavior was familiar. King Basil's, on the other hand, was unsettlingly unpredictable. Her eyes rested on the Entolian, wondering how his first impression of her compared with her reaction to him. As if he could sense her thoughts, the young king paused in the doorway, glancing back. For a moment their eyes met, a slight frown creasing King Basil's forehead. His eyes were again uncomfortably searching as they studied Wren's face, and she was the first to turn away.

"Well." The gruff voice of the general pulled Wren's thoughts from the departing Entolians. "It seems we'd be foolish to hope that this new king has come, cap in hand, to humbly ask our forgiveness for his father's aggression."

A glance around showed Wren that the Entolians had been the last to leave. No one remained with the royal family except the general, her father's steward, and the various servants already beginning to clear the table.

"Hardly," said King Lloyd, his expression dark. "Did you hear his comment when he first arrived? And then again after the meal. He seems to think he can order my time how he pleases."

Wren frowned. Little as she wanted to agree with the Entolian king about anything, her father's attitude didn't seem reasonable. With no courtiers to sneer at her, she pulled out her slate.

I thought you intended to negotiate with him.

Her father's scowl grew as she thrust the slate under his nose, but his eyes skated over the words in spite of himself. "Of course I do," he said impatiently. "But not at all hours of the night."

Wren glanced pointedly out the window, where the sun had barely sunk below the horizon, then gave her father a look. He ignored it.

"I don't want him to think that just because he's come to us, he can set the terms of our discussions," he said to the general.

The older man nodded curtly. "I agree, Your Majesty. He's little more than a child. And from what I can see, he brought no advisors with substantial experience. However much he thinks he understands of military matters, he must defer to you as an established and experienced monarch."

From the little she'd seen of him, somehow Wren doubted King Basil would see it that way.

"Since he's in such a rush," said King Lloyd crisply, "I'll meet with him before breakfast. Wren," he turned abruptly to his daughter, "you will attend."

Wren began to scrub her slate clean, ready to protest. She

always visited her brothers before breakfast—what would they think if she didn't show up?

But her father didn't stay to see what she would write. Without another word, he held his arm out to his wife, and he and the queen left the dining hall together. Frowning, Wren watched them go, noting the tension in her father's shoulders, and the uncharacteristic slump to her mother's elegant frame. A pang went through her at the sight. Her father had his faults, but he wasn't usually unreasonable. She'd been too quick to let her own frustrations blind her to what must be happening within her parents. In her irritation at not being understood, she so often forgot that the king and queen truly thought all six of their sons had been murdered. The last time they'd received an Entolian envoy in Myst had been on that horrible day. Their loss was probably feeling more vivid now than it had in years. No wonder her father was quick to find fault with King Basil, and in no humor to be polite.

Sighing, Wren stowed her slate again, and hurried to the opposite door. She would speak with her brothers now, let them know not to expect her in the morning.

"Come, Your Highness." Wren's governess swooped in out of nowhere, thwarting her plans. "An early night is precisely what you need to prepare yourself for entertaining foreign royalty."

Leaving the disgruntled princess no opportunity to protest, she shepherded her charge toward the royal wing.

Wren stood in the council room, hands clasped a little too tightly in front of her as she waited. Having forced her to attend a state meeting barely after dawn, and on an empty stomach, the least her father could do was to arrive on time. Was it possible she'd misunderstood the summons, and was in the wrong room?

Unlikely. She moved to the window, gazing out at the part of the gardens visible from the council room. Nowhere near her usual haunt, unfortunately. Lost in wondering if Caleb had been able to sleep on the pond the night before, she barely heard the opening of the door.

The sound of a throat being cleared made her turn quickly, ready to reproach her tardy father with her eyes. But she stopped short at the sight of a much slighter figure than her father's, belonging to a much younger king.

"Oh."

King Basil was clearly also surprised to find himself alone in the room with the princess. Well, alone for five seconds, until he was followed into the room by the nobleman who had been staring at Wren the night before, and a man in military uniform whom she hadn't noticed at the welcome dinner.

For a moment Wren just blinked at the Entolian king, but he recovered himself quickly. Giving her a tight half-bow, he said, "I must be in the right place, then. Has King Lloyd been delayed? I had some trouble finding the room, and I expected to find him already here."

Wren raised an eyebrow at this blunt speech. Not that she was inclined to make her father's excuses, given he'd kept her waiting as well. It was as well she couldn't blurt out her thoughts, she reflected—in her irritation, she might have shown a hint of disrespect which would damage the united front the Mistrans must present to Entolia's new king. Shrugging one shoulder, she let her gaze pass back to the window.

King Basil didn't seem discomposed either by her silence, or by her unhelpfulness. He strode across the room, pausing beside her with his hands clasped behind his back, and his feet slightly apart, just as he'd stood after the dinner the night before. She thought he intended to ask her for further information, but instead he just surveyed the view.

"Pleasant enough garden," he said, after a moment. "But far too tame for my taste. And everything feels a little too enclosed here. I suppose it's because I'm so used to seeing the ocean when I look out the window."

Wren raised both eyebrows this time, torn between offense at his lukewarm praise of what was considered the finest garden in Mistra, and curiosity at the idea of a coastal castle. She'd seen the sea only a handful of times in her life, and she couldn't help feeling a little jealous. Pushing that thought aside, she focused instead on King Basil's impolite words. No reason to be jealous of his second rate Entolian castle, she told herself firmly. There wasn't anything to admire either in his kingdom or in him. He was clearly overconfident, to the point of being brash. He reminded her of Averett who, even after the mellowing influence of six restricted years, had a tendency to say exactly what he thought regardless of how it would make others feel.

Glancing at her, the king took in her expression. His own eyebrow went up, a slight smile tugging at one side of his lips. It made him look younger, and Wren suddenly remembered that he was barely older than she was.

"You think I spoke too plainly?" he said, surprising her with the hint of a laugh behind the words. He glanced back at the two men still hovering awkwardly near the door. "My advisors probably agree." The Entolian king's expression suddenly became more serious. "But I don't think my purpose here will be served by dishonesty. Not even polite dishonesty."

Before Wren could think of a response to this somewhat startling speech, the door opened once again. Her father strode in, followed by the general, and several advisors from the Council of Lords. Their synchronized appearance, plus the king's utterly unhurried demeanor, convinced Wren that their late arrival had been intentional. A power play, presumably.

A flicker of irritation passed over her as she wondered whether she'd been omitted from the plan on purpose, or because they'd forgotten about her. She wasn't sure which option would be worse.

"King Basil," said King Lloyd, as the Entolian advisors scurried around the table to join their king near the window. "I trust this time for our meeting was acceptable to you."

"Very much so, Your Majesty," said Basil promptly. "I'm grateful for the opportunity to discuss our situation with you without delay."

"You clearly consider your time to be very limited, King Basil," said Wren's father, his lip curling slightly. "An unusual attitude in one so young."

If King Lloyd had hoped to offend his counterpart with the slur on his youth, he was disappointed. There was no anger in King Basil's voice as he replied, only a grim humor.

"I've never had the luxury of time like others my age, Your Majesty," he said simply. "I've had—not an ax, perhaps, but a crown—hanging over my head since I was child. And as you know even better than I, the position I've come into involves many responsibilities, and the transition from one king to the next is complex even in the best of circumstances. The circumstances surrounding my own coronation are far from what I would call the best. I've left many pressing tasks to wait for my return, but I'll consider it time well spent if we can make some progress to untangling the mess in which we find ourselves."

For a moment King Lloyd was silent, probably as taken aback as Wren was by this calm and direct speech. Unbending slightly, the Mistran king gestured for the Entolians to sit, and settled himself in his own gilded chair.

Instead of immediately doing likewise, King Basil glanced toward Wren, and she realized he was courteously waiting for her to seat herself first. Perhaps he wasn't so much like Averett after all—it was hard to imagine her second brother showing so much consideration to the princess of an enemy kingdom.

Speaking of enemies...with a swift glance around her, Wren realized she had somehow ended up on the Entolian side of the table. Moving as gracefully as she could manage, she made her way around the room, taking a seat next to one of her father's advisors.

King Basil seated himself at last, but Wren didn't miss the way his eyes flicked from her position to the empty seat at her father's right, where his heir should be placed. The Entolian king's brow furrowed slightly, but he made no comment. Apparently there was a limit to his forthrightness.

"You called our conflict a mess, King Basil," said King Lloyd, his tone less aggressive than it had been when he entered the room. "I'm glad to hear we agree on something."

"I hope we'll find we agree on many things," said King Basil evenly. "Although I suspect we'll need to agree to disagree on others if we're to negotiate peace."

"Peace?" King Lloyd laid one hand along the table, considering his counterpart through narrowed eyes. "Is that your wish? An end to the hostilities entirely?"

"Of course," said the young king, with a hint of impatience. "Surely that's what we all wish for. This war is a waste of life and resources, and I don't see how we can in good conscience allow it to continue."

One of his companions shifted slightly, and he paused as he glanced at the man. Seeming to realize he was speaking too freely for the opening exchange of a negotiation, King Basil drew a deep breath.

Taking advantage of the silence, the Mistran general spoke. "If you wish to sue for peace, Your Majesty, I have with me the true borders, as set in place by our ancestors over a century ago."

He started to pull out a map, but stayed his hand at a swiftly disapproving look from King Lloyd.

Wren wasn't surprised by her father's reaction. Clearly King Basil was one to speak for himself rather than rely on advisors, and she didn't think her father would wish to come across as less in control than an eighteen-year-old monarch.

"I doubt the original position of the border is one of the things we are likely to agree on," King Basil said dryly. "However, one thing we can surely all acknowledge, is that this conflict has involved blame on both sides."

"You think I'm going to acknowledge blame?" King Lloyd asked angrily. "Mistra has done nothing to provoke your aggression."

A harsh frown flitted across King Basil's face. "Having watched my father die for six long years, I find that statement a little hard to swallow."

"Your father's injury was a direct result of the unprovoked and barbaric attack he launched on my family." King Lloyd's aggression was back in full force. "And you can be certain I would not treat with the Entolian crown if the murderer Thorn still wore it."

For a moment King Basil was silent, and Wren braced herself, certain an explosion was coming. Anyone with half Averett's temper would never swallow such an insult. But King Basil once again surprised her.

"There's no use in pretending this matter isn't personal," he said tightly. "For both of us."

Wren saw the muscles in his arm tighten, and was sure he was clenching his fist under the table. But whatever emotion he was feeling, he was keeping it well in check. Grudgingly, she found herself applauding his restraint. Despite appearances, he clearly had the ability to *not* speak his mind, the difficulty of which Wren could appreciate better than anyone.

"But," King Basil continued, "I don't think we'll get anywhere by dwelling on the emotional ramifications of—"

"Emotional?" King Lloyd roared, suddenly on his feet. The other Mistrans in the room scrambled to mirror him. "Your father orchestrated the murder of my children, and you tell me I'm being emotional?"

King Basil stood as well, although his movement was slow and controlled. "Of course not, Your Majesty. But one thing must be understood before we can continue. Whatever his faults, my father was not a murderer. Entolia had nothing to do with the tragic deaths of," his eyes flicked unexpectedly to Wren, "most of your children."

She felt herself flushing, and cursed the telling gesture. Had he also caught the inflection in her father's voice? Had his ears also tricked him momentarily into thinking her father had said *all* his children were murdered?

"I don't know if you're a liar or a fool, King Basil," said King Lloyd, breathing hard. "But this meeting is finished." He turned as if to leave, then paused, looking back over his shoulder. "I have a great deal to attend to today. I will not be at liberty to meet with you again until tomorrow. Princess Wren will act as your hostess in the meantime."

Without another word, he swept from the room, his advisors hurrying after him. King Basil remained motionless, staring at the doorway, but not as if he really saw it. Wren could see tension on the face of the nobleman beside him, and open anger radiated from the military officer. But King Basil remained calm.

She shifted uncomfortably, annoyed with her father for leaving her to babysit the slighted king, and embarrassed for him that his inability to control his words and emotions had made him show to poor advantage against his much younger counterpart. The movement drew King Basil's eyes to her, and a rueful expression passed over his face. Knowing how forthright he was capable of being, she half expected him to complain to her face about being fobbed off on the mute princess.

But when he spoke, his tone was self-deprecating more than anything.

"Well." He met her eyes. "That went well."

CHAPTER NINE

Basil

The silent princess blinked at Basil. If tension hadn't still been coursing through him from the encounter with King Lloyd, he would almost have laughed at her expression. She looked like she wasn't sure whether to be offended or amused.

She's not on your side, he reminded himself firmly. *She's Mistra's future ruler, and Entolia is her enemy.*

"Did I hear His Majesty correctly that you've been assigned to host me?"

Princess Wren nodded, her expression giving little away. Basil kept his own reflections to himself.

"Well then," he said instead, spreading his arms wide. "I'm in your hands, Princess."

She considered him for a moment then, with a graceful tilt of her head, she stepped toward the door. Basil moved around the table to join her, Lord Baldwin and the military advisor behind him. As they passed out of the room, two men in the livery of Mistran royal guards fell into step behind the princess, apparently having been waiting for her to emerge.

"Your Majesty," Lord Baldwin spoke quietly in his king's ear, "should we not retire? To debrief that...discussion?"

Basil almost smiled. "Plain speaking, Lord Baldwin, I beg you."

"All right then," said the nobleman, his voice rising slightly in volume as he slowed his steps, so they fell behind Princess Wren and her guards. "I want to debrief that utter disaster of a meeting with you."

"We will," said Basil soothingly. "But other things can come first." He saw Lord Baldwin's confused look, and chuckled. "I don't know about you, but I'm starving. I'm assuming the princess is leading us to breakfast."

"Your Majesty, this is a clear insult." The military officer joined the discussion, his eyes settled angrily on the princess now halfway down the corridor ahead of them. "It's a sign of how little respect King Lloyd has for you, that instead of treating with you himself, he pushes you off onto..." He jerked his head in Princess Wren's direction, apparently sensible enough not to say his thoughts aloud.

Basil came fully to a stop, considering his companions thoughtfully. "I don't know King Lloyd well enough yet to know if he intends it as an insult. But I certainly don't take it as one. Princess Wren is the future of Mistra. I'd prefer to treat with King Lloyd directly, but in the meantime, I'm not at all reluctant to get a sense of where his heir stands."

"How are you going to do that?" snorted the military officer. "The girl's not just mute—they say she's addled in her mind."

Instead of answering, Basil looked up. Alarm spiked through him at the sight of Princess Wren, standing motionless now and looking back at them. Once again, her face was hard to read, but he had the uncomfortable impression that she'd heard the murmured conversation. Would she be offended enough to report it to her father, and make successful negotiation even harder than it already was?

"My apologies, Your Highness," he said more loudly, starting back into motion. Sending a glower at his military advisor, he muttered, "Don't be absurd. She might be mute, but any fool can see her mind is sound."

Princess Wren gave no outward response to any of it, but as soon as they reached her, she began to walk again. As Basil had predicted, she led them directly to a dining hall, smaller than the one in which they'd eaten the night before. From the doorway, Basil could see steam rising in spirals from an impressive array of dishes. His appetite flared at the smells wafting out to him, but he stepped back, politely waiting for the princess to precede him into the room.

To his surprise, Princess Wren stepped back as well, gesturing for the Entolians to enter. Basil hesitated for a moment, but figured she would be a better judge than him of Mistran etiquette. Once he stepped through the door, he glanced back and was astonished to see that instead of following him into the room, the princess was already walking away. If Basil's memory of the castle was correct, she was heading in the opposite direction from any accommodation suites.

After only a moment's hesitation, he turned away from the food, hurrying back into the corridor. Both of his companions made as if to follow him, but he turned to them with a frown.

"No need to follow me. Eat your breakfast."

"But Your Majesty," protested Lord Baldwin.

Basil scowled from him to the military advisor. "I was grateful for your support in my meeting with King Lloyd. But your presence isn't likely to make any discussion with the princess easier, given the obvious discomfort that emanates from you both every time you're in her presence. If you want to be any use to me, get a hold of yourselves."

Without pausing to see the effect of this severity, Basil swept after Princess Wren. She had just disappeared out of sight around a corner, her guards still behind her, but his long strides allowed him to catch up to her without difficulty.

"Your Highness!" he called, when he had almost reached her.

She turned, looking startled.

"Thank you for showing me the way to the dining hall," he said courteously. "But if you're not inclined to take your breakfast, I would prefer to continue negotiations."

She was staring at him with open astonishment now. Basil looked her over, noting that she wasn't wearing a tiara today. Instead her hair was pulled up on top of her head in a bun, and tied with a large ribbon of the same bright blue as her gown. He doubted the hair would stay in place for the whole day, but at present the effect was very elegant. The dress fanned becomingly around her slim form, and like the pink gown of the day before, this bodice was again cut wide across the shoulders. He met her dark eyes, and saw that their gaze had become uncomfortably searching. Had his thoughts been too transparent as he looked her over? He was still adjusting to the reality of a crown princess who was a woman rather than a child.

"It hasn't escaped my notice," he said, smiling wryly at her, "that I haven't had the best of beginnings with your father. But I hope you'll still be willing to hear me out."

The princess considered him for a long moment. There was a frown on her face, but she didn't look angry. Basil suspected it was more that she was trying to figure him out. And not having much success, if her expression was anything to go by. The thought struck him as humorous—no one had found him hard to read before. His habitual bluntness took care of that. Meanwhile, in spite of Princess Wren's silence, he found her much more accessible than her father. Her eyes were bright and intelligent as she looked him over, and he was sure she was debating whether to give him a chance.

He was overcome with the sense that they could communicate successfully with each other, if she would only let him in. Her silence wasn't the issue. But there was most definitely a reserve, a suspicion that held her back from trusting him. Not surprising, given their kingdoms' history.

Basil had stood patiently through her scrutiny, and he was rewarded by the sight of her frown fading away. With a jerk of her head that seemed to invite him to follow, she turned and continued walking.

Elated, he matched his pace to hers, slowing his strides and glancing curiously at the passageway they'd entered. Frequent windows interrupted one wall, giving constant views of a large and appealing garden. If it was the same garden he'd seen from the council room, it must be a large one indeed, since they had crossed half the castle.

Just as he was concluding that it was indeed the same garden, the princess turned abruptly, sweeping out through open double doors into the chill morning air.

"Your Highness." The greeting came from one of two guards stationed on either side of the door, and the princess inclined her head in a graceful acknowledgment.

Trying to ignore the hardness in these new guards' eyes as they rested on the foreign king, Basil kept his eyes on Princess Wren. Her pace had picked up now, and he could feel eagerness radiating from her. Clearly this wasn't a pleasant garden stroll. She had a specific purpose for coming here, one that made her willing to delay her breakfast. As he followed her, Basil glanced around, still trying to get his bearings. The council room had looked out on the garden, but this time they'd entered it from quite a different part of the castle. He suddenly realized that the garden didn't line one side of the castle as he'd supposed, but instead occupied its very center, enclosed by four corridors. He could see two of the castle's four turrets from where he stood, poking through the foliage. He reassessed his half-hearted compliment to the garden earlier. It was quite a marvel.

It quickly became clear that Princess Wren was heading for the enormous pond that dominated the center of the garden. With amazement, Basil saw her reach the water and throw herself down onto her knees at the edge, leaning forward and scanning the surface. From his angle, he couldn't see what she was looking at, given the rushes growing around most of the pond. When he caught up to her, he was greeted with a peculiar sight.

"The swans," he muttered aloud, watching in fascination as the princess physically helped one out of the water. "I should have realized." Several more swans were gliding toward the kneeling princess, but she hardly seemed to notice them, her eyes fixed on the swan in front of her, and her forehead creased with concern.

Distracted as he was by the bizarre tameness of the swan, which was allowing Princess Wren to lay her hand on its side like it was her pet, it took Basil a moment to notice that something was off with the bird. Its wing was bent at a strange angle, perhaps broken, and it moved with less grace than its fellows.

His gaze drawn from the bird to its companion, Basil considered the princess thoughtfully. Judging by the way she was fussing over the bird, she was clearly compassionate in nature. Could her compassion extend to his own, enemy kingdom? Surely she'd be more sympathetic than most courtiers seemed to be about the plight of the soldiers fighting and dying needlessly, on both sides of the battle lines.

The other swans had reached the edge of the water now, and they jostled against each other as they moved onto land. Basil's gaze flicked back to the injured swan, and he was unnerved to see the bird looking directly at him. Why it was so unsettling, he couldn't say, but the swan was watching him with an intentness that made him feel like he'd been caught in wrongdoing. He could have sworn the bird was irritated, but surely swans couldn't communicate emotion to humans merely by the look in their eyes.

Suddenly the bird gave a loud, grating bugle. To Basil's alarm, all of the other swans' heads snapped instantly around, and six pairs of beady eyes settled unblinkingly on him. A couple of them flapped their wings, and a smaller one strutted toward him, clicking its beak in a clear sign of aggression.

A stifled choke made Basil look quickly at Princess Wren. To his mingled amusement and annoyance, he saw that she was holding back laughter at his predicament. He suddenly realized he'd taken a few involuntary steps back, and he let out a chuckle himself.

The birds did not like this show of mirth. Several of them waddled forward, trumpeting in their clear avian voices, and flapping their wings angrily. Basil glanced helplessly at the princess and saw that she was no longer trying to hide her humor. Her face was split in a genuine smile, the first he'd seen on her. For a moment he froze, taken aback by how dramatically it changed her features. He'd thought on first sight that she was attractive, and he'd formed the impression since that she was both intelligent and graceful.

When she beamed like that, however, with the morning light softening her features, and her exuberant hair already beginning to pull free around her face, she was downright stunning.

Without thinking about it, Basil hurried back toward her, past the two guards who were hanging warily back from the strange birds.

"Save me, Princess," he joked. "I'm under attack without even a single one of my guards to defend me."

The injured swan—who alone had stayed by her side—snaked its long neck forward and nipped at Basil's doublet. Instinctively, and again without thinking it through, Basil grabbed at Princess Wren's arm as he jumped back from the bird. It was the kind of gesture he would have done with one of his sisters, and he recollected too late that it was completely out of place with a foreign princess. Out of the corner of his eye, he caught the swift movement of her guards as they stepped aggressively forward, and winced at his blunder.

But someone else was ahead of them. If the swans had been unhappy about him laughing with Princess Wren, they were absolutely livid about him touching her. He didn't need to be an expert in swan behavior to interpret their intent as they flocked toward him, honking angrily and waddling as quickly as their flat feet would let them. A couple of them beat their wings so furiously in their rage, they actually lifted slightly from the ground.

Letting go of Princess Wren's arm, Basil lifted both his own over his head, genuine alarm coursing through him as the birds converged upon him.

"Dragon's flame!" he exclaimed involuntarily, as several wings beat against him, and he felt the nip of at least one beak. "If they kill me, do I take it as an act of war against Entolia?"

That seemed to snap Princess Wren out of her entertainment, and she waded into the fray, laying her hand on each swan in turn. Her touch stopped their attack so effectively, Basil could almost have believed she was using some kind of magic. Could that be the purpose of the artifact she wore around her neck?

He dismissed the thought with a flash of humor. It was a little hard to imagine the austere King Lloyd giving his heir a signet ring that was enchanted to give her authority over waterfowl.

The birds were no longer assaulting Basil, but they were still very menacing as they milled around him, all those beady eyes fixed suspiciously on his face.

Glancing up at Princess Wren, he saw that she was pulling something out of a pocket at her side. Basil brightened at once at the unexpected sight of a slate. The princess scribbled something on it, and held it out for him to see. He looked from her face—still warmed by uncontained humor—to the words curling elegantly across the surface.

If they kill you, I guess you won't take it as an act of anything.

"True," he said, smiling in spite of himself. "But I absolutely refuse to be assassinated by swan attack. Can you imagine? I'd be remembered as the king with the least dignified death in Entolian history. I'd much rather not be remembered at all."

Princess Wren looked like she was trying not to smile, but she couldn't quite manage it. Shaking her head, she wiped her slate clean and returned it to her pocket. Basil felt a surge of disappointment at this evidence that she was done conversing with him, followed instantly by a determination to make her change her mind.

"The slate is an excellent notion," he said cheerfully. "It will make things much simpler."

The princess raised one eyebrow in an expression that made him think she was still deciding whether to be offended. Disregarding this, Basil pushed on.

"I'm honest enough to say that I wasn't expecting to negotiate with you rather than your father," he said. "But I hope that means you'll trust my honesty when I say that I'm pleased for the opportunity. I think you may be able to help me more than anyone else, actually."

The princess managed to look both pleased and skeptical, but the swans just rustled their collective feathers suspiciously.

"Plus," Basil added, thinking he may as well put it all on the table, "I've come to realize that my hastiness in wanting to engage in immediate negotiation has...displeased King Lloyd."

Princess Wren made a noise in her throat. After only a moment's hesitation, she dove back into her pocket for the slate. Basil hid a satisfied smile at his success.

Nothing gets past you, does it?

He laughed aloud at her quip. "Was it really worth the effort of writing it out just to poke fun at me?"

The princess responded with a definite nod, once again not quite able to restrain a smile. One of the larger birds hustled up to her, pressing against her side and snaking its head back so as to give her a look that really could only be described as a glare.

"They're unusual birds, aren't they?" Basil mused, his gaze passing curiously over the gathered swans. He regretted his words a moment later, when a glance back up showed him that the cautious mask had once again descended on Princess Wren's face.

"No offense," he added evenly. "I can see that you're very fond of them. And they're certainly graceful creatures."

One of the swans seemed to take great offense at what Basil had intended as a compliment, waddling forward with an aggressive honk. Bizarrely, the bird slowed at a mere glance from Princess Wren. Basil grinned at the sternly unyielding look on her face. There was the commanding presence of a future queen. Even if it was a little wasted on waterfowl.

Looking up, the princess caught him watching, and Basil

dropped the smile. Not quickly enough, it seemed. Her suspicion was back, and her movements were clipped as she wrote again on the slate.

Why do you think I can help you?

Basil took a moment to consider his answer. He knew what he wanted to say, that wasn't the issue. But even he recognized that the topic might be sensitive. He glanced at Wren's guards. They'd fallen back when the swans attacked him, and were hovering just out of earshot, in the accepted manner of most royal guards he'd come across. It was as much privacy as he was likely to get with the princess. Which meant that now was as good a moment as any to speak his piece.

"Well," he said at last, trying to speak more diplomatically than normal. "I've never really thought this war was about iron ore. As both your father and I demonstrated a little painfully in this morning's meeting, the conflict is personal. Which makes it hard to find a way forward, or even to reach an agreement regarding the ore itself. I've suspected for years that we won't actually end the war until we address its true origins."

The princess tilted her head slightly down, drawing her brows together in an exasperated look. At the same time, the swan nearest Basil flapped its wings rapidly, for all the world like it was also expressing impatience at Basil's meandering speech.

Basil smiled. "You're telling me to get to the point?"

Princess Wren nodded, showing a hint of pleasure at his understanding. Again, it softened her delicate features, increasing Basil's impression of her underlying reasonableness.

"Thank goodness for that," Basil laughed. "I hate trying to speak carefully, and the worst of it is, kings have to do it all the time." He drew a breath, taking encouragement from the fact that Princess Wren seemed to be holding back a laugh of her own.

"I want to know what happened the day your brothers died," he blurted out.

His abrupt speech froze the laughter on the princess's lips. Her dark eyes were once again unreadable as she stared at him —even the swans had all become unnaturally still, although Basil had to assume they were reacting to her body language, rather than his words.

"I know it's an insensitive question," Basil went on. "And I can understand if you don't want to talk about it. But to be frank," he held her gaze, "I think you should talk about it even if it's uncomfortable. Because that's when it all started, and from what I understand, you're the only one who can tell me what really happened."

The silence following this pronouncement was broken by an angry honk from one of the swans. Basil didn't look at the bird, instead keeping his eyes on Princess Wren. She did shift her gaze to the swan, her face marred by a thoughtful frown as she shook her head once. The rest of them were ruffling their feathers, clearly still not sure whether Basil was an enemy against whom they needed to defend their territory, but they remained otherwise silent.

Princess Wren turned, and Basil's heart plummeted when he realized she was walking away from him. But a moment later she seated herself on a stone bench not far from the water's edge, and shot him an expectant look. Her guards mirrored the movement, once again choosing positions just out of earshot.

Hurrying forward, Basil sat beside her, watching her face with rapt attention. Her manner had given little away when he first arrived in Myst, but it hadn't taken much observation to realize she was capable of being very expressive with her features when she chose to be. It made sense—six years of silent communication must have made her an expert.

The princess had placed her slate beside her, but she made no immediate move to write on it. Basil waited patiently, content to try to read her expression as she decided what to write.

The swans had all gathered around her once again, and without any change to her distantly thoughtful expression, she pulled some grapes from her pocket and held them out. The birds snapped them up eagerly, and Basil's stomach gave an audible grumble. He wasn't in the habit of skipping breakfast, but it was well worth it for this bizarre but hopefully telling private interview with the princess.

Princess Wren leaned forward slightly, laying a hand on the flank of the injured swan. Her expression was oddly intense as she locked eyes with the creature, and Basil watched, fascinated by her strange behavior. He could see why rumor called her eccentric, but even while communing silently with a swan, she gave no hint of having lost her reason. And he'd still seen no sign of the awkward child he'd expected—she was as graceful as her avian companions.

Basil couldn't deny to himself that he was fascinated by her. A sudden desire to unravel her mysteries for her own sake momentarily consumed his mind. But he pushed it away, surprised at his distraction. He was here to end a war, and nothing was more important than that.

Picking up her slate at last, Princess Wren scribbled a short message.

You answer my questions first.

"Try me," said Basil promptly. He wasn't going to promise anything, but he could see her request was reasonable.

She thought for a minute before once again scratching out a message.

What do you know about that day?

Basil raised an eyebrow. "Only what rumor says. That all of your brothers were killed by a mad enchantress with a spell so vicious no bodies even remained, and only you survived. Somehow unharmed." He narrowed his eyes at her. "Or so the story goes."

Princess Wren didn't immediately respond, but he noticed that her hand strayed to the red and gold signet ring around her neck. Realizing he was looking, she dropped it quickly. She wiped her slate clean and wrote two words.

Your father?

Basil frowned at the message, trying to make sense of it. What about his father? He looked up to see her watching him expectantly, and understanding hit.

"My father didn't tell me anything about it," he said calmly. "He didn't know anything beyond the rumors we all heard."

One of the swans chose that moment to let out an angry trumpet, but the princess's eyes never wavered from Basil's face.

He smiled ruefully. "Perhaps you're thinking he just didn't confide in me. But that's not the case, I assure you. I didn't always agree with my father's decisions, but he wasn't cunning or underhanded. He held the basic belief that as king, whatever he did or said was right, and he would never have thought he needed to hide his actions from me."

Princess Wren was frowning at him, clearly unsure what to make of his words. Basil shifted on the bench, so that he was facing her. If he'd dared, he would have taken her hands, but he was afraid of being savaged by the swans as much as of rousing her displeasure or that of her guards. Instead, he put all the sincerity he had into his voice as he spoke.

"I'm glad to get to the heart of why I came so quickly. Most of my advisors think the claim of Entolian involvement in your brothers' deaths is a ruse by your people to justify the Mistran attack that started the war. I don't know whether I believe that. But the one thing I know with certainty—the one thing I'm so determined to convince you of that I've traveled across two kingdoms to do it—is that the Entolian crown had no hand in the attack that killed your brothers."

CHAPTER TEN

Wren

Wren sat frozen, her eyes fixed on King Basil's face. She felt almost hypnotized by his unblinking gaze, and for a long moment her thoughts just swirled meaninglessly.

"If my predecessor had murdered six Mistran princes," King Basil went on steadily, "do you really think I'd come here, putting my life in the hands of the ones we had so grievously wronged?"

Even if Wren had been given her voice back, she would have remained silent. She simply had no words to express the turmoil happening within her.

Could it be true?

Could they all have been wrong? Could the war be based on nothing more than a misunderstanding? But the mad enchantress had definitely spoken of provoking war.

He's clearly lying.

The dismissive words came from Conan, who had waddled forward and was leaning his bulk against Wren's legs to enable communication. Soft honks sounded from the other swans, which Wren took to betoken agreement.

Do you think so? she asked doubtfully. She looked down at Caleb, who was standing very close to her knee. In a mute invitation, she reached out her arms, and he leaned into them. Lifting him with a grunt, she deposited him on the bench beside her, like he'd been when she spoke with Lady Anneliese.

What do you think? she asked anxiously.

He took a moment to answer. *Honestly, I don't know what to think,* he admitted at last. *Which means you'd do best to trust your own instincts.*

Wren stared at him, alarm coursing through her. Caleb was putting the responsibility on her to decide whether King Basil was trustworthy? The well-being of the whole kingdom might ride on the decision. She wasn't knowledgeable enough—or confident enough—to shoulder that kind of responsibility.

But as she searched King Basil's face, she could see no sign of duplicity. In her silent observation of two years' worth of council meetings, she'd had plenty of experience in watching people hide things. And of course, no one was hiding as much as she was. But the Entolian king's gaze was open and clear, his eyes met hers unhesitatingly, and he showed no signs of tension.

For a moment, she allowed herself to entertain the idea that Entolia really wasn't behind the attack on her and her brothers. She supposed it should be good news, but the truth was it filled her with horror.

What have I done?

As always, Caleb responded reassuringly to the whisper in her mind. *You haven't done anything wrong, Wren.*

But she took no comfort from his encouragement. He was always going to look out for her, but this situation was bigger than her feelings.

Almost without thinking, Wren found herself writing on her slate, the terrible thoughts in her head too potent to keep inside.

If you're telling the truth, this war is my fault.

Of course it's not your fault, Wren! Caleb protested from beside her, having read the words as she scratched them out. *None of this is your fault. You were a child!*

Wren didn't respond, her eyes fixed on King Basil. Being, of course, oblivious to Caleb's comment, he was frowning down at her words, confusion etched across his face. He looked up to meet Wren's eyes, his expression serious.

"Do you believe that I'm telling the truth?" he asked simply.

Wren considered him, feeling strangely pleased that he hadn't tried to reassure her about her culpability. Instead he'd asked her a serious question, and she intended to give a serious answer. Her eyes raked over his face, noting irrelevantly that a rebellious tuft of hair had curled down over his forehead, and that one of his hazel eyes had a larger patch of bronze in it than the other.

But more importantly, she saw that he once again sat straight and expectant, his expression somber, but his posture relaxed. Maybe Caleb was right. Maybe it wasn't a matter of training or prowess. If all she needed to do was listen to her instincts, there could be only one answer. She'd never met someone as direct and free of dissimulation as King Basil.

Slowly, heavily, she nodded.

King Basil's face lightened at once. Wren's brothers weren't so pleased with her response. Caleb remained silent, but a few of the others bugled indignantly. Averett pushed Conan out of the way, flapping his wings in an agitated manner, so that Wren caught only the odd word, as the feathers brushed against her.

Don't be...fool, Wren. Just because...pair of pretty eyes...lying through his teeth.

Wren shot her brother a look that spoke volumes. She wasn't sure whether it was her eyes that were supposed to be pretty or King Basil's, but she didn't appreciate the insinuation that she was letting some shallow attraction impact her thinking. King Basil was still an Entolian, no matter how handsome he might or might not be. And although he seemed much more comfortable to engage with her than almost anyone she'd met in the last six years, she was still a silent, eccentric oddity. She couldn't be further from the forthright nature he clearly preferred. Neither of them were thinking of the other in that light, and it was unhelpful of Averett even to suggest it.

Very unhelpful, she reflected, surprised and a little ashamed at the hint of wistfulness that passed over her as she looked again into King Basil's eyes, and saw how his smile transformed his face. It was impossible to know whether he was serious by nature, or simply forced to be due to his early ascension to the throne. But when he smiled, the cheerful glint in his eyes convinced Wren there was more to him than his role.

If only she could show him more than the reserved facade she was forced to maintain.

She was being ridiculous. King Basil didn't care about her personality. He cared about ending the war between their kingdoms, and she applauded him for it. Pushing such foolish thoughts aside, she turned her mind to the unanswerable question of who had been behind the enchantress's attack if it hadn't been the Entolian crown.

"Thank you." King Basil's voice startled her, its quiet tones so unlike what she'd so far heard from him. "For believing me," he added, seeing her confusion.

She nodded again, even more slowly. She was uncomfortable with how much his gratitude warmed her, but she couldn't help it. She'd absolutely assumed the king would be offended at being expected to communicate with her in place of her father, and instead he was genuinely trying to negotiate with her.

"So," the Entolian prompted, in a return to his normal, somewhat brusque, manner. "Are you going to answer my original question? About what happened when your brothers died?"

Impertinent, isn't he? demanded Lyall, sounding offended.

Wren bit her lip. She wasn't offended, but a measure of wariness had returned nonetheless. She tried to avoid communicating anything about that day, for fear she'd let something slip that would trigger the curse.

Slowly, regretfully, she shook her head. It was a reasonable request, but it was one she couldn't fulfill.

"Is it too insensitive of me to ask?" King Basil prompted at her prolonged inactivity. There was no hint of sensitivity in his voice.

Wren shook her head impatiently, hoping he would understand that wasn't the issue. Clearing her slate, she wrote two words.

This afternoon.

King Basil looked perplexed, but before he could ask for clarification, a voice hailed him.

"Your Majesty!"

Wren didn't need any special skills of observation to see that the guard—decked out in Entolian livery—was annoyed. It was written plainly across his face.

"King Basil, I must protest," he said, scowling. "I objected to you attending the council without protection—"

"Yes, I remember," King Basil cut him off dryly. But the guard wasn't to be deterred.

"But to go wandering around the gardens, Your Majesty, without even alerting your guards as to your whereabouts—"

The man blustered on. Raising an eyebrow, Wren looked between the guard and the young king. She couldn't imagine any guard ever speaking so to her father, who would certainly never tolerate it. Clearly King Basil was facing the same attitude in his own people that had irritated her on his behalf when coming from her father and the general. She thought of the formidable King Justin of Albury, who had come into his role even younger than King Basil. From all she'd heard of him, she was sure he would have been furious to be disrespected because of his youth. But King Basil just sat, patiently allowing his guard to let out the burst of frustration. When he spoke, his voice was as calm as ever.

"I appreciate your concern, but other than almost being mauled by these swans—I promise their docile appearance is deceiving—I've been perfectly safe here speaking with Princess Wren, I assure you."

Bram clicked his beak menacingly, as if to prove the king's words, and King Basil let out a chuckle.

"I've kept you long enough, though," he said amicably, rising to his feet.

Hiding a smile, Wren reflected that the audible grumble of his stomach may have had something to do with his readiness to leave. She remained seated, inclining her head in acknowledgment of his words.

"I'll look forward to further discussion this afternoon, then," King Basil said. He gave her a pointed look. "As promised."

She nodded slowly, her thoughts wandering to the records room which she intended to visit immediately after breakfast.

She thought King Basil had said all he wanted to, so she was startled when he turned back to address her.

"I don't know why you would think the war was your fault," he said frankly. "I've heard reports from the front lines of soldiers who survive when the rest of their unit doesn't. People tell them they're lucky, but some of them say the guilt of surviving is worse than facing death like their companions." His eyes were thoughtful as they rested on her face. "I have twelve sisters, so perhaps I can begin to imagine what you experienced when your brothers died. I'm no expert, of course, but you seem too sensible to me to extend whatever you might feel about that day so far as to blame yourself for the war."

Wren felt her lips fall slightly open at this direct speech. King Basil's eyes flicked down to them, and she clamped them quickly shut again. She had no response, and he seemed to realize it, because after another inclination of the head, he strode back toward the castle, his guard hovering disapprovingly beside him.

That has to be the most insolent person I've ever met.

Wren had barely noticed Averett placing his webbed foot on top of hers, but his voice rang clearly in her thoughts.

Well, she replied reasonably, *strictly speaking, you haven't ever met him. I thought introducing you as my swan-brothers might possibly break the conditions of the curse.*

Averett clearly had no time for her jokes.

I've never heard such a load of manure, Wren. Claiming he knows nothing of the attack except what rumor says. We all heard that enchantress say she'd been sent to provoke war!

Wren frowned. *She didn't exactly say that.*

Conan bustled up to her, pressing against her leg to make himself heard. *I agree with Averett. What gives the Entolian the right to talk so casually about what happened that day? He didn't even try to be sensitive, or tell you he was sorry for what you've been through.*

Wren cast her mind back over King Basil's words, the smallest of smiles curving her lips as she remembered what he had said. Conan was right that he hadn't exactly been sensitive. But she found she didn't mind his plain speaking. He might be direct, but that didn't mean he was rude.

He called me sensible, she mused, to no one in particular.

Averett let out an angry bugle. *So that's it, then? A handsome young man calls you* sensible, *and that's enough to turn your head, and make you decide he's trustworthy? He's our enemy, Wren! You're not a child anymore—stop mooning.*

Rett, interjected Caleb, reproachfully, but Wren found she had no desire to shelter behind her oldest brother.

I know I'm not a child, Averett. The tone of her thoughts held a snap as she glared at Averett's avian form. *And I resent the suggestion that I'm* mooning *over anyone! I just appreciated the compliment, that's all. If you'd spent six years being followed everywhere by whispers about how you'd lost your wits, you might appreciate being called sensible, too.*

We're supposed to feel sorry for you because of a few whispers? Conan demanded, his weight pressing so heavily on Wren's leg that she was losing feeling. *We've spent those years stuck as* birds, *in case you've forgotten! All because of your stupid prattling about swans that day!*

That's enough, Conan. This time Caleb beat Wren to a response. *I won't tolerate any criticism against Wren, or any belittling of what she's been through.* Caleb's habitual authority radiated from him, and the group fell instantly still and silent, not a feather rustling in the morning air. *We've all suffered, but she's the only one who has a choice. And she's chosen to sacrifice for us. I'm inclined to think it's a count in King Basil's favor that he's intelligent enough to see that there's nothing wrong with Wren's mind.*

So you believe him as well? Wren asked eagerly, bolstered by her brother's praise.

Caleb stretched out his neck, weaving his head slowly from side to side as he thought. *Honestly, I'm not sure*, he said at last.

Wren deflated a little, disappointed. She wanted so badly to be right that King Basil was trustworthy. Her own eagerness alarmed her a little, if truth be told.

Bram waddled forward, unhesitatingly shoving Conan out of the way and pressing his own wing against Wren's leg.

What was he saying about a promised discussion this afternoon? he demanded. Clearly he hadn't been close enough to read Wren's written message to King Basil.

She sighed. *I said I'd tell him this afternoon. About what happened that day.*

You're going to tell him the truth? Bram repeated, his voice horrified in her mind. Only those touching her had heard her comment, but the others could hear Bram's words even without contact, and a chorus of alarmed trumpets instantly surrounded her.

Of course not, she reassured him, shaking her head soothingly at the others as well. *I'm just going to show him the official report. I fobbed him off until this afternoon so I could go to the records room and get it, instead of having to write it all out for him on my slate. If he's telling the truth that all the Entolians know about the attack is what they've heard via rumor, who knows how garbled their account might be?*

You're going to the records room? This time it was Ari who'd nudged his way in, displacing Averett, somewhat to Wren's satisfaction. *Can I come? I want to look over your notes about enchantments again.*

Several of the others clicked their beaks impatiently, and Wren didn't need contact to know what they were thinking.

What's the point, Ari? Bram sighed, his wing still resting against Wren's leg. *We've pored over those notes a hundred times. If there was a way around the curse, we would have found it years ago. We just have to wait—it's only a couple more months.*

Ari made no reply, ignoring his older brother as his eyes rested expectantly on Wren.

All right, she told him with a shrug. *Everyone's pretty distracted by the Entolian delegation, so we might get away with it. Give me fifteen minutes to eat some breakfast, then meet me at the window.*

Ari pulled away from her, giving a happy bugle that she assumed contained a thanks. Flapping his wings, he made his way toward the pond, presumably to forage for his own breakfast. Wren tried not to think about what he would be eating. Grateful as she was for Caleb's defense, she couldn't help but agree with Conan that there were definite perks to being the silent human in the group rather than one of the enchanted swans.

Wren. Caleb's soft voice in her mind drew Wren's attention down to him. The others had begun wandering away, but he remained on the bench with her, looking up at her out of eyes that seemed troubled.

She raised an inquiring eyebrow.

Be careful, all right? I want to believe King Basil. I want peace as much as he seems to, and that will be much easier to achieve if it turns out his father didn't try to murder us all. But you don't need me to remind you what your research has found. That was a powerful enchantment that woman threw at us.

Wren nodded slowly. Caleb was right—she remembered perfectly what she'd learned. The magic required to turn six humans into swans for as long as six years was even more potent than what she would have needed to kill them all.

I'm going to keep an eye on the Entolian king. The new voice surprised Wren. She hadn't noticed Bram coming back, but he'd clearly been listening to Caleb's words. *I'm not ready to just trust him. But I'm also not sure Averett and Conan are thinking clearly. It didn't seem to me like King Basil was trying to offend you with what he said about that day.*

He wasn't, Wren agreed confidently. *He was trying to encourage me—to reassure me that it wasn't my fault.* She sighed. *But he doesn't know the full story.* For a moment she fell into melancholy. King Basil was no fool. Once he read that official report, he'd understand exactly why she was to blame, if it was really true that Entolia hadn't ordered the attack.

Follow him around if you like, she told Bram. *But don't get yourself into any trouble, all right?* She glanced toward the lake. *I'd better go. I only have fifteen minutes before Ari will be pecking at the window to the records room, bringing down the wrath of the record keeper if I'm not there to cover for him.*

Neither of her companions said anything, but in her mind she could almost hear the smiles that would have curved their human faces. Ari might technically be eighteen now, but sometimes he was as impulsive as the twelve-year-old boy who'd bickered with his sister that day in the woods.

CHAPTER ELEVEN

Wren

Wren's thoughts were on Ari as she hurried into the castle. Physically, Caleb might be the most vulnerable of her brothers, but she worried more about Ari than any of them. Lyall wasn't much better—he'd been only fourteen when the curse hit. What would the impact on their development be, to have made the transition from childhood to adulthood while in the body of a bird? They'd certainly matured—impulsive though he might be, Ari didn't actually behave like a twelve-year-old. But would he ever truly catch up? He'd missed such crucial experiences during the last six years.

She avoided the dining hall, assuming that King Basil was eating there, and not yet ready to face those perceptive eyes again. As hotly as she'd refuted it at the time, Averett's quip about her mooning over the Entolian king still lingered uncomfortably in her mind. She couldn't afford to become self-conscious around the foreign king, though, not with so much at stake. Surely if the two of them could communicate even without the assistance of her voice, the two kingdoms could come together for long enough to negotiate an end to the war.

She dismissed her guards with a gesture, and they were only

too ready to melt away. It wasn't normal practice for her to be followed everywhere through her own castle—it was purely a condition of her new role as King Basil's guide. Without the Entolian's presence, she was free to dispense with her minders.

Sidetracking through the kitchens, Wren swiped a few pastries from the Chief Under Chef. The bewhiskered redhead winked at her as she bore her spoils out through the servants' entrance. A man of few words himself, he'd always had a soft spot for the silent princess, and took no issue with her invasions of his territory any time she felt particularly hounded by disappointed expectations.

Still finishing the pastries, she made her way toward the royal records room. Hindered by nothing more than the appraising look of one of the record keeper's assistants, she wandered through the area containing the public records. At the door to the sealed records, however, the way was barred by an armed guard. Wren raised an expressive eyebrow, and taking in her identity, he quickly stepped aside. She had no doubt her visit would be reported, however.

"Princess Wren!"

Wren's heart sank at the surprised exclamation. If the record keeper was pottering around the small chamber, she wouldn't be able to let Ari in. But luck was with her. Just as she inclined her head in acknowledgment of the greeting, the assistant hurried in from the main records room, asking his superior for help with a document that was proving difficult to categorize.

Wasting no time, Wren hurried to the far side of the room, where a small window looked out onto a somewhat overgrown corner of the castle's sprawling gardens. Next to the window was a bookcase containing many bound volumes, each with the name of a monarch. Her fingers slid over the one marked King Lloyd III, settling on the rolled up bundle of parchments next to it.

She pulled out the notes on Caleb's life up until the curse, prepared by some organized scribe in advance of the day when Caleb would be the monarch, and require a record of his own life. The project had been abandoned six years before, although the record keeper clearly didn't have the heart to throw the notes out. Wren smiled to herself as she slid the ribbon off and unrolled the wad of papers. Once completed, the future King Caleb's record would probably be the most sensational volume on this bookshelf.

Nestled in between the various papers were Wren's own notes, where neither her nosy governess nor the gossiping maids would ever "accidentally" see them while tidying up Wren's suite. Even with that precaution, Wren had never been willing to put the full truth to paper, afraid even that would offend the magic of the curse. Most of her scribblings didn't relate to the day her brothers had been turned into swans, but rather to her own research into enchantments.

Sighing, she cast her eyes over the section labeled "counterforce". Not much encouragement to be found there. She'd established to her own satisfaction—or rather dissatisfaction—years before that since the enchantress had built in a counterforce to the curse, there was no other way to break it. The consequences of Wren's slip had demonstrated undeniably that the enchantress had managed to mold the natural counterforce to her magic into a defined and binding remedy to the enchantment's intention. In short, Wren had no choice but to honor the madwoman's demand for six years of silence.

You said I couldn't possibly do it, Wren thought fiercely, as she stared down at the enchantress's name in her own notes. *But you were wrong. In two months, you will have failed, and we'll all be free.*

An insistent tap at the window drew her eyes. She hurried to the casement, laying her papers down on the small table pushed up against the wall just in front of the window.

Unlatching the lock, she slid the window upward so that Ari could climb in. He did so a little awkwardly, the space barely large enough for him. It was a good thing he was the smallest member of the bevy.

Here you go, she told him, pressing the side of her hand against his webbed foot where he stood on the table. *You wanted to look over the notes on enchantments?*

Ari nodded his head eagerly, causing his long neck to fold in strange ways. Hiding a smile, Wren spread the papers out so that Ari could see multiple entries at once, then made her way to a nearby shelf.

This one was covered not with properly bound volumes, but with wads of paper tied together with simple ribbon, allowing new pages to be added with ease. She found what she was looking for quickly. The rustle of feathers and the padding of webbed feet warned her of Ari's approach, and she hurried back to the table before he could wreak havoc in his attempt to flap over to her in an enclosed space.

Dropping the papers onto the surface so that Ari could lean in for a look as well, she rifled through them, making sure everything she wanted was there. The record keeper kept well organized accounts, she had to give him that.

So you're going to show these to the Entolian king? Ari asked, extending his wing enough to rest it on her shoulder. He sounded neither angry like Conan had done, nor hopeful like Caleb. It didn't surprise Wren that Ari seemed not to have a strong opinion regarding King Basil. Politics had never been of any more interest to him than it had been to her. Back when she had the luxury of not caring about such things, that was.

That's my plan, she said lightly. *Find anything of interest in my notes on enchantments?*

Ari's avian form deflated slightly. *No.*

Is it so hard to wait two more months? Wren asked, trying to keep the hint of laughter from her mental voice. *After almost six years, it doesn't seem long.*

It's not, Ari acknowledged. *I don't really mind the waiting that much. But it's always worth checking—you never know when something new will occur to you.* His voice dropped to a mutter in Wren's mind. *And I'm sick of Conan saying I don't have a sensible thought in my head.*

Wren couldn't help grinning at this revelation of Ari's true reason for wanting another crack at her notes. No doubt he had visions of heroically breaking the curse and impressing all five of his brothers. Privately, Wren thought that this close to the six years, they would be annoyed more than anything to discover that there was an alternative solution none of them had identified before now. But she didn't say as much.

Don't mind Conan, she said instead. *He's been sour with everyone since his old sweetheart and her husband had their baby.* She sighed. *I can't help feeling a little sorry for him.*

Me too, admitted Ari. He tilted his head to one side, causing his long neck to rotate. *Why didn't she wait for him, like Lady Anneliese has waited for Caleb?*

Wren snorted before she could stop herself. *Because she and Conan weren't genuinely in love like Caleb and Lady Anneliese were. Conan was only sixteen when the curse hit, and she was even younger! It was a teenage infatuation, and wouldn't have lasted above two months even without the curse. I'm almost certain he was cooling off before he became a swan, and I'd bet my crown she was only interested in him because she liked the idea of being a princess.*

Don't say that to Conan, Ari said dryly.

Wren shook her head, smiling. *Contrary to popular opinion, I'm still in possession of my senses, remember?* She glanced back at her own notes. *Are you done with these? I'd better pack them up before the record keeper comes back in.*

Ari bobbed his head gracefully, and Wren rolled the papers

back into a scroll with deft fingers. Her instinct hadn't erred, because she'd just deposited the rolled bundle back in its place when the door opened without warning.

The theatrical gasp prepared her for the record keeper's inevitable reaction to Ari's presence.

"Your Highness! A bird inside the castle! Inside the records rooms!" He paused dramatically. "Inside the inner chamber of the sealed records! I really must protest."

Ari had begun to bugle softly, in a sound Wren was sure would be a chortle in her mind if she hadn't broken contact with him. She sent him a quick grin before turning to the record master. Folding her hands in front of her, she dipped her head in a silent apology. Then she made as if to shoo Ari toward the window, but the record keeper protested again.

"Your Highness! The swan's too large—it will break the casing if it tries to squeeze through the window again. You'd best take it out through the doors."

Wren debated arguing, but decided it wasn't worth it. At a jerk of her head, Ari flapped down from the table to land by her side. She offered the bundle of loosely tied papers to the record keeper, and he held out an imperious hand to receive them.

"Ah yes, I can re-shelve those for you, Your Highness."

Wren drew the parchments back, shaking her head. She gestured toward the desk just inside the chamber door, where a paper sat with a neat list in the record keeper's somewhat fussy handwriting.

He frowned. "You wish to check those documents out of the record room?"

Wren nodded serenely, and the man fidgeted.

"Princess Wren, permission is required from the king to check out documents from this room."

Wren raised a sculpted eyebrow, touching a finger to the signet ring dangling around her neck.

"Ah," said the record keeper awkwardly, "yes. The crown prince—or princess, in our case, of course," he added hurriedly, "has authority to remove...quite right." He cleared his throat, making a show of pulling a quill from the inkwell on the small desk. "If you'll pass me the documents, Your Highness, I will note their removal from the chamber." He sent her a hard glance. "Their *temporary* removal, I should say."

Wren gave a nod, trying to make her expression as reassuring as possible. She hoped word of her intended use of the papers didn't get back to the record keeper. Or her father, for that matter. She doubted either of them would approve of her showing sealed records to King Basil. It wasn't as though they contained anything genuinely sensitive though, she reasoned with herself.

Oblivious to her silent wrestling, the record keeper made a meticulous entry in his logbook. Then he handed the parchments back to Wren, not quite able to hide his reluctance. With Ari waddling comfortably at her side, Wren made her way through the public records room and out into the corridor.

She'd intended to head straight for the nearest exit into the gardens, but a familiar voice pulled her up short.

"You're too kind, Sir Gelding."

Wren paused, peering around the corner ahead of her. Lady Anneliese sounded uncomfortable to Wren, but it might just be the noblewoman's habitual reserve. Wren's eyes fell on Lady Anneliese's companion with interest. It seemed Sir Gelding had arrived in Myst for his promised visit.

Casting an eye over him, Wren realized he looked faintly familiar from her childhood memory. Lady Anneliese had been right about one thing, she realized. Sir Gelding didn't look old. His dark hair was barely streaked with silver, and his frame was strong. To her irritation, Wren had to admit that, smiling attentively down at Lady Anneliese, he looked quite dashing. The lady's pale coloring and the baronet's dark good looks certainly made a striking picture. Unease curled through Wren's stomach. It was uncomfortably easy to imagine Lady Anneliese—who'd been lonely and sad for far too long—being swept off her feet by this charismatic enchanter.

She could only see Sir Gelding's profile, but Lady Anneliese was angled toward Wren, and she suddenly caught sight of her audience.

"Princess Wren," she said brightly, her manner suggesting she'd just spotted a much-needed ally.

The sight bolstered Wren, and she stepped fully around the corner, summoning a smile. Ari waddled beside her, seeming impatient, but evidently intending to stick with his sister. Lady Anneliese's eyes widened a fraction in surprise at the sight of the swan cruising calmly down the corridor, but she made no comment.

Sir Gelding, on the other hand, froze midway through the bow he'd begun at sight of Wren. His eyes darted between the bird and the princess, and the poise Wren had observed in his interaction with Lady Anneliese a moment before seemed to have fled. Wren stared at him. It wasn't unusual for people to be thrown a little off balance when meeting her, but his reaction seemed extreme. Then it suddenly hit her. Sir Gelding was an enchanter! Could he sense the magic that coated Ari's every feather? And if he somehow figured out who Ari really was, would that violate the terms of the curse?

Panic coursing through her, she inclined her head in what she hoped was a gracious acknowledgment of Lady Anneliese's greeting, then hurried past the pair to the entrance into the garden which stood not far down the corridor.

Ari hurried at her side, his wings flapping as he tried to keep up with her near jog. She didn't pause to explain. She had to get to Caleb, and make sure he hadn't suffered further injury. Her heart didn't begin to slow until she finally reached the pond, and caught sight of her oldest brother gliding calmly—if a little awkwardly—across its surface.

She let out a long breath, turning to Ari, who had sidled up to plonk one broad foot on top of her slipper.

What was that about, Wren?

She shook her head, not sure if she wanted to alarm the boys with her fears. *Doesn't matter.*

Ari narrowed his beady eyes at her, but didn't press for more information. *Keep your secrets, then,* he said, a little huffily. *I think I'm going to go for a fly over the woods, maybe visit the clearing, check if there's anything to see.*

Be careful, said Wren anxiously. She knew it wasn't the season for hunting swans, but she still felt nervous any time her brothers mingled with their truly avian brethren. *And Ari?* she added, as he spread his wings for take off.

He looked questioningly back at her, and she felt her heart speed up again at the memory of Sir Gelding's astonishment.

No more trips into the castle.

CHAPTER TWELVE

Basil

Basil frowned to himself as he paced down the corridor. After only a day, the castle was already becoming familiar. Once he'd grasped the layout, with the central garden, it became quite easy to navigate the four main wings.

Not that his thoughts were on the architecture. They were on Princess Wren. She'd never showed up to breakfast, even though he'd lingered uncharacteristically over his food in the hope that she was still coming, and he'd seen no sign of her since. He certainly hadn't seen King Lloyd, or anyone else who could actually assist him in his goals.

And now it was almost time for lunch. What if the princess didn't attend that meal, either? She hadn't told him where to meet her, or what time. Was she intending to honor her offer to speak further that afternoon? Or had she given him an empty promise to get rid of him?

He didn't think so. She might not use many words, but her communication still seemed too direct for such stratagems. And she hadn't seemed uncomfortable in his presence. Surprised, certainly, by his brazen questions. But if he was reading her correctly, she hadn't been offended.

The desire to understand the secret of her restraint was becoming more consuming by the second. He half wished he hadn't called a meeting of his team, so that he could go looking for her right away. But that would be losing sight of his objective —he needed to know what his people had discovered.

He'd barely reached his rooms when there was a smart rap on the door. One of the advantages of being king was that no one ever kept him waiting. At his curt command, Lord Baldwin entered the room, followed closely by two of the guards, the enchantress merchant and her husband, and three servants from the delegation.

"Thank you for coming," said Basil promptly, casting his eyes over the assembled group. "What do you have to report?"

The enchantress cleared her throat. "We believe we've discovered the purpose of the artifact the princess wears, Your Majesty."

"We?" Basil asked.

She nodded her head toward one of the servants, and the girl stepped forward with a curtsy. "We teamed up, Your Majesty. We thought people might not want to talk to us Entolians, but servants always chatter. It wasn't hard for me to hear things that others wouldn't." She smiled tentatively at the enchantress. "With a bit of guidance about what I was looking for, of course."

"An excellent notion," Basil said, with an approving nod. He was pleased to see such initiative in his companions. "And what's the purpose of the artifact?"

"Supposedly, it carries a basic protection charm," the servant said.

The enchantress made a noise of protest, a smile curling her lips. "There's nothing basic about it, Your Majesty," she told Basil. "A protective enchantment strong enough to leave someone unharmed by a curse intended to kill them would require very strong magic. The artifact must have cost a small fortune."

Basil frowned. "And the princess was wearing it when she and her brothers were attacked?"

"Apparently there's quite a drama around that," the maid chimed in again, an eager tinge to her voice. "The crown prince—Prince Caleb, his name was—always wore it. It's the ring traditionally carried by the king's heir, although King Lloyd apparently had it reset before he presented it to his son. But the rumor is that when the group was attacked, Prince Caleb put it on his little sister, to protect her."

Basil frowned as he thought this over. Princess Wren's words in the garden came back to him. No wonder she felt a survivor's guilt.

"They say," the maid continued, "that everyone knows even King Lloyd wishes it had been Prince Caleb who'd been wearing it, not Princess Wren."

Basil's frown grew. He sincerely hoped the king had never said anything of that nature to his daughter. In spite of King Lloyd's anger at their early morning meeting, he'd formed a better impression of the Mistran monarch than that. He thought of his own father's unwillingness to accept Zinnia as a back up heir, and let out a sigh. Clearly Mistra's princess had plenty to contend with. Was her silence some kind of bizarre response to all the opposition?

"Thank you," he said aloud. "You've done well." He turned to the two guards standing next to the merchant. "Anything you wish to report on?"

One shook his head. "Nothing of note, Your Majesty. We spent most of the morning in the barracks. But while we're speaking of the princess...I've gotten the impression that the local guards are very loyal to King Lloyd, but not overly eager about the prospect of serving the princess as queen one day. I think the crown prince was very popular."

"All of which puts the kingdom in a weak position, Your Majesty," the other guard pointed out. "Which can only work in our favor, surely."

Basil shook his head. "I disagree," he said flatly. "Perhaps if Mistra intended to annex our kingdom, we might not wish to see them in a strong position. But I hold to what I've always said—if King Lloyd had dreams of conquest, he would have moved against us a long time ago. A weak kingdom is an unstable kingdom, and I don't want that for a neighbor."

The guard looked chastened, but before he could respond, the young servant cleared her throat nervously. Basil looked back at her expectantly, and she spoke in a rush.

"I heard another rumor you might be interested in, Your Majesty. About the possibility of an invasion."

Basil straightened, and the rest of the group went still. It was a little hard to believe the servants would gossip accurately about military plans, but he supposed he shouldn't dismiss whatever the maid had heard too quickly.

"It's all over the castle that when your father died, the king's advisors suggested he march on Tola," the servant said, seeming nervous at everyone's unwavering attention. "Apparently it was the princess who stood against it, and convinced her father not to consider that course."

Basil lifted his eyebrows. He felt a flare of warmth somewhere in the region of his chest at the idea of Princess Wren defending his kingdom before they'd ever even met. He remembered the seemingly incongruous impression he'd formed almost upon first meeting her, that she was his ally, not his enemy. He wanted her to be his ally, somehow even more than he wanted it from King Lloyd. From everything he was hearing, he was becoming more convinced that the king had indeed meant it as an insult when he fobbed Basil off on his heir. But Basil was better pleased with the arrangement than ever. Surely if they were left alone, he and Princess Wren could get something done. At least the silent princess, alone of all Mistra, seemed willing to talk to him.

Somewhat ironic, really.

"And King Lloyd listened to her?" he mused aloud. "Well, that's a count in his favor, if nothing else is."

Lord Baldwin raised an eyebrow. "Is it a count in his favor if he was swayed by sentiment, Your Majesty?" he asked delicately.

"Being willing to listen to counsel has nothing to do with sentiment," said King Basil dryly, his thoughts flying to his own father. "And everything to do with humility. An important virtue in any leader." He sighed, running a hand through his hair. "All right, Lord Baldwin. I daresay it's too soon for you to have had much success—"

"Not at all, Your Majesty," Lord Baldwin interjected. "I've made inquiries about the princess, as you requested."

Basil blinked at him, surprised. "You're efficient. What did you discover?"

Lord Baldwin rolled one shoulder uncomfortably. Just as with the nobleman's reaction to the front line, Basil found Lord Baldwin's overblown discomfort whenever the princess came up to be inconsistent with the rest of his behavior.

"Well, she's certainly considered eccentric, to use the more polite term. The rumors are true, that she's been thoroughly examined for any sign of injury, or any magical blockage to her speech. There was nothing." He cleared his throat awkwardly. "It seems the damage is to her mind. Apparently it's not unheard of, if there's been trauma..."

Basil frowned. "Do you mean that the trauma makes her unable to speak, or unwilling?"

"Apparently the line between the two can be a little hard to determine in such cases," shrugged Lord Baldwin. "But it seems to be generally accepted that her mind has been affected in some way by what she witnessed."

Basil shook his head incredulously. "I don't know what that means. She seems to me to be a perfectly rational person who just...doesn't speak."

One of the guards cleared his throat. "What about that is rational, Your Majesty? If she *can* speak, but won't, surely that's a sign of...damage."

"It's certainly a sign of something," Basil muttered to himself.

"Then there are the swans, of course," Lord Baldwin said, wincing slightly as he said it.

Basil chuckled. "Yes, I met them, actually. Unless I'm mistaken, they didn't like me much." He bit his lip thoughtfully. "And one of them seems to be following me."

"What?" Lord Baldwin asked, looking perplexed. "Through the castle?"

Basil shook his head. "It stays outside, but I've spotted it multiple times throughout the morning. Any time I'm near a window, it seems to kind of...keep an eye on me."

He couldn't help but laugh at the looks on his team's faces. They ranged from offense to open alarm.

"I don't mind it," he reassured them. "At least the bird makes no secret of its surveillance. Honestly, it's less irritating than the guards who are clearly tracking my every step, but still try to look like they're just going about their business."

"Yes," I'd noticed that, Your Majesty," said one of the guards grimly. "In light of that, don't you think it would be wise to have your own guards with you at all times?"

"No, no, it doesn't trouble me, really," Basil said, waving a dismissive hand. "It's no more than I expected. The guards aren't going to attack me. They're just making sure I'm not snooping anywhere I shouldn't be." He smiled. "And the swan isn't going to hurt me, either. It's probably just curious. They seem to be incredibly tame birds, probably domesticated enough to recognize a newcomer to the castle."

"Yes, the princess has well and truly domesticated them," Lord Baldwin confirmed. "It is the strangest of her oddities. I mean," he sounded pained, "they say she even knits them clothes."

"That is certainly unusual," Basil acknowledged dryly.

Lord Baldwin seemed emboldened by the agreement, and he hurried on. "Apparently..." He winced slightly, as if not wanting to say his next words, but Basil fixed him with an expectant stare. "Apparently," Lord Baldwin tried again, "people think she's sort of...replaced her brothers with them."

"How do you mean?" Basil demanded.

Again Lord Baldwin rolled his shoulders in obvious discomfort. "Well, there are six of them. According to general reports, the group were on their way to hunt swans when the incident occurred all those years ago. The princess seems to have sort of adopted some of those swans, and general opinion is that she tried to replace her lost brothers with them."

Basil rubbed his hands together absently, turning this information over. "That suggests an unbalanced mind, though," he said, more to himself than anything.

"I've heard of such things before," the merchant chipped in unexpectedly. "People who've lost a child adopting a dog in its place, encouraging the creature to sleep in the child's bed, that sort of thing. And to not just suffer the loss of all her brothers, but to actually witness their violent deaths at the tender age of eleven...well, it would be enough to overset many people."

"But she's not overset," Basil said, with conviction. "I just can't believe that."

One of the guards cleared his throat. "Just because she's... well, pretty, Your Majesty—"

"Dragon's flame, man!" Basil interrupted with a laugh. "Do you suspect me of an entanglement?" He sighed, running a hand down his face. "That sounds very pleasant—if only I had time for something like that." His voice turned dry as he thought of all the mess his father had left him, which he had in turn left behind in Tola. "Maybe in ten years."

He scanned the group, looking for any sign that there was more information to come. But everyone remained silent, watching him expectantly. His eyes settled last on Lord Baldwin.

"You've been very successful at ferreting out information in no time at all," he said mildly. "How did you manage it?"

Lord Baldwin bowed slightly. "I'm glad to be of service, Your Majesty. I found that people are willing enough to talk, if you know how to go about it."

Basil felt a slight crease form between his brows. Thinking of all Lord Baldwin's comments of "general opinion" and "people think", he wasn't entirely satisfied. He had no difficultly believing that a servant had gleaned gossip from her counterparts, but that locals would be as willing to speak to a visiting Entolian lord seemed less likely. But he decided not to press the matter at present.

"Well," he said curtly, his gaze encompassing all of them. "Thank you for your reports. I'm expected at lunch in a moment, so we can discuss these matters further tomorrow."

Everyone filed out quickly at the dismissal, and Basil was soon striding for the dining hall, flanked by the two guards who'd remained outside his chambers while the group spoke. Basil again caught a glimpse of a swan through the window, flying alongside his path. It wasn't on the garden side of the castle, but on the outside. The birds couldn't be that tame, then, if they still roamed beyond the castle walls.

Basil chuckled at himself. The bird was following him around like a spaniel. Clearly it was extremely tame. Thinking humorously of the protective way the swans had flocked around Princess Wren when he'd dared to laugh with her, he sent his avian companion a jesting wave. For a moment the bird seemed to stare at him, then it angled its sleek body upward, disappearing from view as it flew toward the sky.

Still smiling to himself, Basil entered the dining hall. His heart lifted at the sight of Princess Wren, already seated in the place she'd occupied at dinner the night before. Not waiting to be told whether he was also destined for the same place, he hurried to her side, seating himself before he could be directed elsewhere.

"There you are, Princess Wren," he said cheerfully, as she bent her head in greeting. "I was beginning to fear your swans had turned on you, and dragged you into the lake."

She shook her head, not managing to check the smile of amusement that blossomed on her face. Something in her expression told Basil that she had no fear of her birds turning on her.

Basil had barely sat down when everyone around him hastened to their feet. Seeing King Lloyd and Queen Liana entering the room, he copied the motion, his gaze resting thoughtfully on the monarchs. In appearance, Princess Wren was quite like her mother, he noted. Although she owed her rather determined chin to King Lloyd.

The Mistran king's gaze moved over the assembled group, his eyes resting briefly on Basil before he inclined his head. Basil returned the gesture, unconcerned by his counterpart's coldness. He'd already decided, in conference with Lord Baldwin, that he would be wisest to wait a day or two before broaching the topic of the war with King Lloyd. Clearly he'd set the other king's back up, and needed to give him time to cool down.

The idea of such a delay would have chafed Basil unbearably only days ago. But now he found that with the prospect of negotiating with Princess Wren in the interim—not to mention the challenge of unraveling her secrets—he was quite content to let King Lloyd's anger wear itself out.

The princess had one thing going for her, he reflected, as he enjoyed some particularly well cooked venison. She didn't distract from the food with polite chatter. Basil spoke little either to her, or to Lord Baldwin on his other side, during the course of the meal. But he was keenly aware of the princess's presence all the same.

As soon as King Lloyd rose, signaling the end of the meal, Basil turned expectantly to Princess Wren. But before he could ask for her promised explanation, he realized that the Mistran king hadn't left the room as he'd supposed, but was moving toward his guest. Basil pushed himself to his feet in an unhurried motion, facing his fellow monarch eye to eye. Or as close as possible given that King Lloyd was several inches taller than Basil.

"Your Majesty," Basil said, inclining his head.

King Lloyd didn't return the gesture or the greeting, instead watching Basil with hard eyes. A man Basil didn't recognize was hovering just behind the king. His dark hair was streaked with silver, but he was clearly much younger than his sovereign. A nobleman, perhaps. Certainly not a commoner. His jewelry was too ostentatious for that, Basil thought, casting a glance over the red gemstones glittering on the man's hands and lapels.

"Care to explain, King Basil," King Lloyd said tightly, "why you've brought an enchantress into my kingdom with you?"

Basil blinked, taken off guard by the question. "There isn't much to explain, Your Majesty. I thought it might be useful to have someone who's able to sense magic accompany the delegation, and she kindly agreed to come." He looked between the two men before him. "If I've erred in not registering her presence, I apologize. I didn't think any kingdom but Bansford required such a process."

"Of course we don't require registration," said King Lloyd impatiently. "But I would like to know what your intent was in failing to mention her magic to me."

"No ill intent," Basil said lightly. "Merely thoughtlessness. I don't know about Mistra, but enchanters are common enough in Entolia that their presence isn't considered especially remarkable."

King Lloyd looked less pleased than ever, as though he resented the suggestion that Entolia had more enchanters than Mistra did. Basil looked again at the man standing behind the king, who was now staring at Princess Wren. Raising an eyebrow in surprise, Basil followed his gaze and realized that he was looking not at her, but at the red and gold ring she wore around her neck. Sudden understanding blazed.

"I take it you're an enchanter?" he said, causing the man's eyes to flit back to him.

The Mistran bowed a little stiffly. "I am, Your Majesty," he confirmed.

Basil hid a smile. He shouldn't be surprised that King Lloyd had asked an enchanter from his own people to check Basil's delegation, much as Basil had brought an enchantress in an attempt to check over the Mistrans' mysterious princess.

"This is Sir Gelding," King Lloyd said, sounding a little begrudging at being required to perform the introduction.

"Well, Sir Gelding," Basil said amicably, "if you'd like to... look over any others from my group, I'm sure they'd all be glad to cooperate."

King Lloyd narrowed his eyes, perhaps trying to decide whether Basil was being insolent. But he made no comment.

"I trust you are comfortable," he said instead, in clipped accents. "As you are already aware, I am not at liberty to meet with you again today. I expect I will be similarly occupied all of tomorrow, as well."

"I understand perfectly, Your Majesty," said Basil cheerfully. "There are many demands on a king's time. I'm sure I'll occupy myself quite effectively while I await your convenience."

King Lloyd looked more annoyed than ever, but apparently he could think of no appropriate retort. With a stiff incline of his head, he turned on his heel and strode from the room, Sir Gelding in his wake.

CHAPTER THIRTEEN

Basil

"Well," Basil said, turning to Princess Wren, "if I didn't know better, I'd—"

He broke off. Wren was watching the retreating pair, her eyes fixed on Sir Gelding's back. Basil would have described her expression as fearful.

She seemed to suddenly notice his regard, because she turned to him, looking flustered. She raised an eyebrow in a clear question, gesturing for him to finish his thought.

"Oh," said Basil slowly, pulling his thoughts back to the conversation he'd just had with King Lloyd. "I was just saying that if I didn't know better, I'd think your father was disappointed I wasn't more offended by his unavailability."

He saw a tiny wince cross Wren's face before she smoothed out her expression. She put a hand in the pocket where Basil knew her slate rested, but paused, biting her lip.

Basil smiled. "It's all right," he said softly, having no difficulty reading the conflict in her eyes. "You don't have to defend him, I understand." His gaze became unseeing for a moment, and he let out a sigh. "Heaven knows my father was much more unreasonable than yours, and I still loved him."

Pulling himself together, he gave his head a little shake before focusing back on Princess Wren. Those dark eyes were at their most expressive as she watched him. He could see her sympathy, and it sent a strange thrill up his spine. But he could also see uncertainty, even confusion. He smiled ruefully.

"I imagine you were brought up to think of my father as a monster. But he wasn't, I assure you. He was just much too short-tempered a man to bear a debilitating injury with patience."

A cleared throat reminded him that they weren't alone, and he turned to see a disapproving Lord Baldwin on his other side. Clearly the nobleman thought it was unseemly for Basil to speak so honestly about his late father, and perhaps he was right.

"Thank you, My Lord," he said lightly, "you're free to pursue your own activities. The princess and I intend to further discuss our situation."

"King Basil," said Lord Baldwin, a definite scold in his tone. "You intend to once again go off without any other member of our delegation? I must protest in the strongest—"

"Yes, thank you, Lord Baldwin, I understand perfectly," Basil cut him off genially. "Your counsel is noted. That will be all."

The nobleman's jaw worked for a moment, but in light of Basil's unequivocal dismissal, there was nothing he could do but take himself off. Basil watched him go with a small twinge of regret. He wanted his people to trust him, and to feel that he valued their input. But remembering their conversation in the garden, he considered it unlikely Princess Wren would confide in him if he had his retinue in tow.

Turning back to the princess, he saw that one elegant eyebrow was arched slightly. He couldn't quite resist flashing her a grin.

"There are some perks to being king," he commented. "Now,

Princess. I'm once again in your hands. I will simply have to trust that you won't set your swans on me this time."

She smiled, shaking her head and rising to her feet at last. As she stepped out from behind the table, she tilted her head, inviting Basil to follow her. The gesture drew Basil's attention to the elegant line of her neck. Sometime since he'd last seen her, someone had rearranged her hair, because it was once again drawn up onto her head, the two ends of the blue ribbon dancing becomingly against the warm brown skin exposed by her elevated hairstyle and her scooped neckline.

He realized she was staring at him in confusion, and he hastened to follow her, feeling uncharacteristically wrong-footed. He thought she would lead him back to the garden where they'd sat that morning, but she instead made her way around the castle's inner perimeter, taking him all the way to the furthest point from the dining hall, on the opposite side of the complex. A few times, as they walked, Basil once again caught sight of a swan mirroring their progress from the outside of the building. He wondered if it was the same one as before, or one of the others. He couldn't tell them apart, but he had a feeling Princess Wren would be able to.

The princess paused in a doorway he'd never seen before, fixing the two guards behind her with a stern look as she flicked her eyes first to the room beyond, then to the ground under their feet. They exchanged glances, clearly confused.

Basil smiled. "I could be wrong, but I think Princess Wren is requesting you to stay here."

The guards observed him with hard eyes, but any offense they might have taken at him speaking for Princess Wren was rendered foolish by her emphatic nod of agreement. The two men shifted on their feet, clearly unsure whether to do as instructed.

With a sigh, the princess pulled out her slate and dashed out a few words. Basil pretended to be absorbed in looking through the doorway in question, but when no one was watching him, he snuck a glance at her message.

So you can watch not listen. We want our guest to speak freely.

After another moment's hesitation, the guards stepped back, their eyes settling on Basil with suspicion.

He ignored them, following Princess Wren through the doorway in question. He looked around in wonder at a large room made entirely of glass, right up to the panels of the domed ceiling. It was unseasonably warm inside, and palm fronds draped lazily over the path. The crunch of pebbles sounded beneath their feet as the princess crossed the space toward a bench situated by a small pond, the surface of which was covered with large flat lily pads. Basil followed her slowly, distracted by the exotic flowers which introduced bright splashes into the otherwise overwhelming impression of green.

"This is an incredible hothouse," he said. "I've never seen one so magnificent."

The princess's face softened in a genuine smile which made her eyes sparkle. She nodded her agreement. Clearly this was a favorite place of hers. The hothouse and the garden...Princess Wren seemed to like being surrounded by nature. Basil found himself wondering, irrelevantly, what she would make of his seaside home. He pushed the thought aside.

"How do you keep it so warm at this time of year?" he asked, genuinely fascinated by the phenomenon. The princess gestured to something in the middle of the space, and Basil walked over to have a look. It was a cunningly wrought bronze basin, covered with interlocking beams which gave it the appearance of a wicker basket turned to metal. Inside flickered a flame, and on closer inspection, Basil realized why it was familiar.

"That's dragon flame!" he exclaimed, noting the hints of green among the weaving orange fire. He scanned a small placard attached to the basin, which described the dragon flame as a coronation gift given to a king whose name Basil didn't recognize. One of King Lloyd's predecessors, presumably.

"What an amazing gift," he said, impressed. He looked over at Princess Wren, and saw that she looked pleased with the effect of her exhibit. There was a hint of smugness in her face, and Basil couldn't help grinning. It wasn't like the lofty pride King Lloyd would surely have felt the need to display if he'd been showing off this treasure to a foreign king—if anything, it was endearing.

"Don't think you're the only one whose castle has wonders to show off. When you visit Tola, I'll show you the caverns, and you'll be just as impressed as I am by your hothouse."

Princess Wren stilled, looking as surprised as Basil felt by the unplanned invitation. He told himself firmly to focus on the task at hand. They had a great deal of ground to cover before the Mistran princess would be able to visit his kingdom. He had been able to defy his father's prohibition for visiting the enemy by the simple expedient of outliving him and claiming his crown. But something told him there was no force in Solstice that would convince King Lloyd in his current frame of mind to let his daughter set foot in Entolia.

"We're straying from the point," he said quickly, seating himself beside the princess. Some of her hair had already come loose again, joining the ribbons dancing around her shoulders.

Basil tried not to notice the way the moisture in the air made the tendrils curl across her exposed collarbones.

He'd have to remember, if he ever received a state visit from anyone he approved of as little as King Lloyd approved of him, to burn any of his grown up sisters' dresses that had these scooped necklines that seemed to be the fashion in Mistra. It was hardly the way to avoid attracting attention.

"Are you going to answer my question now?" he asked seriously. "About the day your brothers died?"

Princess Wren nodded, her expression somber. She reached for her pocket, but instead of her slate, she pulled out a bundle of papers, tied together with ribbon.

Basil reached out to receive them, but he was momentarily distracted by movement just outside the glass walls. The hothouse opened not into the gardens, but outward, into what seemed to be a small wood. And a now-familiar shape was hovering in the air just beyond the glass.

Basil gave a small chuckle. "We have an audience."

The princess looked around, startled, but relaxed at sight of the swan. Basil glanced at her in time to see her roll her eyes at the bird, and his grin broadened.

"It's been following me all morning, actually."

Looking unsurprised, Princess Wren sighed, but made no attempt to explain. Instead she gestured at the papers in Basil's hand.

He looked down, momentarily confused by the scrawled notes. The princess leaned toward him, frowning at the topmost paper. Reaching over him, she flipped the page over, exposing the one underneath. As she tucked the top page around the back of the bundle, her hand brushed against Basil's. He noted in a detached way that her skin still felt cool, in spite of the heat of the room. But a moment later he caught sight of the neat title on the newly exposed page, and everything else fled from his mind.

.   .   .

Attack on Mistran princes and princess—official report

Basil read eagerly, his eyes widening as he took in the details of the bizarre and vicious attack against Princess Wren and her brothers. He winced slightly at the opening comments regarding the visit from the Entolian envoy. It was certainly an unfortunate coincidence of timing. He scanned several pages, his eyes settling on the summary at the bottom of the report.

All those present at the time of the attack report the same thing. The enchantress appeared from among the trees, made accusations against the king, and declared her intention to kill the six princes and the princess. When the guards tried to intervene, she unleashed an enchantment on the entire group which rendered all witnesses uncon-scious. When the group awoke, it was to discover the enchantress dead, no sign of the princes, and the princess in a state of great distress. An exhaustive search was conducted, but no further external evidence was located. For an account of what occurred during the lost time, investigators were reliant on the testimony of Princess Wren, who was either unable or unwilling to give any kind of coherent account of what happened.

Basil glanced at Princess Wren. She wasn't looking at the page, but her carefully averted gaze, and the slight flush on her neck convinced him that she had been reading over his shoulder a moment before, and knew that he'd just read the comment about her unhelpfulness. He felt a wave of pity for her. He didn't understand her secrets, but any fool could see that she was neither oblivious to, nor entirely hardened to, the general disdain her people held for her.

He cast his eyes back up the more detailed report. She'd obviously said something, though. Her written messages to her father had been copied out.

The woman attacked us, it said. Basil's eyes skated over the part about the woman intending to kill them all in revenge, and how it hadn't fully worked. Clearly not, as Wren had emerged unharmed. Physically, at least.

"She said she had help," he read in a mutter. "She talked about others, and extra power. She said 'they'll still get their war'."

Basil frowned at Princess Wren, who was sitting beside him with ramrod straight posture. "Extra power?" he repeated. "From where?" He didn't wait for a reply, continuing to think aloud. "I suppose that makes sense. Surely that killing curse was much too powerful for one enchantress working alone."

The princess nodded vigorously. She pointed to another spot on the paper, and Basil nodded.

"Yes, I saw the comment about war." His frown grew. "So someone was trying to provoke conflict. But if not us, then who?"

He glanced at his companion, noting the defensive look in her eyes. Her comment from that morning suddenly made sense to him, and he drew in a breath.

"That's why you think it's your fault! Because it was your comment that made your father think Entolia was behind it, when in fact it wasn't us."

She hesitated for a moment, then nodded, pulling her bottom lip between her teeth as if desperately trying to keep her emotions in as well as her words.

Without thinking it through, Basil reached over and laid one of his hands over hers, where they were folded in her lap. He heard the shuffle of the guards' feet outside the door, but neither of them actually entered, and he did his best to ignore their disapproval.

"The war isn't your fault, Wren." He didn't even notice he'd dropped her title until after he spoke, and the princess didn't call him on it. "If that woman was speaking the truth, someone was actively trying to provoke conflict, and they played all of us for fools. You certainly can't be blamed for being among the first of their victims."

To his astonishment, Wren's eyes suddenly brimmed with moisture. Sensing that she needed a moment of privacy, he released her hand and looked back down at the page. But his thoughts were on her, and the intensity of the emotions that came through every time she let her guard down. The princess might not say anything, but it hadn't taken long for him to realize there was always a lot going on behind those eyes. And she had clearly been through a great deal, some of it probably self-inflicted, if her unnecessary guilt over this account was anything to go by.

"The question," he said briskly, surprised by the gruff note in his voice, "is where this extra power actually came from. And who was really behind the attack." He looked up, and was pleased to see that Wren had regained her poise. "Who was this madwoman?"

Wren leaned over him again, rifling through the pages. She pointed at one in the middle of the pack, and Basil skimmed it quickly. It was another report, this one the result of an investigation into the woman who had killed the princes. She was a disgruntled former employee of the crown, hired to provide minor magic-related services. She'd been relieved of her position six years before the attack because of misconduct, and had appealed to the king without success. Apparently she was known to be unbalanced, but hadn't been considered dangerous because—

"Her power was assessed as weak to middling?" he read aloud. He looked up at Wren's piercing expression. "There can be no doubt she had help, then," he mused. "From someone much more powerful than herself. But it definitely wasn't us."

He ran a hand over his face. What a mess. He was convinced King Lloyd wouldn't be ready to negotiate a true peace until he believed that King Thorn hadn't killed his sons. And it seemed that in order to clear his father's name, Basil would have to discover the true source of the extra power used by the enchantress. But he didn't know anything about such things. He'd had no idea one enchanter even *could* give their power to another to use. Or possibly multiple enchanters, judging by the strength of the curse.

He saw that Wren was watching him with an expression that hovered somewhere between hope and frustration, and he forced his own discouragement down.

"Well," he said with determination. "It seems our task is to discover who's been plotting against our two kingdoms, so we can end this misguided conflict between us. And we'll probably have to do it quietly, as neither your people nor mine are likely to be on board. Still, between us, we should be able to make some progress. Want to fix this together?"

Wren didn't need words to express her response. The dazzling smile that lit her face and made her dark eyes shine, told Basil all he needed to know.

CHAPTER FOURTEEN

Wren

A ha!

Wren's silent exclamation roused her companion, and Lyall gave a sleepy honk.

What is it? He glanced around the darkened room, his eyes alighting on Wren's half-burned candle. *What time is it? You should be sleeping.* He flapped his wings guiltily. *And I should be out on the lake with the others.*

Sleep in here in the warm if you want, Wren shrugged. *No one will mind.*

Lyall sighed into her thoughts, shaking his graceful head rapidly as if to clear it. *I can't bring myself to do it, not when Caleb refuses to even though he can hardly float straight.*

Yes, Wren agreed, her tone a mixture of fondness and exasperation. *I wish I could convince him not to be a martyr.*

So what's your revelation? Lyall asked, still sounding drowsy. *Are you still researching combined power?*

Wren nodded, her eyes remaining fixed on the page on her lap.

Lyall extended his neck, leaning down for a closer look at the page. *Is that from the records room? I thought you'd trawled *through every record in the castle even vaguely related to magic years ago.*

I have, confirmed Wren. *And I've just finished re-trawling through them. What I'm looking at now is from Basil's records.*

Basil, is it? Lyall fixed her with an uncomfortably human look.

Wren just rolled her eyes. She knew most of her brothers were still suspicious of Basil—and more protective of her than ever—but she didn't have time for Lyall's quips right now.

That's his name, last time I checked, she deflected. *He sent an express to his sister back in Tola two weeks ago, asking her to send him anything on combined power, and her reply arrived this afternoon. There wasn't a lot, but we thought we'd split it, make sure we don't miss anything. Look here.*

She pointed at an entry on the page, and Lyall blinked at it, looking for the moment no more intelligent than a standard swan.

What does it mean?

Wren sighed, impatient of her brother's lack of knowledge. Most of the boys had shown an unsatisfying disinterest in her and Basil's research. Caleb was on board, of course. And Ari was theoretically supportive, but utterly uninterested in the dry details of magic theory. Both Averett and Conan, however, were determinedly insisting that Basil was a snake in hiding who was perfectly aware that his father had planned their supposed murder, and Lyall and Bram seemed to be reserving judgment.

She wished Basil was there—he would understand the significance of her finding. She briefly considered looking for him right away, then remembered that it was past midnight.

Probably not, then.

It's an explanation of how one enchanter can store magic to enable its use by another magic-user, she said, for Lyall's benefit.

Store it like in an artifact? he asked, sounding confused. *But I don't remember the enchantress using an artifact.*

Wren shook her head. *Neither do I. That's why I'm excited. I'd never heard before that magic-users can pour their power into each other like this. It seems it's not common practice, and I can see why. It looks risky if you don't do it right.*

So who was the other magic user who poured his or her power into that madwoman? Lyall asked skeptically.

Wren sighed, rolling up the parchment. *It's a clue, not a solution to the whole mystery.*

If you say so, said Lyall vaguely.

Wren swallowed her exasperation. Given that figuring out who had empowered the enchantress's attack would do absolutely nothing to break the curse, she couldn't really blame her brothers for their tepid interest. Perhaps if she and Basil were still investigating once they'd returned to their human bodies, they might care a little more about solving the mystery.

The information in Basil's records might be only a clue, but it was tantalizing enough to keep Wren lying awake for some time. This must be the solution to the enchantress's incongruous power. But unless the person who'd given her access to their own magic was incredibly powerful, it still seemed like too much. Could it have been multiple people? It was a chilling thought. She was impatient for the morning to come, eager to share her discovery with Basil, but eventually she drifted into an uneasy sleep.

She all but pounced on the visiting king at breakfast the next morning. Basil had beaten her to the dining hall, and he looked up as she hurried across the room, smiling a greeting in his open way. When she slid into the seat beside him, he just nodded at her. They'd spent at least some of each day together for the previous two weeks, and Wren had noticed that he'd fallen into some non-verbal habits of communication.

When she gave him a meaningful look, however, he seemed to realize she had news to share.

"What is it?" he prompted eagerly. "Did you find something in Zinnia's notes?"

Wren nodded her head minutely, aware of several pairs of eyes on her. One of those pairs belonged to her father, who was watching her with a frown between his brows. She tried to smooth out her features, focusing on the plate in front of her.

Basil was apparently oblivious to their audience. "What was it?" he pressed. "I pored over every word of my half, but there was nothing we didn't already know."

Wren cast a quick look up at her father. He was still watching, and his frown had turned to a scowl. She returned her gaze to her plate, but she could still sense Basil's shift as he glanced between her and the king.

"He's the one who organized for you to be my minder," he said mildly, but when Wren didn't respond, he let the matter drop. "We can talk after breakfast," he said instead.

Wren nodded again, turning her attention to her food. She could feel Basil's impatience as the meal progressed, and she didn't blame him. In all their discussions over the past two weeks, they hadn't found a hint of any solutions to the mystery. Wren had been surprised—and pleased—to discover just how extensive an investigation her father had launched at the time, in spite of being convinced that Entolia was behind the attack. She'd assumed no one had looked into other options, but hours spent perusing the sealed records demonstrated that wasn't so. Nevertheless, the investigations had found no evidence of foul play closer to home, and neither had Wren and Basil.

The confirmation that another enchanter could indeed have given their attacker extra power might be small in the scheme of things, but it was at least a step forward.

Wren had intended to make her way to the hothouse with

Basil immediately after breakfast. Or perhaps the gardens—this find might be worth sharing with her other brothers. Lyall hadn't cared much, but Caleb would.

To her frustration, however, she wasn't at liberty to go to either place. King Lloyd summoned his daughter imperiously the moment she rose from her seat. With an exasperated look back at Basil, she followed her father to his private study, her mother walking serenely alongside them.

"What are you doing, Wren?" King Lloyd demanded, as soon as the door was closed behind them.

She stared at him blankly, waiting for more context, and he gave a huff of annoyance.

"You're too friendly with King Basil."

Goaded, Wren pulled out her slate. Her father made another impatient noise in his throat, which she ignored.

You assigned me to babysit him, remember? Or was I just a way to insult him?

"Of course not," blustered the king, not entirely convincingly. "I thought he might treat better with a counterpart of his own age."

Wren spread her hands appealingly. What grounds did he have to complain when that was exactly what was happening?

Her father seemed to realize the same thing, and he leaned back against his desk, taking a moment before speaking again.

"I realize I asked you to be his guide of sorts, and at first I was pleased you were taking the duty seriously. But it's been more than two weeks, and your guards report that you still meet with him every day. Are you sure your loyalties aren't becoming divided?"

Wren glared at him, genuine offense radiating from her at this questioning of her devotion to Mistra. Her irritation drove away any guilt she might have felt about concealing from her father the investigation she and Basil were attempting. It wasn't as if she was doing anything to harm Mistra's interests. Quite the reverse. The kingdom would be best served by an end to the war, and a true understanding of the enemy who had attacked her brothers and started the conflict in the first place. If she thought she could safely tell her father what she was up to, she would have done so in a heartbeat. But his unreasonable behavior since Basil arrived convinced her that it would be a bad idea. She wasn't going to let her pursuit of the truth be impeded by her father's inability to put his personal feelings aside and listen to what Basil had to say.

"All right," said the king, raising his hands defensively under the force of her glare. "I suppose it's good if you can gain his trust enough to soften him to our cause. He must be made to see that there can be no progress without an Entolian admission of wrongdoing, and reparations. Understood?"

Wren barely refrained from rolling her eyes. Utterly convinced as she now was that Entolia hadn't launched the attack, she could see the folly of her father's stubbornness. But his words had prompted something in her mind. She'd been putting all her energy into researching enchantments with Basil, but her single-minded focus had caused her to miss another crucial opportunity. She had the access her father was denying the visiting king. She should be trying to use her influence to soften *him*, not Basil.

The thought daunted her more than she wanted to admit to herself. She knew her father cared about her, but she'd never felt that he took her seriously, and she didn't have the confidence to try to influence him. Her intervention on the proposed invasion of Entolia had been her only victory in that area. And now that he seemed to suspect her of being too soft toward Basil, she was afraid he would be even less likely to take her counsel on board.

Locking the thought away for later, she cleared her slate.

May I go?

King Lloyd waved his dismissal, and to Wren's surprise, her mother walked with her out of the study. The queen seemed ill at ease as they traversed the corridor, and it took her a full minute to address her daughter.

"I've also noticed that you seem to be on good terms with King Basil, Wren," she commented softly. "What's your impression of him? Is his desire for peace genuine, do you think?"

Wren stopped walking, waiting until her mother looked her in the eye. Then, putting all her sincerity into her face, she nodded earnestly.

The queen nodded as well, her expression troubled. "I hope so," she said, her voice little more than a whisper. She looked exhausted as she held Wren's gaze. "I miss your brothers as much as your father does," she commented unexpectedly. "But I'm weary of conflict. There's been too much fighting already."

With a quick squeeze of her daughter's hand, she turned, making her way toward the royal wing. Wren stared after her mother, her thoughts swirling. Perhaps she would have an unexpected ally in any attempt to soften her father.

Still turning the matter over, she hurried toward the hothouse. It was little used, and she and Basil had adopted it as a base of sorts. Her guards no longer protested her restrictions on them. They hovered in the doorway willingly enough, clearly finding her constant one-sided conversations with Basil neither interesting nor a threat to her safety.

She hoped Basil would be waiting for her there, and she wasn't disappointed. As soon as she entered the room, she saw him, examining the pond with his back to her, feet planted apart and hands clasped behind his back.

He turned at her approach, his face brightening at the sight of her. "Is everything all right?" he asked. "I know my father only ever called me to his study like that when I was in serious trouble."

His smile lightened the words, and provoked an answering one in Wren. She shook her head to show all was fine. She wasn't about to recount her conversation with her father to Basil. He'd already become more of a friend than she would have considered possible a fortnight before, but telling him that her father had instructed her to try to gain his trust and manipulate him would be taking things a little far. She didn't have any intention of trying to convince either Basil or her father of anything to do with the border. She couldn't care less about the iron ore. Her only interest was in holding on until the curse lifted, and finding out who had been behind it in the first place.

"What did you find in Zinnia's notes?" Basil demanded, his mind clearly also returning to their main concern.

Wren joined him at the bench, sitting down and waiting until he did the same. She pulled the parchment in question from her pocket and held it out to him, not bothering to point out the relevant section. Basil would understand its significance without her help.

Sure enough, only a moment after his eyes scanned the page, he drew in a sharp breath. "So it's definitely possible!" he exclaimed. He frowned as he ran his eyes over the whole entry again. "But not something to be done lightly."

Wren nodded her agreement, and Basil looked up at her, his expression troubled.

"It would have to be someone powerful though," he said. "To enhance her magic enough for that curse."

Wren held up one hand, using a finger from the other to tap each digit in turn.

"You think more than one other enchanter poured magic into her?" he asked, grasping her meaning at once. She nodded, pleased, and Basil looked thoughtful. "Possible," he mused. "But an alarming thought. Imagine an entire group of enchanters bent on provoking conflict between our kingdoms. That's a formidable opponent."

Wren drew in a deep breath then let it out. Her thoughts had gone along much the same track the night before.

"And," Basil added, sounding angry, "whoever they are, they must be incredibly irresponsible to give that kind of power to someone so clearly unbalanced. How dare they play with people's lives like that? It's not a well-planned attack, is it? It's more like they didn't care about the consequences, and just wanted to wreak havoc."

Wren frowned. He was right, and it didn't make sense to her either. Her eyes strayed to the glass walls, and the winged figure loitering in the woods just beyond them. Bram had been determined in his surveillance of Basil, she had to give him that.

"It's almost a shame your father *doesn't* keep a register of all the enchanters in Mistra," Basil muttered. "Might make it easier to identify whom we should be investigating."

Wren shook her head, pulling out her slate. Basil waited with his usual patience while she laboriously wrote out a longer message.

Remember the investigation—we know
she spent time in Entolia. Maybe the
magic-user who helped her was
Entolian.

"That's true," Basil sighed. Wren knew him well enough now not to be surprised by the total lack of defensiveness in his voice. "It's equally possible."

Wren ran a hand through her hair, which was unrestrained today, as she liked it best. She noticed Basil's eyes following the gesture, and was suddenly reminded of the first time she'd showed him the hothouse. He hadn't repeated the action since then, but she could still feel the pressure of his hand as he'd laid it reassuringly over hers.

He seemed to realize she was watching him, because he forced a smile.

"Don't worry, Wren," he said firmly. "We'll find out who orchestrated that attack." His face set into hard lines. "And we'll make them regret it."

~

"If you didn't bring anything to offer, King Basil, I don't know why you came all this way to treat with us."

Wren sent the general a glare that he naturally didn't see, since he was as usual paying her no attention. Had all her father's advisors only recently become so petty, or was she only just noticing it now that she was painfully aware of Basil's presence? If anyone had asked her—which of course they didn't—she could have told them that their attempts to project strength made Mistra seem weak compared to Basil's steady and unemotional calm.

"I'm not unwilling to negotiate, General," Basil said, in an excellent display of that calm. "But your demands are unreasonable, as I think you know. Surely we all know that neither kingdom is going to cede the entire ore field to the other. That would amount to a surrender, and if either of our forces were in a position to compel that outcome, we would have reached it years ago."

"So you admit that your army isn't strong enough to overcome ours," said the general quickly, his eyes gleaming with the imagined hit.

Wren sighed, putting her elbow on the table and resting her chin in one palm. Her father frowned at her, but she ignored him. If anyone's behavior was making them look bad in front of their foreign guests, it wasn't her posture. This council was a waste of her time. Her scheduled meeting with Basil in the afternoon was sure to be much more worthwhile. Even if they hadn't found anything new since their one breakthrough a fortnight before, at least they were learning to communicate effectively with each other, which was more than she could say for those present in the council room.

"Only inasmuch as your army isn't strong enough to overcome ours," retorted Lord Baldwin, the one representative of Basil's Lords' Council.

Basil held up a hand, and Lord Baldwin fell silent. "If there's nothing further to discuss, Your Majesty," he said, his eyes on King Lloyd, "I don't wish to detain you from more important matters."

Wren's father narrowed his eyes suspiciously. It wasn't the first time Wren had observed how much he was irked by Basil's patience in face of the king's continued obstruction. She wondered if her father really knew what he was trying to achieve. He'd said he accepted Basil's request to visit only because he couldn't politely refuse, but what was the point in making the Entolian king kick his heels in Myst? It was probably the general, constantly in her father's ear about how important it was for Mistra not to appear weak by ceding any ground.

Wren's eyes passed from her father to Basil, who was the picture of calm. He'd been in Myst for a month now, and when he arrived, he'd been so insistent that they negotiate immediately, and not waste time he could little spare from all his pressing obligations back in Tola. Surely he would lose patience at any moment, give up on negotiations, and ride back to Entolia.

The thought made Wren feel unspeakably depressed, and not just because of what it would mean for the war. She desperately wanted him to stay another month, so she could show him who she was, underneath the reserve enforced on her by the curse. But it was foolish to expect it. She was amazed he'd stayed as long as he had. He was unlikely to extend his visit by as much time again.

"Very well," said King Lloyd at last, rising with a little less dignity than normal. "If you have nothing new to say, I do indeed have other things to attend to." He swept from the room, clearly expecting his retinue to follow. Wren did so reluctantly, casting a glance back at Basil. He remained where he sat, looking a little weary. He sent her the briefest of smiles, but he was swamped by his own companions before she could respond.

CHAPTER FIFTEEN

Wren

Wren had no expectation of seeing Basil again before lunch, so she was surprised to see his now familiar figure striding toward her not an hour later, as she knelt by the garden pond.

What's the Entolian doing out here? groused Conan, with whom she had been speaking.

Ignoring him, Wren straightened, her smile of welcome dimming as she took in Basil's companion. He'd never brought anyone else to speak with her before, and she wasn't sure she liked it. Especially since her own guards were, for once, absent.

"I hope you won't mind Lord Baldwin joining us, Wren," said Basil briskly, once the pair had reached the pond.

I mind both of you joining us, Conan shot back. Wren stepped away from him so she wouldn't have to hear his complaints in her mind, inclining her head in an insincere acceptance of Basil's words.

The young king seemed to read her reluctance, because his brow furrowed slightly. "I'm sorry if you don't like it," he said softly, in a pointless attempt to speak privately. "But I have no new avenues of inquiry. We're not getting anywhere, and I can't afford to wait around here forever."

For some reason he glanced up at the sky as he spoke, but Wren barely noticed. Her heart sank. He'd shown a remarkably patient front every time her father was present—suggesting he wasn't entirely ignorant of how to play politics—but she'd known he must be chafing underneath. He was eager to leave her—to leave Mistra—and she couldn't blame him.

He glanced back down at her, his brows drawing further together as he took in her expression. He opened his mouth to speak, but she cleared her throat, not wanting any more forthrightness just now. Raising her eyebrows expectantly, she looked toward Lord Baldwin.

The moment she did so, his head whipped away in a painfully transparent effort to hide the fact that he'd been staring at her. She held in a sigh. The Entolian nobleman was as awkward around her as any of her own people. Mistrans who were disappointed in their future monarch she could understand, but she found it hard to grasp what about her made the Entolian so very uncomfortable.

"Ah yes," said Basil, sending a small frown his companion's way. "Lord Baldwin has shown himself particularly effective at finding information, and I asked him to keep an ear to the ground for any whisper of discontented magic-users." He gave Lord Baldwin an expectant look. "Well, share your discoveries."

The nobleman cleared his throat. "Yes, King Basil." Although Wren was presumably the only one present for whom his information was new, he couldn't quite fix his eyes on her. "I didn't hear anything concrete, but there are rumors that a group of both Alburian and Mistran enchanters were involved in the attack that transformed Albury's crown prince. Apparently they showed a general antagonism toward royalty, so it's possible someone among them may have wished to target Mistra's royal family as well."

Basil looked at Wren expectantly. "What do you think?"

She frowned. That wasn't what she'd heard—she was aware that a Mistran had been behind the attack on Albury's now-monarch, but the report her father had received had claimed it was only one enchantress, acting alone. And that woman certainly wasn't the same one who'd attacked Wren and her brothers.

She reached for her slate, then hesitated, glancing at Lord Baldwin. She felt self-conscious to use it in front of him, but Basil was still watching her searchingly, and she couldn't think of any other way to say what she wanted to.

If Albury identified these enchanters, what became of them?

Basil read the message quickly, and turned to Lord Baldwin, waiting for him to answer. With clear reluctance, the nobleman leaned forward far enough to read Wren's words.

"Pardoned," he said concisely. "So they're still at large."

Wren considered his words, trying to put the timing together. She remembered the sensation it had caused when rumor had reached Myst of the attack on Prince Justin of Albury. It was hard to forget—it wasn't every day a royal got turned into a beast and disappeared from the face of the continent. But she and her brothers had already been two years into their curse by then. If the same enchanters were behind both attacks, they'd moved against Mistra first. Perhaps they'd been emboldened by their supposed success, and carried on to Albury?

"What are you thinking, Wren?" Basil's eyes studied her face, and he tipped his head encouragingly toward her slate, which she hadn't even realized she'd been tapping with her fingernails.

Again Wren glanced at Lord Baldwin, but there was no help for it. She stepped over to her usual bench. If she was going to be writing prolonged messages, it would be easier if she could lean on her lap to do it. Seating herself, she held up a single hand to tell Basil she would need a minute, and he nodded accommodatingly.

Our agent reported that it was a single disgruntled Mistran behind that attack,

she wrote.

Although it's true that, according to him, the enchantment was stronger than anyone would have expected from one enchantress.

She frowned, leaning back and mulling it over. Basil stood nearby, his hands clasped behind his back as usual, making no attempt to hurry her. Almost absently, she handed him the slate while she thought.

He read it quickly, and she noticed that Lord Baldwin's apparent reluctance didn't stop him from reading over his sovereign's shoulder.

"Interesting," said Basil.

Wren's thoughts solidified, and she gestured impatiently for him to return her slate. Once he did so, she rubbed the first message out and scratched another.

It's a similar inconsistency to my own attack, isn't it? Our enchantress threw something at my brothers and me which should have been beyond her power.

Basil's expression became keen as he scanned her words. "Perhaps there is a connection," he breathed. "Foolish of us not to think of it before."

Wren nodded emphatically, her mind whirling with possibilities. Should they approach Albury's monarchs, and ask for any information they might have? The thought was intimidating. Perhaps that would be a mistake—was it possible the Alburian crown had been involved? But that made no sense. Not when King Justin had himself been a victim.

A sudden thought occurred to her and she gasped. Bending over her slate, she scratched out another message.

And it was shortly after the attack in Albury that the Listernian princess fell afoul of her own curse, which everyone said was an incredibly strong one!

She pushed the slate back into Basil's hands, then paused. That wasn't quite right, though, was it? Because the Listernian princess's curse had been cast a long time before, when she was an infant. Surely the same group of enchanters weren't working against royalty as long ago as that.

Lord Baldwin cleared his throat, his expression more uneasy than ever. "Your Majesty," he said, looking only at Basil, although he was clearly responding to Wren's scribbled message. "I think you may be creating connections that aren't there."

Basil stared at him. "But you're the one who said the same enchanters might have targeted both Albury and Mistra."

"I know I did," Lord Baldwin said hurriedly. "But I merely meant that if the enchantress who attacked the Mistran princes was aided by another unseen attacker, as you seem to suspect, that person might have been involved in the attack on Albury's prince as well. I wasn't suggesting some vast conspiracy."

Wren frowned. She and Basil had only suggested that there might be a connection between the various attacks against royalty. It was a bit much for Lord Baldwin to talk as though they were letting their imaginations run wild.

"Well, if I'm not to draw connections, what *were* you suggesting I do with your information?" Basil asked his advisor mildly.

"That's a matter for you, Your Majesty," said Lord Baldwin with a shrug. "I suppose I was merely suggesting that it might be worth looking in Albury for renegade enchanters as well as in Mistra."

Wren considered him. It wasn't hard—she could stare at him with impunity given he seemed to be avoiding looking at her. She'd had the same thought herself, about going to Albury. But somehow the fact that Lord Baldwin had suggested it made her less inclined to actually do it.

"It's a worthwhile suggestion," Basil said lightly. "We should go. My head guard wishes to meet with me." His eyes met Wren's, and she read their silent message. They would discuss this matter further at a later time, without Lord Baldwin's restrictive presence.

The private communication warmed Wren—she couldn't help but be pleased to know Basil trusted her, and considered her his primary ally in his goals, in spite of their kingdoms' situation. She gave him a nod, and a smile that she rarely bestowed on anyone else.

Glancing at Lord Baldwin, she saw he was watching the two royals, his discomfort even more clear than before. But he followed his sovereign's lead and took his leave, hurrying alongside Basil toward the castle.

Wren sat on her bench for a long time after they left, thinking it all over. If Lord Baldwin's information was a lead, it wasn't a terribly encouraging one. The idea that they needed to consider every magic-user in Albury as well as Mistra and Entolia didn't exactly get them closer to their goal.

Pushing herself to her feet, Wren wandered toward the pond. For once, none of her brothers had tried to push their way into her conversation with Basil and Lord Baldwin, and she wanted to at least check on Caleb before going inside again. Standing by the reeds, she could see a few of them far out in the center of the pond, but she was too far away to recognize who was who. She glanced around, her eyes alighting on a small path which wound its way up a rocky ledge. The gardeners had used ingeniously disguised pumps to create a small waterfall which fell in a constant cascade from the top of the ledge into the pond. Wren stepped onto the path, thinking that she'd get a good vantage point from alongside the waterfall. There was no need to disrupt whatever her brothers were doing.

She reached the top of the ledge quickly, and turned her eyes back to the swans. Ah yes, there was Caleb, floating lopsidedly with his bad wing out at its usual strange angle. He seemed to be in conversation with…was that Bram? No, Averett. Bram was probably off spying on Basil through a window somewhere.

Wren was leaning forward, trying to identify a smaller swan which had just come up from a dive, when it happened.

She had been standing on flat rock a moment before, but she

suddenly felt her slipper snag on a trailing root, and she wobbled dangerously. Just as she regained her balance, she felt another root connect with her other foot, which she hadn't even moved. As she waved her arms wildly, trying to right herself, she felt the roots actually wrap around her ankles and tug.

Only just remembering not to scream aloud, she toppled from the edge of the ridge, too stunned even to take a preparatory breath before she hit the water.

It wasn't a dangerous height to fall from, but it was enough to send her deep into the pond. She flailed her arms wildly, her body responding to the unpleasant cold of the water. Her head had just broken the surface when she once again felt something around her ankle.

She pulled her leg up frantically, wondering how she'd become so entangled that she'd ripped the root out with her as she fell. But her foot wouldn't come loose, and a moment later, she was tugged back below the surface. Opening her eyes, she strained to see through the murky water. Catching sight of her ankle, she let out an involuntary gasp that filled her mouth with pond water.

It wasn't a root tangled around her foot. It was the weeds growing from the bottom of the pond, reaching up impossibly, wrapping themselves around her ankle and attempting to pull her down. As she thrashed wildly and ineffectually, already desperate for air, another weed shot out and wound around her other ankle.

Wren fought her panic, trying to make the movements of her arms precise and deliberate. She just had to propel herself back to the surface. The weeds surely weren't strong. But she could make no progress against them, and a desperate glance upward showed that the surface was higher above her than she'd realized.

She bent her body in the water, trying frantically to pull the weeds off her, but she was running out of time. Her body started convulsing, and her mind wouldn't work properly. She let go of the weeds, drifting back into an upright position as blackness threatened.

Suddenly a sharp pain at one ankle brought her back to full awareness. She looked down to see a white shape gleaming through the murkiness. Another swan arrived, and another, and soon four of them were pecking and tugging viciously at the weeds, ripping the plants apart with their beaks. They accidentally pecked her more than once, but she welcomed the pain, knowing it was all that was keeping her conscious. Within moments, the four of them had her free, and they swarmed around her. Lyall and Averett snaked their way under each of her shoulders, and she felt the water churn as their powerful feet propelled her to the surface.

When her head broke, she gasped and spluttered, still not immediately able to get air. She could see Caleb across the pond, swimming in her direction as quickly as his injuries would allow.

Averett and Lyall didn't wait for him. They kept swimming, tugging Wren toward the shore. Ari swam ahead, his wings beating the water in agitation, and Conan brought up the rear. When they deposited Wren on the shore, she pulled herself onto her hands and knees, coughing up the last of the water.

Wren! Ari's terrified voice sounded in her mind as he huddled against her. *Are you all right? What happened?*

I fell, she rasped, her internal voice somehow as hoarse as her audible one would be if she could speak aloud. *From the ledge with the waterfall.*

Ari turned away, presumably to communicate this information to the others, but Wren seized his leg urgently. She could already hear shouts, and she could see the guards from one of the castle entrances hurrying toward her. She needed to tell the truth to someone who'd believe her.

Ari, she said urgently, *it wasn't an accident. The plants—the roots on the ledge, and the weeds in the water—came for me.*

Her brother's beak fell open, and he seemed lost for words. There was no time for more. The guards converged on Wren, followed closely by a maid who seemed on the verge of hysterics.

Before Wren well knew what was happening, she found herself in her own rooms, with her feet in a bucket of hot water, a stern but pale-faced governess plying her with towels, and her father's physician bending over her.

"She'll be fine," he said soothingly to Wren's parents, both of whom were watching him anxiously. He smiled at Wren. "You're none the worse for wear, Your Highness. But perhaps stay away from any water-facing cliffs for a while, hm?"

She gave a weary smile, nodding her thanks.

Her mother hurried in to take the physician's place, clasping Wren's hand in one of her own.

"You'll not be going anywhere near the gardens at all," King Lloyd said, his voice strained.

Wren gave a protesting gasp, frowning at him. He couldn't take away her sanctuary. How would she see the boys if she wasn't allowed out there, and they weren't allowed in the castle?

"I mean it, Wren," said King Lloyd. "Do you realize you almost died?"

She gave him a look. Of course she realized. But the terror in his eyes made her rein in her exasperation. He thought he'd just come close to losing his last remaining child. He was allowed to be upset, even a little unreasonable.

She fished her slate out of her sodden pocket, using a corner of the towel wrapped around her shoulders to dry it off.

I'll be more careful, I promise.

Her mother squeezed her hand, looking close to tears, but the king wasn't mollified.

"What happened, Wren?" he demanded. "How could you be so careless in the first place?"

She shook her head, scribbling again.

Not careless. Not accident. Weeds came after me. Magic.

Queen Liana gave a gasp, her eyes flying to her husband as one hand jumped to her mouth.

"What?" King Lloyd roared. "You were attacked?" His face darkened. "I knew we couldn't trust King Basil. I'll have that snake arrested immediately." He turned to the guards hovering just outside the door.

Wren leaped to her feet, water splashing over the floor as she lunged across the room and grabbed her father's arm before he could issue any commands that might plunge them into true war. Forcing him to look at her, she shook her head emphatically. Her father's face was as hard as flint, but she dragged him back across the room, making him look at her slate as she once again wrote.

Not Basil. He wasn't with me.

"Who then?" her father demanded furiously.

Wren gave a helpless shrug. She had no more idea of that than her father did.

"You've let his air of candor fool you, Wren," her father growled. "No one's tried to harm you in six years, and I'm supposed to think it's coincidence that you're attacked the moment the Entolians arrive?"

Wren scratched hastily, desperate to make him understand. Never had the glacial speed of her words been so infuriating. Her mind ran miles ahead of her hand, longing for the instant communication of verbal speech. At last she finished her message, thrusting the slate into her father's face.

They've been here for a month, Father, with no sign of aggression. Basil's had lots of chances to harm me if he'd wished. He truly doesn't want war. Attacking your heir is the last thing he'd do.

Wren's governess cleared her throat. "I feel bound to say, Your Majesty," she said, not quite looking at Wren, "that two of the maids saw the incident from an upstairs window, where they were cleaning. They say that the princess was alone, and that she simply fell into the water. She seemed to struggle to stay afloat, and her pet swans helped her to the bank." She gave a delicate cough. "I wonder if it is perhaps possible that Princess Wren is a little overwrought, and is imagining things."

Wren scowled at her, but didn't immediately contradict. Of course she knew she hadn't been imagining the unnatural behavior of the weeds, but for the moment perhaps it was better for her father to believe that than to arrest Basil for her attempted murder.

"Don't do anything irrevocable," said Queen Liana pleadingly to her husband. "If you arrest King Basil because Wren fell into the pond when he wasn't even with her, you'll be the one provoking war. I'm as frightened by Wren's accident as you are, but Lloyd...I'm so weary of the fighting."

Her shoulders sagged at the last sentence, and Wren's father hesitated. Taking advantage of this sign of softening, Wren hastily scribbled another message, her writing becoming sloppy in her urgency.

Listen to us, Father. I just almost died, and even I'm calling for restraint. We're all so sick of the conflict. Can't you at least try to give Basil the chance to demonstrate good intentions?

For once her father gave no sign of impatience as he waited for her to scratch this message out. He read it slowly, his expression still hard, but his eyes thoughtful.

"Of course I don't wish to be hasty," he said curtly. He paused, his eyes narrowing as he stared at Wren's neck. "Where's your signet ring, Wren?"

Wren's hand flew to her throat, startled to discover the chain was gone. It hadn't even occurred to her before now that the protective enchantment on the ring should have prevented her from being fatally attacked. But it had been no use at all when the weeds were dragging her under.

"Well?" the king pressed, a hint of anger in his voice. "Why did you take it off? You know you're supposed to wear it at all times."

Wren shook her head, rubbing her slate clean so she could write out a new message.

I didn't. Must have fallen off in the water.

The king was still frowning, but some of the anger was fading from his eyes. "Perhaps it really was an accident," he said, mostly to himself. "No one would have been able to push you into the pond while you were wearing it."

Wren bit her lip, confused. Was it possible she really had imagined the magic? She gave her head a little shake. No. That had definitely been an attack. How had it gotten around her ring? She relived the short fall into the pond, and her flailing attempts to reach the surface. She'd always worn the ring on a long chain, so she could hide it below her gown when desired. It wasn't hard to imagine it coming off. The enchantment didn't prevent it being removed—it was intended to be worn snugly on a finger, where it was less likely to be dislodged.

Remembering her first reaction on falling into the water— surprise, but no real fear—Wren thought she understood why the ring hadn't protected her from the roots. The danger of falling into the pond from that small height wasn't great. It wasn't life-threatening, or even likely to lead to serious injury, and it was therefore insufficient to activate the protective enchantment. The weeds that pulled her below the water would have been, but by then her ring was gone. Did the person who planned the attack know that, or did they just get lucky?

"The ring must be found, and resized for your finger."

Wren shook her head frantically, but her father's expression was unyielding. "I don't want to hear any more arguments about it, Wren. I should have done it years ago."

He cast a glance over her sodden person. "And accident or not, from now on, at least two guards must accompany you everywhere, not just when you meet with King Basil." He frowned. "And when you *are* with King Basil, it will be four guards." He shot a meaningful look through the doorway at one of Wren's guards, standing to attention in the corridor.

The man nodded. He would no doubt relay the order to the head of Wren's guard, and she would never be allowed to go anywhere alone again. Her heart sank. It would make her investigation with Basil considerably more difficult. But it was better than her father openly accusing Basil of attacking her. And maybe it would discourage whoever had attacked her today from trying again.

When Wren nodded a reluctant acknowledgment, her father immediately turned and strode from the room. Wren stared after him, taken aback by his abrupt exit. Swiveling back around, she saw her mother watching her heavily.

"Can we have a moment, please?" the queen said softly, without taking her eyes off her daughter.

Everyone in the room hastened to leave, with no protest beyond a disapproving sniff from Wren's governess. In moments, they were alone.

"Wren," said Queen Liana, tears standing in her eyes as she clasped Wren's hands between her own. "I was so terrified when we were summoned..." Her voice trailed off, and she took a moment to collect herself. "You will be careful, won't you?"

Wren nodded, returning the pressure of her mother's hand, and trying to communicate with her eyes that she took her mother's fears seriously.

"And you truly believe King Basil had nothing to do with your accident?" her mother asked.

Wren nodded emphatically.

"You're absolutely certain?"

Again, she nodded, her expression solemn.

The queen let out a long breath. "I want to trust him," she mused, her eyes unfocused. "I want to believe he's not like his father, and peace is possible." Her gaze returned to her daughter. "You know why your father ran away like that, don't you?"

Wren shook her head, her eyes full of questions.

The queen sighed again. "Because he loves you as much as I do, and the thought of losing you as well terrified him. He didn't want you to see his emotion, so he left while he could still contain it."

Wren blinked. Was her mother right? Her father always held himself so rigid, it was too easy to forget what a heavy load he was carrying. She felt a trickle of sympathy, and determined to bear being shadowed by guards with good humor.

"Do you know why we had so many children?" her mother asked unexpectedly.

Wren shrugged, lifting an inquiring eyebrow.

"Because I wanted you," smiled the queen. "I wanted a daughter." She squeezed Wren's hands, and again Wren returned the pressure. "I wanted the boys as well, of course." Her eyes grew distant. "And they were wonderful sons, each and every one of them. But when you were born," her gaze returned to Wren, a misty smile on her face, "I was so happy. There were strict requirements for the upbringing of Mistran princes, especially Caleb. But I hoped that I would be allowed more rein in how I raised you. I hoped you would enjoy the things I enjoyed, that I'd be able to spend more time with you." She sighed. "I hoped you could escape the burdens of politics and rigid protocols, and everything that comes with ruling." She smiled again, but this time it was strained. "Things don't turn out quite like we plan, do they?"

Wren shook her head sadly. So often she kept hope by telling herself that everything would be fixed once her brothers returned to their true forms, and her parents knew they hadn't lost their sons. But her mother's words reminded her of the truth she already knew. The lifting of the curse wouldn't turn back the clock. Her brothers were alive, but many things had been lost to the curse that couldn't be recovered once it was defeated.

"One of the things I hate most about everything that's happened," her mother went on, "is the distance I feel it's created between us. Sometimes it seems like I spend all my time trying to convince you to undertake a role I never wanted you to have. Trying unsuccessfully, I should add," she amended dryly.

Wren grimaced apologetically. If she could explain, she would, but since she couldn't, there wasn't much to say.

"I couldn't bear to lose you, Wren," the queen said simply. "I know you feel like an unwanted replacement, and I don't know how to change that. But I need you to know you're loved for being yourself. If I sometimes seem grieved that you've taken your brother's place, it's not because you're inadequate. It's because I never wanted this life for you." She let go of Wren's hands and wrapped her arms around her. "It shouldn't have taken you nearly dying for me to tell you that, and for that I'm sorry."

Wren leaned into her mother's embrace, tears standing in her own eyes. She didn't know who'd tried to do her an injury today, but she knew she couldn't let them win. Their unseen enemies had taken too much from Wren's family already, and she wasn't going to let them take anything more.

CHAPTER SIXTEEN

Basil

Basil tried to be attentive to the report being delivered by his head guard, but his mind kept straying to Lord Baldwin's information, and the possible connection he and Wren had identified between the attack on her brothers and the attacks suffered by the Alburian and Listernian royals.

What did Wren really think about it all? It was clear she'd been holding back, not comfortable to share her thoughts freely in front of Lord Baldwin.

Basil shot a sideways look at the young nobleman, who'd accompanied the king to his suite to receive the guard's report. Once again, Lord Baldwin's discomfort around Wren had been painfully palpable. No wonder she didn't want to communicate with him present, Basil thought with a flicker of annoyance. Why couldn't Lord Baldwin pull himself together? Basil had come to enjoy the nobleman's company, and would have liked him as an ally in the investigation he and Wren were undertaking. But Lord Baldwin's inability to behave naturally around the silent princess was too great a barrier to allow his inclusion.

"In short, I've observed nothing to concern me, Your Majesty," the guard finished. "The Mistrans may not be welcoming us with warmth, but I can't see any sign that they intend us harm."

Basil nodded. "Thank you for your report. I'm pleased to hear you're at ease with our situation."

The thickset guard gave a rare smile. "I don't know if I'd go as far as at ease, Your Majesty," he said. "If I'm honest, I didn't expect such a long visit, and I wish I'd brought more guards, to keep everyone sharp. But it's my job to be wary. I can at least acknowledge that nothing in the Mistrans' behavior has so far justified that wariness."

Basil smiled. "As always, I appreciate your honesty. And I'm pleased to hear your scout has reported the ceasefire at the border continues to hold steady."

"Yes." The guard hesitated. "If I may be bold, Your Majesty, I don't believe it can stay steady forever. Without a proper resolution to the conflict, tensions on the front lines will reach boiling point eventually."

"I know," Basil sighed. "We must hope we can reach a proper resolution before that happens."

The guard bowed and withdrew, leaving Basil alone with Lord Baldwin. Basil's eyes strayed to the stack of letters and reports sitting on the desk in his suite. A response to his mother's latest request for instructions was well overdue, and he hadn't even glanced at the agricultural report which he was supposed to be approving by return courier. He'd never expected ruling a kingdom to be easy, but attempting to do it from a distance was a nightmare.

Basil was just thinking that he'd better start with a response to the letter from one of his more influential advisors, once again condemning the whole visit to Mistra, when the nobleman beside him cleared his throat.

"Speaking honestly, King Basil, I also didn't expect such a prolonged visit."

Basil gave him a weary smile as he tugged on the stiff fabric of his sleeve. "Pressing matters to return to, My Lord? It's inconsiderate of me to keep you away from your lands for so long without fair warning."

"Not at all, Your Majesty," said Lord Baldwin hastily. "That's not what I was getting at. I just had the impression when we were leaving Tola that you were determined to finalize the matter with all speed."

"I was," sighed Basil, rubbing at his chest, over which his tunic was tightly laced.

He still wasn't convinced by the cultural advisor who'd insisted he would make a better impression if he donned the clothes favored by his hosts. The weather was growing far too warm for these restrictive Mistran garments.

"And I didn't plan to be here nearly this long either, if *I'm* honest," he went on. "But it's been borne in upon me that my attempts at efficiency were a touch...naive." Plus he'd begun to pin his hopes on the dragons providing him with answers, and was trying to linger long enough to coincide with their promised visit. Not that he intended to tell Lord Baldwin that.

"But you also seem quite happy to linger here," said Lord Baldwin carefully, looking sideways at Basil. "You and the princess seem to be on excellent terms."

Basil shot him a searching look, wondering what was behind the question. It wasn't that he was surprised Lord Baldwin had noticed the easy friendship that had so unexpectedly developed between him and Wren. But Lord Baldwin was so uncomfortable whenever the princess came up, Basil was taken aback to hear the nobleman raise the topic himself.

Basil hesitated, not sure how to answer. If his reasons for staying in Myst so long were easy to explain, he would have answered the irate letter on his desk long before. But he hadn't wanted to articulate to himself, let alone to Lord Baldwin or the nobleman back home, that his growing enjoyment of Wren's company was a substantial factor in his willingness to extend his stay. He wasn't usually one to shy away from confronting truths, but he had a vague sense that if he looked this one in the eye, the whole precarious balance of his and Wren's relationship would collapse very quickly. And he didn't want that.

Before he had figured out what response to give, an urgent knock sounded on the door, and both men turned.

"Enter," Basil called calmly.

One of the servants from his delegation threw the door open, almost falling into the room in her haste.

"Your Majesty!" She bobbed a hasty curtsy. "Have you heard what happened to the princess?"

"What do you mean?" Basil demanded, a potent shot of fear racing through him. "What happened?"

"She was just pulled from the garden pond by her guards, sopping wet and half-drowned!"

"What?!" Basil was barely aware of his movements as he stepped toward the door. "But we were just with her!" He glanced at Lord Baldwin, whose face was frozen in horror at the news. "Moments ago!"

"I know," the maid breathed, her eyes wide. "I heard one of the other servants say the king isn't convinced it's an accident, and I thought I'd better come and warn you, in case anyone accuses..."

She trailed off, but Basil didn't need her to finish her sentence. Anyone could predict that at the first suggestion of foul play, King Lloyd's mind would turn immediately to his unwelcome guest.

"Surely they couldn't accuse us," spluttered Lord Baldwin. "She was fine when we left the garden!"

"And nowhere near the water," said Basil, still too alarmed

by the news of Wren's accident to care much about any accusations. "What happened?"

"I don't rightly know, Your Majesty," admitted the maid. "Someone told me she fell from a cliff, but I didn't think there was a cliff in the garden."

Basil cast his mind hastily over the layout of the pond. There was a small ridge there, with a waterfall. But it wasn't high enough for a fall from it to be dangerous. He relaxed slightly. "Is she all right?"

"I don't know that either," the maid said apologetically. "She was taken to her rooms, and her maids have been bustling in and out warming water and bringing towels."

Basil nodded distractedly. That sounded like she'd suffered nothing worse than a dunking. But still...how had it happened? He'd never seen her climb that ridge before. And why did her parents suspect foul play?

With a great effort of will, he curbed his first impulse, which was to rush to her immediately. Something told him King Lloyd would not take well to Basil presenting himself at Wren's suite, demanding to see for himself that she was unharmed.

He had little choice but to wait. Any ability he had to think strategically about Lord Baldwin's information had fled, however, as had his desire to respond to his various urgent correspondence. Once the maid had bowed herself out, Lord Baldwin hurrying to do the same, Basil found himself pacing his room for almost an hour. He remembered when his sister Violet had fallen from a horse and broken her arm. Given that she'd been in no danger of lasting injury, he'd surprised himself with how much it had distressed him.

Eventually he'd realized that logical or not, he felt responsible, as though he should have been there and somehow prevented it. He knew his parents didn't have the time or attention to properly supervise all their children, and as far back as he could remember, he'd felt a flicker of guilt every time circumstances prevented him from filling that gap. It was a feeling he'd striven to overcome as his duties increased. Now that he was king, he needed that detachment more than ever—there was no way he would be at liberty to play father to his sisters.

The impotent frustration he felt now, knowing Wren had suffered an accident moments after he'd left her, was similar to that old feeling. But at the same time it was different, and alarmingly intense. He knew she was fine, and that whatever happened hadn't been his fault. But he was still filled with a restless energy that would allow him to think of nothing else.

He was disappointed but unsurprised when the princess made no appearance either at lunch, or for their afternoon rendezvous. He was perfectly content for discussion of their new information to wait, but he wished he could have spoken to her, assured himself that she wasn't in any danger. Thankfully the weather had become considerably milder since his arrival in Myst, and he didn't think she'd be in danger of illness from submersion in the pond.

When she didn't attend dinner either, Basil gave up on the evening altogether and retired to bed. He lay awake for some time, trying to reassure himself first that her prolonged absence just meant she was tired from her ordeal, not that her injuries were worse than reported, and second that his own overblown reaction was no cause for concern.

When Basil arrived in the dining hall the next morning, he took one look at Wren's empty seat, and turned back toward the door. He refused to be dismayed—it wasn't unusual for the princess to skip breakfast. But he had no interest in a solitary meal, and he determined to go looking for her himself, whether or not her parents would like it. He hadn't missed the hardness in King Lloyd's eyes every time he looked at Basil during the previous night's dinner, or the suspicious glances being thrown at his delegation by Mistran nobles and servants alike. The rumor that Princess Wren's fall had been no accident had clearly spread through the castle with predictable speed.

It was equally clear that Basil's own people were on edge. No accusation had been made against him, and he'd issued no new orders to his guards, but two of them trailed him as he made his way through the castle. It irked him, but he made no attempt to send them away. He knew they were only trying to protect him, and with suspicions running high, perhaps it was wise to have witnesses around when he ran Wren to ground at last.

Not bold enough to seek the princess at her rooms—wherever they even were—he made his way instead to the gardens, hoping she was up and about and simply disinterested in breakfast.

To his mingled delight and annoyance, he spotted her as soon as the pond came into view. She was sitting on her usual bench, the lame swan cuddled up beside her. He hastened toward her, calling a greeting.

"Wren! You're still alive, it seems."

He regretted his flippant words as he rounded the large bush between him and her location, and realized she wasn't alone. Not only were two guards standing behind her bench, glaring suspiciously at him, but a young woman with honey colored hair was seated on her other side, turned slightly toward the princess. At Basil's arrival, she stood hastily, curtsying.

"I beg your pardon," he said pleasantly. "I've interrupted."

"Not at all, Your Majesty," she said politely, curiosity in her eyes as she cast a surreptitious look over him. "I was just on my way to breakfast."

"No need to leave on my account," said Basil, and she smiled.

"I'm expected." Her voice was a little strained, and Basil noticed that Wren's expression had become troubled as she watched the other woman. She scratched a message on her slate, and tapped her companion's arm.

The young woman looked down at the words, and gave another strained smile. "I would like that, Your Highness." She gave an unconvincing laugh. "I'm afraid I need all the counsel I can get."

Basil barely glanced at the other woman as she took her leave, inclining his head vaguely. His focus was on Wren's face, intrigued by its expression. She was looking at her departing friend with distress in her eyes.

At least, he assumed the other woman was Wren's friend, since she'd been writing on her slate. He'd noticed that the princess was sparing in who she used the tool with. It had certainly made her uncomfortable to use it in front of Lord Baldwin, but Basil had seen no sign of embarrassment on her face as she scribbled a message for this woman.

"Who was that?" he asked amicably, seating himself beside Wren without waiting for an invitation.

She didn't answer immediately, and Basil took a moment to glance at the slate still sitting beside her. It held a curious collection of messages.

What do you think of Sir Gelding?

What's your father's hurry?

You are <u>not</u> old.

And finally, the last message, that Basil had seen her write after his arrival.

We can talk more later.

It seemed he really had interrupted something. He pictured Wren's expression as she'd showed her last message to her companion. Her eyes had seemed to plead with the other woman not to do anything hasty, and glancing over the messages gave Basil a fair idea of what she'd meant.

"Is Sir Gelding courting her? That enchanter who was suspicious of me because I brought an enchantress with me from Tola?"

Wren started at his question, pulling her eyes from her retreating friend and looking rapidly between Basil and the slate. Glaring pointedly at him, she snatched it up and scrubbed it clean.

"Sorry," he said, nothing particularly repentant about his grin. "It's rude of me to eavesdrop, I know. But I've always been bad-mannered."

Wren rolled her eyes, the smile tugging at her lips telling him she wasn't really offended. She dashed out a few words onto her now empty slate.

That's Lady Anneliese, a friend, and yes, Sir Gelding is courting her.

"He seems too old," Basil commented, picturing the streaks of silver in the enchanter's hair. "Although he was very polished, and good-looking enough, I suppose."

Wren's hastily suppressed snort of laughter made him throw another grin her way, but her expression sobered quickly.

I agree that he's too old.

She hesitated, then added another sentence.

Lady Anneliese was going to marry my
oldest brother, Caleb, before…

She left the sentence unfinished, but Basil understood perfectly. His own mirth dropping away, he laid a hand over hers. She stilled at his touch, her expressive eyes finding his immediately. Basil was aware of her guards behind the bench, shifting disapprovingly at the contact, but he ignored them.

"I'm sorry," he said sincerely. "The whole thing must be very painful for you."

Wren hesitated again, then extricated her hand to write another message.

For her, more than me.

Basil was silent. He knew better than anyone that tact wasn't his strength, and he thought it better not to say anything than to fill the space with awkward words.

"What's Sir Gelding like?" he asked eventually.

Wren shrugged.

"You don't know much about him?" Basil guessed.

She nodded, then rubbed her slate clean. Basil waited patiently while she scratched out a longer message this time. His sisters would be amazed at how patient he'd become, he reflected. But he never found it frustrating to wait for Wren to write out her thoughts. She was always so absorbed in what she was doing, it gave him frequent opportunities to study her without being caught at it.

Today, he noticed that she was wearing a gown unlike her usual style, with long sleeves and quite a high neckline. She looked well, with no sign of illness or injury from her accident the day before. Her hair was pulled back from her face in many intricate braids, and the style was very becoming on her. He supposed her maids had time to do such an elaborate hairstyle when she spent a whole day hiding away in her rooms, he thought, still a touch resentful about his anxious night. But he couldn't really feel annoyed, not when she was so clearly blooming with health.

She held out her slate at last, and he took it, glancing down at the words. The whole slate was covered, the letters small and tight.

All I really know is that Sir Gelding voted against attempting an invasion back when the war started. I found a record of that council meeting recently. He lives far south, but he and a number of others traveled to Myst for the council, and he was against full scale war.

"Interesting," Basil mused. He laid the slate down. "Not my primary concern right now, though." He pinned her with a hard look. "What's this I hear about you falling into the pond yesterday?"

Wren grimaced, shrugging one shoulder, but making no move to pick her slate back up.

"Seriously, what happened?" Basil pressed. "I was frantic when I heard—the maid made it sound like you'd fallen to your death."

With a sigh, Wren picked up her slate at last.

I'm fine. Not a big deal.

"Then why have you been hiding away in your room since it happened?" Basil demanded, aggrieved.

Pressing down on the slate with unnecessary force, Wren added to her previous words.

Because everyone in my life is overly protective.

For some reason, she cast an exasperated look from the swan still huddled at her side to those on the surface of the lake as she said it. But Basil wasn't interested in her swans at that moment.

"You could at least have let me know you were all right. I was picturing all kinds of disasters."

Wren shot him a surprised look, her hand hovering as if unsure what to write in response to that. Basil met her gaze steadily, not at all embarrassed to have her know he'd been worried about her.

It was Wren who dropped her gaze first, fidgeting with her skirt for a moment. Then, with a furtive look behind her, she angled her body so that it was between the slate and her guards, and scratched something in letters so tiny Basil had to lean right over her to read them.

It wasn't an accident. Magic was involved. I would have drowned if my swans didn't save me.

"What?" Basil demanded, and Wren sent him a glare as she scrubbed the words away hastily.

Remembering the presence of the guards, he dropped his voice. But he couldn't keep the intensity out of his words—all the previous day's alarm had returned with twenty times the potency. Someone had tried to kill Wren when his back was turned? He should never have left her side!

"Why did you say it's no big deal?" he demanded. "Why pretend?"

With a grimace, Wren wrote another minuscule message, which she erased the moment he'd read it.

Because if I say it was an attack, my father will arrest you for it.

"Ah." Basil sat back, understanding rushing in. "I see the dilemma."

There was no need for Wren to explain further. He knew King Lloyd was unlikely to see reason where he was concerned. The Mistran king had clearly been expecting something duplicitous since the moment Basil arrived. And if he thought Basil had attacked Wren, they'd never be allowed to exchange another word again.

That would be unacceptable.

Seized by a sudden thought, he sent Wren a concerned look. "But you know I had no part in it, don't you?"

She smiled softly as she nodded, the look in her eyes causing something uncomfortably warm to lodge in Basil's chest. He smiled back at her, for a moment losing the thread of their conversation. Knowing that she trusted him made him feel lighter than he had in a long time.

Before either of them could say more, an insistent honk from the pond drew both their attention. Wren started up at once, abandoning her slate and hurrying toward the water. The lame swan began to struggle down from the bench, and without thinking about it, Basil paused to help it, as he'd seen Wren do many times.

He barely noticed the startled look the bird threw at him as his eyes were drawn back to Wren, now kneeling by the water. Her guards had hurried after her and, bemused, Basil did the same.

When he reached Wren's side, it was immediately clear that she was excited about something. The other five swans had all gathered at the water's edge, and she had a hand laid on two of them, looking between them. As Basil watched, he realized one had something dangling from its beak, flashing with red and gold. Before he could get a good look, Wren seized it. Just as Basil realized it was a chain, Wren threw it over her head, glancing surreptitiously at her guards. Basil didn't think they'd seen—they were hovering several paces back, eyeing the nearest swans warily.

Wren looked over at him, a smile of satisfaction curving her lips. Basil was staring at her in confusion, but he hadn't yet formed a question when she reached over and grabbed his wrist with one hand. He froze at her touch, thrown as much by her happily expectant expression as by the contact. His confusion only grew when, after the briefest of moments, Wren drew in a sharp breath and dropped his wrist as if it had burned her.

She pushed herself clumsily to her feet, her breath coming quickly as she hastily stowed the chain under her gown. In a detached part of his mind Basil noted that this must be why she'd worn a high-necked gown. It wasn't hard to guess that the ring with the protective enchantment had fallen off when she went into the pond, although he had no idea why she was trying to hide the fact that her swans had found it again.

He suddenly realized that he shouldn't be staring at her as she put something down the front of her dress, and looked away quickly. His thoughts were churning, many loose threads dancing tantalizingly before his mind's eye. He was on the cusp of something, he was sure. Lots of isolated pieces of information wove through his awareness, trying to connect.

Wren's bizarre behavior as she held on to him just now, looking at him almost like she looked at those ridiculous swans.

The impressive training that allowed the swans to search for and retrieve her lost jewelry from the pond.

The fact that there were six of them.

Wren was still avoiding his eye as she hurried back toward the bench, meeting the injured swan partway. Strange that the swan hadn't improved in the whole time Basil had been in Myst. How long did it take for a swan's broken wing to heal?

As he watched Wren kneel down beside the swan and lay a hand on its feathers, he felt a tickling at the edge of his awareness, an inkling of something he couldn't quite pin down.

Without warning, the injured swan collapsed onto its side, letting out a high-pitched trumpet of clear agony.

Wren's panic was instant and palpable. She seized the bird, her own mouth open in a silent scream as she clutched it, almost as though she was trying to protect it from harm by sheer force of will. Basil had assumed the bird had somehow agitated its injury, but the princess's reaction was so over the top, he thought she must know something he didn't.

The bird was still trumpeting in agony, and the sound cut through Basil like a knife. As if sensing his gaze, Wren suddenly whipped her head around to face him, her eyes wide and terrified as she took in the confused way he was looking between her and the swan.

With a movement so abrupt it made him jump, she pushed herself off the ground and threw herself at him. Before Basil knew what she was about, she was beating his chest furiously with her open palms, her eyes filled with blind panic as she communicated a silent plea he couldn't understand. The breath was knocked from him, and his hands flew up in an instinctive gesture of defense, seizing her wrists and stilling them with an iron grip.

He was vaguely aware of Wren's guards, who'd taken a half-step forward then stopped, clearly unsure whether to intervene when their charge was the one launching an attack. One of Basil's own guards started forward with a cry, and Basil shot him a furious look that communicated more clearly than words that he was to stand down. The man fell back, his eyes wide and uncertain.

Basil looked back at Wren, and once again the breath left his body, although this time it had nothing to do with being pounded in the chest. He still held both of Wren's wrists, and his defensive instinct had been to pull her within reach, where her movement was too restricted to allow her to resume her assault.

Her eyes were wide with terror as they stared into his, and her emotion was so potent, he felt fear clawing at his own mind as well. In the space of a heartbeat, she'd gone from striking him to being pressed against him, her face upturned to his, mere inches away. She was still panting from the exertion of her attack, and her breath almost intermingled with Basil's. For a wild moment, he had the impulse to lean down, touch his lips to hers, wipe the panic from her eyes. He couldn't remember ever feeling so unmoored in his life, and it took all his willpower to restore reason and beat the compulsion back.

For an endless moment they both stood, locked in their strange embrace as they stared wordlessly at each other.

And then Basil came to his senses and released Wren's wrists, taking a swift step back. The swan on the ground was still now, except for the laborious rise of its chest as it breathed, and the guards and even the other swans still seemed too stunned to move.

Wren barely caught her balance as she stumbled backward, looking as dazed as Basil felt. She knelt beside the injured swan.

"Wren," said Basil shakily, taking a step toward her and again looking in confusion at the swan.

At her name, Wren whipped around to face him. She pointed one trembling finger to the castle, and her meaning was as clear as if she'd spoken the words aloud.

You need to leave.

Basil didn't hesitate. Still barely in control of his own reactions, he strode from the garden, his mind whirling with all kinds of chaos. What in dragon's flame had just happened?

Once again, he found himself pacing his room, and when Lord Baldwin came to speak with him, he sent him away without even a pretense at politeness.

Something unnatural had happened in that garden, and Basil had no idea what. The most obvious explanation was that Wren truly had lost her mind, as everyone had long suspected. But he couldn't believe it. And it wasn't just Wren's behavior—he was equally overwhelmed and perplexed by his own emotions. He could still feel the pressure of her frantic hands on his chest. What kind of a fool wanted to kiss a girl who'd just attacked him?

But remembering Wren's utter panic, he found he bore no anger for her charge. It had clearly been as unreasoning and instinctive as his own reaction when he seized her wrists and pulled her against him. It was the memory of the terror in her dark, speaking eyes that wreaked havoc on his mind. What secret burden was she carrying? What disaster had he unleashed? Because whatever she was afraid of, he'd clearly had a hand in it. It was the only explanation for her instinct to turn on him. Being her ally had become such a central part of his life. He couldn't stand the idea of becoming her enemy again.

After the previous day's experience, he fully expected Wren to hide herself away once more. He was therefore stunned when, a mere hour after the incident, she sought him out. Assuming at first that the curt knock on his door was one of his own people, he barked out permission to enter in a less than welcoming tone.

The door didn't open, however.

"Princess Wren wishes to speak with you, Your Majesty," called a gruff and unfamiliar voice.

Basil threw the door wide to see Wren standing several paces back into the corridor, flanked once again by her guards. She couldn't quite meet his eye, but she had clearly come prepared, because she handed him not her slate, but a parchment covered in her now familiar writing.

I wish to apologize, and to ask what will seem a strange favor.

Favor? Basil looked up at Wren, but her eyes remained on her slippers. Rapidly, he read the rest of the short letter.

I know my behavior must have seemed very strange. I'm extremely sorry that I struck you, and I know I have no right to ask anything of you. Nevertheless, I must ask you to put the matter from your mind, and try not to think about it at all.

Basil's eyes flew back to Wren's face, noting that she looked close to tears. He took a step out into the corridor, and her guards drew slightly closer to their charge. Basil threw them a wry look before focusing all his attention on the princess before him.

"I find it difficult not to think about you, Princess Wren," he said softly, hardly knowing what made him say the words.

She looked up at last, her face flooding with color. Seeing her confusion, he smiled reassuringly and lifted her letter.

"But I will do my best to comply. It's not a strange request at all. I'm not hurt, so you don't need to apologize for anything. And I can certainly understand you wishing to put the incident in the past."

She nodded gratefully, although Basil couldn't help but notice that the lines of anxiety remained on her face. With a graceful curtsy, she turned and hurried away down the corridor, her guards trailing behind her.

Basil looked from her retreating form to the letter in his hand. Her request was a near impossible one. If anything, he now had more questions than ever.

CHAPTER SEVENTEEN

Wren

The next fortnight passed interminably for Wren. Now that the end of the curse was so close she could no longer count it in months, she should have felt on the verge of victory. Instead, she was more terrified of its power than she had been since the early days.

Less than a month left, and this had to happen now? Why did the maddening, perceptive, uncomfortably honest, inconveniently attractive Entolian king have to come to Myst now, and overset everything she'd been working for?

Even after two weeks, she could still feel the suffocating, stomach-churning panic rising every time she thought about that moment by the pond. When she'd seen Caleb collapse, she'd lost her wits completely, convinced that he was at last dying before her eyes, with her other brothers soon to follow. The remembered panic was always followed by a hot rush of shame at what she'd done in response. She hadn't even been aware of deciding to lunge at Basil like that. Robbed, as always, of her voice, her body had simply expressed her desperation for Basil to stop what he was doing in the most immediate way it could find.

What must he think of her?

She knew what had happened. Basil had started to figure it out. It was the only explanation for Caleb's sudden deterioration. She supposed she had her answer to the question of whether someone else figuring out her brothers' identity would be enough to activate the curse. She'd almost been able to see the dots beginning to connect in Basil's mind, but the dominant expression on his face had still been confusion. She just had to hope that meant he hadn't actually put the pieces together.

Was her cryptic request of Basil going to work? If he thought too hard, figured it out fully, would Caleb die?

She had thought, after her own slip ups back at the beginning of the curse, that one more blow would be enough to kill Caleb. She could only be profoundly grateful she'd been wrong. But still, it was hard to keep the tears back every time she watched Caleb floating on the pond, moving in slow circles as he paddled with the one good foot left to him. He could no longer get out of the water and waddle without pain, and he was more helpless and vulnerable than ever.

They'd been so close.

So close to reaching six years without further incident.

She walked around now in a constant state of fear, so terrified to communicate anything that she felt she was truly becoming the spineless, timid, damaged princess her kingdom had long believed her to be.

And the worst of it was, even in the midst of such a crisis, she couldn't seem to keep her thoughts from things they had no business dwelling on. The strength of Basil's hands as he gripped her wrists, unyielding enough to restrain her mad attack, but gentle enough not to hurt her. His warm breath on her face as he held her against him, staring searchingly into her eyes, his own gaze straying to her lips almost as if he was about to...

She pulled her thoughts from that quagmire with a snap, a shudder running over her at her own weakness.

Are you all right, Wren?

Caleb's concerned voice sounded in her mind, and a wave of remorse washed over Wren, threatening to drown her. As always, her brother was trying to protect her, but he was the one in danger, and it was her fault.

I just can't believe how stupid I was, she responded, turning to him where he sat huddled against her on their bench. *It was me grabbing his wrist that set him thinking. I don't know what came over me. I just forgot for a moment that he wasn't one of us. I thought I could speak into his mind if I was touching him.* Her mental voice was bitter. *I'm an utter fool.*

You're not a fool, contradicted Caleb patiently. *And it's not your fault. King Basil must be very sharp to figure it out after a month, when no one's come close in almost six years.*

Wren didn't answer. She knew why Basil had started to see what no one else had. It was partly her fault, in that she'd let him in much more than she had anyone else. But it was also just the way Basil was. Unlike almost everybody else, he'd never been hesitant to spend time in her company, even when she was with her strange pet swans. And he'd really looked at her, so unflinchingly that it made her feel seen in a way she'd almost forgotten was possible.

Loneliness welled up within her, and she closed her eyes, furious with herself.

Wren? Caleb had clearly sensed her shift in mood.

I'm so selfish, Caleb, she whispered into his mind.

Don't you dare ever call yourself selfish again. The anger in Caleb's voice made Wren's eyes fly open, and she stared at him, confused. *You are the least selfish person I have ever met, Wren*, he added.

His tone was perfectly serious, but Wren rolled her eyes. *That's ridiculous.*

It isn't. I doubt one person in a hundred could do what you've done for us, and probably fewer than that would be willing to try. His voice softened slightly, and he stretched his neck up to lay his head on her shoulder. *Wren, you said something a while ago that made me think you don't understand what you mean to us all. We're not protective of you because we're worried your safety will affect ours. We're protective of you because you're incredible, and we're so grateful for everything you've sacrificed for us.*

It's true.

Wren felt the touch of a wing before she heard the new voice in her mind. Clearly Averett had been listening to Caleb's words from nearby, even if he hadn't been able to understand Wren's replies.

She was so stunned by the affirmation from the usually critical Averett, she couldn't think of anything to say.

Even Conan knows the sacrifices you make for us, Averett continued, *even if he's not likely to thank you to your face. If I'm honest, I didn't think you had a hope of making it when we were first cursed, but you proved me wrong a long time ago. We all think you're incredible—not to mention you're our little sister—and we'd never let anyone hurt you if we could help it.*

Wren bit her lip, trying to hold back tears at the unexpected compliment. Her brothers' approval meant more to her than they'd ever know, and she could hardly believe that was how they saw her.

Lyall waddled up alongside Averett, laying one webbed foot over Wren's so he could join the conversation. She wasn't surprised that the other swans had been hovering nearby. With still no idea who had been behind the magical attack that sent her pitching into the pond, her brothers had all been even more protective than usual. Whenever she was outside, she could barely move for the feathers that hemmed her in on all sides.

Now we've cleared that up, Lyall said briskly, in reference to Averett's words, *can someone explain what triggered all this emotion? Did I hear Caleb saying something about you calling yourself selfish, Wren? Why would you think that?*

Wren hugged her shoulders uncomfortably, not really eager to discuss her weakness with her brothers and tarnish their image of her as "incredible". But all three of them were watching her expectantly, and there was no help for it.

Even though I know how dangerous it is, I have to stop myself every day from seeking Basil out, she explained miserably.

You want to continue your investigation into the source of the enchantress's power? Averett asked.

Wren shook her head. *No, it's not that.* She'd accepted that further investigation with Basil was too risky. Those answers could wait—would have to wait—until the curse was lifted. Then Caleb could take the reins and salvage the mess she'd made of it all. Just two more weeks to last.

I just... She hesitated, trying to figure out how to put into words the sudden return of all her feelings of isolation. She sighed. *Your lives are on the line, and all I can think about is how much I miss his company. I've obviously been avoiding him since the incident, and I'd forgotten how lonely it is when no one actually wants to speak to me.*

She felt small and pathetic saying the words, but at the same time, it was a relief to express her feelings.

I guess I didn't realize how much his friendship meant to me until I lost it.

There was a moment of silence as her three listeners seemed to struggle for what to say.

King Basil is certainly not what I expected, Averett admitted at last.

A honk drew Wren's attention to another sleek white form hastening to join the group.

Are you talking about the Entolian? Conan asked, shoving his head into the mass of feathers so that it connected a little painfully with Wren's knee. *Have you finally come to your senses and realized he's the one who tried to kill you in the pond that day?*

Wren frowned at him, but she didn't even need to come to Basil's defense.

Enough with this, Conan, Lyall cut in wearily. *King Basil had nothing to do with Wren's accident. Bram was following him, remember? He was completely unaware of what was happening, and when he found out, he paced his room for an hour.*

So Bram claims, scoffed Conan, clearly unwilling to see reason where Basil was concerned. *Even if that's true, there's still what he did to Caleb. When we're free I'm going to make that worm answer for it. I knew he came here to do us a mischief! Probably wanted to finish the job.*

That's not fair, snapped Wren, knowing there was no point engaging, but unable to stay silent when Basil was so wrongly attacked. *What happened to Caleb wasn't Basil's fault.*

Or yours, interjected Caleb firmly, clearly guessing her thoughts. *No one bears any blame for this except the evil madwoman who cursed us.*

Is that true, though? Averett mused. *If Wren is right, and that enchantment was too great for her power, maybe someone else was involved. Someone who's still alive, and possibly still working against us.*

So you believe Basil and me, Averett? Wren pressed eagerly.

Averett rolled his sleek head thoughtfully. *I'm starting to see that something doesn't add up.*

At this defection by his one ally, Conan made a noise of disgust and broke away from the group, taking to the air, presumably to let out his frustration in a good long fly.

And the attack on you has made me nervous, Averett continued, ignoring his brother's departure completely. *Someone was behind it, and it terrifies me to think that it might be the same someone who was willing to kill us all.*

Wren nodded, pulling her bottom lip between her teeth. It was another fear that haunted her every day. There'd been no sign of further attack, but that didn't reassure her. With her father's attitude toward Basil unchanged, she'd been unwilling to insist that her near drowning hadn't been an accident. But she'd made some discreet inquiries, with the help of Lady Anneliese, who'd proven herself delightfully willing to ask questions *for* Wren, without asking questions *of* Wren.

Based on Lady Anneliese's innocent inquiries of her suitor, the ability to control plants was quite a specific type of magic, one which none of Myst's resident enchanters were known to have. Sir Gelding's power, Wren had already discovered, had nothing to do with plants.

She wondered if there were any such magic-users in Tola, but asking Basil that question would require communicating with him, which Wren was too terrified to do. What if some look or gesture of hers was the final piece he needed to solve the puzzle of her swans?

Well, Lyall sighed, the sound coming out as a soft bugle. *Without any resources behind us, it's hard to see how we can effectively investigate the incident.*

Wren sighed as well. He was right, and they all knew it. So now they were all just waiting, waiting, waiting. Two more weeks, and everything would become much simpler.

Lyall wandered off, followed by Averett, back to the pond to forage for some food. Wren looked down at Caleb, stuck at her side until she helped him down.

I understand why you miss him, Caleb told her softly. *He treats you like a real person. Like a normal person. I like him for it, and I hate that his perceptiveness is forcing you to distance yourself from him.* He leaned forward and nipped her sleeve affectionately. *But it's not for much longer.*

Wren gave him a weak smile. She didn't say as much, but she had little hope of being able to continue her friendship with the Entolian king. She knew how much his lack of progress had frustrated Basil before she'd cut him off from continuing their investigation. Now that he didn't even have that, she couldn't see him sticking around in Myst for two more weeks. She was honestly amazed he'd already stayed an extra fortnight since she flew at him and made a fool of herself.

A sudden shadow overheard made both her and Caleb look up, and Wren felt her mouth fall open in astonishment at the unexpected sight of a dragon flying low over the castle. Another shape followed, scales glittering in the sunshine. Two dragons!

Wren stood abruptly, breaking her contact with Caleb. She took a step toward the castle, then remembered that he needed her assistance to get down from the bench. She leaned down hurriedly, lifting him bodily with a grunt.

I'm too heavy for you, he protested.

No you're not, she contradicted cheerfully. *Not for a short distance.* Just as she deposited him in the water, a series of flapping splashes alerted her to Bram's arrival. He landed on the water, swimming swiftly to meet her.

Wren kept one hand on Caleb's side, and placed the other against Bram.

Two dragons have just landed in front of the castle! he announced eagerly. *I was watching King Basil as usual, and I saw them! He ran straight out to watch them land, but I thought I'd better tell you before following him.*

Thanks for the thought, answered Wren. *We saw them fly overhead.* She fixed Bram with a hard stare. *Now stay here.*

But—!

She cut off his protest. *It's too dangerous for you to be near Basil. Or anyone else who might figure out who you are, which definitely includes dragons. I'll check it out and let you know what I find out.*

Bram rustled his feathers in agitation, but Wren didn't stay to argue. Picking up her skirts, she ran toward the entrance into the castle, her attendant guards following at a smart trot. The palpable excitement in the corridors showed how quickly news of the dragons' visit had spread.

Wren hurried through the bustle, eager not to miss whatever greetings her parents might be exchanging with the unexpected visitors. Mistra was perfectly friendly with their draconic neighbors, but actual visits to the castle were rare. Although the beasts flew overhead frequently, shedding their magic, Wren had only seen one up close a handful of times in her life.

When she reached the castle's huge front doors, she had to push her way through the gathered throng of servants to get outside. After a short while, her guards became impatient of the chaos, and one of them barked out an order. Once the crowd realized it was their princess trying to elbow her way through, they parted quickly.

Wren emerged into the afternoon sunshine, blinking at the impressive sight before her.

Her parents stood regally near the top of the broad staircase, backs straight and eyes up. With a flash of pride, Wren noted that her father lost none of his commanding presence in spite of being dwarfed by the creatures before him.

The two dragons had alighted shoulder to shoulder, and were both regarding King Lloyd and Queen Liana fixedly. They were very similar in size—on the smaller side for dragons, if Wren was assessing them correctly. One was quite a bright yellow, with a purple edge to his scales, and the other was purple all over. Their expressions were serene, no hint of aggression in either form. She relaxed slightly, as a fear she hadn't known she was holding leaked out.

She moved forward to stand beside her parents, not about to miss such an exciting event.

"Ah, Wren," said her father, extending an arm toward her. "We are honored by a visit from Dannsair and Rekavidur of the dragons."

Wren dropped into a curtsy. For a moment the silence stretched out, then she saw her father shift uncomfortably.

"Allow me to extend greetings on my daughter's behalf," he said, clearing his throat. "She would wish to greet you with the honor you are due, were she not..." He trailed off awkwardly, and both dragons swiveled their heads to look at Wren.

She quivered slightly under the unblinking gaze of four orb-like eyes, but forced herself to hold her head up. Whatever her father thought, she had nothing to be ashamed of.

"Greetings Princess Wren," said the purple dragon in a musical voice that revealed her to be a female. She glanced at King Lloyd. "We are not offended by your daughter's silence, king of men."

The yellow dragon made a strange guttural noise in his throat that caused many in the crowd to draw back in alarm. After a moment, Wren realized it was laughter.

"Offended?" he said, his voice gravelly. "On the contrary. Given that we have traveled to Myst specifically out of a desire to see the silent princess for ourselves, we would have been more likely to be offended had she spoken, and proved our journey futile."

Wren had been drilled in the importance of upholding etiquette when interacting with dragons, but not all her training could prevent her mouth from falling open. The dragons had come to see her? To...to gawk at her like an oddity?

"You wished to witness my daughter's silence?" her father asked, his voice not quite steady.

The female dragon tilted her head to one side, studying him. "It is perhaps we who have offended?"

"Of course not," said the king quickly, although his bow was a little stiff this time. "You are most welcome here, as any repre-sentative of your colony will always be. We are, as I said, honored by your visit."

"We do not represent the colony, precisely," said the female dragon placidly. "Merely our own curiosity."

This time Wren was sure that her father was offended, but of course he knew better than to ever say so. Representatives or not, dragons were still dragons, and even kings didn't mess around with that.

"Are we mistaken in thinking you have another visitor already?" the yellow dragon, the male, asked.

He swiveled his head around, and Wren followed his gaze to see Basil, standing a short distance behind and to one side of the Mistran royals. Wren's heart squeezed painfully at the sight of the Entolian, all her regret at their enforced separation rushing back.

"Ah, King Basil," said the dragon. "Well met."

Basil bowed curtly. "Greetings, Rekavidur, Dannsair. I am glad to see you."

In spite of the polite words, Wren didn't think he looked too pleased. It was interesting that he knew the dragons by name, however. A sudden suspicion sprang into her mind. Had he somehow known they were coming? Was that what he'd been waiting around Myst for? And if so, what did that mean?

"And I you," said the male dragon calmly.

He stared at Basil for one more unblinking second, then his head swung abruptly back around to Wren. She forced herself to hold his gaze, even though it felt like the mental equivalent of being seared by dragon flame. The dragon—Rekavidur, her father had said—lowered his reptilian head until it was just before hers. She felt so hypnotized by his scrutiny, she barely noticed the other dragon joining him.

For a long moment they both stared at her, taking deep breaths which she could have sworn were designed to smell her.

Then they straightened, exchanging a brief glance before turning to King Lloyd.

"We thank you for your hospitality," said the female dragon formally. "We won't linger, but we are glad to have met you, King Lloyd. May your kingdom prosper, and the ties between our kinds be always strong."

Wren's father looked more perplexed than ever, but he bowed more gracefully this time.

"Mistra's favor goes with you," he said solemnly. "We are honored by your visit."

Wren wondered if the words were sincere. It was exciting to have dragons visit, and most royals would welcome it. But at the same time, she could see at a glance that her father was trying to hide his usual embarrassment over Wren's situation. Having the dragons not only notice it, but declare that they came specifically to marvel at it, must be igniting all his mortification. Underneath her dignified front, she was squirming herself.

With the formal exchanges, Wren expected the dragons to take off immediately, and she couldn't help but be glad. Honor though it might be, she didn't want them to hang around. Surely if they got anywhere near her brothers, they would recognize the magic clinging to the swans. What if they told her father? What if everything was revealed, and her brothers fell one by one with a mere two weeks to go?

Dragons were a perceptive danger she couldn't afford at this moment.

She was therefore extremely nervous when Basil stepped forward and cleared his throat. "I wonder, Rekavidur, Dannsair, if you might honor me with a few private words."

CHAPTER EIGHTEEN

Basil

From the corner of his eye, Basil saw Wren start at his request. And unless he was mistaken, King Lloyd was as displeased as he was surprised. But Basil kept his focus on Rekavidur and Dannsair, not quite able to keep the irritation from his eyes. A month and a half he'd waited for their arrival, and this was what they came up with?

"Certainly, King Basil," said Rekavidur, with dignity. Then, without warning, he pushed off from the flagstones, his wings whipping out in the same moment as his taloned front feet clutched hold of Basil's shoulders.

Before Basil could do more than give an involuntary gasp, he went shooting up into the air, his legs dangling sickeningly below him. He could hear the shouts of his guards, and he grimaced against the rushing wind. He was going to get quite a scold when they got hold of him.

Rekavidur didn't ascend high or fly far. They landed on the grass just outside the closest city wall, with the mountains rising up behind them. Dannsair alighted a moment later, and the two dragons fixed Basil with identically expectant expressions.

Basil ignored them, bending over double and taking a

moment to catch his breath. When his stomach no longer felt like it was going to surrender his lunch, he straightened.

"A little warning would be nice next time."

Rekavidur cocked his head to one side. "You are asking for another such journey at a later time?"

"No," said Basil quickly. "I'm definitely not." He drew in a breath, eager to get straight to the point. "I'm glad you came. I've been lingering here, hoping to see you."

Dannsair sat back on her haunches, looking surprised. "You were lingering for us? Does that mean you would otherwise end your visit so soon?" She shook her head in amazement. "Humans certainly are hasty."

"Time moves a little differently when you're not immortal," said Basil dryly. "I never dreamed I'd be here for a month and a half without even making progress on negotiations."

"Give it time, young king," said Rekavidur soothingly.

Basil wasn't soothed. "Never mind the negotiations," he said curtly. "They're not your problem, after all."

"True," Dannsair agreed, nodding wisely. "We just came to examine the princess, for our own investigations."

Basil was about to speak, but he paused. "Your own investigations? Investigations into what?"

"That is no more your concern than your political negotiations are ours," said Rekavidur. There was no anger in his voice, but Basil knew he would discuss the topic no further. Something tickled in his mind, but he didn't have the space to pursue it right now.

"Wasn't there a more surreptitious way to conduct your investigations?" he asked instead. "Did you have to make such a spectacle of Wren?"

"Spectacle?" repeated Dannsair, blinking in confusion. "We just looked at her."

"Yes, but you declared to the whole kingdom that you'd

come to—" Basil cut himself off and ran a hand through his hair. There was no point trying to explain these kinds of subtleties to dragons. He knew Wren well enough now to have noticed her mortification—not to mention her father's painfully obvious embarrassment—but in his experience, dragons were so entirely devoid of self-consciousness, they were almost incapable of understanding human sensitivities.

"Never mind," he said hurriedly. "Are you willing to share with me what you observed?"

The dragons looked at each other, as if communicating silently. It reminded Basil of Wren for some reason. Probably just because everything reminded him of her lately. The last two weeks, when she'd barely looked at him during meals and avoided him altogether at every other time, had been more tortuous than he cared to admit.

"Yes, we'll share our observations with you," said Dannsair at last. "Although not our conclusions. You can make of the information what you will."

Basil nodded eagerly. He'd take what he could get.

"Did you sense any magic? Do you think the princess is under a curse?"

Dannsair gave a guttural chuckle. "Two questions, with entirely different replies. Which do you wish us to answer?"

Basil forced back his impatience. He'd forgotten how infuriating dragons could be to communicate with.

"Both, please."

"I see you are in a hurry," said Dannsair, sounding more amused than ever. "So I will be as precipitate as a human. As to your first question, yes, we did sense magic. As to your second, no, she does not appear to be under a curse."

"What magic did you sense, then?" Basil asked, frowning. "Was it just the artifact around her neck?"

Dannsair wove her head from side to side in a slow denial.

"No, it wasn't just that. We sensed it, of course, and its enchantment is strong, of its kind. But there was other magic that...lingered."

"What do you mean by lingered?" Basil demanded.

Dannsair gave a draconic shrug, the ripple passing over her scales from her shoulders to the tip of her tail.

"I don't know how else to explain it that will make sense to you."

"But what kind of magic is it?" Basil pressed. "What makes you so sure she isn't under a curse?"

"The magic is too faint for that," Rekavidur explained. "Faint enough that I doubt a human enchanter would even detect it."

Dannsair nodded sagely. "Especially when masked by the powerful enchantment on that artifact. Besides, it's not just that it's too faint to be a curse on her. It's not molded to her form at all."

Rekavidur gave a grunt of agreement. "It's not targeted at her, like a curse on her would be. It makes no attempt to wrap around her. It is connected to her only faintly, and the wonder is that it lingers so persistently around her at all."

"But it is connected," Dannsair interjected. "Like one end of a line, connecting her to...something. Its purpose is not clear."

Basil deflated, disappointed. He could make no sense of any of that, and it brought him no closer to figuring out the mystery of Wren's silence. Having kicked his heels so long in expectation of the dragons' arrival, he couldn't help but feel a definite sense of anticlimax.

"Well, thank you for sharing your discoveries, anyway," he said, figuring he'd better observe the niceties.

The dragons both dipped their heads in gracious acknowledgment of his thanks.

"Did you find enough information to satisfy you on your own...inquiries?" he asked curiously.

Rekavidur gave a snort that actually emitted a tiny spurt of flame. "Satisfy? We gave the situation a preliminary examination. We will discuss what we have observed, consider its ramifications, and pursue further inquiries when we have determined the best avenue to do so."

So, in about twenty years? Basil thought sarcastically. But he didn't speak the words aloud—even he knew not to be too forthright with dragons. He thought they would take off at once, but Dannsair spoke again.

"We came here directly from Tola."

"You did?" Basil looked quickly up at her, a prickle of alarm shooting through him. It had been several days since his last letter from home. "Was all well with my mother and sisters?"

"We saw only Zinnia," said Dannsair. "But she appeared to be in good health." Her thin lips curved in a slightly unnerving smile. "At least, so I infer from her excess of energy when she was prompting us to pay our visit here."

Basil let out a soft groan. He would really have to speak to Zinnia about the proper respect to show dragons. She was going to get herself flamed one of these days. "Please allow me to apologize for my—"

"I don't think I will allow it," interrupted Dannsair, a touch haughtily. "The level of friendship between your sister and I far exceeds that between us, and therefore I would consider it an impertinence for you to speak to me on her behalf."

Basil froze with his mouth still open, completely nonplussed. He'd gathered that Zinnia was friendly with these dragons, but clearly it went much further than he'd imagined.

"I apologize," he said at last, bending in a bow.

"Accepted," Dannsair said, with a return of her good humor. "I only brought up the matter of our route because I thought you might be interested to know what we observed when we flew over the site where you humans are waging your foolish little battle."

"The front lines?" Basil asked sharply. "What did you observe?"

"Magic." Rekavidur jumped in with the simple word. "Radiating up from the location."

Basil stared at them. "Magic? But...are you sure?" He regretted the foolish words as soon as they were out, but to his relief the dragons just laughed rather than getting offended again. "What type of magic was it?" he pressed.

The did a synchronized rippling shrug. "We didn't stop to investigate," said Dannsair, with the hint of another smile. "Zinnia had given us to believe our errand here was of great urgency. We agreed that we would inform her if we found you in danger of any kind. Since you seem to be well, it appears we are free to return to our colony." She dipped her head slightly. "Well met, King Basil. Until our paths next cross."

And with an abruptness that always perplexed Basil in the otherwise unhurried creatures, the two dragons shot into the air, sending such a ferocious wind whipping around the grassy knoll that Basil was almost knocked flat.

"Don't feel like you need to, you know, return me to where you found me or anything," he muttered futilely to the two shapes receding rapidly into dots in the sky. He let out a sigh and looked around him. He'd have to walk halfway around the city wall to reach the main gate, and then he'd have to trek through the city to reach the castle again. It would probably take him the better part of an hour.

Not that this information would have swayed the dragons, of course. His desire to save an hour would be incomprehensible to the immortal creatures.

With another sigh, Basil started walking along the line of the city wall, wondering first whether his guards were going to be angry enough at his defection to murder him themselves, and second whether any other king in Solstice had ever had to trek through a foreign city alone and on foot.

"Less ego, more stability," he reminded himself in a mutter.

As it happened, the walk was actually quite grounding. Fortunately the guards on the city gate recognized him, and—although clearly utterly bewildered—let him in without protest. And by the time Basil finally reached the castle courtyard from which Rekavidur and Dannsair had spirited him away, he'd had plenty of time to think about their revelations.

He didn't know what to make of the dragons' vague comments about magic lingering around Wren. He supposed it confirmed his theory that her silence wasn't entirely a matter of choice, but that didn't really help him solve the mystery.

What they'd said about the front lines concerned him more. He knew his father had considered the idea of using magic in the fight with Mistra, but as far as he was aware, the suggestion had never gone anywhere. Enchanters' skills were in too great a demand for many of them to choose the uncertain life of a soldier. And civilian magic-users were often conscientious about their own codes of conduct, which would preclude them from using their magic for war.

If Entolia wasn't using magic in the war effort, did that mean Mistra was? But it couldn't be anything too potent, or surely it would have enabled the Mistrans to force a victory years ago. If she wasn't so studiously avoiding him, Basil's first instinct would have been to tell Wren what he'd discovered, and ask whether she knew anything of magic on the Mistran side of the front lines.

He decided he would speak to her about it at dinner. She would probably refuse to engage with him, but even her reaction might be telling. His heart lifted slightly at having a justifiable excuse to speak to the princess.

But when he arrived in the dining hall, slightly late due to his unplanned trip outside the city wall, he was disappointed not to see her in her seat. And she didn't show up for the entire meal.

He couldn't help the flicker of alarm that awoke at her failure to attend. The astonishing scene that followed hadn't made him forget what Wren had confided in him—her accident at the pond had been no accident at all. The knowledge that someone might be trying to kill her had made her distance over the last fortnight even harder to bear. He knew there was no point pushing his company on her, but he often wandered the castle's second story, hoping to catch a glimpse of her down in the gardens through a window, just to assure himself that her continued absence was the result of her choice, not something worse.

But he told himself he was being foolish to read anything sinister into her decision not to come to dinner on that particular night. All the chatter in the dining hall was about the dragons' visit, and Basil well remembered the discomfort he'd read behind Wren's carefully cultivated expression. Was she hiding away in her rooms out of mortification at being made such a spectacle? The thought was a little heart-wrenching, but also exasperating. He'd thought she knew him well enough by now to know there was no need to be embarrassed with him.

After the meal, Basil sought out the enchantress who had accompanied him from Tola. He hadn't seen a great deal of her and her husband in recent weeks. He knew they were making the most of the rare opportunity to form connections with Mistran merchants, clearly hoping that the two kings would reach an armistice, and that they would be in a strong position to open trade. He didn't begrudge them the head start on their counterparts back in Tola. They had done him a favor by accompanying him on a trip most Entolians believed fraught with peril.

To his astonishment, when he mentioned magic at the front lines, the enchantress nodded, unperturbed.

"Yes, Your Majesty, I felt it when we passed the battlefield."

"Why didn't you say anything at the time?" Basil demanded.

She looked perplexed. "I assumed you knew, Your Majesty. All I could feel was a faint sort of protective power, and I thought you must have arranged for a general protection over our forces. Similar power covered the whole region, so I figured it was common practice in times of war, and that the Mistrans must have done the same." Seeing Basil's astonishment, she pressed on anxiously. "I'm sorry if I did wrong, Your Majesty. If I'd felt anything that seemed dangerous, I would have mentioned it, but it never occurred to me that you were unaware...I mean, it was just the sort of basic hedge enchantment that many wealthy nobles pay enchanters to place over their homes."

Basil shook his head. "It's not your fault. I didn't think to ask about magic outside of Myst." He ran a hand thoughtfully through his hair. "We certainly haven't put such an enchantment up, but the Mistrans might have, I suppose." He frowned. Could that be all the dragons had noticed? "Not that I can expect a straight answer from King Lloyd, of course."

Not for the first time, frustration welled up within him at the counterproductive attitude of the Mistran king. It hadn't chafed him nearly as much when he and Wren had been locked in their own investigation. But now that her assistance—and if he was honest, her company—was denied him, he was struggling to find reasons to stay.

His time was split between wandering the corridors aimlessly—usually accompanied by Lord Baldwin—and sitting in his suite for hours at a time, reading reports and answering correspondence from home. He had a rotation of couriers going back and forth on a practically constant circuit, and he knew that his communication was still far from adequate. It would all be so much simpler if he was at home. From all he could make out, his mother was doing an excellent job of keeping things running in his absence, but she wasn't the monarch, and there were limits to what he could delegate. It was difficult enough to keep vaguely on top of the practical things. He was floundering completely in other areas of equal importance, such as reading the mood of his court.

Not to mention that it was clear from Zinnia's letters—Basil's only source of information about the state of his family rather than his kingdom—that the queen's new duties led to her spending even less time with her children than normal. Guilt lanced through Basil at the thought. But what else could he do?

He could just go home, he supposed. But he couldn't bring himself to do that just yet. In spite of Wren's avoidance of him, it was her presence that kept him from giving up on negotiations, packing up and returning to Tola. It wasn't just about solving her mysteries, either, or completing their interrupted investigation. He'd seen her crushing isolation, and he simply couldn't bring himself to leave with things as they were.

Over the several days following the dragons' visit, Wren continued to dodge his company. She had begun to sit with her friend, Lady Anneliese, for meals, in a gesture that clearly indicated her unwillingness to be seated near Basil. The noblewoman hadn't previously eaten in the royal dining hall, so Basil could only assume her presence now was the result of a specific plea from Wren.

The thought wasn't heartening.

Still, he took every opportunity to watch her from a distance, and what he saw was both reassuring and deeply concerning.

It was reassuring because, although she might do her level best not to interact with him, she couldn't quite keep her eyes from straying to him every time they were in the same room. There was no anger in these glances, and somehow Basil didn't believe that their strange and painful scene by the pond had given her a dislike of him that made her shun his company. There was something else behind her distant behavior, some new layer of mystery that separated her from him as surely as her silence seemed to separate her from most of her fellow Mistrans.

Fools, he thought, as he had so often done before. Quite a small amount of effort had allowed him to see the vibrant and intelligent person hiding behind Wren's silent mask. It was absurd that so few seemed to have made the effort before him.

The aspect of Wren's new demeanor that was deeply concerning was the fear. She exuded it, moving around the castle as if in constant expectation of disaster, jumping at every noise, and often fidgeting with the ring hidden under her gown. When she glanced at Basil, thinking herself unseen, he could see the fear rising in her eyes, and it broke his heart a little every time. At first he'd thought it was just the expectation of embarrassment from the dragons' words, but as the days turned into a week, it became clear to Basil that it was something more than that. What had her so terrified?

With Wren's assistance denied him, Basil attempted to renew his efforts with King Lloyd, hoping that Rekavidur and Dannsair's recognition might have given him greater credibility with the older king. But it quickly became clear that Wren's father was more inclined to blame his royal guest for the humiliation he and his daughter had supposedly suffered from the visit than to respect him for being on good terms with dragons who, by their own admission, did not represent their colony.

All inquiries into Lord Baldwin's suggestion about renegade enchanters in Albury yielded nothing. A week after the dragons' visit, Basil had to face the reality of the situation. He'd been in

Myst for almost two months, and not only had he failed to end the war, he'd made no progress whatsoever in that direction. He supposed his visit was worthwhile purely for the fact that as long as it continued, so did the temporary ceasefire. But he couldn't kick his heels in Myst for that reason forever, and he didn't want to. He had no armistice, no solution to the mystery of who had killed Wren's brothers and sought to create conflict between the kingdoms, and not even a lead to pursue. And with the dragons having come and gone, and Wren's company denied him altogether, any reasons he'd had to stick around were fast evaporating.

Pacing his room one evening, he reached a decision. He would leave first thing in the morning. He'd tell King Lloyd he needed to speak with his general, at the front lines, and would go to investigate the dragons' comments himself. He dispatched one of his guards to take a message to the Entolian enchantress, and to Lord Baldwin. They'd only be gone a matter of days. The rest of his delegation could await their return in Myst, so that King Lloyd knew he wasn't planning a flight back to Tola with the state of the border still unknown.

With that decision made, Basil sank into his bed more ready for sleep than he had been since Wren had flown at him in such desperation by the pond, three weeks before. His last thought, as he drifted into unconsciousness, was of the feel of her pressed against him, held in place by his instinctive grip, her expressive eyes full of unreadable emotions, and her breath coming in gasps as she tried desperately to tell him something he simply couldn't understand.

CHAPTER NINETEEN

Wren

Wren woke to the sound of a curtain being vigorously pulled across its rail. Blinking in the bright light that flooded the room, she pushed herself up into a sitting position.

"For shame, Princess Wren, to be still abed at this hour," scolded her governess, moving from the window to Wren's enormous four poster bed.

Wren just yawned, and the governess gave a sniff of disapproval.

"If you didn't sit out in the damp air to all hours, you wouldn't wake so late that you missed breakfast."

Wren made no effort to respond. Her governess knew perfectly well that she wasn't usually such a late riser. She'd sat with her brothers until after midnight—much to the displeasure of her attendant guards—because she wanted to sleep late, specifically so that she could miss breakfast. Lady Anneliese had been incredibly accommodating in helping her avoid Basil at lunch and dinner, but the noblewoman didn't actually live in the castle, and it was a little much to expect her to be present in time to break her fast every morning.

A maid sailed past, bearing a silver tray, and Wren sniffed hopefully at the steam rising from it.

"Compliments of the Chief Under Chef, Your Highness," said the girl with a smile. Wren returned it, warmed enough by the thoughtful gesture to ignore her governess's snippy comments about servants forgetting their station and encouraging the princess to become slovenly.

Wren picked up a bread roll that was still hot from the oven, but it was only halfway to her mouth when the maid sent her a significant look. She nudged something else on the tray, and Wren was surprised to see a thick white envelope. Picking it up, she recognized the Entolian royal seal holding it closed.

"Found it pushed under your door when I came to light the fire this morning, Your Highness," the maid said in an undertone. "It's not my place to say it, but I know the signs of a lovers' quarrel as well as anyone. And if I may be so bold, I don't like to see Your Highness wafting around the castle so morose."

Wren felt a flush rising up her neck at the implication that she was avoiding Basil because of some argument between sweethearts. If only it were as simple as that. But she couldn't deny she was greatly intrigued at what would have caused him to push a note under her door. Waiting until her governess bustled into her own adjoining room, Wren ripped the envelope open and scanned the short letter inside.

> Wren,
> I would have liked to
> say goodbye and tell
> you all of this in
> person. But I wasn't sure
> you would welcome it.

For a moment Wren's vision spun. Goodbye? Had he left, then? She should be glad, she supposed. His presence was such a danger to the boys. But she'd been so close to showing him her true self. Not even a week remained of the curse's six years! She looked down at the page again.

> By the time you read this, I
> will have left, and I wanted to
> at least tell you that I'm not
> going back to Tola yet. I haven't
> given up on solving our
> mystery, or—speaking as the
> brutally honest man you know
> I am—on figuring you out.

The dragons gave me a great
deal to think about when we
spoke, and I'm following up on
a lead they gave me. I won't put
more in writing, but I hope to
return soon.
Basil

Wren stared at the page in growing horror. He was trying to figure her out? Of course he was. And the dragons had given him a lead! Had they been able to tell, then, just from looking at her? She'd been afraid they would sense the subtle thread of magic that presumably connected her to her brothers' curse, not compelling her silence, which was purely voluntary, but allowing her to join their silent communication. The question was, had they been able to discern from that subtle thread the truth of her brothers' situation?

She flew from her bed, dressing more quickly than she ever had in her life. Ignoring her maid's astonishment, and the governess's protests from the next room, Wren dashed into the corridor. The guards stationed outside her room sprang into action, hastening after her as she sped toward the gardens. She didn't breathe properly until she caught sight of Caleb, floating lopsidedly across the surface of the water. It seemed whatever the dragons had told Basil, it hadn't been enough for him to fully solve the mystery yet. But she couldn't let him follow up on that lead, whatever it was!

Scanning the water, she recognized the sleek form of Bram, ducking down below the surface in search of food. Confirmation, if she'd needed it, that Basil had left Myst.

She waved her arms over her head, and her third brother

finally noticed her hovering by the water. She could barely contain her impatience, but finally Bram was close enough for her to make contact.

Bram, did Basil leave Myst this morning?

He nodded his head in a decidedly non-avian gesture. Wren frowned at him, hoping that the guards hovering several feet away weren't as perceptive as Basil had been.

Where was he going?

Not sure, Bram replied. *I followed him far enough to see that he really was leaving the city. But he didn't have his whole delegation with him, just that nobleman, the merchant enchantress and her husband, and a couple of guards. I assume they're coming back.*

It was Wren's turn to nod. *That's what his letter said. But it might be too late by then.* She chewed on her lip anxiously. *I think I have to go after him.*

That's ridiculous, Bram told her flatly. *Father will never allow that, and he'd be right.*

Wren scowled. Her brother wasn't wrong—she doubted there was any argument that would convince her father to allow her to go chasing after the Entolian king. But that was because he didn't know what was at stake.

Do you think I'm going to sit here and watch for Caleb to die when Basil figures it out? Who knows what these dragons told him? He might be on the cusp of solving it right now!

It will all be over in a week, Bram argued. *Maybe he won't make any headway before then.*

That's not a chance I'm willing to take, said Wren flatly. She fidgeted with Caleb's ring on its chain, her mind turning over rapidly. Who could she turn to for assistance? *I'm going,* she decided, an idea occurring to her. *Tell the others I might be gone a few days, but I'll be back as soon as I can.*

I'll tell them, but then I'm coming with you, said Bram, clearly recognizing the futility of further argument. *If I can't stop you—*

which I absolutely would if I wasn't stuck as a stupid bird—I can at least keep an eye on you.

Suit yourself, shrugged Wren. *But I'm not waiting.*

With the words, she pushed herself to her feet and hurried into the castle. She was fortunate, and ran her quarry to ground quickly. Lady Anneliese was, as she so often seemed to be these days, strolling down the corridor with Sir Gelding in attendance. Her arm was in his, and he was smiling down at her with a particularly satisfied expression.

Wren felt a flash of impatience. Why did the dashing enchanter always have to be where he wasn't wanted? She thought Lady Anneliese had said he was coming to Myst for a couple of weeks at most, but he'd been there two months. As glad as Wren was that Lady Anneliese wasn't giving in to his wooing too quickly, she wished the baronet would go back south, to tend to his duties with the Blacksmiths' Guild.

Dismissing the matter from her mind, she hurried up to the pair, nodding her head distractedly to Sir Gelding and tapping Lady Anneliese on the arm. The noblewoman turned, surprised but apparently pleased to see Wren. Disregarding Sir Gelding's piercing—and rather irritated—gaze, Wren pulled out her slate.

Can I speak to you privately?

"Of course," said Lady Anneliese, dropping her voice. She took a hasty leave of Sir Gelding, who made quite a show of bidding her farewell. Wren could barely contain her impatience as he bent over Lady Anneliese's hand, several showy rings glittering red on his own fingers as he pressed his lips to the back of the noblewoman's hand. They reminded her a little of Caleb's signet ring. At last, Lady Anneliese was free to follow Wren down the corridor to an alcove with a bench seat. As soon as they were out of Sir Gelding's sight, Wren wrote four words.

Do you trust me?

"Of course I do," said Lady Anneliese, clearly astonished.

And will you help me, without me being able to explain why?

Lady Anneliese studied Wren's face for only the briefest of moments before giving a decisive nod. "You know I will."

Wren sagged slightly in her relief, then scrubbed her slate clean and scribbled another rapid message.

Can you tell my father your parents have invited me for an immediate visit to your manor just outside Myst? But can you actually prepare for a longer journey?

Lady Anneliese blinked three times in quick succession, but made no comment. With a reassuring nod, she pushed herself to her feet and strode away down the corridor. Wren felt a rush of gratitude as she watched the other woman's graceful form disappear around the corner. She had preparations of her own to make, but she needed to be careful not to let anyone see her doing so before the official invitation had been received.

As it happened, Lady Anneliese achieved that in an astonishingly short time. She exceeded Wren's expectations by actually acquiring the invite from her parents. Wren expected to have to work hard to convince her father, but her mother came unexpectedly to her assistance. Her parents had always thought well of Lady Anneliese, and they could hardly fail to have noticed that Wren had few friends among her peers. It seemed her mother had noticed her recent melancholy more than Wren had realized, as well. Once Wren revealed to her father that she'd found and was wearing her enchanted ring, and even agreed to let him resize it upon her return to Myst, the matter was settled.

By mid-afternoon, Wren's baggage and one of her maids were settled at Lady Anneliese's manor house an hour's ride from the city. Lady Anneliese's parents were even too polite to comment on the unexpected addition of a swan to the party. And by late afternoon, Wren and her hostess had left again, heading south on a supposed ride of leisure.

Once out of sight of the manor, the two women exchanged a look, spurring their horses on. Bram, flying above them, matched their pace. By the time the single guard accompanying them realized they were not in fact on an outing of pleasure, but were actually riding hard toward the border, they were more than two hours away from the capital.

"Your Highness," he protested, when Wren refused for a fourth time to turn around and head back to her lodgings. "It will be dark soon."

Wren pulled her horse to a walk, letting the animal rest as she balanced her slate on the saddle in front of her. Her message scratched out, she held it up for the guard to see.

We aren't going back tonight. You can either ride back to Myst and tell my father I've absconded, or you can stay with me to guard me. Your choice.

The guard stared, aghast, but he had little choice, as Wren had been perfectly aware. By the time they were forced to stop due to the darkness, he had made his peace with his likely dismissal enough to begrudgingly light them a fire. Knowing that he would take any opportunity to send a message back to Myst, Wren had steered clear of any inns or posting houses. The weather was mild, and the country was pleasant. She had no fear of sleeping in the open for one night, not with an armed guard and her brother to act as sentry.

Two of her brothers, that was. They were just laying their extra cloaks out on the grass for makeshift beds when a gleam of white shone through the darkness. Before Wren realized what was coming, Ari had dropped to the ground at her side, flopping against her in exhaustion.

Phew, he said, his voice cheerful in spite of clearly being winded. *I found you. I thought if I just flew south east, I'd surely catch up before dark. If I hadn't spotted your fire, though, I'd probably have flown all the way to the border.*

What are you doing here, Ari? bugled Bram in irritation, from where he was nestled on Wren's other side. *You're supposed to be keeping an eye on Caleb.*

The others will do that, trumpeted Ari dismissively. *I didn't want to miss the action!*

Wren rolled her eyes, but she wasn't actually averse to the

extra company. Two pairs of eyes in the sky would hopefully make it easier for them to catch up to Basil the next day.

So where exactly are we going? Ari asked brightly.

Wren toyed with her chain anxiously. *Lady Anneliese found out that Basil told Father he was going to meet with his general at the front lines. It may have been just a story, to cover up whatever lead he's following, but we're hoping he is at least going that way.*

He was definitely headed south east when he left Myst, Bram interjected confidently.

Wren nodded, a shiver going over her that had nothing to do with the cool night air. She just hoped that they weren't too late to throw Basil off whatever track he was on. And that Caleb didn't suffer any more for her failures.

CHAPTER TWENTY

Basil

"Lord Baldwin, how about we pick up the pace now? Your horse looks fine to me." Basil tried to keep the exasperation from his voice.

He was as reluctant to push an overworked horse as anyone. But given he could see no signs of injury or exhaustion in Lord Baldwin's steed, he suspected that the animal's supposed struggle had something to do with its rider's evident lack of enthusiasm for the venture. He was starting to regret asking Lord Baldwin to come. The nobleman's constant delays had made the journey to the border take almost twice as long as Basil had expected. And now that it was finally within sight, Lord Baldwin was once again slowing them down. Perhaps he should have kept it to the enchantress and her husband. And his guards, of course, whom he knew he would never have been able to shake off.

"Forgive my denseness, Your Majesty," said Lord Baldwin, dodging the question in a way Basil found infuriating, "but I still don't really understand why you wish to visit the front lines. I thought your priority was negotiating with King Lloyd."

Basil drew a deep breath, willing himself to be patient.

"Negotiations which were going swimmingly." He regretted the petty words straight away. Sarcasm was a crutch for those too insecure to speak their minds. "Lord Baldwin," he tried again, "we both know I wasn't getting anywhere with King Lloyd. If there's something happening at the front that I don't know about, then having that information can only strengthen my position for negotiation. Besides, I needed a break from Myst as desperately as this poor horse of mine needed to try his paces." He ran a hand down his mount's neck. "I've used you poorly, haven't I, friend? Two months stuck in that city, with scarcely a chance to stretch your legs."

"If you were after fresh air, Your Majesty," Lord Baldwin pressed, "wouldn't a ride near the city have been more pleasant than a visit to a war ground?"

Basil shot him a disbelieving look. Did the nobleman really think he'd come here out of idle curiosity? He knew Lord Baldwin didn't like seeing the effects of battle, but that didn't justify being this obstructive to his king's plans. Basil certainly didn't feel he owed Lord Baldwin an explanation of what had sent him here. He hadn't confided the dragons' words to anyone, wanting to make his own observations before deciding whether to share the discovery.

"Time to move, everyone," Basil called to the group at large, turning from Lord Baldwin. "We should be there within the hour, and I don't want any more delays. The sooner we conduct our business, the sooner we can be on our way back." At the mention of returning to Myst, his thoughts flew instantly to Wren, and some of his misgivings about his absence from the city flooded back. What if whoever had attacked her by the pond tried again while Basil was away? Not that his presence was much protection, he thought ruefully, since she wouldn't let him near her.

They'd just joined company with a scout from the outermost

Mistran camp—the man turning to ride back with them, his eyes fixed suspiciously on Basil—when a cry from one of Basil's guards made him turn in the saddle.

The whole group pulled up, waiting warily for the approaching trio of riders to be close enough for identification. They were coming from the north, so it was unlikely they originated from the front lines. Something in the air above the riders caught Basil's attention, and he blinked at the two white forms against the blue sky. His eyes flew down to the riders, one of whom could now be seen to have a distinct mane of dark hair...

"Surely not!" he exclaimed, spurring his horse into action, back the way they'd come.

One of his guards made a noise of chastisement as he kept pace, but Basil ignored him, his eyes fixed on the arrivals now almost within hailing distance.

"Wren!" he cried, as the two groups converged.

The word had barely left his mouth when the princess drew her horse alongside his, reaching out to grip at his arm. Her eyes were brimming with more intensity than ever, and he once again had the feeling that she was trying desperately to communicate something straight from her mind into his.

"Wren," he repeated, still struggling to comprehend her sudden appearance. "What are you doing here? Is everything all right?"

She let go of his arm and rummaged in one of her saddle-bags for her slate. Scribbling quickly on it, she held it across the space between their sidling mounts.

Basil snatched it up and read her message.

Basil, you have to stop.

He blinked at the message, then up at her. "Stop what?"

Impatiently, she clicked her fingers, gesturing for him to return her slate. Basil heard one of his guards give a disapproving grunt, and Basil shot him an irritated look as he handed Wren the slate. It was so typical for his people to be more concerned for Basil's dignity than the obvious urgency of the situation. If only they were as circumspect when they were the ones failing to show him the respect of a sovereign.

By the time he turned back to Wren, she was already holding the slate out again. Her words were barely legible, but he supposed it couldn't be easy to write neatly on horseback.

Do you trust me?

Basil didn't hesitate. "You know I do." He glanced from Wren's companions—the honey-haired noblewoman whose name he'd forgotten, and the tensest guard Basil had ever seen in his life—to his own group, whose watching faces ranged from suspicion to astonishment. "Dismount," Basil said, turning back to Wren. "We can't talk properly up here."

With the words, he slid from his horse, handing the reins to the nearest guard, who received them with a bad grace. Basil didn't stay to hear the man's protests. He'd already approached Wren's horse, and was holding out his hands to help her dismount. After a moment's hesitation, she accepted the offered assistance, and swung herself down. She landed so neatly in Basil's arms that for a moment he started to close them around her slim form unthinkingly. But reason reasserted itself quickly, and instead he made sure she was steady on her feet before stepping back.

Wren clearly wasn't as easily distracted as he was. She'd already lifted the slate, and even as he tugged at her arm, leading her to a more private distance, she was writing furiously on it. A minute later she flipped it around so he could see her message.

I can't explain, but I'm begging you to stop and come back to Myst with me. I don't know what the dragons told you, but you <u>cannot</u> follow whatever lead they gave you. If you trust me, please, just let it be.

Basil stared from the words to Wren's face, his mind registering nothing but astonishment. He thought back over the letter he'd slipped under Wren's door. Never in his wildest imaginings could he have predicted that his simple message would provoke such a response in her. She'd ridden helter-skelter out of Myst—giving her usual minders the slip to do it, judging by the expression on her guard's face—to stop him following Rekavidur and Dannsair's lead?

Her words seemed to dance before his eyes, even as he watched her face. *I'm begging you.* Her eyes mirrored the plea, beseeching him to trust her. He wanted to, but he was only human. He wasn't restrained enough to just lock all his questions instantly away, and tamely turn back toward Myst without even attempting to understand.

"You don't want me to follow up on the dragons' information about the border conflict?" he asked slowly. "Does that mean you know about the magic at the front lines? Is it a Mistran enchantment, then?"

It was Wren's turn to stare at him, her mouth hanging open.

Looking dazed, she rubbed the slate clean with a sleeve of her already disheveled gown and wrote again, her hand shaking slightly this time.

The dragons' lead was about the war?

"That's right," Basil nodded, feeling utterly bemused. Had his letter not made that clear?

Wren hesitated, a worried look in her eyes as she bit on her lip, clearly debating whether to write more. After a painful moment, she added three words below what was already there.

Not about me?

Basil stared at her, his mind working furiously. She'd thought the dragons had told him something about her? Well, they had, now he thought of it. And he'd hoped all along that they would, that they might have answers about her silence. But their comments about magic that lingered around her had been too vague for him to make any use of. He couldn't help but be desperately curious to know why the idea of the dragons giving him a hint of her secrets evoked such terror within her.

"No," he said, belatedly realizing that she was still waiting for a response to her question. "But I'll admit I asked."

Her eyes widened in horror, and he seized her hand convulsively. He hated to see her so afraid.

"Wren." His voice was barely above a whisper. "Isn't there some way I can help you?" He could hear the pleading in his own voice now, and he didn't try to hide it.

She shook her head emphatically and pulled her hand away.

And still, in her eyes, that frantic, silent entreaty that he couldn't decipher.

"I think there's been a misunderstanding," he said, taking a step back and trying to speak more normally. "I came here purely because the dragons told me they sensed magic radiating from the front lines when they flew over on their way to Myst."

Wren blinked at him in silent astonishment.

"So you didn't know about it, after all," Basil said grimly. "Do you think your father might have had an enchantment placed on the Mistran forces without you knowing about it?"

Frowning, Wren considered the question thoughtfully. At last, she shook her head.

Basil wasn't sure whether to be excited or alarmed that there wasn't any such easy explanation for the supposed magic. But he had no difficulty recognizing the little thrill that came from once again working with Wren to solve a mystery.

"Well, someone has," he said. "And I intend to find out who, if I can. Or at least what the enchantment is." He glanced at Wren's guard, who'd been inching closer as they spoke, and was now only a few feet away. "If your...fears are allayed, I suppose you should head back to Myst now. I promise I'll tell you what I discover."

He looked back at Wren, and couldn't help grinning at the look on her face. He'd take it. At least the death glare had driven away the fear for the moment.

"Well obviously I don't object to you coming with me," he said amicably. "But something tells me your father might."

Wren waved a dismissive hand, then marched back to her horse. Basil kept pace with her, offering his cupped hands to throw her into the saddle. As soon as she was settled in place, she turned her steed's head toward the now visible outskirts of the army camp.

Her poor guard gave what could only be described as a piteous groan. "Your Highness, please."

Raising an eyebrow, Wren made a chivvying motion back toward the distant capital, then lifted one shoulder in a shrug. The message was clear. *Go back if you want.* Basil chuckled as he climbed back into his own saddle. He knew as well as Wren must do that her guard was in an impossible bind. He wasn't going to leave her and her noblewoman friend with no one but the distrusted Entolian group.

"I'm not sure how it will go down when we try to cross the border," Basil admitted to Wren, as they nudged their horses forward. "Obviously I intend to commence my inquiries on the Entolian side, and an unannounced visit from the Mistran princess might create a bit of a reaction."

Wren frowned thoughtfully, then reached into a saddle bag and pulled out a long scarf. With some difficulty, keeping one hand on the pommel for balance, she wound it around her head, effectually trapping her wild hair.

Basil studied her dispassionately. "Hm," he said. "It might work."

He glanced overhead, where the two swans who'd accompanied Wren were cutting gracefully through the air. One sight of them, and it wouldn't be hard for people to guess her identity, of course. But there wasn't much to be done about that. And they weren't sticking very close to her, like they normally did. He'd been surprised at the distance they'd kept, circling at a significant height the whole time the two groups spoke.

"Your Highness, I can't allow it."

Basil turned to see a look of great determination on the face of Wren's sole guard. He'd pressed his horse up against Wren's other side, and the poor man looked so harried, Basil couldn't help feeling sorry for him.

"With respect, Your Highness," he said firmly, his gaze on

Wren, "I've gone along with this mad scheme of yours only because I believe the king would prefer me to accompany you than leave you unprotected while I ride back to Myst for backup. But," his face set in unyielding lines, "I cannot allow you to cross the border out of Mistra. If you attempt to do so, I will be forced to prevent you."

Wren raised an expressive eyebrow, looking far from impressed. Her own determination radiated out from her, as did the poise Basil had always admired. Even the guard seemed to see it, because he quailed slightly—clearly not relishing the idea of hauling the princess bodily away from the border—but he stood firm. And Basil had to acknowledge that in doing so, the man was only honoring the duty he'd been given.

"He's right," Basil interjected. He winced internally at the betrayed look Wren directed at him, but continued steadily. "It won't help anyone for you to start an international incident by crossing the border—and through a battleground—without your father's knowledge. It's actually better for us to split up. Now that you're on board, we can investigate either side of the battleground simultaneously."

Wren frowned as she thought it over, but she seemed to see the sense of the argument, because eventually she nodded.

His point carried, the guard fell back slightly as they urged their horses to a faster pace, and Basil took the opportunity for more private speech with Wren. "I'm going to ride ahead, get to my general as quickly as I can. If you find any hint of magic, follow it to its source, as best you can. I'll do the same on my side, if there is any. I'll return as soon as possible, and we can discuss whatever we've found."

Wren looked confused, but the guard—clearly still suspicious—had drawn close again, so Basil just gave her a reassuring nod and redirected his horse toward his own group.

Unsurprisingly, the arrival of the silent princess had made

Lord Baldwin more uneasy than ever, but Basil had no time for his vaguely formed protests. Cutting him off without compunction, he turned to the merchant woman.

"I want you to stay with Princess Wren," he said curtly. His eyes flicked to the enchantress's husband. "Both of you, if it would make you more comfortable. See if you can help her find any magic on the Mistran side."

"Stay in Mistra?" the enchantress repeated nervously. "But she'll think I'm plotting something if I follow her instead of you."

"No she won't," said Basil confidently. "She's an ally in the effort to end the war, not an enemy. I trust her implicitly. I want you to do whatever she asks you to do, and you can consider that an order from your king."

Both husband and wife looked taken aback at his strong words, but they didn't press the matter.

"But how will you find anything without a magic-user with you?" the enchantress pressed. "What's the point of you crossing to the Entolian side at all?"

"I'll manage," said Basil, shrugging a shoulder. He turned to see his guards watching him expectantly, and Lord Baldwin, predictably, hovering reluctantly behind. "Come on, My Lord," Basil said imperiously. "You're with me." There was no way he was going to subject Wren to Lord Baldwin's company. The enchantress and her husband might be strangers to her, but Basil had every expectation they would treat her with respect.

With a final murmured protest, Lord Baldwin joined him, and together with Basil's guards, the two men spurred their horses into a canter. They skirted around the main Mistran camp and made for the checkpoint they'd passed through on their way to Myst. By the time they reached the long trench cut across the Mistran side of no man's land, they'd gathered a sizable escort of Mistran soldiers. Basil knew where they could cross the trench, but he slowed his pace, recognizing that he would need to make his intentions known to whichever senior officer was sent to intercept him.

Sure enough, his horse had barely dropped to a walk when a rider approached from the main camp, flanked by half a dozen others. Basil didn't recognize the officer, who wore the uniform of a colonel. Most likely the return of the enemy king would normally be enough to bring the general himself—whom Basil knew had returned to the front lines from Myst—but Basil suspected he was currently occupied dealing with the unprecedented event of Princess Wren showing up at the battlefield without even a proper escort.

"Your Majesty," the colonel said, his horse stamping restlessly beneath him. "We received word from King Lloyd that you wished to pass through." His eyes scanned the small group, and Basil could see his confusion. "Are you returning to Entolia? Are your negotiations complete?"

"No, Colonel," Basil said reassuringly. He could understand why the soldiers, having loitered for two months of uneasy armistice, would be vitally interested in a precipitate flight back over the border by the Entolian king. "Negotiations are ongoing. I merely wish to speak with my general regarding the matters under discussion."

The colonel nodded. "Allow us to escort you."

In spite of the formal words, the group of Mistran soldiers barely saw Basil over the trench before they came to a halt, spreading out into a line to watch Basil and his companions cross the empty space between the two army camps. Basil was aware that in the last six years of fighting, the line between the armies had moved many times. At one point, he understood that the Mistrans had managed to occupy the entire ore field. But the Entolians had immediately mounted an offensive which had pushed their enemies back further even than their original position. No one had yet managed to hold much ground.

For now, though, both forces had withdrawn enough to leave a wide space of currently unclaimed land. They'd even been in position long enough for permanent structures to be built, dotted some distance behind the trenches.

Basil led his horse into the dividing space at a walk. It wasn't safe to go faster. The once fertile ground had been churned by many hooves and tramping feet into something unrecognizable, barren mounds of mud and debris stretching out ahead of him. There had been no rain for at least a week, but every now and then he caught sight of a puddle of fetid water sitting unmoving in hollows that had probably once been bright with wildflowers. There were still some stumps and fallen trunks dotted around, showing that this land had once supported trees, and the horses had to step with care.

Eventually, feeling disheartened and faintly ill, Basil reached the first checkpoint of the Entolian side, where ten uniformed soldiers awaited him, clearly having spotted his approach. They led him quickly to the general's tent, right in the heart of the army camp. The Entolians had also constructed buildings, used for storage, and surveillance, but all of the troops—even the general—still lived in the tents, ready to move at a moment's notice if fighting resumed.

Basil couldn't help but notice on the way through the encampment, that the general state of the army had deteriorated since he'd ridden through all those weeks before. Then the soldiers had all stood to attention as he passed, their swords gleaming and their uniforms tidy. Now many of them were just milling around. More than one soldier started at sight of their king, hastening to tuck in uniforms, or even stow away dice, clearly having been whiling away the time with games of chance. Apparently two months of inaction had taken its toll.

There was nothing sloppy in the appearance of Basil's general, however. His tent was as orderly as Basil remembered from his previous passage, and his posture was just as ramrod straight. He wasn't a tall man—shorter in fact than Basil—but he was wiry, and there was strength in every muscle.

"Well, Your Majesty," he said, bowing a little mechanically. "I was surprised to receive your courier's message, but I am glad to host you here once again."

Basil gave a wry smile. "Glad to see me emerge alive, General? I know you disapproved of my visit to Myst."

The general observed him out of unblinking eyes. Basil half expected him to point out that not just he, but everyone had disapproved of Basil's plans. But he should have known better. His general wasn't such a plain speaker.

"I am of course pleased to see you in such excellent health," was all he said.

Basil nodded briskly. "Thank you. I don't intend to make a long visit," he explained. "A couple of days at most. I'm expected back in Myst, where I still have hopes of negotiating a permanent armistice. In the meantime, however, I wish to examine our encampment for signs of magical interference."

The general started visibly. "Magical interference, Your Majesty?" He looked perplexed. "King Thorn never authorized the use of magic on the battlefield. It was discussed, I believe, but the resources were not forthcoming."

Basil nodded. "That's what I thought as well. And I wish to confirm the truth or otherwise of my belief. A similar investigation is currently being conducted in the Mistran encampment."

The general actually raised an eyebrow this time. "By whom, Your Majesty? Surely not our people?"

"A combination of Entolians and Mistrans," said Basil, as if it was the most natural situation imaginable.

The general looked more bewildered than ever, but Basil gave him no time to ask further questions.

"The trouble is, I need assistance to examine our camp for magic." He studied the general's face. "I've heard rumors in the past...do you have an enchanter in your army, General?"

The general gave a grunt. "I wouldn't pin your hopes on Sergeant Sid, Your Majesty. Strictly speaking he has magic, but if he's to be believed, it's not strong. And he's always so reluctant to use it, it's not worth the effort." He grunted again. "Amazing how obstructive a man can be without ever actually saying no."

Thinking of the journey from Myst to the front lines, Basil cast a wry glance at Lord Baldwin beside him. "Yes," he agreed. "Amazing."

The nobleman had the grace to look ashamed.

"Well, I don't think it takes very strong magic for an enchanter to simply be able to sense the presence of other magic," Basil said, his attention back on the general. "I'd be grateful if you'd take me to this Sergeant Sid."

"No need for you to go to him, Your Majesty," said the general firmly. He nodded at an orderly in the corner, and the man took off out of the tent. He returned a few minutes later with another soldier in tow.

"Your Majesty," said the general. "This is Sergeant Obsidian."

The sergeant sprang to attention at the general's words, throwing up and holding a salute so tight it looked painful.

"At ease," Basil remembered to say, and the man relaxed only marginally.

Basil studied him curiously. He was younger than Basil had expected, probably only a few years older than the king— although the prominent scar on his face made the sergeant look slightly older than he probably was. The jagged white line started just below his ear and ran halfway down the soldier's jaw. His skin was as pale as Basil's own—perhaps a little tanned from an outdoor life—but other than that, his coloring was dark. His short hair stuck out in sharp black spikes, and his eyes were so dark Basil could barely make out the pupils.

Obsidian, the general had said? Basil restrained a smile. The young soldier was aptly named.

"Are you an enchanter, Sergeant Obsidian?" he asked genially.

Only by the slightest twitch of an eyebrow did Sergeant Obsidian betray his distaste for the question.

"Yes, Your Majesty."

"What form does your magic naturally take?" Basil asked curiously.

"Nothing remarkable, Your Majesty," said Sergeant Obsidian in clipped accents. "I possess the ability to identify deception."

Basil thought this over. It wasn't the first time he'd heard of enchanters who could tell when someone was lying. "Sounds remarkable to me," he commented mildly. "I can imagine it might be very useful, although that's not what I'd like your help with today."

"No, Your Majesty?" The soldier visibly brightened, and Basil's curiosity was roused. Why was this young sergeant apparently reluctant to use his magic? But he didn't have time to ferret out Sergeant Sid's secrets.

"I'm just looking for assistance to identify magic," said Basil. "And from what I understand, all magic-users can do that, regardless of the form their own power takes."

Sergeant Obsidian's face was once again an expressionless mask, from which Basil deduced that he was disappointed to be wanted for his magic after all.

"That's right, Your Majesty."

"Well then," said Basil briskly. "Shall we begin?"

Sergeant Obsidian once again showed a flicker of emotion. Surprise this time. "Right now, Your Majesty?"

"Of course," said Basil briskly.

"I trust you won't object to me joining you, King Basil," said the general. It didn't sound like a request.

Basil restrained a sigh, resigned to the unwanted addition. "Certainly you may join me, General." He looked back at the sergeant. "I've received information, Sergeant Obsidian, that there may be magic in use here at the battlefield."

Sergeant Obsidian's face became veiled. "Are you making an accusation, Your Majesty?"

For a moment Basil was bemused, then understanding dawned. "Against you? Not at all."

He paused. Was it possible that the dragons had simply sensed Obsidian's presence? He hadn't considered that possibility. But it didn't seem likely. They'd said magic was radiating from the area—surely the magic contained in one ordinary enchanter wouldn't have been notable to them. Dragons must fly over enchanters all the time.

"Because I have often been required to use my magic as part of my duties," said Sergeant Obsidian, with a touch of bitterness.

The general shifted. "Often?" he repeated, with an impatient noise.

"I wasn't referring to that," said Basil decisively. He crossed his arms, pinning the sergeant with his gaze. He didn't understand the dynamic between the magic-using sergeant and his superior officers, and he didn't especially care to. "Have you sensed any other kind of magic in the camp?"

Sergeant Obsidian rubbed his clean-shaven jaw with one hand. "In the camp? No."

"Anywhere nearby, then?" Basil prompted, with a touch of impatience.

"Well, there's the general protective enchantment over the whole battleground, but I assume you mean other than that."

Basil uncrossed his arms, staring at the sergeant. "She was

right," he muttered, thinking of the merchant woman's words. Sergeant Obsidian looked confused, so he hurried on. "What general protective enchantment?"

The sergeant frowned. "I don't know how else to describe it. It's a little like a building protection, but different. I mean, it would have to be different, wouldn't it? Protecting a battlefield must be quite a different task from protecting a home or store."

"I know nothing of a protective enchantment over my camp," the general said, turning his sharp gaze on Basil. "Your Majesty, if you put something like that in place after you ascended the throne, I really think you should have warned me, at the very least."

Basil shook his head. "I didn't put it in place. I had no knowledge of it at all until recently."

The sergeant looked startled. "Was it the Mistrans, then?" he asked, frowning. "I've wondered what the point of it was sometimes...it certainly feels like a protective enchantment, but I've seen men die while fighting right above it, so it can't be that powerful."

"Above it?" Basil asked, perplexed.

The soldier shrugged. "It's soaked into the ground or something. It sort of...emanates up from the battlefield."

Basil stared at him. "Can you take me to where it's strongest?" he asked. "I mean, are you able to, I don't know...follow the trail of it like a dog following a scent?"

He could have sworn a flash of amusement passed through Sergeant Obsidian's dark eyes, but they were so unreadable again a moment later, he couldn't be sure.

"I can try, Your Majesty. But like I said, it always seems to kind of come from the ground. What will you do, dig down to it?"

"If I have to," said Basil grimly, "then that's exactly what I'll do."

CHAPTER TWENTY-ONE

Wren

Wren held herself as straight as she could, meeting the general's eyes unflinchingly. It wasn't exactly a surprise that he wasn't supportive of her desire to scour his camp for secret magic in company with an Entolian enchantress. But Wren had never been more determined in her life. If the dragons themselves had told Basil they'd felt magic at the front lines, she didn't doubt for a moment it was there. And if neither the Mistran nor Entolian crowns knew anything of it, there could be little doubt its purpose was nefarious.

Here at last was a substantial lead. Surely whoever was using illicit magic on the battlefield was connected to whoever had launched the magical attack against her and her brothers in order to provoke war.

Either that, or they had more than one group of renegade magic-users on their hands, and that possibility didn't bear thinking about.

"Your Highness, I simply cannot allow you to wander around the army camp unaccompanied. It's not safe, and it's not seemly." The general's tone was clearly intended to be final, but as always, he had underestimated Wren.

Pulling out her slate, she wrote one simple sentence.

To stop me, you will have to physically restrain me.

The grizzled man before her scowled at the words, his agitation growing. Wren could see in his eyes that he would like very well to do exactly that, but she was fairly confident he wasn't going to dare. It was as well that Ari and Bram hadn't accompanied her into the camp. She'd told them to keep their distance given the Entolian enchantress's presence, and the associated risk of discovery. The fact that their absence made her seem slightly less of a lunatic in front of the general was just an added bonus.

"Your Highness," the general said gruffly, his eyes still on her slate. "This is not your place."

Serenely, Wren added two words to her message.

I disagree.

She lowered her slate and folded her hands over it, raising an eyebrow expectantly. The general let out a frustrated grunt as he turned helplessly to Wren's solitary guard. The man shrugged his shoulders, and Wren allowed herself a tiny smile of satisfaction. Her father's general had never taken her seriously, but the assumption that nothing was going on behind her silence had been his mistake, not hers.

Her thoughts flew to Basil, who must be undertaking a similar process in his own army camp right now. Similar, but entirely dissimilar, she guessed. It was almost laughable to imagine Basil groveling for permission to search the battle-ground. He would listen calmly to whatever his general had to say, then do exactly what he wanted.

Well, she might not be the unassailable sovereign of her kingdom, but she was its princess—as far as the general knew, its crown princess—and she wasn't going to be intimidated.

As obtrusively as possible, she reached up and adjusted the chain around her neck. As she'd hoped, the general's eyes were drawn to the signet ring lying against her gown, and she saw him fidget. She stared at him until he reluctantly met her eyes. If the general was going to refuse to recognize her rank, he would have to do so to her face.

The general's scowl was back as they locked gazes, but still he didn't outright refuse her. How could he? Impatient as she was to get started with the search, Wren felt a glow of satisfaction. It was hard to believe that such a short time ago she'd felt guilty at the very idea of using her supposed position to influence matters of state. She'd always felt it would be self-aggrandizing, and had dreaded having every word she'd spoken thrown back at her once Caleb's presence was revealed to the court.

She thought very differently now. She wasn't usurping Caleb's place—she was minding it for him. If he could still speak into matters of import, he would, but his beak rather got in the way of that.

It was Basil who'd made her see her own folly. Not intentionally, of course. But like her, he'd been thrown into a position he wasn't ready for—and by her guess, didn't especially want. And it was clear that he was surrounded by people who didn't have confidence in him, thanks to his youth. But he hadn't let that lack of confidence cow him, as Wren had done. He had faith in himself, and was unhesitating in using his position of power to effect the change he thought was needed.

He didn't always get it right, of course—he'd mishandled her father from the beginning, and she'd heard him acknowledge it more than once.

Nevertheless, somehow, even with all that confidence there was nothing self-aggrandizing about him. How many times had Wren seen him calmly take disrespect, or even outright insults, without letting it sway his decision? No, if there was one thing Basil had taught her, it was that ruling well wasn't about ego. She'd thought that by not putting herself forward, she was being humble, and respecting Caleb's claims instead of stealing his position. But she'd let her own doubts—and those of others—make her value herself too low. And that wasn't humility. It was just a different kind of pride from rating her importance too high.

Caleb couldn't do what needed to be done right now. Wren could, and neither the general's disdain, nor her own doubts were going to stop her.

"Your Highness," the general tried again, breaking their silent stand off at last. "Will you at least wait until I can send a courier to your father, to confirm—"

He broke off as Wren wrote calmly on her slate.

No, I will not.

She had no doubt that the general would send a message to her father immediately—if he hadn't already—but she didn't intend to wait for a reply. It would take the better part of two days.

The general looked more frustrated than ever, but he made no more protests. "Then I will, of course, accompany you," he said stiffly.

Wren inclined her head graciously. She'd prefer not to have his escort, but she couldn't exactly prevent him. Without another word, she sailed out of the tent, to where Lady Anneliese and the two Entolians were waiting for her. Wren gave a firm nod in response to her friend's questioningly raised eyebrow, and a flash of admiration crossed Lady Anneliese's face.

Bolstered, Wren turned to the enchantress Basil had left with her. She was about to pull her slate out, when the woman spoke.

"Your Highness," she bobbed a quick curtsy, "I can feel it faintly even from here. Shall I lead you in the direction it seems to be coming from?"

Wren smiled encouragingly, and the two Entolians turned eastward.

Half a dozen soldiers accompanied the group, clearly bent on protecting their general as well as their princess. Wren could hear the older man muttering angrily alongside her, suspicious of their Entolian guides, but she ignored him. The enchantress led them through the camp, her eyes a little unfocused as she followed that extra sense that only magic-users had.

At the edge of the camp, there was a long trench, dug parallel to the invisible and contested border between the two kingdoms. Its edge was lined with lances jutting out at an angle toward the Entolian side, and it was a grim sight. Wren wondered if it might be the enchantress's destination, but the woman turned to one of the soldiers, clearly seeking a way across. At his direction, they all climbed down into the trench. Wren had assumed it to be merely a physical barrier, so she was surprised to find it peopled with soldiers. They probably didn't recognize her on sight, but they all stared wide eyed at the spectacle of the merchants leading two titled women through their battleground. The general, however, they certainly recognized. Every one of them sprang to attention when he came into view, and Wren saw a couple surreptitiously smoothing their uniforms.

The soldiers weren't quite what Wren had expected. They didn't look afraid, although that might have been because of the two month break from hostilities. Neither did they seem filled with determination to win, like the general was. They looked… settled, as if this was simply what they did every day. She realized, with a wave of sadness, that it was. How long had these men been here? Years of a barely moving war must take a strange kind of toll on a life. She set her face determinedly to where the two Entolians were climbing up a roughly dug earth staircase to the other side of the trench.

All the more reason to end this conflict.

Reaching the top of the steps, Wren glanced back at the soldiers in the trench. Their apathy was gone, a row of fearful faces turned toward her. She supposed it must be strange for them to see someone as important as their general heading out into no man's land. They knew, of course, that the two armies were in a temporary ceasefire. She could only assume that going past the trench was so strongly associated with danger, they couldn't help the instinctive reaction.

Wren felt a certain foreboding herself, as they moved out into the scarred and damaged landscape of the space between the armies. They didn't strike out into the unclaimed ground, instead moving alongside the trench. Nevertheless, the surface was so uneven, they had to move slowly. Wren could see signs of previous trenches, only partially filled in, presumably marking earlier battle lines.

"Princess Wren."

Lady Anneliese's soft voice startled Wren, drawing her gaze from the barren landscape. The other woman looked troubled, and Wren wondered if she was uncomfortable to be so near the battleground. With a flash of remorse, Wren reflected that she'd never really given the noblewoman the opportunity to bow out of the adventure.

"This may not be the best time," Lady Anneliese continued, picking her way carefully around a patch of foul-smelling mud. "But I don't feel right to keep it from you. I had hoped opportunity would present itself when we were at the manor, but..." She drew a deep breath. "I've accepted Sir Gelding's offer."

Wren swung around to stare at her friend, stumbling on a hidden hole. Her guard appeared from nowhere to steady her, and she gave him a distracted nod of thanks. Most of her attention was on Lady Anneliese, who looked even paler than usual at Wren's response.

"I'm sorry if you're disappointed in me, Your Highness," she said, sounding almost tearful. "And I will miss you very much when I leave Myst. But..." She swallowed. "I don't think I can stand to stay in the capital forever. Not when every time I turn a corner, I'm reminded of..." She paused, pulling herself together. "I don't think there's any other way I can get this kind of distance."

Panic was rising in Wren—she should have been paying more attention to Lady Anneliese's situation, but she'd been so distracted by her own troubles. They were days from Caleb's release! She knew with horrible certainty that Lady Anneliese was much too honorable to pull back from a betrothal, even once Caleb's survival was revealed.

She could see that the noblewoman was on the verge of tears at her prolonged lack of response, so she reached out and gave her friend's arm a tentative squeeze. She didn't want Lady Anneliese to think she blamed her for any of this mess. But it was still the last thing she'd wanted to hear at that moment.

The matter was driven from her mind as the enchantress in front of her suddenly stopped walking. Wren was so distracted, she almost bumped into the back of the woman. Her guard was once again forced to steady her.

"What is it?" The question came from the Entolian merchant. If Wren was remembering correctly, he was married to the enchantress. "Did you lose the trail of the magic?"

She shook her head, looking confused. "No, it's definitely been getting stronger. The source must be nearby. But it's like it's coming from underneath us."

"You mean it's soaked into the ground or something?" her husband pressed.

She frowned. "I don't think so. The closer we get, the less it feels like a general enchantment that permeates everything in its vicinity. It's more like a sharp source, but that source is just...under us."

Not being able to sense magic, Wren couldn't really grasp what the woman was describing. But she looked at the ground beneath her feet, along with the rest of the group.

"Under us?" The general's gruff voice broke into the silence. "We all know what's under us, and it's not magic."

"What is it?" asked the enchantress blankly.

The general made a derisive noise. "What is it? What are we fighting this blasted war over all these years?"

"Mistran pigheadedness?" The merchant's mutter was clear enough for everyone to hear, and his wife shot him a reproving look.

"Iron ore," snapped the general. "The ore field is under us."

There was a moment of silence, as everyone stared at each other. The general looked between them, his brow becoming more furrowed by the second, as even he seemed to consider the apparent connection.

"You say there's magic coming from the ore?" he asked the enchantress slowly. It was the first sign he'd shown that he even believed the Entolian had magic. "How is that possible?"

"No idea," she answered with a shrug. "And I didn't say it's coming from the ore. Just that it's coming from underneath us."

"Is there an entrance somewhere?" Lady Anneliese chimed in.

"An entrance to what?" Clearly the general wasn't just exasperated with the Entolians. "It's not a mine. It's an untapped ore field."

"But they must have dug somewhere to discover the ore initially," said the enchantress. She hesitated. "Mustn't they?"

The general grunted. "I'm not a miner."

Wren noticed that Lady Anneliese was looking very thoughtful, and she nudged her friend.

"I don't know anything about mining either," said Lady Anneliese, meeting Wren's eyes with a slight flush, "but Sir Gelding has mentioned the iron ore more than once."

Wren nodded. Of course. She'd almost forgotten that the Mistran enchanter oversaw the Blacksmiths' Guild. She frowned thoughtfully. It was a little surprising that he'd been so silent on the war. She would have guessed he'd be more eager than anyone for the war to end, so they could start the mining. Although that depended on the outcome of the war, of course. If the Entolians won, or even just came out with more ground, the Blacksmiths' Guild would be disappointed. Was that why he'd stood against a full scale war in the first place? Because he didn't think the Mistrans could win, and was worried they'd lose all the ore?

She looked up, to see Lady Anneliese watching her expectantly. Wren nodded, encouraging her to go on.

"Well, he just made it sound like he's seen the ore," the noblewoman said, with a shrug. "He must have gotten to it somehow."

The general was frowning at Lady Anneliese, but more in concentration than in anger, Wren thought.

"Sir Gelding? That baronet who runs the Blacksmiths' Guild? He's been here a few times, to inspect the site." He jerked his head further along the trench. "There's some kind of inspection point where they can look at the ore."

Wren's slate was out before he'd finished speaking.

Take us there.

With only a token show of reluctance, the general led them back into the trench. Clearly his curiosity was roused now, as well. This part of the man-made ravine held fewer soldiers, and they passed only a few sentries as they continued along the line of the border. The space was too small for the general's bodyguards, so the soldiers walked along the uneven higher ground, scanning the area for threats. Wren noticed that they often looked anxiously toward the Entolian side, as if fearing their enemy would discover the general's proximity to the battle line, and be tempted to break the ceasefire. Wren's thoughts flew over the unclaimed land as well, although not in fear of an impending attack. Where were Basil's inquiries leading him?

When the general at last stopped walking, Wren looked around her, trying to spot the inspection point he'd mentioned. All she could see was a little hollow dug into the outside edge of the trench, coming up no higher than her waist.

"That's it?" The enchantress sounded as confused as Wren felt.

The general grunted. "This is where they come to inspect the ore. I don't usually accompany them, though." He shot a look at one of the soldiers on the higher ground above. "You've brought Sir Gelding here before, haven't you?"

The soldier nodded. "Yes, sir. This is the place."

"But what do they do?" the Entolian merchant asked skeptically.

"I don't know," said the soldier with a shrug. "They sort of have a look, and mutter to each other, and then leave."

Wren frowned at the hollow. Have a look at what? Disregarding both her gown and her dignity, she knelt down before the spot, examining the dug earth.

The enchantress knelt beside her. "Whoa," she muttered. Wren shot her an inquiring look, and she hastened to explain. "There's definitely magic concentrated in this area, Your Highness. I can feel it pouring through the earth. There's something behind there. Or, I don't know...under there."

Wren put a hand out in front of her, laying it on the dirt. She couldn't feel anything unusual, but she wouldn't expect to, not having magic in her own blood. But as she leaned in for a closer look, a draft of air hit her from the side. Sticking her head into the hollow, she was amazed to see a narrow opening on one side. It wasn't large enough to crawl through, but the air coming from it definitely suggested something beyond solid earth.

She pulled out her slate, trying to be as brief as possible while still making sense.

Tunnel maybe? Can your magic enlarge the hole?

"Maybe, Your Highness," said the enchantress, sounding nervous. "But it might be unstable. I wouldn't want to risk anyone getting hurt."

Especially you, was the unspoken addition. Wren could sympathize with the Entolian's hesitation to endanger the foreign princess into whose company she'd been pitched, but as with the general, Wren had no intention of taking no for an answer.

I'm going to try anyway. Your help will make it safer.

The enchantress fidgeted on her knees. Her husband, standing behind the pair, gave a grunt.

"Go on. King Basil told us to do anything she asked, remember?"

"Hang on." The general's sharp voice cut into the conversation, and he pushed his way to Wren's side. "What are you planning to do?"

But Wren had already rubbed her slate clean, and she ignored him. She was the smallest in the group, but that wasn't the only reason she was determined to be the one to investigate. She touched the chain around her neck, making sure Caleb's ring was still in place. Whatever was inside that hollow, she didn't anticipate serious injury.

She nodded encouragingly at the enchantress, and the woman screwed up her face in concentration. Wren had expected her to wave her fingers and just make the hole bigger, but instead she began to dig with her actual hands. She muttered as she did so, and Wren watched in amazement as the thickly packed, root-crossed dirt fell away like sand. In moments, the hole in the side of the hollow was large enough for Wren to fit. She heard Lady Anneliese's gasp as a draft of stale air rushed out at them all.

With a smile of thanks to the enchantress, Wren thrust her head into the hole, crawling quickly before her guard could grasp her intention. Sure enough, she heard his shout of protest as her hips squeezed through the narrow gap, but it was too late for him to pull her back out. She wondered fleetingly if the enchantress would widen the hole even further, so that the others could chase her through it, but she didn't pause to find out.

She'd emerged into a space barely larger than the opening the enchantress had made for her, and she felt uncomfortably hemmed in as she crawled forward. She continued moving, however, following the line of the tunnel out toward no man's land, and steeply down. She was just debating how difficult it would be for her to crawl backward to safety if she hit a dead end when the tiny tunnel suddenly opened up. Feeling around her hesitantly, Wren pushed herself to her feet. A small beam of light filtered in from the hole where she'd entered, allowing her to make out what looked like a tunnel, running perpendicular to the small track she'd come through. Shouting sounded faintly from behind her, and she glanced back over her shoulder, trying to figure out if anyone was coming after her.

At a sudden rumbling sound, the shouting ceased abruptly. Wren stepped hastily away from the tiny tunnel, but not quite quickly enough. With a groan, a whole section of earth fell away from the ceiling above her. She could barely make out what was happening, but she threw her arms over her head, fully expecting to be struck by the falling clumps.

But she felt nothing. After a moment, she lowered her hands cautiously. The rumbling had stopped, and all was still. Her first impression was of total blackness. Fighting panic, she scanned the area, noting from the movement of air that she wasn't stuck in too small a space. Slowly, her eyes adjusted, and she realized she could still make out the shape of her surroundings.

It seemed the enchantress had been right about the ground being unstable. The tiny tunnel through which Wren had entered was gone, buried by huge chunks of dirt. Broken clumps lay all around her, and for a moment she marveled that she hadn't been struck at all. Then she remembered the reason she'd been determined to take the risk herself, and touched a grateful hand to the powerful artifact around her neck.

Thanks, Caleb, she thought silently. *Now can this thing help me get out of here safely?*

Wherever here was. She stepped away from the cave-in, searching for the new source of light that was allowing her to still see. As her eyes continued to adjust, she realized that the tunnel into which she'd emerged was much broader than she'd first supposed. And, more significantly, it was clearly man-made. Not only was it straight and even, but its sides had been reinforced with timber structures.

Wren felt a chill that had nothing to do with the draft still emanating from further down the tunnel. Who had made this place, and for what purpose? It was surely a sinister sign that her own general didn't know about it—he certainly wouldn't have brought her to it if he did. Did the Entolians know? But Basil was the king. If something was happening behind his back at the front lines, it could be nothing good.

Choosing the direction where the light seemed brightest, Wren followed the tunnel. She felt a twinge of guilt for the turmoil she had surely left behind in the trench, but she didn't see any option but to keep going until she found an alternative way out. A short distance down the tunnel, she came across what looked like a wooden torch mounted on the wall, although instead of fire, it had a large stone, from which emanated a faint white light. She paused to examine it. She'd heard of such things. Natural objects which, while not exactly magical themselves, had a susceptibility to magic, making them ideal for use in enchantments, as they needed to be infused with only limited power. She saw that similar stones lined the tunnel all the way ahead. It might not take much magic to power them, she reflected, but it certainly took some. Could they be what the Entolian enchantress was sensing?

Wren continued walking for what felt like an age, although the semi-darkness of the tunnel was so disorienting, she had no real idea of time. Occasionally she saw smaller tunnels branching off from the large one, but she stayed on the main track, thinking that if the worst came to it, she could try to find her way back to the starting point, where she knew it was a limited distance to dig in order to break back out into the trench.

She'd just started to slow her pace, squinting in the low light in an attempt to identify the objects which were appearing scattered along the side of the tunnel, when voices reached her ears.

CHAPTER TWENTY-TWO

Wren

For a moment Wren froze, afraid in spite of her protective talisman of who she might find down here. The tunnel curved ahead, and looking up she realized that a brighter, yellow light was leaking around the corner from that direction. Then a new voice rang out, clear and heart-stoppingly familiar.

"Well. It seems you were right, Sergeant. There most certainly is something down here."

Basil!

With a gasp, Wren stumbled forward. She rounded the corner so rapidly, she almost fell into the group of men standing just past the bend in the blaze of several lanterns. She barely saw the others, her eyes drawn instantly to the tall man at the center of the group, his light brown hair sprinkled with dirt, and his hazel eyes full of shock as they latched on to her.

"Wren!" Basil started forward, reaching out to steady her as she pulled herself abruptly up. "What are you doing here?" His eyes searched vainly in the semi-darkness behind her. "Surely you're not alone?"

Wren nodded, a slight shiver running over her frame,

followed quickly by a flush of heat. Perhaps she'd been more unnerved by being trapped in the tunnel than she'd let herself acknowledge. Although that didn't explain why the heat seemed to have localized at the points where Basil still gripped her shoulders steadyingly.

She forced herself to look away from him, taking in the identity of his companions. Basil's guards she recognized, and Lord Baldwin, although she didn't linger on him. He was watching her with even more discomfort than usual—he looked almost horrified. The rest of the group were all in military uniform. One was so decorated, Wren suspected he might be Basil's own general. He was flanked by two soldiers, but a third stood next to Basil, his dark eyes showing mild surprise at Wren's abrupt appearance.

Pushing down a strange and embarrassing impulse to curl up against Basil's chest, Wren took a step back and straightened her spine. She was a princess of Mistra, and she fully intended to show these Entolian soldiers a strong front. Surreptitiously, she shook a few clumps of dirt loose from her hair.

Basil cast an appraising glance over her. "You look like you got in here by crawling through a hole," he said bluntly.

Feeling slightly resentful, Wren acknowledged it with a quick nod. Basil chuckled, and Wren couldn't help scowling as she flicked her chin toward his own disheveled appearance.

"I know, I know, I'm not much better," Basil acknowledged comfortably. "We did have to dig a bit, but at least we didn't have to crawl." His expression turned grim as he turned his head toward the nearby wall of the tunnel. "It was certainly worth the effort though, wasn't it?"

Following his gaze, Wren felt her eyes widen at the sight of another one of the objects she'd been passing. In the light of the lantern being held by the third soldier, she could clearly make out the small wooden cart, piled with chunks of dirt and rock, with a series of unfamiliar metal tools sitting on top. Suddenly the reinforced tunnels made sense, and she felt like a fool for not recognizing it immediately.

They were standing in a mine.

"We've found the source of the magic," Basil said darkly. "It seems someone is mining the iron ore out from underneath the battlefield. By the looks of things, they've probably been doing it for years. Maybe the whole duration of the war. And I can only assume they're using magic to do it so clandestinely, and so successfully."

"It's not just iron they're mining, Your Majesty," chimed in the dark-haired soldier. "But yes, they're certainly using magic to do it. This place is coated with magic. Not just the protective enchantment I felt from above—which I assume operates to protect the mine from being damaged by the fighting—but other magic as well. Even the lights," he nodded toward the stone-topped torches, "have latent power."

Wren looked him over, intrigued. It seemed Basil had found another magic-user to act as his guide after he left the merchant enchantress with Wren.

"What do you mean they're not just mining iron, Sergeant Obsidian?" Basil asked, frowning.

In answer, Sergeant Obsidian lifted a pick from the cart and swung it into the wall of the tunnel, which in this area seemed to be primarily rock. He chipped away for a moment, then pulled off a chunk of something red. Raising his lantern in his other hand, he held up his prize for everyone to see.

Wren wasn't the only one to gasp as the lantern threw its light not just onto the item in the sergeant's hand, but on the vein of dull red threading its way across the rocky tunnel wall behind him, enlivened by the occasional sparkle of gold.

"Is that ruby?" one of the other soldiers asked, sounding awed.

The sergeant shook his head. "Much more rare than that. It's fire jasper." He pointed to the piece in his hand. "See the thread of sparkling gold that runs across it? That's how you tell it apart from regular jasper."

Fire jasper. The name tickled something in Wren's memory, although she couldn't immediately identify it.

The Entolian general raised an eyebrow, a definite hint of suspicion on his face. "I didn't realize you were well versed in matters of mining and precious stones, Sergeant."

The young soldier gave a humorless smile. "I don't know anything about mining, sir. I know about magic. Fire jasper has a latent affinity with magic, and can be useful in all kinds of enchantments. It makes sense that there's some in this area actually. We're not so far from the dragons' realm, and everyone says their colony was built on a bedrock of fire jasper." He tossed the piece he'd mined to Basil. "Now I think about it, I've heard that it's sometimes found alongside iron ore. But as you can probably guess, Your Majesty, it's about a hundred times as valuable as iron."

Wren's eyes widened as she remembered where she'd heard about fire jasper before. It had been mentioned in the notes Basil's sister had sent, as a tool that could be used in combining the power of more than one enchanter. The notes had tallied with the sergeant's account—apparently fire jasper was particularly effective in carrying magic of various kinds.

Basil's face was set in grim lines. "Well, now we know the what and the why. What still remains is the who."

"I'm more interested in the how!" snapped Basil's general. Studying him quietly, Wren detected mortification beneath his outrage. It seemed he truly hadn't known about the secret mine under his own battlefield, and he must be deeply embarrassed to have his obliviousness paraded in front of his king. "As for who, it's clearly the Mistrans behind this," the general blustered on. "Just the kind of duplicity I would expect from them, waging battle for the mine above land, and all the while sneaking under our feet to steal what's rightfully ours!"

"General," interjected Basil mildly, "this might be a good moment to formally introduce you to our new companion." He cleared his throat. "Princess Wren of Mistra."

The general's eyes seemed to start from his head, and to Wren's amusement he reached for the hilt of his sword.

"Oh, don't be absurd," said Basil impatiently. "She's not here to attack any of us. She's been investigating the source of the magic, same as I have."

Ignoring the protests clearly building on the general's lips, Wren pulled out her slate. She was aware that the soldiers were all watching her in fascination, but the time for embarrassment was long past.

This wasn't us.

"I know it wasn't," said Basil reassuringly.

But even as the general frowned over her words, Wren felt a jolt of unease go through her stomach. She'd bet her life that her father knew nothing of this secret mine. He hadn't even visited the front line in years. But she knew of another Mistran who definitely had. One who even had magic. She gasped as the baronet's image flashed before her mind's eye—the ostentatious jewelry he wore! She'd assumed the stones were rubies, but were they actually fire jasper? Fire jasper which he'd had harvested from this very mine?

Wren's eyes widened as she realized why the dull red stone looked familiar. Caleb's ring! She remembered her father telling her how expensive it had been to acquire an enchantment so powerful. Had the use of precious fire jasper in the protective magic been part of what made it so expensive? If Mistra claimed some of this mine, could her father have such artifacts made for all of his children?

But the value of the fire jasper wasn't important right now. What mattered was establishing who was stealing it.

Scrubbing out her message, she hastily scrawled two words and thrust it back in Basil's face.

"Sir Gelding?" he read aloud, sounding confused. "The one who's courting your friend? What about him?" He frowned. "He has magic, doesn't he? Do you suspect him of involvement?"

Wren nodded emphatically, frustration flaring at her inability to quickly communicate her thoughts.

"I thought he was against the war, though," Basil mused.

Wren nodded once more. She pulled back her slate, but Basil caught up with her thoughts before she had to write anything down.

"Of course," the king mused in sudden understanding. "It wouldn't serve his interests for Mistra to invade Entolia, and drive the battle beyond the border. Because then the Mistran crown could begin mining."

Wren nodded grim agreement. The baronet wouldn't want either full scale war, or a stable peace between the two kingdoms. Either course would expose what was happening on the site of the ore deposit. If he was behind this secret mine, the current situation was ideal for him. The ongoing skirmishes prevented the site from being properly explored by either crown.

With a sudden thrill of fear, Wren realized that he'd been speaking to Lady Anneliese when she approached her friend. He must know about her supposed visit to Lady Anneliese's manor. Would he go to visit his betrothed, and discover that they'd actually left the manor? Would he figure out where they'd gone? He wouldn't be happy about either her or Basil examining the battlefield.

In fact, he was probably less than pleased about them working together at all.

She looked up to see Basil watching her closely. Whether his thoughts had followed the same route as hers, she didn't know. But he seemed to have reached a similar destination, judging by the anger growing in his eyes.

"He's been in Myst all this time, too, hasn't he?" Basil asked sharply.

Wren nodded slowly, her eyes narrowing. She'd thought Sir Gelding was staying in the capital purely to press his suit with Lady Anneliese. But perhaps he'd had a different motive as well, to keep a wary eye on the visiting king. Perhaps it was no coincidence that his stay had been unexpectedly lengthened just as Basil's had.

"Do you think he's the one who tried to drown you in the pond?" Basil pressed. "There can't be that many enchanters with access to the castle—why didn't we think of him before?"

Shaking her head, Wren scratched out a new message.

I did think of him, and I made discreet inquiries. His magic isn't the type that can control plants.

"Controlling plants?" the Entolian sergeant chimed in unexpectedly. He'd clearly been reading Wren's words over his king's shoulder. "That's a rare power. I've only ever met one person who can do that."

"Who?" Basil demanded. "When did you meet him?"

"Years ago," said the sergeant. "We enchanters do tend to rub shoulders with one another, whether we want to or not." For some reason there was bitterness in his voice.

"Yes, but who was he?" Basil demanded impatiently.

"I don't remember his name, Your Majesty," said the sergeant with a shrug. "He was the son of a farmer—magic hadn't been seen for three generations in his family, so it was quite a surprise. Their lands were near here, actually." He frowned. "Most likely they've been overrun by the war, now I think about it."

Wren and Basil exchanged a glance, and as so often seemed to be the case, she knew he was thinking the same thing she was. It sounded like this enchanter had a reason to be angry at the royals who'd thrown his kingdom into war. Maybe even angry enough to attack the princess of his enemy kingdom? But how would he have gained access to the castle to attack her in the first place? Surely he could have found a more direct way to express his anger.

She thought back over the incident, and the conversation that had come before it. She and Basil had been speculating about a link between the attacks on various royals across Solstice. She'd wondered afterward if it was possible they were onto something—that her attacker was part of some kind of shadowy league of enchanters, and had heard somehow, and wanted to stop them pursuing the lead. But then Basil had started figuring out the secret of the swans, and it had driven all thought of a possible continent-wide conspiracy of magic from her mind.

It still seemed to her that the most likely motive for stopping her and Basil from working together was to hide the mine in which they now stood. Which brought her back, not to the unknown Entolian farmer with plant-based power, but to Sir

Gelding, whom she knew for a fact didn't have magic that controlled plants.

Suddenly, the entry she'd read about combined power danced once again before her eyes, and she stiffened. Basil was still watching her, his expression intense, and she knew the moment they locked eyes that he'd caught her change in posture.

"Everyone," Basil said, keeping his eyes on Wren, "I want you to go back the way we came, make sure our tunnel in is clear enough for the princess to comfortably accompany us back to the surface."

"But Your Majesty—" started several voices at once.

Basil cut them all off. "That's an order." He turned at last, pinning first the general, then his own guards, with an unyielding stare. "To every single one of you. We will join you momentarily."

"King Basil..." The last weak protest came from Lord Baldwin, but Wren wasn't surprised when he quailed under Basil's glare. The nobleman had never seemed to her to have a great deal of resolution.

Reluctantly, their companions all moved away down the tunnel, casting frequent glances back. Once they'd disappeared around a corner, Basil turned to Wren.

All at once, it hit her that they were alone, for the first time since before she fell into the pond. The hard stare was gone from Basil's face, and his eyes were softer than she'd ever seen them.

"Are you all right?" he asked quietly.

Wren realized she was trembling slightly. Making an effort to pull herself together, she nodded, then tilted her head to one side.

Clearly understanding the unspoken question, Basil smiled. The intimacy of the expression sent another quiver over Wren's frame. "Yes, I'm fine. This is a grim discovery, but I'm inclined to think that making it constitutes an enormous step forward."

Wren nodded slowly. She was also glad they'd found the secret mine, but her thoughts still swirled uneasily around Sir Gelding, and his possible role in her accident. She only realized she was biting her lip when she saw that Basil's eyes were drawn by the gesture. Flushing slightly, she reached for her slate.

Before she could get there, Basil stretched his arm across the distance between them. He stilled her hand with his own, that knowing smile back on his face. "You're going to mention combined power, right? You're thinking the enchanter Sergeant Obsidian mentioned could have given his power to Sir Gelding, who could have used it to attack you. I've even been wondering whether those jewels Sir Gelding wears might be fire jasper, which he's using to channel additional magic."

It took Wren a moment to respond. She wasn't startled by the accuracy with which he'd read her. He'd developed quite a knack for figuring out what she was thinking. But she was distracted by the feel of his hand on hers, the warmth of his skin such a contrast to the chill air of the mine. The departing group had left them only one lantern, and in the dim light the moment felt intimate, important.

Gathering her thoughts with difficulty, she nodded. She wasn't oblivious to the full implications of the idea. It meant Mistran and Entolian enchanters were working together against the combined crowns, which suggested a more organized—and more formidable—enemy than she'd previously guessed. But she couldn't seem to make her thoughts focus.

Basil was still smiling, his eyes searching her face. "You know," he said, his tone conversational, "it's remarkable how much you can say even when you don't actually say anything."

Wren didn't even know what made her do it. No thought preceded the action. Her hand just acted of its own accord, twisting under Basil's so they were palm to palm. His own movements seemed equally unconscious as he interlocked their fingers and lifted their hands so they met in the air between them.

For a breathless moment they stood there, Wren's palm tingling from the sensation of her fingers interwoven with Basil's, the heat of his skin on hers sending out little trails of flame that seared her consciousness.

Then Basil took a small step toward her. Wren tried to remind herself that he was dangerous for some reason, that she'd been avoiding him for fear of...something.

She couldn't for the life of her recall what. All she could comprehend was Basil's closeness, the dirt still clinging to the waves of his hair, the broadness of his chest up this close, the frank way he looked her full in the eye, with no hint of self-consciousness, or of discomfort at her secrets. Few people looked at her so closely, and *no one* looked at her like that. No one before Basil.

As if in a trance, Wren moved forward as well, so that they were mere inches apart. Basil's free hand came up, and a rush of heat passed over Wren as he cupped her cheek.

"Wren." His voice was as soft as silk, muffled in the close air of the tunnel.

She turned her face up invitingly, her heart picking up speed and her breath coming more rapidly. She saw Basil's eyes dart to her lips, and he shifted toward her. But just as her eyelids flickered, preparing to close, he released her abruptly and stepped back.

As he dropped their interlocked hands, mortification rushed in to take the place of his warm touch. Wren's eyes dropped to her feet, her stomach churning horribly. She'd been so sure he was going to kiss her. What a fool she must look.

"I'm sorry," Basil said, running a hand through his hair.

Whether he was apologizing for almost kissing her, or for pulling back, she didn't know. "I shouldn't have...I know I can't..."

He drew a deep breath, meeting her eyes and trying painfully to smile. "It's all a bit of a mess, isn't it?"

Wren said nothing, of course, but Basil read her as easily as he always did.

"Wren," he said quickly, stepping forward again and taking her hands in a reassuring grip. "Surely *you're* not embarrassed! You have nothing to be ashamed of. I'm the one who..." He grimaced. "I mean, you know I *wanted* to kiss you, don't you?"

Wren flushed at his plain speaking, glad for once of her iron-clad excuse for silence. She didn't have any words, even if she'd been allowed to use her voice.

"I'm not trying to make a secret of how I feel," Basil pressed. "I wanted to kiss you desperately."

His voice wasn't emotional, exactly, but Wren couldn't doubt the earnestness that radiated from him. So why *hadn't* he kissed her?

"But thanks to who I am, we both know I can't," he went on matter-of-factly. "So I shouldn't have put us both in that position. I'm sorry. You're just...so hard to ignore." His eyes burned into her, and Wren dropped her gaze to her feet again.

His words warmed her for a moment, but the feeling soon fell away, leaving utter confusion in its wake. If he wanted to kiss her, if he had no hesitation in communicating how he felt, why was it so impossible for him to follow through? What was it they supposedly both knew?

"Wren." She felt yet another change in mood, and looked up carefully, to see a sincere but less intimate expression on Basil's face. "I've grasped the implications of this combined power possibility as clearly as you must have. If there are Mistrans and Entolians working together against peace, we have to be very careful whom we trust." Seeing that Wren was about to look down again, he reached out a gentle hand and tilted up her chin. "If any Entolians were involved in the attempt to kill you, Wren, I don't know how I'll forgive myself."

The words were spoken simply enough, but the intensity of his expression sent strange flutters throughout Wren's body. She stepped back, still wrestling with all the abrupt changes of the last few minutes.

"Come on," said Basil briskly, clearly sensing that the moment was over. "Let's get back above ground, then we can figure out what to do next."

CHAPTER TWENTY-THREE

Basil

Basil made no attempt to break the silence as he led Wren back through the tunnel and up to the surface. He was surprised to find that it was dark outside—they'd been down in the mine longer than he'd realized. He cast a glance at his companion as they rejoined the rest of the group and picked their slow way across no man's land and into the Entolian camp.

He wasn't sure what was more heart-breaking—the fact that Wren had retreated into the careful facade she'd worn when they first met, or the fact that he knew her well enough now to still read the anguish underneath. He'd hurt her when he drew back, and that was exactly what he hadn't wanted to do. What he *had* wanted to do was to throw all considerations of responsibility to the wind and kiss her senseless, there in the privacy of the temporarily abandoned mine. What would her lips have felt like on his? Would she have let him bury his hands in that delightfully wild hair of hers, let him pull her flush against him?

He pulled his mind from those thoughts, struggling to keep his eyes on the uneven ground in front of him, instead of on the slim figure beside him. At this moment, she was about as far from the warm armful of his imagination as she could be. She held herself stiffly, looking anywhere but at him. He knew he'd made a mess of explaining himself, but she surely understood why they couldn't be together.

Given that there was no future for them, would she really want to start something they couldn't finish, guaranteeing further pain down the road?

Remembering his scornful response to the suggestion that he might become entangled with the princess, Basil almost groaned aloud. He was entangled, all right. Well and truly. And he had no idea what he would do when he inevitably had to return to Tola, leaving her behind in her silent, lonely world.

Determination raced through him. First, they would get to the bottom of whatever plot they'd stumbled on. It wasn't just about uncovering who had been stealing the precious fire jasper, and inciting conflict in order to do it. It wasn't even just about stopping the war. It was about making sure whoever had attacked Wren paid for it. If nothing else, he would ensure she was safe before he left Myst again.

He wasn't surprised when Wren refused the offer to spend the night in the Entolian camp. Thinking of the relative proximity of Tola, Basil wished fleetingly that he could take her back to his castle, let her sleep in comfort in one of the lavish guest suites. But he knew she wouldn't accept, and he didn't really want her to. It was abundantly clear that her entire trip had been undertaken without the approval of her parents, and King Lloyd would assuredly accuse him of kidnapping her if he got wind of her making it as far as the castle in Tola.

Promising to follow her back over the border as soon as it was light, Basil sent her off with an escort made up of soldiers whom the general swore on his life could be trusted.

"Well," he said, as soon as he and Lord Baldwin had reentered the general's tent, "it's quite a discovery we've made."

"To put it mildly," growled the general. He still looked furious about the clandestine activities happening right under his feet. He threw a look at Sergeant Obsidian, whom he'd obviously ordered to remain in the tent. "Care to explain why you didn't share your information earlier?"

The sergeant shrugged. "I didn't know about the mine, Sir. I only knew there was a general presence of magic, and like I said, I didn't think it was anything sinister."

"So you say," grunted the general, but Basil's sense was that he was irritable more than actually suspicious. "In any event, I've called for a patrol to explore the mines further. You will join them, Sergeant Obsidian."

"Yes sir." The young soldier sprang into a salute. The general dismissed him with another grunt, and turned to Basil.

"I anticipate returning to Myst tomorrow," Basil said, before the older man could speak. "I would like to take Sergeant Obsidian with me. I have my suspicions about who might be involved with the mine, and his particular abilities may come in very useful."

"As you wish, Your Majesty," said the general curtly. "He is yours to command."

Basil sighed. If only his position as king gave him half the authority everyone seemed to think it did. He felt like everything important to him remained utterly out of his control. His thoughts flew inevitably to Wren, but he forced them back to the present.

"Lord Baldwin and I are going to cross back to the Mistran camp now," he said decisively. "But send Sergeant Obsidian to me at first light. I'll speak with the Mistran general about letting him through. He can bring me a report about this patrol he's joined."

The general nodded, and Basil turned to take his leave before a sudden thought occurred to him.

"I should visit the wounded while I'm here," he said, turning back. "Perhaps I could do so tonight, rather than returning in the morning?"

"There aren't any, Your Majesty," said the general simply.

Basil blinked. "What?"

The general shrugged. "Any with injuries requiring ongoing care were moved to Tola soon after your last visit. And there are no new injuries, because there's been no fighting since then."

"Oh," said Basil, "of course." He felt heartened. "Well, that's something."

Glad to be away, he exited the tent. There was a dizzying amount still to be discussed and figured out, but it would have to wait. He wanted to make sure Wren wasn't spirited away before he could join her.

"King Basil," said Lord Baldwin, the moment they were clear of the general's presence, "are you sure it's a good idea to return to Myst? We're not exactly welcome there, and—"

"Of course I'm going back," said Basil impatiently. "My business there is unfinished, and I'm not going to run off like a thief in the night after telling King Lloyd I'd be returning."

"Well then, Your Majesty," said Lord Baldwin, with an edge of desperation, "perhaps you could give me leave to remain in Entolia."

Basil frowned at him. "You don't wish to join me? I never forced you to come to Myst, My Lord. You volunteered, remember?"

"I know I did, Your Majesty," said Lord Baldwin. "But I didn't expect to be gone so long from my holdings, and to be frank, after seeing that mine, I have no desire to be mixed up in whatever's brewing. I would be grateful if you would give me leave to return home."

Basil considered him with a frown. A week ago he would

have granted Lord Baldwin's request with a good grace, but something made him pause.

"I'm afraid I'm not willing to give you leave," he said bluntly. "I expect you to return to Myst with me, and see out our visit."

Lord Baldwin looked crestfallen, but he made no further attempt to argue.

The soldiers at the Mistran checkpoint didn't look excited to see the Entolians, but they made no attempt to hinder their passage. If nothing else, it was encouraging that Wren's return from the Entolian camp hadn't triggered the Mistran general to bar Basil's entry.

Basil had hoped for further speech with Wren, but he soon discovered that she was closely guarded. He still hadn't heard the full story of how she'd ended up in the tunnel all alone, but he could only assume that her disappearance had thrown her companions into a panic. Having ascertained that she was still in the camp, closeted in the largest tent on site, he had nothing to do but pass the night in an uneasy rest of his own.

In the morning, Wren's guardians were no more inclined to let Basil get near her than they had been in the evening. He did see Lady Anneliese coming and going from the princess's tent, and he debated hailing her. She was being courted by Sir Gelding, wasn't she? Should he warn her of their suspicions regarding the enchanter? Unsure of how deeply Wren trusted her, he decided to hold his peace. Surely Wren would tell her friend if she wished to.

Basil had expected Sergeant Obsidian to arrive early in the morning, but it was past noon when the young soldier finally appeared. Fortunately the Mistran group hadn't departed yet, although Basil wasn't sure what they were waiting for.

The sergeant had a good reason for his tardiness. He had spent most of the night patrolling the mines, and was able to give Basil a full report. From what the Mistran forces had discovered, the mine seemed to be fully empty for the present. Whoever was excavating it must be doing so in shifts, rather than constantly. The soldiers had explored many of the tunnels, and had followed them all the way to secret entrances, hidden well beyond the boundaries of the battlefield. Obsidian's presence had clearly been valuable—he'd been able to confirm that these entrances were protected by powerful cloaking enchantments, preventing anyone from discovering them from the outside who hadn't already passed through the tunnels.

Shortly after Sergeant Obsidian arrived, Basil received a different report, this one from the Entolian enchantress whom he'd left behind with Wren.

"Well," he said dryly, once he'd heard the details of Wren's exploits, "I'm no longer surprised she's being held captive by her own guards. They must have had heart failure when she disappeared into that tunnel."

The enchantress nodded. "There was quite a scene, Your Majesty. To tell the truth, I was detained myself until she reappeared."

"I'm sorry I put you in that position," said Basil with a grimace. "And I'm relieved they let you out when she returned."

"She wrote an epic on that slate of hers," smiled the enchantress. "I didn't see it, but she won them over. I didn't really blame them for being angry with me. I was terrified myself when the tunnel collapsed. I suspect her protective artifact saved her, but it didn't seem that the general knew about that. I suppose there's no way to hide something like that from people who actually live in the castle, but it seems it hasn't been widely advertised."

Basil nodded. "I'm sorry to ask it of you," he said, his gaze encompassing the enchantress's husband as well, "but are you willing to return to Myst with me?"

"Of course, Your Majesty," said the merchant. "We want to see this through."

Basil nodded gratefully.

"But if you're wanting to travel with the princess's group," the enchantress chimed in, "I suspect you'll have to wait a little while. Unless I'm mistaken, the Mistrans sent for reinforcements the moment the princess arrived at the camp, and they're making her wait until some of the king's guards arrive."

When the day wore away into evening, with still no sight of Wren, Basil didn't doubt the enchantress's guess. He toyed with the idea of getting a head start back to Myst, but decided it was best to wait for Wren, even if they weren't going to be given the chance to actually interact.

"Are those swans some kind of guardians for the princess?" Sergeant Obsidian asked, as the small group of Entolians shared a simple meal around one of the Mistran campfires.

Basil followed the sergeant's gaze upward, to where two swans were circling around the large tent in the center of the camp. Their presence, more than anything else, had convinced Basil that Wren was still on the site.

"I think they are, in a manner of speaking," he said. "Why do you ask?"

The sergeant frowned. "I can't really tell what's going on from this distance, but there's some kind of magic around them. I wondered if they'd been enchanted to follow her, or something."

"Is that possible?" Basil asked, intrigued.

Sergeant Obsidian shrugged. "If you have the right kind of power. I don't think anyone can control animals with the certainty one might control plants, for example. But some enchanters can influence them."

"I hadn't thought of that," mused the merchant enchantress, her eyes also on the swans. "There's definitely something strange about them, though, isn't there? I've never been up very close to them. They always fly away when we approach." She gave a chuckle. "They're as suspicious of Entolians as the rest of Mistra is. But even from here, I can sense some kind of magic around them."

Basil was giving the conversation only cursory attention, his thoughts having dropped to the occupant of the tent below the swans. Did she know he was out here, waiting for her? Was she still upset with him for what had happened in the tunnel? He wasn't even sure whether she was annoyed with him for pulling back, or for trying to kiss her in the first place. All he knew for certain was that when they'd parted, she'd barely been able to look him in the eye.

Half a dozen members of the royal guard arrived early the next morning, and in an impressively short time, the group from Myst were all ready to depart. The Entolians, although receiving no invitation, gathered in readiness as well. The captain of the royal guards acknowledged Basil's presence with appropriate respect, but his gaze was heavy with suspicion as it rested on the young king. Basil had no doubt that he'd been given a report of Wren's adventure over to the Entolian side of the battlefield, and that he didn't plan to let the foreign king near his charge.

It didn't really matter. There wasn't much Basil could say to Wren, given how things stood. It was enough to finally see her as she emerged from the tent at last. Her eyes scanned the group, and he was gratified to see them stop as they reached him. She sent him a wan smile, but she looked worn. No doubt she'd been severely lectured for her dangerous activities.

Basil returned her smile reassuringly, his eyes flicking up to the two swans once again circling above her. Wren seemed to follow his gaze, and in a familiar gesture, she pulled out her slate. A moment later, she was in silent conversation with the captain of the royal guard. The man approached Basil as the riders started to move, and requested politely but firmly that the two groups travel with some distance between them.

Although he acquiesced with outward calm, a frown creased Basil's eyebrows as his gaze traveled to Wren. The obvious conclusion was that she'd sent the guard to make the request. But why? Was she really so angry at him she didn't want him anywhere near her?

It was a full day's ride back to Myst, and Basil became increasingly discouraged as the day wore on. By the time they made their way through the city gates in the early evening, he was utterly weary and disheartened. Wren had made no effort to approach him during the journey, and the Mistran guards were watching him like they might watch a prisoner. What exactly was waiting for him back in Myst?

Any hope of speaking either to Wren or to King Lloyd on arrival evaporated the moment they entered the castle. Basil's suspicion that Wren had left Myst without her parents' knowledge or approval was confirmed as the king and queen surged into the castle's entryway and converged upon their daughter. Queen Liana's strained face showed fear and relief in equal measure, but King Lloyd looked furious. And he'd barely satisfied himself of Wren's well-being when he turned his gaze on Basil, entering the building with his small entourage.

"What is the meaning of this?" hissed the Mistran king, striding across the space. "You needed to visit your general, did you?" His voice was heavy with sarcasm. "I don't know by what means you lured my daughter out of the city, but—"

A loud clap startled both the kings. They turned to see Wren, looking mortified, and quite as angry as her father. Her eyes were fixed on King Lloyd, and her brows were drawn together.

Basil, who had stood solidly in the face of his host's wrath, took the opening afforded by the king's distraction.

"You're under a misapprehension, Your Majesty. Far from luring Princess Wren from Myst, I was completely unaware of her decision to leave the city until our paths converged at the front lines. But I daresay she'll explain all that to you, if you give her the chance."

King Lloyd's eyes narrowed in anger. "Do you think I need you to tell me how to communicate with my own daughter?"

Basil blinked in surprise. "Of course not."

"Guards." The king turned to the Mistran guards standing nearby. "Escort King Basil and his companions to their rooms, and ensure that they stay there."

"Lloyd!" The warning in the queen's voice was clear, but her husband paid her no heed.

"I will not be your prisoner, Your Majesty," Basil said firmly. "If we are no longer welcome here, my people and I will leave."

But even as he said the words, his eyes slid past the king to rest on Wren's face. Their gazes locked, and he paused, taken aback by the longing in her eyes. For weeks she'd avoided him, and on the journey back to Myst she'd had nothing to say to him. So why did her eyes beg him not to leave, as clearly as if she'd spoken the words?

"No one is going anywhere until I get to the bottom of what's going on," said King Lloyd grimly.

Forcing down his own anger, Basil brought his eyes back to the king's face. "I can understand that, Your Majesty. It's not that I wish to leave—I have a great deal I need to discuss with you. My visit to the front lines was...illuminating." Again his eyes sought Wren's, and he was heartened by her nod of encouragement. Looking again at her father, Basil added, "I hope what I have discovered will help bring us closer to peace."

King Lloyd still looked angry, but his frown also showed confusion. After a moment of hesitation, he seemed to find a way to save face. "The dinner hour has past, King Basil. I will have food brought to your rooms, and those of your people."

Without another word, he turned and swept back across the entrance hall, his wife and daughter carried along with his entourage as they all retreated further into the castle. Right before she passed through a doorway, Wren turned slightly back to Basil, sending him the smallest of smiles.

He returned it, but she was already gone.

"Your Majesty," muttered Lord Baldwin from Basil's side, sounding more agitated than Basil had ever heard him. "Surely we're not going to stay under such conditions." He glanced up at the guards looming over them. "King Lloyd fully intends us to be his prisoners. All that talk of sending dinner to our rooms was merely dressing up our captivity in fancy wrappings."

Basil didn't immediately answer, his thoughts swirling. He pictured the hesitant smile on Wren's face as her father had swept her from the room, and suddenly the memory of her nearness in the tunnel overwhelmed him, making it hard to think straight.

"Your Majesty?" Lord Baldwin prompted. "We should leave at once, return to Tola while we still can."

Basil turned to his advisor with a rueful smile. "We're not leaving, My Lord."

For once, he thought the nobleman might be right, that the treatment of the other king was genuinely inconsistent with Basil's dignity as king of his own people. But Basil was honest enough with himself to know that while Wren begged him— however silently—to stay by her side, he wasn't going anywhere.

Lord Baldwin looked even more agitated, but he couldn't speak freely in front of the guards. He waited unhappily while Basil requested an additional room be prepared for Sergeant Obsidian. Then, looking like a whipped puppy, he followed Basil up the stairs to the second floor passage where their suites were located, the guards shadowing them too closely for politeness.

Food was indeed brought to Basil's rooms, but he could hardly sit still long enough to eat it. His thoughts were with Wren, and whatever conversation she was having with her parents. Had she told them all about the mine yet? Would their suspicions about Sir Gelding be enough to convince King Lloyd to arrest the enchanter that very night?

Hours passed, and still Basil heard nothing. Feeling nowhere near sleep, he paced his room, certain that at any moment a message would arrive for him, if not from King Lloyd, at least from Wren. But when a knock finally fell on his door, shortly before midnight, he was disappointed to discover only Lord Baldwin on the other side.

A quick glance past the nobleman showed a silent face off between the Mistran guards who seemed to have trailed Lord Baldwin from his suite to Basil's, and Basil's own guards, who were standing to attention outside his room.

With a grunt, Basil stood aside and gestured for Lord Baldwin to enter, shutting the door on the territorial display.

"What brings you here, My Lord?" he asked Lord Baldwin impatiently. "Surely it's almost midnight."

"Half an hour from it, Your Majesty." Lord Baldwin's arms were crossed, and he twisted his sleeve nervously in his hand. "And I came because I need to speak with you."

Basil resumed his pacing, irritation flickering to life inside him. "I don't want to hear any more about how we should turn tail and run home to Tola. I'm committed to this course, and I intend to see it through, no matter how unreasonable King Lloyd is being." He shot Lord Baldwin a look. "And I'll acknowledge that he's been extraordinarily unreasonable." He stopped pacing with a sigh. "Although I suppose it's to be expected. If Wren disappeared without his knowledge, he must have been terrified he'd lost the last of his children. Who knows what tale the Mistran guards have told him about her disappearing into the mine, and emerging from the Entolian side with me in tow?"

He chewed his lip thoughtfully, almost forgetting his companion's presence.

Lord Baldwin cleared his throat, sounding more uncomfortable than Basil had ever heard him. "Your graciousness toward King Lloyd is commendable, Your Majesty. I don't think I would be half as understanding in your position."

Basil just blinked at him. Lord Baldwin hadn't so far been one to try flattery to get what he wanted, but it was clear he hadn't yet reached his point. The nobleman walked stiffly across the room, pausing at one of the tall windows that looked into the castle's central garden.

"I didn't come to talk about King Lloyd, Your Majesty," Lord Baldwin said at last, his back still to Basil. "Or to urge you once again to leave."

"What did you come to talk about?" Basil prompted, when Lord Baldwin fell silent.

The nobleman turned to face him. "I wished to tell you that I have come to greatly respect you, King Basil. You are a good leader. And, if I'm honest, you're not at all what I expected when I agreed to come on this journey." He gave a rueful smile. "Knowing how you value honesty, I will acknowledge that at first I thought the same as the rest of the Lords' Council, that in addition to being too young and inexperienced for your role, you were rash and without tact, and would almost certainly make a mess of the whole business."

Basil took no offense at the honest words, but he couldn't help grimacing at the blunt but undoubtedly accurate description of his advisors' view of him.

"But I've learned more of you in these past weeks than I expected to in a lifetime. Although I don't always agree with your decisions, I can say without reservation that you've proved us all wrong. And I hope the other lords will be brought to recognize it as well."

Basil frowned. It wasn't that he didn't appreciate the praise, but there was no doubt in his mind that Lord Baldwin was still building to his point, and Basil couldn't help feeling apprehensive about what it might be. He moved toward the nobleman, and as he did so, his eyes were drawn to the window behind Lord Baldwin.

No servants had attended him since his arrival, other than the one who'd brought him food, and Basil had been too distracted to pull the curtains closed himself. The window afforded him a clear view of the garden, bathed in spring moonlight, quiet and unmoving save for the dark silhouettes of the trees swaying gently in a light breeze.

That and a figure, descending the wall of one of the castle's other wings. With a sharp intake of breath, Basil stepped up beside Lord Baldwin, his eyes riveted on the form. Dark as the shape was against the darkness of the night, there was no mistaking that figure. Or that exuberant hair.

"What is she doing?" he muttered involuntarily, hardly knowing whether to be entertained or alarmed by the sight of Wren climbing precariously down the stone walls from her second story window. He would hazard a guess that her door was being guarded as closely as his own.

"Is that the princess?"

Lord Baldwin's startled question belatedly reminded Basil of his company. He nodded vaguely, his eyes still fixed on Wren's form. When she reached the ground without incident, he let out a sigh of relief.

"But why is she climbing out of her window?" Lord Baldwin asked, sounding aghast.

"I have no idea," said Basil. A moment's reflection, however, made him think he might. He knew better than anyone how fond she was of her swans, and how protective of the injured one. She'd been away for almost a week. She probably wanted to check on them, and he was guessing that outing wasn't sanctioned by whoever had charge of her right now. She'd disappeared from sight now, but there could be little doubt she was heading for the big pond in the center of the gardens.

He chewed his lip again. "I wonder if I should go to her."

"You can't go into the gardens now, Your Majesty," protested Lord Baldwin. "I doubt the guards will let you stir from your room at this hour of the night, and they certainly won't let you anywhere near the princess."

Basil didn't answer, barely listening to the nobleman's words. "I hope her parents weren't too harsh with her," he mused, still staring into the garden, although he could no longer see Wren. "I'm pretty sure her whole outing was based on a misunderstanding from my letter to her, so it's really more my fault than hers."

"King Lloyd will have no difficulty believing that, Your Majesty," said Lord Baldwin dryly. "If you come out of this in one piece I'll be relieved, and if we leave Myst without war being reignited, I'll own myself astonished."

Basil turned from the window at last, frowning at his advisor. "I'm not leaving until we've reached peace, My Lord." He glanced back into the night. "I'm more determined on that than ever." He didn't add the thought in his mind—that if true war broke out between the two kingdoms, he'd lose any hope of continuing his friendship with Wren—but Lord Baldwin seemed to understand anyway.

"You've come to care very deeply for her, haven't you, Your Majesty?"

Basil turned at the soft words, frowning as he tried in vain to read the expression in Lord Baldwin's eyes. He had no patience right now for the nobleman's overblown discomfort regarding Wren's reputation.

"I have no hesitation in saying that I consider her more deserving of my respect than almost anyone I've ever met," he told Lord Baldwin shortly.

To his surprise, the nobleman responded with a wry smile. "I didn't ask if you respect her, Your Majesty. I asked if you care for her." He gave Basil a meaningful look. "Deeply."

Basil turned back to the window, frustrated with the heat he could feel rising up his neck. For once, he had no desire to be forthright. Politics and military strategy were one thing. Matters of his heart were quite another. It wasn't that he was rattled by Lord Baldwin's blatantly poor opinion of Wren. That reflected badly on the nobleman, not the princess. But Basil was fully aware of the futility of his cause when it came to Wren, and it made him anything but eager to discuss it.

"I will say no more, Your Majesty." Lord Baldwin gave a deep bow, his tone respectful. To Basil's surprise, he began to move toward the door.

"Wait," said Basil, and Lord Baldwin paused. "What did you come in here to tell me?"

"What I've already said," Lord Baldwin answered, not quite meeting Basil's eye. "That I have great respect for you, and great confidence in your rule."

"Lord Baldwin." Basil made no attempt to hide his exasperation. "Have you forgotten how much I dislike anything less than total honesty?"

Lord Baldwin's smile was pained. "In this case, Your Majesty, you wouldn't like total honesty either."

And with those cryptic words, he bowed himself out of the room.

Basil stared after him, bemused and frustrated. He wished he hadn't drawn the nobleman's attention to Wren's descent from her window, because before that point he'd been sure Lord Baldwin had nerved himself up to say whatever was on his mind. Basil's gaze drifted back to the moonlit gardens. The obvious conclusion was that whatever Lord Baldwin had left unsaid had related to Wren. Basil felt his face set in grim lines. Perhaps Lord Baldwin was right, and this was one occasion where he didn't want to hear the other man's honest opinion.

Dismissing the matter temporarily from his mind, he let his thoughts fly back to Wren. If he strained his ears, he thought he could hear distant splashes, like wings on the surface of a pond.

He sighed. Lord Baldwin was right. An attempt to wander through the castle and join the princess for a midnight tryst would surely lead at best to conflict between the Mistran and Entolian guards currently outside his rooms, and at worst to a full scale war between the kingdoms. He pulled the window up, wincing as it groaned loudly, and peered down the wall. There were solid looking vines growing up this section of castle. He could probably climb down just as Wren had done, and no one would be the wiser.

After a moment's consideration, he reluctantly abandoned the idea. His own experience had just proved that anyone could be watching from the many windows that faced inward into the gardens. If he was observed meeting the princess in the dead of night, it would do neither Entolia, nor Wren herself, any favors.

He didn't intend to tamely sit by and let King Lloyd prevent contact between him and Wren though, he thought with determination. He had enough propriety to avoid doing so at midnight, but at first light, he was climbing down the creeper and going looking for her, without the escort of either set of guards.

CHAPTER TWENTY-FOUR

Wren

Wren lay unmoving in her bed, her eyes squeezed shut a little too tightly to be convincing. She couldn't help it—inwardly she was still fuming too violently to fully relax her body.

She tried to make allowances for her father's fears, but this was a new level of unreasonable. Confined to her room with armed guards at the entrance to keep her in...she may as well be locked in the dungeons.

As her father most likely intended Basil to be, come morning.

Wren's stomach churned uncomfortably. The trouble she'd brought down on Basil's head was the worst part of her whole adventure. She'd forced her father to read her meticulously written out description of what really happened at least five times, but he was still determined to behave as though Basil had deceived him with his plans, and abducted Wren right from the castle.

Not to mention poor Lady Anneliese was now in disfavor with the king and queen. The noblewoman's own parents had looked just about ready to murder her. Not that Lady Anneliese had shown much distress over that. Judging by the rigid air of shock she'd worn for the last couple of days, Wren deduced that her friend was still reeling from the accusations Wren had confided in her regarding the man she'd just agreed to marry. Not that she'd be marrying Sir Gelding once Wren's father had him arrested.

Which brought Wren right back to the source of her frustrations. She could still see the impatience in her father's eyes as he probed her story over and over, demanding what proof she had against the enchanter. Truth be told, Wren hadn't realized until her father pressed her just how little proof she actually had. It had seemed so clear, and so obvious, when she'd been down in the mine with Basil. She'd had no doubt whatsoever that the enchanter was behind it all, or at the very least involved.

But it seemed that King Lloyd didn't consider Basil's word that the Entolian crown hadn't built the mine very convincing evidence.

Wren had tried arguing that the general himself told her that Sir Gelding had visited the site. While her father assured her he would be discussing the matter extensively with the general himself, he found even that information less compelling than Wren had hoped. According to her own account, the spot Sir Gelding had inspected hadn't been a true entrance to the mine. The only entrance she'd actually found had been on Entolia's side of the battleground.

That point had certainly made Wren pause. For a while she'd been stumped as to why Sir Gelding had visited that particular point. But eventually it hit her—it must be the place where the army's territory came closest to impinging on the mine. Presumably Sir Gelding's visits to "inspect the ore" were actually intended to check whether the mine was secure, and not at risk of discovery by the army. Wren had no doubt Sir

Gelding's visits had also included actual attendance at the mine via a clandestine entrance on the Mistran side.

However, given this argument was not only speculation on her part, but was a theory she'd clearly come up with in the course of their conversation, Wren wasn't really surprised her father hadn't given it much weight.

She wasn't sure what frustrated her more—her father's flat refusal to believe her, or her mother's refusal to weigh in at all. Worse than either, though, were all her father's comments about Basil being a snake who had clearly intended from the beginning to lure away Wren's allegiance. She squirmed in her bed at the memory. Although he hadn't used the words, he clearly believed that Wren was besotted, and that it was a result of some kind of attempt by Basil to seduce her.

If only, Wren thought, her mind flying to the moment she and Basil had shared in the mine, and his outright declaration that they couldn't be together. The thought was flippant, but it nevertheless sent a flush of embarrassment over Wren. Of course she was glad Basil wasn't trying to seduce her. But the memory of his hesitation still stung more than she liked to admit to herself. When he'd laid his hand against her cheek, and looked into her eyes with that steady gaze of his, any remaining denial within her had fled. She'd fallen hard for Entolia's young king, and there was no turning back. And for a moment, she'd really believed that he felt the same, that he saw past her enforced oddities enough to actually want her.

He'd said he wanted to kiss her, hadn't he? The answer came back immediately. Whatever he'd said, he hadn't kissed her. He'd said she was hard to ignore, as well. Clearly he was trying his utmost to ignore her, to ignore the attraction he claimed to feel.

Thanks to who I am, we both know I can't, he'd said, so simply, as if he was in no doubt that she understood.

But she hadn't understood, not at the time. It had taken her an embarrassingly large portion of the ride back to Myst to grasp what he'd meant. He was the king of Entolia. She knew he felt the connection between them as strongly as she did. But he was also one of the most practical people she knew, and she didn't doubt that he would put the interests of his kingdom before his own heart. And while personally he might be willing look past her eccentric silence, and her pet swans, he couldn't do so on behalf of Entolia. She wasn't a fit queen for his kingdom in her current state.

She understood the reasoning. She could even respect it. But it stung, nonetheless. And the knowledge that she would soon be able to emerge from her self-imposed silence didn't remove that sting in the least.

And as if she didn't feel wretched enough already, the betrayal in her mother's eyes as she read Wren's confession about how she'd given them all the slip made Wren feel worse than all the rest. Her mother had opened up to her about how terrified she was of losing the daughter whom she believed to be her only surviving child, and Wren had thrown it in her face by running away and putting herself in harm's way. *Tomorrow,* Wren promised herself. *Tomorrow you'll be able to explain it all, and she'll understand that you wouldn't have put yourself in danger for any less cause than keeping the boys safe.*

And with that thought, all other considerations melted away. She'd pushed hard on the journey home for good reason. She wasn't likely to lose track of the date, not with the six year deadline so close. She'd been determined to make it back to Myst in time for the day she'd waited for all those years.

And now it was mere minutes away.

With an enormous effort, Wren forced her breathing to slow, and her limbs to relax. She wasn't sure if the curse would lift at midnight, or would wait until dawn. But she fully intended to be by the lake when the clock struck twelve, just to be safe. She had no illusions that the guards outside her door would allow her to simply walk out of the room, so she would have to do something she hadn't attempted in years, and climb out her window straight into the gardens. And in order to do that, she needed her governess to be convinced that she was asleep, and retreat for the night.

The next time the older woman poked her head into the room, it was to see a serene princess breathing steadily and lying unmoving under her covers. Still muttering disapprovingly about Wren's misadventure, she withdrew to her own room for what Wren trusted would be the final time that night.

Waiting another twenty minutes, Wren slid carefully out of her bed. She crept across the room, pausing to slip a cloak over her nightdress, and shoes on her feet. After a moment's thought, she tied on her pocket as well, just in case she needed her slate. She eased up her window without eliciting any noise from her governess's room, and a moment later she was lowering herself down the wall outside.

She'd expected it to be harder than when she was eleven, given she wasn't as active as she had been in her childhood. But in actual fact it was considerably easier, due to the longer reach of her limbs. In minutes, she was safely on the ground, amid the quiet rustlings of the moon-bathed garden. Pulling her cloak tightly around herself, she hurried between the bushes, avoiding the marked paths in case anyone was watching from a window. Ari appeared beside her as she moved, and she sent him a quick smile. She'd seen him from her window earlier in the evening, and it had been heartening during her painful interview with her parents to know she had an ally nearby, however little use he could actually be to her.

The two of them reached the pond mere minutes before

midnight. Alighting beside her, Ari pressed his sleek body against her legs.

Do you really think it's going to work?

Underneath the deeper voice of the eighteen-year-old, Wren could hear the eagerness of the twelve-year-old boy she'd last seen in the woods that day.

It's going to work. She tried to inject more confidence into her words than she felt. But surely it would work. It had to.

Midnight, do you think? Ari asked.

Wren shrugged. *I don't know. It might be dawn. But I'm pretty sure it will be one or the other.*

The other swans had spotted them, and were gliding across the smooth surface of the pond, leaving silent ripples in their wake. They all huddled around Wren, even Caleb flopping awkwardly onto the shore without her assistance.

Many familiar voices sounded in her mind as they all pressed against her.

We didn't think you'd make it back in time!

Bram told us what you found! Do you really think it was Sir Gelding?

Almost midnight, Wren. You're almost free.

The last voice was Caleb's. Wren smiled mistily at him. It was like her oldest brother to think of her, but they were the ones who would soon be free. Things would change for her too, of course. Wren's thoughts flew unbidden to Basil. Would the recovery of her voice, and the revelation of who her swans were, be enough to overcome his scruples about her suitability to stand at his side in Entolia?

Surely it would be. But somehow the thought didn't erase the ache she felt whenever she remembered the sensation of him stepping away from her in the mine.

Suddenly, the great castle clock began to chime. They all froze. Nothing in the garden moved—even the breeze had died down, and the very plants seemed to be holding their breath. The air was thick with some terrifying mix of excitement and nerves as one girl and six swans stared at each other in wordless anticipation.

One. Two. Three. Four. Five. Wren counted the strokes in her mind, tension rising within her. *Six. Seven. Eight. Nine.* Without deciding to do it, she found she had squeezed her eyes shut. *Ten. Eleven. Twelve.*

She suddenly realized she was holding her breath, and she drew in a shuddering gasp of air as her eyes flew open.

Nothing had happened.

Six swans still clustered around her, their feathers pressed against her nightgown, their beady eyes fixed unblinkingly on her.

Well, Averett's matter-of-fact voice sounded in her mind, *that was anticlimactic, wasn't it?*

It didn't work. Ari sounded panicked. *Why didn't it work?*

Don't worry. Wren fought back her own rising terror. *Midnight clearly isn't the trigger. It will most likely be at dawn. I've read a lot about enchantments, remember. Sunrise and sunset are significant times, and enchantments are often tied to them.*

She's right. Caleb's calm voice sounded in her mind as a soft bugle wafted out from him around the group. *Which means tomorrow will be a big day for us. We should all try to sleep for a few hours.*

In tense silence, the other swans detached themselves from the huddle and drifted back out onto the water. Caleb turned to Wren.

Our last night on the water. Quite momentous.

What if it didn't work because of me? Wren whispered into his mind, disregarding his attempt at lightness. *What if I broke the counterforce when I spoke that time? Or when I wrote about your fate? Or when I accidentally started showing Basil the truth?*

It's going to work, Caleb told her firmly. *Dawn, like you said.*

Wren didn't reply. She was too wound up, too full of fear to have reassuring words. And she didn't want to infect him with her panic. Whatever she said to her brothers, she'd really thought it would be midnight.

She helped Caleb back into the pond, then sat down at the water's edge. For a long time she just sat, watching her brothers floating on the surface, out in the middle of the pond. She heard the clock strike one, and pulled her cloak more tightly around her. She couldn't imagine she would be able to sleep, and didn't even intend to try. But the day's hard ride, and the various stresses of the preceding weeks had made her weary in mind, and she was glad enough to lay herself along the ground and let her thoughts drift while she waited for the sun.

"Wren. Wren?"

The familiar voice broke into Wren's consciousness, and she shifted slightly. A warm hand gripped her arm, its touch reassuring somehow. But why was her bed so hard and uncomfortable?

"Wren, wake up."

Basil. Her thoughts caught up with a jolt. What was Basil doing in her bedroom? Her eyes flew open, and she gasped at the tanned face hovering above her, hazel eyes piercing her, and disheveled waves of brown hair glinting in the light of early morning.

Early morning! Everything came rushing back, and Wren pushed herself upright with another gasp. Disregarding Basil, she spun wildly on the spot, her gaze fixating on the surface of the nearby pond.

With a sickening thud, her heart plummeted into her stomach.

Six swans floated on the surface of the water. Five of them were still asleep, heads tucked under their wings. But one was awake, a wing bent away from his body at an awkward angle, and his eyes fixed on Wren with a look that was much too knowing for a bird.

There was so much in that look. Reassurance, understanding. Devastating grief.

Wren could barely take any of it in. All she could comprehend was the horrible truth that it hadn't worked. Dawn had unarguably arrived, and her brothers were still trapped in their avian forms. For six years she'd given it everything she had, and it hadn't been enough.

"Wren? Are you all right?"

Basil's tentative voice reminded her of his presence. Wren felt the tears welling up, and without even thinking about it, she turned and threw herself onto his chest. His arms flew up as instinctively as they had the time she'd attacked him on this very spot, but this time his grip didn't restrain. Instead his arms closed around her, and he pulled her close.

Wren was hardly aware of the gesture. A storm had broken upon her, and she could do nothing but let it lash her with its fury. Abandoning any pretense of dignity she wept brokenly against Basil, her face buried in his chest, and her tears saturating his tunic.

He didn't seem to mind. He just held her tightly, saying nothing and asking no questions as he let her ride the wave of her anguish. Finally, tortuously, her sobs slowed, and eventually stopped. She sniffled herself into stillness, but made no attempt to draw back from the warm security of Basil's embrace.

Pressed flush against him as she was, she could feel the steady beat of his heart, and feel the warmth of his breath in her hair. In spite of everything, she felt safe. The last time she'd felt so safe had been when she was a child, who didn't understand the dangers around her, and thought her big brother could protect her from everything.

The safety she felt in Basil's arms wasn't like her blind trust in Caleb, though. She knew perfectly well how dangerous her world was. And she knew that Basil couldn't protect her from the storms, either physically or emotionally. But his steady presence told her that he would weather the storm with her, not flinching away either from her limitations or her pain. And that was a kind of security she'd never known before. The kind that had seemed impossible in her years of isolation. The kind that made her believe she had the strength to withstand whatever was thrown at her.

She straightened her back at last, lifting an arm to wipe the tears from her face.

But Basil beat her to it. His hand suddenly cupped her head, like it had done in the mine, and his thumb moved gently across her cheek, wiping away the moisture. The simple tenderness of the gesture made tears pool once again in Wren's eyes, but she didn't let them fall.

She met Basil's gaze, and held it. His hazel eyes were clear and unblinking, and when she nodded in a silent gesture of gratitude, she knew he understood her. Basil asked her no questions, but suddenly the urge to bare her heart to him overwhelmed her, and she stepped out of his arms, pulling out her slate.

I know I can't lean on you, but thank you for being here. With me.

Basil frowned at the words, his clear gaze passing back up to her. "Why can't you lean on me?" he demanded unexpectedly. "I'd like nothing better." His lips quirked up in a half smile that drew Wren's eyes inevitably to them. "I don't mean to belittle your distress, but it felt pretty nice when you leaned against me just now."

Wren shot him an exasperated look. She was trying to be sentimental. Of course he had to ruin it with his bluntness. Resisting the urge to roll her eyes, she scrawled another message.

I meant emotionally, obviously. I know
I'm not good for Entolia, but I can't tell
you what your friendship means to me.

That sobered him at once. "What does that mean, you're not good for Entolia?"

Wren shrugged. Was he really going to make her explain it, when he was the one who'd declared it to be an insurmountable barrier? That was hardly chivalrous.

"No, don't fob me off," said Basil sharply. "What do you mean you're not good for Entolia?"

Wren frowned, a little bewildered by his manner. She raised her hands helplessly, then tapped her throat to indicate her silence. And, unable to bring herself to look at them in their current form, she waved an arm back at her swan brothers.

Basil's eyes followed her gestures, then settled back on her face. His evident confusion turned quite suddenly to a look of horror as he once again understood more than what she'd said.

"Wren!" he gasped, clearly aghast. "Is that what you thought I meant when I said we can't be together? That your silence and your ridiculous birds somehow make you inadequate to be my queen?"

Her gaze shifting back and forth between Basil's eyes in

consternation, Wren nodded. Of course that was what he'd meant.

"That's outrageous!" Basil cried, his voice loud enough to wake those of the boys still sleeping.

Wren heard an angry honk that sounded like Conan, but she didn't look around. Her eyes were fixed on Basil's face in fascination.

"Wren." He took her hands, the warmth of his fingers sending sparks shooting all the way up her arms. "That's the last thing I was thinking. I don't know why you're silent, but I do know it makes no difference to how incredible a person you are." His gaze flicked to the pond. "The swans I understand even less, but to have you with me, I could live with a thousand of them."

Wren didn't know whether to laugh or cry. Even as she attempted a chuckle, a tear leaked out. Basil saw it and immediately released one of her hands so he could once again wipe it away. His palm enveloped Wren's cheek, making it hard to think straight.

"Wren, I love you," said Basil simply, knocking the breath from Wren's body. "I don't know when it started exactly, or when I knew it for sure. I think I got an inkling when I heard about your accident in the pond. And the fury I felt when I discovered it wasn't an accident..." He shook his head slightly. "Certainly I knew it by the time you appeared in that mine, wandering in as if it was normal for you to be exploring abandoned tunnels alone." He gave her a wry smile. "I definitely didn't come to Myst looking to fall in love. To be frank,"—of course he had to be frank—"I really don't have time for romance." The tenderness of his smile robbed the words of any insult. "But I couldn't help it, not once I got to know you."

Wren leaned into him, everything else temporarily forgotten

as she gloried in the wonder of being not only seen but loved by this incredible man.

"I thought I was being responsible by not saying all this in the mine," Basil went on. "That I was saving us both pain. But if the alternative is you thinking you're not good enough, then clearly I should have done this in the first place."

And without another word, he pulled her tightly against him once more, and crushed his lips to hers. Wren's gasp of surprise was swallowed in the insistency of his kiss, and after the first moment of shock, she felt the tension drain from her body as she molded herself against him and returned his kiss unreservedly.

If she'd thought about it—which in all honesty she had—she would have imagined Basil to be a methodical, no-nonsense sort of kisser, like he was in speech.

He was nothing like she'd imagined.

His hold was so possessive she felt utterly wrapped up in him, and his lips moved against hers with an abandon that sent heat shooting through every inch of her. She leaned up on her toes to reach him better, her hand sliding up his neck. One of Basil's arms was wrapped around her waist, still holding her against him, but she felt the other one tangling in her unrestrained hair.

Somewhere behind her, Wren heard a loud trumpeting sound, but she had no space in her mind for anything but Basil, the feel of him, the warmth of his breath, the—

"Ow!" The cry came from Basil, his voice still breathless from their kiss. Before Wren knew what was happening, his arm had fallen from her side, and he'd stepped back. "Ouch!" he yelled again. "Stop that!"

Blinking in confusion, Wren looked down to see a flash of orange in a blur of white as a sharp beak lashed out again at Basil's legs.

Scowling, Wren dropped to her knees and reached for the bird.

That's enough, Conan! Leave him be!

That's my little sister your hands are all over! Conan snapped, even though he must know Basil couldn't understand him. He puffed out his chest, his feathers all ruffled as he attempted to lunge free of Wren's restraining arms.

Suddenly the humor of it all hit Wren, and she rocked back on her heels, laughter bubbling up uncontrollably. Basil had been wincing as he examined his injured leg, but at her laughter he looked up. A rueful expression passed over his face, and the next moment he joined her mirth. Conan flapped his wings in agitation at being laughed at, but even he seemed to realize that further attacks against Basil would just make him even more ridiculous. An admonitory honk from Caleb on the water was the final straw, and he slunk away, back toward the pond.

Still chuckling, Wren pushed herself to her feet again. She grimaced when she saw that Basil was actually bleeding, her gaze apologetic as it traveled up to his face.

He was smiling at her with such a spark in his eyes that she felt heat once again rush up her cheeks. Not least because of the timely—and somewhat horrifying—reminder that she'd just been passionately kissed for the first time in her life, and her brothers had watched it happen.

Basil stepped back toward her, but Wren had returned to reality now, and the need to understand had driven away the abandon of those reckless moments in Basil's arms. She picked her slate up from where it had fallen beside her, and scribbled five words.

I still don't understand why.

Basil frowned at the message, his face settling once again into serious lines. "Why we can't be together?" he asked, and she nodded. "I thought it was obvious. I'm Entolia's king. I will always have to live in Tola, and give my life in service to its people."

Wren lifted her eyebrows in a silent prompt, still not sure of his point.

"Well, you're...you're the future monarch of Mistra," said Basil, clearly confused as to why he had to explain it. "You are your father's heir. Your life belongs to Mistra, so you can never belong to me." His voice softened, a husky note entering it. "However much I might want you to."

He stepped close again, and one hand traveled up to cradle the side of her neck. "Your father would probably have me arrested for conspiring against his crown if he knew how desperately I wish I could carry you away to Entolia with me forever."

For a long moment, Wren just stared at him, her mind whirling. What a fool she'd been! Of course it was obvious, just as he'd said. He thought she was as tied to the Mistran crown as he was to the Entolian one, so he'd thought there was no hope for a future together. She couldn't very well rule Mistra from Tola.

A little overwhelmed by the parade of emotions she'd been whisked through, she let out a sudden laugh. Relief washed over her as she realized that Basil hadn't held back because he thought she wasn't enough—he thought she was too much, too important. He thought she was something she wasn't, and once he understood that she wasn't her father's true heir, there would be no more barrier to—

The reality that had temporarily fled at Basil's touch came rushing back with triple the potency, and Wren's laughter died on her lips. She felt so crushed by the memory of her brothers' state that she actually swayed on her feet. Basil's arms steadied her at once, his expression concerned and confused, but Wren couldn't look him in the eye anymore.

He might be right after all. For six years she'd stubbornly refused to train to be queen, insisting in the privacy of her mind that Caleb would take his rightful place. But six years was up, and he hadn't been freed from the curse. And even she had to acknowledge that a swan couldn't become king of Mistra. Would she have to be her father's heir after all? A position which she didn't want, which she'd refused to prepare for, and which might now separate her from the man she loved?

She raised her hands to cover her face as a fresh wave of despair washed over her. She was so caught up in her anguish, she hardly heard the loud cracking sound above her. Looking up in a daze, she could do nothing but stare stupidly at the enormous branch dangling loosely directly above her head.

CHAPTER TWENTY-FIVE

Basil

Basil's eyes darted up as a loud snap rent the air. At sight of the massive tree limb hurtling toward Wren, he let out a cry and dove at her. But Wren had stepped away from him when she'd been gripped by whatever silent realization had turned her laughter into despair, and in the split second before the branch hit her, he knew he wouldn't be fast enough.

Except, the branch didn't hit her.

She was too stunned to even leap out of the way, staring up at it like a moth hypnotized by flame. But instead of crushing her, the huge branch seemed to glance off an invisible shield just above her head. It fell at a strange angle to one side of her, crashing harmlessly into the reeds at the water's edge.

Wren's wide eyes passed from the branch to Basil's face, nothing in her expression except shock. Then, slowly, she moved one hand up to her throat, and tugged at the chain around her neck. The heavy signet ring popped out from under her gown, and Basil stared at it, his breath coming in uneven pants.

The protective enchantment on the artifact had saved her.

Basil felt weak with relief, but the emotion was mingled with horror at the realization that if she hadn't been wearing it, he wouldn't have been able to prevent her being crushed before his eyes.

And there was no way that branch had fallen by mere chance.

As that certainty grew within him, so did the anger. Someone had just tried to kill Wren, right in front of him. And it wasn't the first time, either. He stepped instinctively toward her, one arm shooting out to pull her close even as his head whipped around them, searching for any sign of someone lurking nearby.

"Plants again," Basil muttered darkly. He wondered if their guess was correct, that Sir Gelding was somehow using the power of the Entolian enchanter whose farm had been overrun by the battlefield. Was Sir Gelding here right now, lurking out of sight somewhere, wielding his borrowed magic? Basil wished Sergeant Obsidian had been with him. He might have been able to follow the magic back to its source, like he'd done at the battleground.

He'd barely grasped hold of Wren when the pair of them were mobbed by a flurry of feathers. The swans had obviously witnessed what had happened, and it had set off their bizarre protectiveness for Wren. They clustered around her, trumpeting and flapping their wings in agitation. The strangeness of her manner as she laid a hand against each of them tugged at Basil's mind, but he didn't give in to his curiosity. He had much more important things to think about than the swans.

Basil hadn't bothered to count the swans, but he realized when one suddenly dropped from the sky at Wren's side that they hadn't all been hovering around her. The swan pressed itself against the princess's legs, bugling urgently. Basil squinted at it, fairly sure that it was the one which so often followed him around. Suddenly Wren's eyes widened, and she dove for her slate again. Her hands flew over it with such speed that Basil could hardly read the message she shoved toward him.

Sir Gelding. He's here, but he's escaping.

"How do you know?" Basil asked sharply.

But Wren was already running, following the swan as it once again took to the air. Basil raced after her, his heart pounding in his chest at the thought of Wren chasing down the man who might be trying to kill her.

The swan had disappeared now, but Wren seemed to know where she was going. She sprinted through the garden without hesitation, and a moment later, they were rewarded by the sound of an angry trumpet followed by a sharp yell.

A confused mass of limbs and wings appeared from an enormous shrub in the path before them, resolving itself into the form of the dark-haired enchanter wrestling with the swan.

"What...magic...is on...these...birds?" he grunted, apparently not yet aware of his human audience.

Basil saw Wren's eyes widen at the question, and she lunged forward and pulled the bird off Sir Gelding. For a moment she just stared into its eyes, then the swan took off like an arrow, speeding back toward the pond.

Basil was only vaguely aware of Wren's interaction with her bird, his eyes narrowed upon Sir Gelding.

"Going for a morning stroll, Sir Enchanter?" he asked darkly.

The enchanter brushed off his disheveled clothes with unnecessary force. "As a matter of fact, I am, Your Majesty." His eyes rested on Wren, and he made no attempt to hide his distaste. "I'm afraid King Lloyd will have little choice but to have those swans shot if they're going to start attacking members of his court."

"Save the act," spat Basil. "We've seen the mine. We know everything." He was aware that statement was stretching the truth at best, but it wouldn't hurt for Sir Gelding to feel a little fear.

The nobleman froze, but he looked quite calmly between the two royals. "Mine?" he asked smoothly. "What mine?"

"The one where you've been mining not only iron, but fire jasper worth enough to fund a small kingdom," said Basil pleasantly. He took a step forward, and the nobleman's hand flicked toward his pocket, as if in instinct. Basil followed the gesture with his eyes. "What, going to pull out an artifact, Sir Enchanter?" he asked calmly. His gaze rested on the nobleman's hand, and he raised an eyebrow. "Speaking of fire jasper, that's an unusual set of rings. Did you steal them from your king's side of the border, or from mine?"

"Oh, so you've settled on a border have you, Your Majesty?" the baronet asked nastily. "I didn't realize you'd been so productive while in Myst. I thought your time had been whiled away in other..." his gaze passed to Wren, "dalliances."

A growl built in Basil's throat, but he bit it back. He could feel Wren's anger at his side, and his own fist clenched as he took a menacing step toward Sir Gelding. "Don't think I've forgotten your attacks on your own princess," he spat out. "King Lloyd will hear all about that. What did you do? Harvest power over plants from that disgruntled Entolian enchanter whose farm was swallowed up in the war?"

Sir Gelding said nothing, but Basil thought he looked a little rattled at this evidence of Basil's information.

"And yet," Basil pressed, "all you've got to show for it is two failures. Did you forget about the protective artifact worn by the king's heir, or aren't you an important enough noble to know about it?"

That jab brought a flare of anger into Sir Gelding's eyes, but Basil didn't miss the moment of understanding that preceded it. The baronet's gaze flew to the ring now dangling on the outside of Wren's gown, and he let out a small breath. Sir Gelding must have sensed the magic in the ring, but it seemed he'd been unaware of the artifact's purpose, and for that Basil could only be grateful.

"You've concocted some fine tales to cover up your own misdeeds, Your Majesty," said the enchanter smoothly. "But somehow I doubt King Lloyd will give much weight to the word of a deceiver and a betrayer."

He suddenly raised his voice, making both Basil and Wren jump.

"Guards! Over here! King Basil is attempting to abduct the princess again!"

Wren's fury was rolling off her in waves, but Sir Gelding ignored her completely, smirking instead at Basil. Already they could hear the sound of running feet, rapidly getting closer.

"Or didn't you know that the guards are currently scouring the castle for you, Your Majesty? Apparently you went missing from your rooms during the night, and are suspected to be up to no good."

Before Basil could respond, half a dozen guards converged on them, two of them immediately seizing Basil by each arm. He could hear more approaching, and he made a split decision not to resist. It would only make him seem guilty. He'd have to trust that King Lloyd would hear him out.

Wren, however, wasn't taking Basil's arrest so tamely. She flew at the guards, pulling at their arms and stamping on their feet. She looked absolutely fierce, and Basil felt a thrill at the determination in her eyes. She'd certainly come a long way from the princess he'd first met, who'd kept in the background and never drawn attention to herself.

"It's all right, Wren," he said quickly. "We'll explain it all to your father." He shot a venomous look at Sir Gelding.

"We've found the princess as well!" one of the guards called, and the shout was taken up by others out of sight.

"Ah, how delightful," said Sir Gelding quietly, looking between Wren and Basil. "The princess was also missing, was she? How...convenient, to find you both together."

Basil growled at the insinuating tone to the man's words, but a moment later one of the guards seized Wren, and all other considerations fled from his mind.

"What are you doing?" he demanded. "Are you going to arrest your own princess?"

Wren, of course, said nothing, but she turned startled eyes on the guard in question. He had the grace to look uncomfortable, but he didn't loosen his hold.

"King's orders," he said gruffly, his eyes fixed on a spot over Wren's shoulder. "We're to arrest King Basil on sight, and if you're found, we're to take you before him as well, Your Highness." He cleared his throat. "Forcibly if necessary."

Wren's scowl didn't show much surprise, from which Basil surmised that she hadn't left things in a strong position with her father the night before. The guards had just begun to march them both toward the castle when an aggressive bugle sounded behind them, followed quickly by several more.

The swans had obviously realized Wren's predicament, and they'd arrived in force to protest her arrest. They flew at the guard who was holding her, and the man cried out in alarm, releasing Wren's arm. But Wren made no attempt to evade him. She flapped her arms at the swans, for all the world like she had wings as well, her glare clearly telling them to back down.

The guard seized her again, looking nervously at the swans

as he did so, and this time the group made short work of hauling both royals inside. The swans, denied entry to the castle, flew along outside the windows, trumpeting angrily as they followed Wren's progress through the castle.

It was all the most surreal experience of Basil's life, and he hardly knew whether he was awake or dreaming as he was marched into King Lloyd's public audience hall. Sir Gelding, he noticed, slid smoothly into the room before the guards, approaching his king with a spring in his step. Either he truly thought he had the upper hand, or he was extremely skilled at feigning confidence.

Basil straightened his back, trying to reclaim his usual calm. He had barely a thought for his own dignity—he was too outraged by the sight of Wren being hauled before her own father, as if she'd been caught in some wrongdoing. Word of the drama had clearly spread as well, and the room was beginning to fill.

Sir Gelding was already at the front of the long room, muttering in his sovereign's ear. The Mistran king's eyes widened as they landed on Wren, and a look of horror flashed across his face before he could suppress it. Basil was fairly confident that, whatever he'd said to his guards, he hadn't actually intended for his daughter to be arrested like a criminal and brought to a public audience in her nightgown.

"Release the princess, you fools," he snapped at the guards, who hastily sprang back from Wren's side.

King Lloyd's eyes traveled to Basil's face, anger in their depths.

"You were requested to remain in your rooms," he said, in an icy voice that silenced the mutters of the crowd at once. "And yet I am informed that my guards apprehended you wandering around the gardens. What is the meaning of this?"

"Lloyd," muttered the queen, her alarmed eyes on her

daughter who, although no longer being held by the guards, was still standing next to Basil like a second criminal under accusation. But her husband seemed to have dismissed Wren momentarily from his mind after having the guards release her. His narrowed gaze was fixed on his Entolian guest, and he was clearly gripped by whatever pain or anger had always made him unreasonable where Basil was concerned.

"Precisely what I would like to ask you, Your Majesty," said Basil, with a little less than his habitual calm.

"This is no time for games," snapped the Mistran. "You were not in your room this morning, but my guards remained at your door. How did you reach the gardens?"

"I climbed out the window," said Basil matter-of-factly.

There was a little gasp around the room, and King Lloyd swelled in anger. "Fine behavior for a guest," he said darkly. "Care to explain why you considered such conduct appropriate?"

"I have a constitutional dislike of being trailed by guards," Basil answered simply. "My own I tolerate, as a necessary evil that comes with being king. But I draw the line at those of another king."

King Lloyd's eyes narrowed at this casual speech, but he didn't immediately respond. His wife was still tugging on his sleeve, and he looked at her at last. Following her gaze, he seemed to remember Wren's presence, and a scowl crossed his face at sight of his daughter's nightgown, which wasn't entirely concealed by her thick cloak. "Wren," he said curtly, and with a passable assumption of dignity, "come and stand beside your mother."

When Wren made no move, Basil turned his head to look at her. She shook her head firmly, her face set in stubborn lines. A small thrill went through Basil as she took a step toward him, clearly indicating her intention to stand by him through whatever was coming.

"It is clearly necessary to have guards trail you," snapped King Lloyd, his eyes back on Basil. Perhaps predictably, given the public setting, he seemed to be taking out his annoyance on Basil rather than on the daughter who was defying him. "Given you otherwise sneak around my castle like a thief." In spite of his efforts, the Mistran king's eyes flashed again to Wren, and Basil thought he had a fairly good idea what King Lloyd thought he'd been trying to steal.

Basil ignored the irate king, turning to Wren. "It's all right," he told her quietly. "You should go and—"

She silenced him with a glare, then jerked her head toward Sir Gelding, as if to say, *Get on with it*. Basil realized all at once that she didn't have her slate—she'd handed it to him to read, and he'd dropped it by the pond when she took off running—so he would have to be their combined voice for now.

"Your Majesty," he said, turning to King Lloyd. "I had hoped to discuss this matter with you privately, but if this is the setting you choose, I don't want to delay for another moment before telling you what I discovered at the front lines."

"I've already been informed of the mine my daughter discovered under the battleground," said King Lloyd in a hard voice. "A mine from which Entolians have been extracting not only iron, but fire jasper."

Another gasp swept around the room, and Basil bowed his head in acknowledgment. "Both Entolians and Mistrans I believe, Your Majesty. I have reason to think that there's been a collaboration between—"

"I've heard the story you've filled my daughter's ears with," the king cut in over him. "And you'll find I'm not so gullible."

Wren shifted in place, and when Basil glanced at her, he saw she was glaring at her father. But the king didn't look at her, his gaze still fixed on Basil. "If there's a secret mine set up in the ore field, it's a creation of the Entolian crown."

"I assure you, King Lloyd, it is not," said Basil curtly. "I'm embarrassed to acknowledge that neither I nor my general knew anything of it before my recent trip to the battlefield."

King Lloyd's disdain was visible, but Basil's attention was distracted by movement at the side of the room. His own retinue had just edged into the space, Lord Baldwin looking pale and horrified, the merchant couple tense and watchful, and Sergeant Obsidian frankly curious.

"You have taken advantage of my hospitality," said King Lloyd, his voice shaking slightly. "Not only have you deceived me in relation to your activities at the front lines, but you have lured the princess away from the safety of her home, endangering her by placing her in the middle of a battlefield."

A glance over at Wren showed her groping fruitlessly in her empty pocket, practically crying with frustration.

Basil opened his mouth to defend himself, but Sir Gelding beat him to it. "I wish that was all he'd done, Your Majesty," he said, his voice pained. "But I'm afraid what I witnessed in the gardens this morning goes well beyond that."

The king narrowed his eyes at the baronet. "What do you mean, Sir Gelding?"

The enchanter cast a delicate look between the princess and the visiting king. "I wouldn't wish to air, ah...personal matters in a public setting."

Basil gritted his teeth. Sir Gelding was clearly enjoying this.

"Having just done so by implication," snapped out King Lloyd, "I think you'd best set the record straight, Sir Gelding."

Sir Gelding cleared his throat. "Well, Your Majesty, I was walking in the gardens this morning when I stumbled across what I can only describe as a tryst. King Basil was..." he turned a malicious look upon Basil, "in conference with Princess Wren, by the pond."

Wren stood straight, but Basil could see the flush of mortification that passed over her. Anger burned within him as mutters grew in the crowd, many pairs of eyes passing over Wren's attire. Honestly Basil had barely noticed that Wren was in her night-gown when he woke her by the pond. He'd been a little distracted by her throwing herself into his arms and weeping as though her heart was breaking. A mystery he still had no solution for.

"What exactly are you implying, Sir Gelding?" King Lloyd said, through gritted teeth. The baronet clearly wasn't winning any favor for himself, but at the same time, Basil could see in the king's eyes that he was horribly afraid the accusation might be true.

"I was unable to help overhearing their conversation, Your Majesty," said Sir Gelding, casting his eyes regretfully downward. "And with my own ears I heard King Basil seek Princess Wren's acquiescence in an act of treason toward her king."

Basil's mouth fell open in astonishment. Whatever he'd expected, it hadn't been that. He glanced at Wren, and saw that she looked equally nonplussed.

"Treason?" King Lloyd repeated skeptically. "Princess Wren?"

"I'm afraid I have suspected for some time," Sir Gelding said, "from comments I have overheard from others in the Entolian delegation. But this morning's conversation confirmed my fears. King Basil came to Myst with the intention not of ending the war with a mutually beneficial armistice, but of ending the war via a full Entolian annexation of Mistra."

The muttering around the room grew to shocked whispers, and Basil couldn't hold his ridicule in.

"That's preposterous," he said flatly. "King Lloyd, you know from your own experience that from the moment of my arrival,

I've attempted to negotiate with you in good faith. I have no desire to annex Mistra, and even if I did, I would have no way to achieve it, as you must know."

"No way prior to your relationship with Princess Wren," cut in Sir Gelding smoothly. "What better way to combine the kingdoms under Entolian rule than have the Mistran heir defect from her own family and accept a lesser role as a non-ruling queen, standing beside the personable young king with whom we can all see she's besotted."

The crowd was muttering, but Basil hardly noticed them, his eyes locked with his accuser's.

"Don't play games, Your Majesty," Sir Gelding went on smoothly. "I heard you this morning, when you told the princess that if her father knew what you were proposing to her, he'd have you arrested for conspiring against his crown."

Basil stared at the enchanter in growing anger. The man was more devious than Basil had given him credit for. Wrapping his lie so carefully around a thread of truth was a clever trick indeed. The knowledge that he really had witnessed what had passed between Basil and Wren that morning ignited a different kind of anger in Basil, and he took an involuntary step toward the enchanter.

The guards were instantly on him, and Sir Gelding permitted himself a small smirk.

"And what did the princess reply?" King Lloyd's voice was harsh and tight.

"Lloyd," whispered the queen pleadingly. "Are you really going to do this here?"

But the king ignored her, seeming as hypnotized by Sir Gelding's lies as the rest of them.

The enchanter once again looked appropriately pained. "I regret to say, Your Majesty, that she was...enthusiastic in her response."

The whispers had become open gossip, and again Basil could see Wren's embarrassment.

"Lies!" he called angrily. Could any of these fools really have any doubt as to Wren's purity of heart?

The baronet raised an eyebrow. "Do you truly deny, King Basil, that you were seen passionately embracing Princess Wren in the gardens this very morning?"

Basil felt his own face heat, and knew that it must make him look ashamed. But in reality he was simply furious—how dare this snake make the kiss he and Wren had shared seem sordid?

Before he could respond, however, a commotion drew everyone's eyes to the entrance to the audience hall.

Five swans were trying to fight their way into the room, their wings flapping furiously and their angry bugling filling the air. The guards at the doors raised their weapons, shouting in alarm as the birds dove at them with beaks outstretched. With a gasp, Wren ran toward the door, tugging on the arm of the nearest guard, who'd raised his spear as if he meant to use it.

His distraction cost him his ground, and the swans poured into the room, trumpeting loudly as they flew in agitated circles above the shocked crowd. One of them kept dive-bombing people, and Basil had the strangest conviction that it was the same one who'd attacked him when he kissed Wren. In spite of everything, he gave a small grin at the sight of a well-dressed lady hiking up her skirts and running across the room, shrieking wildly as the swan chased her.

Another loud trumpet cut across the pandemonium, and everyone turned to the door to see a sixth swan framed in the entrance. Wren's most petted swan, the injured one, had arrived, and it waddled slowly and apparently painfully down the length of the audience hall. Wren ran to the bird, concern on her face, but it kept coming until it stood right beside Basil. He had to admit, for a bird, it had a real presence.

"Your Majesty," came a pained voice from the crowd, and Basil recognized one of the more pompous of King Lloyd's lords. "Surely the birds must be removed from the building."

Wren glared the man down, and to Basil's surprise, King Lloyd seemed to have little more patience with the complaint himself.

"Leave the birds," he said to the guards in general, several of whom were trying to catch the swans. "They're the least of my concerns. Wren." He fixed his daughter with a hard look. "Is there any truth to what Sir Gelding said?"

Basil could see Wren poised to shake her head vehemently, but the wording of her father's question made her pause. He understood why—there was *some* truth to it. That's what made it such a clever lie. Basil didn't doubt that, like his, Wren's thoughts were drawn vividly to the passionate embrace the baronet had alluded to. But while he applauded Wren's honesty, he winced at the knowledge that her failure to immediately deny it all must make her seem guilty. She again reached for her pocket, apparently forgetting for a moment that her slate wasn't on her.

"Your Majesty," said Basil angrily. "Is the princess truly to be blamed for my decision to declare my feelings to her this morning? I promise you on my honor that I never dreamed of inciting her to treason against you. I have never had the smallest desire to annex Mistra, and whatever my feelings on the matter, I am perfectly aware that as your heir Princess Wren is bound by her duty to her kingdom, and not free to pursue a future in Entolia with me."

"So what you're saying," King Lloyd interjected, his lips compressed into a furious line, "is that with no intention of any honorable proposal, you embroiled my daughter in a public embrace?"

"I...uh..." Basil floundered for a moment. That wasn't at all what he'd been trying to say, but it was, most uncomfortably, accurate. After all, that was the reason he hadn't intended to kiss Wren in the first place. But what could he say? That King Lloyd's overt absence of faith in his own heir had left her with a lack of confidence that was heartbreaking to behold, and filled Basil with a determination to kiss her pain away?

Something told him that wouldn't go over well with the irate king before him.

"By his own admission, Your Majesty." Sir Gelding suddenly reentered the conversation. He seemed a little distracted, however, his eyes on the swans now clustered protectively around Wren. Remembering what the baronet had said about the swans having magic on them, Basil glanced at his own people. Both the merchant enchantress and Sergeant Obsidian were watching the swans as well, their foreheads creased in concentration as if trying to make out a riddle.

"That's nonsense," Basil cut in quickly, making the most of the enchanter's distraction. "I haven't confessed to anything sinister, because there's nothing sinister to confess. Your Majesty, as I believe Princess Wren has already told you, there's considerable reason to think that Sir Gelding is himself behind the mining operation taking place at the battlefield. He's wearing fire jasper on his hands right now!"

"Absurd," snapped Sir Gelding. "These are rubies, family heirlooms. You are merely trying to deflect, Your Majesty, and it won't work. Too many others have witnessed your trysts with the princess." He glanced around the crowd. "Lady Anneliese," he said, his gaze settling on Wren's friend. "I know you've seen them often together."

There was a moment of silence, as everyone turned to the noblewoman. Her face paling under the scrutiny of so many eyes, she moved slowly toward Sir Gelding. But she didn't reach him, stopping instead when she was alongside Wren.

"I do not believe the princess has done, or ever would do,

anything to harm Mistra's interests. I was with her at the front lines, and I trust her when she tells me that there is reason to believe Sir Gelding is involved in the deception there."

The baronet's face went white, then immediately red in his anger. "How dare you?" he breathed. "You promised your loyalty to me."

The noblewoman held her head high. "A terrible mistake," she said coldly. "I don't know how I ever thought I could marry you. Having known what it is to have the love of a good and honorable man, I must have been mad to think I could bear to be your wife."

Wren reached for her friend's hand, her eyes shining with tears, but Basil's gaze flicked warily back to Sir Gelding. He looked furious, and was clearly building to some kind of explosion. Thinking it would be best to say his piece before that explosion came, Basil jumped in once more.

"Your Majesty, there's more than just the mine. The princess and I have been conducting our own investigation into the attack that killed your sons."

"You have, have you?" King Lloyd's growl was low and furious at this mention of his sons' murders. His eyes flicked between his daughter and Basil, and it was clear that he saw her discussion of the painful topic with the foreign king as a betrayal. For the first time, Basil actually saw the crushing pain that he had always suspected hid beneath King Lloyd's anger. The emotion flickered plainly across the king's face, fleeting but raw.

Wincing at his blunder, Basil hurried on, hoping to turn the king's thoughts from Wren's part in the investigation. "I believe, Your Majesty, that the attack was part of an attempt to provoke conflict between our kingdoms."

"We all know that," snapped King Lloyd, his face hard again, but his emotions clearly still in turmoil. "It was your father's main purpose. Who other than him would have wished to provoke conflict?"

"I'll tell you who," said Basil calmly. "Someone who knew that something much more valuable than iron was to be found on the contested land. Someone with links to the Blacksmiths' Guild, who might have heard a firsthand account of the ore. And someone who had the magical knowledge to recognize the value of the red stone. It would be a person with enough influence to form connections with like-minded Entolians, and who lived far enough from the capital to be able to operate without the scrutiny of the crown."

Sir Gelding was growing more and more red by the second, to Basil's satisfaction. King Lloyd's gaze was still as hard as steel as it rested on the visiting king's face, but Basil thought he saw a flicker of doubt in the older man's eyes. Hastening to press his advantage, Basil continued.

"Someone who apparently cared infinitely more for his own wealth than for his kingdom's future."

But at those words, the veil once again descended over King Lloyd's eyes. "Your own crime," he spat. "It seems your crown was willing to engulf your kingdom in war for the sake of your secret mine."

"Neither I nor my father are responsible for the mine," Basil started again, trying to hang on to his patience, but King Lloyd cut him off with a laugh so bitter it could have rivaled the late King Thorn.

"I'm done with your excuses." The king's eyes passed from Basil to Sir Gelding. "And with your blatant attempts to ingratiate yourself. Do you think making these accusations brings you favor?"

A glance at Sir Gelding showed that the enchanter wanted to be angry, but was too wary of his sovereign's suddenly unpredictable temper to express it.

"It hardly matters who built the mine, does it?" Quiet as it was, King Lloyd's voice echoed awfully around the room. "It comes down to the same thing. Greed. Is that the reason my sons are dead?" His frame was starting to shake. "Because of your GREED?!"

The king didn't even seem to know who he was accusing anymore, his eyes flicking between Basil and Sir Gelding as fury long suppressed rushed to the surface.

Basil said nothing, some instinct warning him that he was in genuine danger for the first time since his arrival in Mistra. King Lloyd's loss of control wasn't altogether surprising after Wren's unapproved flight to the front lines. Basil could only imagine that her disappearance must have thrust her parents back into the darkest moment of their lives. And although Wren had returned safely, the relief must be tempered by other emotions, as she instantly became the very public focus of both Sir Gelding's malicious insinuations, and Basil's unsanctioned declaration of affection.

Sir Gelding also seemed to sense the dangerous ground on which they stood. At the king's final roar, the enchanter visibly paled, although his instincts apparently didn't encourage him toward silence.

"Not *my* greed, Your Majesty!" Sir Gelding protested, sputtering. "I would never—"

"ENOUGH!" King Lloyd's shout made even Basil wince, and Sir Gelding fell back a step as his sovereign advanced.

"Duplicity from without and treason from within!"

"Treason?" gasped Sir Gelding. "Never!"

Still Basil remained silent. He glanced at Wren, and saw both fear and grief in her eyes. The watching crowd was as silent as death. It was clear that King Lloyd's subjects were as rattled as Sir Gelding by the uncharacteristic display from their sovereign.

No one knew what to expect, which meant Basil, as an outsider, couldn't hope to predict the outcome.

"I have always cared for Mistra's future, Your Majesty!" Sir Gelding blundered on. He shot a venomous look at Basil. "King Basil's allegations against me are merely his attempt to deflect the blame for his treachery. He covets Mistra—the greatest kingdom in Solstice."

"I'm not the one coveting what isn't mine," Basil said quietly. "And if you care so much about Mistra's future, killing off all its princes and pitching the kingdom into war is a strange way to show it."

For a moment Sir Gelding just stared at Basil, venom in his eyes as his jaw worked. "Ridiculous," he scoffed at last. "Why would I do any such thing?" He made a dismissive gesture with his hand. "The desperate accusation of a guilty man, from a royal house of murderers and seducers."

Basil's temper finally erupted at this open slur against his family and his kingdom. But before he'd done more than open his mouth to bring a hot retort, a cloaked blur launched itself at the enchanter. Basil's anger turned to alarm, a startled exclamation escaping him at the sight of Wren beating her fists against Sir Gelding's suddenly upraised arms. Apparently she could no longer endure standing by—her attempts to communicate the truth dismissed—compelled by some force Basil didn't understand to listen silently to the venomous lies of the man who had taken her brothers from her.

"Get off me!" the baronet gasped. "Someone stop her!"

For a moment the onlookers were all frozen, as stunned by the princess's outburst as they had been by the king's. Basil took a step forward, but he hadn't reached the struggling pair when the king's voice boomed across the room.

"Wren, compose yourself!"

The princess pulled back, her breath coming in pants as she

glared at the enchanter. Basil reached her in two quick steps, placing a hand behind her elbow in a gesture of support. She looked up at him, anger still glinting in her eyes, her chest heaving in her agitation.

"I know," Basil said quietly, nodding at her unspoken protest. "But we'll fix it. I promise. We just need to stay calm, and keep telling the truth of what happened until they bel—"

"DON'T TOUCH HER!"

The roar from King Lloyd made them both jump. Basil dropped his hand from Wren's arm like he'd been burned.

"I have been too tolerant," the Mistran growled, looking anything but. "Guards, seize them. Both of them!"

Basil's eyes widened, and not because of the guards who surged forward to grab his arms. "You're going to arrest your own daughter?" he protested, staring at the king.

"What?" Wren's father looked angrier than ever. "Of course not." He turned his gaze to the guards hovering in confusion just behind Wren. Most of them were eyeing the swans that had gathered around the princess, honking angrily, at the suggestion of her arrest. "Seize Sir Gelding as well," King Lloyd clarified.

"But, Your Majesty!" spluttered Sir Gelding, as the guards dragged him to stand right beside Basil. "I haven't done anything to—"

"Silence." King Lloyd made a gesture of finality with his hand, and the enchanter cut off mid-protest.

Basil, who had made no protest, drew several deep breaths, trying to remain calm in spite of the firm grip of the guards on his arms. Attempting to place himself in King Lloyd's position, he acknowledged that the older king was wise to recognize that he needed to collect himself before going further. Basil could even see the sense in throwing both suspects into the dungeons and sorting it out when heads were cooler. But it was a touch problematic that one suspect was a visiting king. Already Basil could see his own guards struggling through the crowd toward him, and he knew that they all stood on the edge of a cliff, moments from another incident like the one that had ignited war between the two kingdoms in the first place.

Before he could decide what to do or say, Wren once again threw herself forward, her swans clicking their beaks uneasily as they followed. Except this time she didn't attack the baronet. Instead she placed herself in front of Basil, glaring up at her father. In a gesture as clear as any words, she pointed at Basil, shaking her head, then pointed furiously at Sir Gelding, held at Basil's side by the guards.

"We will speak of it later, Wren," said King Lloyd, his anger still close to the surface. With a nod to the guards, he turned his back on the whole group, his shoulders rising and falling rapidly. Shocked mutters swept across the crowd like wind in dry grass, and the guards looked at each other helplessly. They were probably wondering if they were really supposed to drag a foreign king to the dungeons.

"When will you learn not to interfere?" Sir Gelding's hiss was so quiet, Basil actually had to lean sideways to hear it. Wren, who was still silently attempting to protest Basil's arrest, looked around, taking a moment to grasp that the enchanter was speaking to her. "If only that petty fool hadn't gone rogue and ruined the plan, you wouldn't be my problem."

"What does that mean?" growled Basil, his eyes narrowing as they rested on the enchanter.

Sir Gelding ignored him. With malice dripping from every word, he pinned Wren with a glare. "How does it feel to know your brothers were never the target?" he breathed, his words less than a whisper but still seeming to hold Wren in thrall. "That they died in *your* place? The attack was never meant to start full scale war. It was only ever aimed at the unnecessary extra princess no one would be willing to start a true war over."

Basil caught the briefest glimpse of Wren's horrified shock before red filled his vision. Sir Gelding's manner infuriated him almost as much as his words—he clearly meant to deal Wren an unendurable wound, and he just as clearly saw her as no threat, with no chance the monarchs or anyone else would believe a word the supposedly addled princess tried to communicate.

A low growl began to build in Basil's throat, and in the corner of his eye, he saw King Lloyd turn. Although no one but Basil had heard the enchanter's taunts, the king had apparently realized that something was happening with the prisoners. But Basil had no opportunity to act on the rage that had him in its grip, because someone else beat him to it.

Wren's swans had stuck close by her side throughout the whole exchange, and Sir Gelding was suddenly engulfed by beaks and feathers. A chorus of enraged trumpeting filling the room as many pairs of wings flapped furiously around him. Startled, the guards released the enchanter and stepped back, covering their faces with their arms. Basil could understand why. From Sir Gelding's cries of pain, the swans were doing more than just flapping their wings at him. Basil could only be grateful that the birds had forced Sir Gelding far enough away from Basil and Wren that they were clear of the melee.

"Enough with these ridiculous birds!" King Lloyd shouted, descending from the dais at last. "Why are the prisoners still here?" He shot a furious look at the guards. "And why have you released Sir Gelding? I will have order in my castle. Get the swans off him—kill them if you must."

Basil saw Wren start forward, her warm skin blanching in horror. Her eyes were terrified as they flicked between her father and the swans, who continued to pummel Sir Gelding mercilessly, in spite of the guards advancing on them with raised spears. Basil was struggling against the guards' continued hold on his arms, hardly knowing what he intended beyond keeping

Wren out of harm's way, when he felt an invisible ripple pass over the room. It was like nothing he'd ever felt before, and from the gasps around him, everyone else had felt it, too. He heard sharp cries from both the Entolian magic-users in the room, but he didn't turn to look at them. He was much too busy staring at the unbelievable sight before him.

Wren's swans had all collapsed to the floor with trumpets of alarm, and were writhing on the polished wooden surface. Except that their trumpets were turning into shouts, and their figures were growing, elongating, changing.

Basil's mouth fell open in astonishment as the six swans became six young men before his eyes, white feathers rippling and disappearing, and warm brown skin taking their place. Their clothes were fine, but ill-fitting, muscles bulging from overly tight sleeves, several inches of leg showing below some of their leggings. He saw Wren's dark eyes on one man, her straight nose on another, the determined chin she'd inherited from her father on more than one.

The men pushed themselves to their feet, examining their own bodies with cries of delight before rushing as one to engulf the princess. Basil caught the briefest glimpse of Wren's face—tears pouring freely down it—before she disappeared in their midst.

He remained rooted to the spot, barely able to take it in.

Finally, the mystery of the swans was answered. They weren't the attempt of a damaged mind to replace the princess's murdered brothers. They *were* her brothers.

CHAPTER TWENTY-SIX

Wren

Wave after wave of shock rolled over Wren as she was enfolded in the many arms of her brothers. She reached out, trying to grasp all of them at once, hardly able to believe they were real. There'd been no time for a good look at any of them, but there were clearly no twelve-year-olds here. Six strong, whole, *human* men surrounded her, each calling her name in excitement, gripping her arms, ruffling her hair in a very undignified way. One of them even dropped a kiss on the top of her head. She was fairly sure it was Averett, but she doubted she'd ever get him to admit it.

"It's the same time of day, Wren," said Ari excitedly, his voice identifying the tall young man as the brother she knew. "It was in the morning, wasn't it? It must have been exactly this time of day when we were cursed! That's why dawn was no good."

Wren laughed in amazement, wondering why she hadn't thought of that possibility earlier. Suddenly, the mass of writhing limbs stilled, and the sea of brothers parted. Looking past them, Wren saw what had caused them all to stop. Her parents were frozen, staring at their seven children with expressions that cut Wren to the heart. It was the same intensity of emotion she remembered from that terrible day, six years before, almost as if the joy of seeing their sons alive was too potent to settle easily into happiness.

"Caleb?" Queen Liana whispered. Her eyes passed over them all in turn. "Averett? Bram? Conan? Lyall? Ari?" Wren saw the tears begin to well as her mother realized all of her sons truly were there, alive and human. Then she fell on the group, and they all embraced her in turn, laughing and crying themselves.

Wren's eyes slid past the chaos, settling on Basil's motionless form. His gaze passed suddenly to hers, and the shock in his eyes made her grin. She raised a careless shoulder as if to say, *so that's what that was about*, and a smile built slowly on his face as well. She kept watching him in silence while her family talked excitedly all around her, waiting for the realization to hit him that the barrier of her being her father's heir no longer stood between them.

All at once, he got it. She saw the moment it happened, and his eyes lit with a sudden fire that seemed to reach across the room and blaze right into her soul. She felt her cheeks flame with it, but she held his gaze, a tentative smile on her face. Stepping forward, away from the guards who had released him in their shock, Basil put a hand to his heart, his face shining as he raised a single eyebrow. Laughing a little, and feeling strangely shy, Wren nodded. She saw him draw a shaky breath, and her smile grew.

Unless she'd misread him completely, she'd just received a silent proposal.

Her every nerve tingling with excitement, Wren turned back to her family. King Lloyd had waded into the group close behind his wife, his own shock apparently too great for words. He hardly seemed aware of whose arm he was gripping, until his questing hands reached his firstborn son in turn.

"Caleb," he breathed, and the room went silent.

Wren stilled as well, her eyes fixed anxiously on her oldest brother. She hadn't yet had a chance to properly look him over, to ascertain the effects of his injuries on his human body. She saw now that one of his arms was held at an awkward angle against him, clearly useless. The effect of her slip ups the day the curse had hit.

He was also holding all his weight on one leg, the other thin and bent. The price he'd paid for Wren's growing closeness with Basil. A shot of guilt lanced through her happiness, and she looked anxiously to her father, whose gaze was passing slowly from Caleb's feet all the way up to his face.

"My son," whispered the king, his voice catching. "You've come back to me." He pitched forward so abruptly, Caleb actually wobbled under his embrace. But King Lloyd didn't pull back, instead wrapping his two strong arms around his son and holding him upright as he clung to him.

With tears of joy in her eyes, Wren moved through the crowd of her family members until she reached Caleb's side. As soon as he pulled back from her father's embrace, she laid her hand on his arm. He smiled down into her face, with the warmth that had always made her feel special.

"Hey, Magpie."

Wren chuckled as she slipped the chain from around her neck, unclasping it and removing the ring. She offered it to Caleb, and in the midst of a solemn hush, he received it from her and slipped it over his finger.

The crowd started clapping, but one voice rose disastrously above the rest. "But, Your Majesty," Lord Kinley protested awkwardly. "Prince Caleb is...I mean, look at him."

King Lloyd's face went from overjoyed to icy in a heartbeat. "Yes, My Lord?" he prompted, in a tone that would tell anyone but a fool that it was time to stop speaking.

Lord Kinley, unfortunately, was something of a fool. "Well, he's crippled, Your Majesty," he said. "And he has a lame arm."

The crowd seemed to hold its breath as it looked to Caleb. Wren bristled with indignation on her brother's behalf, but the smile that split Caleb's face was one of genuine amusement.

"You're missing the material point, My Lord," he said with a calm that rivaled Basil's unflappability. "My arm may be crippled, but it's an arm. After six years with only wings, I am more than satisfied, I assure you."

A murmur of appreciative laughter went around the room, and Wren's heart glowed with pride.

"That's all very well, Your Highness," blustered Lord Kinley, but Caleb cut him off.

"Of the two of us, My Lord, I believe I am the only one with experience as a crown prince of this kingdom." The tiniest hint of ice had entered his voice, increasing his resemblance to his father beside him. "And I can say with confidence that there is absolutely nothing in my current state of health that will prevent me from fulfilling my role with all the capability I ever had."

Scanning the crowd, Wren's eyes caught on a head of honey-colored hair. Lady Anneliese had melted back into the crowd when Wren ran to the door to greet the swans, and she now stood a short distance away from Lord Kinley. Her eyes were riveted on Caleb's form, and tears poured silently down her face.

"Very admirable, Your Highness, of course." Wren's eyes snapped back to Lord Kinley in disbelief. The man truly didn't know when to shut his mouth. "But—"

"Enough." It was King Lloyd who cut the nobleman off this time, and his voice wasn't nearly as measured as his son's. "Another word against your future king, and I will have you arrested for treason."

Lord Kinley swallowed visibly and subsided. It seemed that

even he knew to be silent in face of that threat. The king's eyes passed to his son, and they softened. "You are wise beyond your years, Caleb. Wiser than I am. Although I hope I'm wise enough not to repeat the same mistake twice." He looked stricken as he turned to Wren. "For too long I've allowed myself to think that the loss of one ability means a total loss of capability. I have no intention of making that mistake when it comes to Caleb's body, and I'm sorry, Wren, that I ever made that mistake when it came to your voice."

Wren's heart swelled at the sincerity in his gaze, but she was aware of every eye in the room on her, and she didn't feel inclined to display her emotion in front of the whole kingdom. "Thanks Father," she said matter-of-factly, her voice coming out a little husky but perfectly functional. "Although of course I can use my voice now."

The sensation caused by the first words she'd spoken in six years was almost as great as that brought on by the swans' transformation into humans. Her mother actually let out a soft scream, and Basil's startled gasp was loud enough to draw Wren's eyes across the distance between them.

But the next moment she was engulfed by her family, and the chattering of the crowd grew so loud she could barely hear Bram's teasing words about how they were all going to have to put up with her incessant talking again now.

"But I don't understand," Queen Liana said, her eyes searching Wren's face. "You knew all along about your brothers?"

"Of course," said Wren. "I was even able to communicate with them, in our minds. Only if we were touching," she added as an afterthought.

The queen's eyes bulged. "But why didn't you tell us? And why didn't you speak all those years if not from the trauma of watching your brothers die?"

Wren drew a deep breath. "It's a long story, Mother. But the basic summary is that those were the terms of that madwoman's curse. The counterforce was that if I could be silent for six years, they'd turn back into humans. And I wasn't just forbidden from speaking aloud. I was also forbidden from communicating what had happened to them in any way. If I failed, they would all die."

Her parents both gasped audibly. "So..." King Lloyd swallowed. "So all those times we tried to push you to speak..."

"Would have killed us if Wren hadn't stood strong," Caleb finished for him. "But she did stand strong. Honestly, I think she must be the strongest person in the kingdom, Father."

His eyes glowed with pride as he looked at Wren, and she felt a curious tangle of joy and guilt. "I didn't always stand strong," she corrected her brother. "Caleb's arm is like that because I slipped up twice on the first day. Once when I shouted at the enchantress as she was dying, and once when I started writing out what had happened."

Her father looked stricken, clearly remembering that moment.

"And his leg is my fault as well," said Wren, feeling the need for full confession. She glanced apologetically at Basil, not wanting to suggest that he was somehow to blame. "Our visitor saw far too much of the boys in their swan forms because of me, and he started to figure it out from watching them." She frowned. "Although I still don't fully understand why him figuring it out breached the curse."

"I think I do," Basil chimed in unexpectedly. He approached closer, and Wren found herself gravitating toward him without conscious thought. He put an arm around her shoulder, pulling her against his side—somewhat daringly, Wren thought, given that he was technically still supposed to be under arrest. "I didn't figure it out from watching them. I started putting some pieces together from watching *you* interacting with them. I think maybe your behavior was communicating the truth, however unintentionally."

Wren nodded slowly, thinking it over. "The curse must have considered that in line with me finding a non-verbal way to tell you their situation."

"That's some seriously strict magic," muttered Ari mutinously.

"My injuries are absolutely not Wren's fault," Caleb said calmly. He bent a stern look upon her. "As I've told her many times. Far from doing anything to harm any of us, she is an absolute heroine for the sacrifice she's made for us for six uncomplaining years."

"Hear, hear," chorused Wren's other brothers, and she felt heat creeping up her neck.

"Wren, my darling," her mother's voice was choked with tears, "carrying that burden all this time, from so young. And we never knew. You are a heroine!"

Wren disclaimed feebly, but it was Basil's voice in her ear that finally stilled her mumbling. "You see, everyone agrees with me. You're the most incredible woman in Solstice."

For a moment Wren struggled vainly for words, then she remembered that she'd never needed words with Basil. It was comforting to realize that even though she *could* speak now, it didn't mean she had to. The thought made her feel slightly more secure in her wonderful but overwhelming new reality. She leaned into Basil's side, relishing in the fact that there was no more need for fear, and no more reason to hide anything from him.

"I love you," she said quietly, and heard his breath catch. She turned her face toward him and smiled up into his awestruck eyes. Some words were worth speaking aloud, of course.

"It still makes no sense," King Lloyd said, thankfully not having noticed his daughter's intimate moment with the king he might still consider an enemy. "Why would the enchantress want to turn the princes into swans? And why would Wren's silence be the counterforce to the curse?"

"She didn't intend to turn us into swans," cut in Averett dryly. "She intended to kill all seven of us. But she was a few turrets short of a castle, if you know what I mean, and we somehow ended up as waterfowl instead." He nodded at Wren. "And Caleb's ring protected Wren altogether, of course. Only then the madwoman got a bit annoyed about Wren talking over the top of her attempts to die in the peace of her successful revenge, and she decided to mold her counterforce into the most random thing she could think of." He gave a grim smile. "She assumed Wren wouldn't be able to do it, of course—who could?—and figured we'd die in the end anyway."

"But she was wrong," said Ari, shouldering Basil out of the way and slinging a proud arm around Wren's shoulder himself.

Basil fell back with a good grace, his eyes laughing at Wren in a way that reminded her he was an older brother himself. A moment later his eyes fell on Sir Gelding, standing wide eyed and shocked between four dazed-looking guards, and his expression hardened.

"The real question, Your Majesty," Basil said curtly, "is who would be irresponsible enough to give such a great amount of power to someone so unhinged."

King Lloyd turned slowly, his eyes passing between Basil and Sir Gelding. Some of his joy melted away, replaced by a pucker of confusion between his brows. "It seems there was a great deal I didn't know," he said slowly, looking between the young king and the white-faced enchanter. "I don't intend to be hasty in my assumptions again." He narrowed his eyes thoughtfully at Basil. "You stand by your claim that it was not the Entolian crown which gave power to the enchantress who attacked my children?"

"Absolutely, Your Majesty," Basil said firmly. "We had nothing to do with it."

Wren's father seemed to measure Basil with his gaze. "Whether or not that is the case, you must realize I cannot simply ignore the allegation made against you, that you attempted this very morning to incite my daughter to treason."

Ari let out a snort, his arm still around Wren's shoulder. "This morning? Personally I found the sight of King Basil kissing Wren a bit nauseating, but treason is a stretch."

Wren elbowed him in the ribs, torn between laughter and embarrassment. Her eyes flicked to Basil's, to find him already looking at her. His expression was one of long-suffering, but there was a warmth in his eyes that sent tingles up her spine.

"He kissed her?" Bram interjected, sounding startled. "In front of you all? That was bold."

"To be fair," Basil pointed out mildly, "I didn't realize all her brothers were watching."

"Not all," Bram corrected. "I left the pond before then. When I woke up and found that I was still a swan, I wasn't inclined to float around and cry about it. I saw that Wren and King Basil were both there, so I did my customary search of the area, to check for any threats." His eyes grew hard as they passed to Sir Gelding. "Which is how I saw *him* hiding behind a hedge, working some kind of magic which sent a branch plummeting toward Wren's head."

"What?!" King Lloyd started visibly, fury once again clouding his gaze as he turned to the enchanter.

"It's not exactly the first time he's tried to kill her, though, is it?" Averett added matter-of-factly. "We all just heard him tell her that she was the actual target of the attack six years ago."

A deathly hush fell over the group, spreading out across the whole room. King Lloyd turned to Sir Gelding, and Wren could see the last of his skepticism fall away. There would be no more wriggling out of it for the enchanter.

Sir Gelding went pale under the look Wren's father was giving him, but this time, the king's voice was quite calm.

"It seems we have our answer as to who would give excessive power to a murderous lunatic and send her after my children."

"I didn't give her any power, Your Majesty," protested Sir Gelding, looking frantic. "I would never gift my magic to a foul, disease-riddled fool like that enchantress."

Wren frowned as she studied his face. He certainly seemed sincere, but that didn't mean much. He'd obviously been successfully deceiving everyone for years.

"Who did, then?" scoffed King Lloyd, clearly disbelieving the denial.

Sir Gelding opened his mouth, then closed it again. A look of frustration passed over his face, and Wren's frown deepened. It was a painfully familiar expression to her.

"Someone...someone else," the baronet managed at last.

"Compelling evidence," said King Lloyd icily. "So you didn't give her your magic to use, but you did craft a plan to murder my daughter and frame the Entolian crown for it, so as to provoke conflict between the two kingdoms that would distract everyone enough to allow you to clandestinely mine fire jasper out from under the contested land."

"Certainly not, Your Majesty!" Sir Gelding tried desperately. "The princes misunderstood me earlier. I only heard of the plan later—I had no hand in it!"

Wren snorted, as a cleared throat made everyone turn toward the small group of Entolians. The one soldier among them stepped forward, bowing to King Lloyd. His eyes sought Basil, who gave him a curt nod, then he faced the Mistran king again.

"My name is Sergeant Obsidian, Your Majesty," he said

smartly, "of the Entolian armed forces. I am an enchanter myself," he grimaced slightly as he said the words, "specifically gifted with the ability to detect deception." His gaze passed dispassionately to Sir Gelding. "And that man just lied to you through his teeth, Your Majesty."

"Thank you, Sergeant," said King Lloyd, his eyes fixed coldly on the protesting Sir Gelding. "I don't even need magic to recognize that. So you did give your power to the woman as well, I take it?"

Again Sergeant Obsidian cleared his throat. "Actually, Your Majesty," he said, sounding a little surprised himself, "that part did not appear to be a lie. Just what came after."

Basil shifted, and Wren looked over to see him raise an eyebrow, studying Sir Gelding thoughtfully. "Are you part of an organized group of Mistran and Entolian conspirators, who came together six years ago to plot against the two crowns and steal the ore out from under our land?"

Sir Gelding opened his mouth as if to deny it, but his gaze flicked resentfully to Sergeant Obsidian, and he nodded instead, his expression sullen.

"And are you in a position to name every one of those conspirators?" King Lloyd pressed.

Again, Sir Gelding nodded sulkily.

"Well." King Lloyd's voice had turned brisk. "Clearly there is more to be learned from you, Sir Gelding." He nodded to the guards. "Take him away."

Wren shook Ari's arm off and turned back toward Basil, not wanting to waste another minute on the traitorous baronet. She could hardly miss his venomous words, however, as he was dragged past her.

"You ruined it all, you pathetic excuse for a princess. One seductive glance from a boy masquerading as a king, and you lose your head and start digging into things that don't concern you. It would have been better for Mistra if you'd died in the first place, like we planned."

Wren felt Basil stiffen beside her, and saw his hands curl into fists at his sides. "Watch yourself," he growled.

Sir Gelding laughed in his face. "You think I attacked your little sweetheart these last months just because the two of you were asking too many questions? I never intended to remove Mistra's heirs, but dragon's flame, I'd rather my king had no successor than be followed by a spineless princess too afraid to open her mouth. I would never have let her be queen!"

Wren stared icily back at him, refusing to let him see how his poisonous insults stung her. "You are pathetic," she said, pleased with how calmly her words came out.

Basil, on the other hand, seemed to have been deserted by his legendary calm. He took a step forward, his frame tense and his hands still balled. But before he could act, a shape hurtled past them both and connected with Sir Gelding's nose. The baronet cried out in pain, and Wren leaped forward to steady her swaying brother.

"Thank you, Wren," said Caleb with dignity, leaning heavily on her shoulder to keep from falling. "That answers the question as to whether I can still throw a punch." Once he was steady on his feet, he stepped away from her. "It's a good thing the curse didn't target my right wing, isn't it?" He shook out the hand of his still-strong right arm, flexing the fingers which appeared to have just broken Sir Gelding's nose.

"Take him away before I lose my patience and execute him on the spot!" growled King Lloyd, who had hurried forward to stand beside his son.

The guards resumed their progress toward the door, but Sir Gelding was still spitting insults, even as blood poured down his chin.

"You think you can all make a fool of me?" he roared, his

eyes on Wren. She read his intent in his eyes a moment before he struck, but there was no time to do more than gasp as he ripped one arm free from the guard who held it and passed his fingers over the rings on his other hand.

His lips were moving, muttering words Wren couldn't catch, and she had the unidentifiable sense of something rushing toward her. From force of long habit, she let out no scream, but Basil's yell sliced through the air as he threw himself in front of her.

The shout turned into a cry of pain as Sir Gelding's magic hit Basil, and Wren's scream was ripped from her at last as she hurled herself toward where he lay on the floor. Her newly righted world spun around her, terror ripping at her chest. It was like the first attack all over again, except this time she had no ring to protect her, and the figure writhing painfully on the floor was Basil. She couldn't lose him!

But as she curled her body protectively across his, she felt only a flicker of pain from Sir Gelding's magic. Her mind quieted, and two voices separated from the general noise, shouting unfamiliar words from behind her. Basil stilled where he lay, his breathing rapid but unlabored. The sergeant enchanter and the merchant enchantress appeared at his side, their eyes scanning their king anxiously as a full dozen Mistran guards converged on Sir Gelding.

"Basil!" Wren cried, anguished.

Basil's eyes snapped open, finding hers at once. To her astonishment, his face split in an enormous smile.

"That's the first time you've said my name," he informed her delightedly. He pushed himself up, clearly unharmed, until he was sitting next to where she knelt. His voice dropped as he reached out a hand to rest on her cheek. "I like how it sounds on your lips," he said, his gaze dropping to the feature in question. "I like it a lot."

"All right," interjected a disgusted voice, as Ari helped Wren to her feet with unnecessary force. "Settle down. That's our little sister you're ogling."

"Ari!" scolded Wren, scandalized. "No one's ogling anybody!"

"Debatable," Averett said dispassionately. "He's certainly not looking at you like one of us would."

"I should hope not," said Basil, laughing as he got to his feet himself. Wren noticed none of her brothers had offered to help him up. "She's your sister! I already have twelve of those—the last thing I want is another one."

A sudden shout near the doorway made them all turn. Sir Gelding, it seemed, was still fighting. And he had more magic up his sleeve. As they watched he made a throwing motion, and the guards seizing him let go at once, grasping their own hands as if burned.

"Stop him!" shouted King Lloyd, as Sir Gelding made a break for the door.

But it wasn't a Mistran who intercepted Sir Gelding's flight. It was Lord Baldwin who stepped forward, extending a foot and neatly tripping the baronet up.

Once again guards swarmed over him, this time wasting no time in binding his arms and legs. One of the guards knelt beside him, grunting as he tugged the rings from Sir Gelding's fingers. They also gagged him, but not before he gave one last shout, his eyes fixed on Lord Baldwin.

"Traitor! You think you can get away with it? I'm going to give them every single name, and yours is top of the list!"

His yells were suddenly muffled by the gag, but the damage had been done. Wren's wide eyes passed from Lord Baldwin, who had gone very pale, to Basil, who now stood stiff as a board beside her.

"Lord Baldwin," he said, his voice calm but intense. "You've been working with Sir Gelding. You're part of this collaboration of Mistrans and Entolians." Neither sentence was a question.

"What a fool I've been," he added, a hint of bitterness creeping into his voice. "So many clues. The ease with which you acquired the local information when we arrived. Your reluctance to spend any time at the front lines. The very fact that you were the only one willing to volunteer to accompany me to Myst. You had to try to contain the risk of my visit, didn't you?" Wren could detect real hurt behind the bald accusations, and her heart ached for Basil's disillusionment.

"Your Majesty," said Lord Baldwin, his lips going white. "Please...let me explain..."

"That's what you came to my rooms to do last night, isn't it?" Basil said slowly. "To confess, and to explain."

Lord Baldwin nodded eagerly.

"But you didn't." Basil's voice was hard.

The nobleman winced. "I was going to, I swear. But then you spotted the princess climbing down from her window, and I saw the way you looked at her. I could no longer deny to myself how deep your affection for her had gone. I knew there was no hope you'd forgive me, not when I'd been involved in a plot to have her killed when she was only a child."

Basil's face was suddenly like flint, and he reached out to touch Wren's arm in an apparently unconscious gesture, as if reassuring himself she was present and whole.

"That's why you were always so uncomfortable around her," he said evenly. "It wasn't her silence that you couldn't handle. It was your own guilt."

Lord Baldwin hung his head. "The guilt has been eating at me for years, but never so painfully as when I saw how worthy you are of my respect. Your father...well, his expectations of his nobles were never reasonable. I don't think it is an exaggeration to say that his treatment of my own father drove him to his grave. When my father died, and I inherited his position, I was young, and foolish, and angry. Young enough to be unfit for the wealth and influence of my new role. Angry enough to be swayed by treasonous talk, and foolish enough to be dazzled by the promise of riches. Sir Gelding recruited me himself."

He raised his face, and his eyes searched Wren's pleadingly. "I never supported the plan for provoking conflict. I never truly wished you harm, Your Highness."

"Don't speak to her," said Basil, his voice steady, but his shoulders shaking. "Don't even look at her. I trusted you, and you stood by while your allies tried to kill the person most precious to me in the world."

"I knew nothing of Sir Gelding's attacks on the princess these past two months!" Lord Baldwin protested. "I was as horrified as you."

"Guards," King Lloyd ordered, "place Lord Baldwin in a cell." He exchanged a look with Basil. "We will consider what is to be done with him later."

Wren remained silent as the nobleman was led from the room, pale but unresisting. She felt torn. She believed that he hadn't meant her harm in any direct way. But he certainly hadn't done anything to protect her. He might not have done much to aid in Sir Gelding's schemes, but neither had he helped Basil with his efforts for peace. From what she'd observed, he'd been obstructive at every opportunity. And although it may be true that he objected to the plan to murder an eleven-year-old princess, he'd apparently been willing for soldier after soldier to die in battle in his pursuit of riches and revenge.

Out of the corner of her eye she noticed Caleb moving slowly across the room toward Lady Anneliese, who still seemed too overwhelmed to speak, but her father's words to Basil drew her attention back to the two kings.

"We have a more pressing matter to discuss," he said

solemnly. His eyes flicked to Wren, and she smiled encouragingly at him. "King Basil, it is now abundantly clear that you spoke the truth when you said the Entolian crown was not behind the attack on my children." He drew a breath. "And I must therefore acknowledge that Mistra was at fault in mounting the attack that ultimately led to your father's death. I must also acknowledge that I have kept you waiting here too long. We can open negotiations tomorrow regarding reparations, and—"

"Your Majesty," Basil cut in quickly. "I am honored by your acknowledgment of fault, and I know my family will also receive it with gratitude. But I'm not interested in reparations. Entolia doesn't need it, and I don't want it. I wish only to move forward into a time of peace between our kingdoms."

"A cause in which I will gladly join," said Wren's father quickly. "But in good conscience, I must urge you not to reject the offer of reparations too hastily. If you wish to take time to think about it, discuss it with your advisors—"

"I know what my advisors will say," Basil interjected. "They would most likely share the view my father would have held. But my father and I never saw eye to eye about the true nature of the conflict between our kingdoms."

King Lloyd frowned, clearly confused, and Basil pushed on. "I've told you before that the war was always personal. To be honest, I wish all war was so personal."

Wren gazed up at Basil's serious face, amazed anew by the maturity his early responsibility had given him. He was meeting the other king's eyes unflinchingly, his voice steady and his back straight.

"Most of the time," Basil explained, "kings wage war from council rooms. They send their soldiers to fight and die in their name, and retain the luxury of lives untouched by war." He shook his head sadly. "But that wasn't true for my family, or for yours. I hope the miraculous return of your sons will help begin to heal the devastation you've experienced. But my father was never able to find healing, and I don't just mean for his injury. He couldn't get over the outrage of being forced to suffer in his own royal body the war that his soldiers should have fought for him."

Basil sighed. "He didn't take it well, but perhaps if every king who sends his people to war had to suffer a wound of his own, we would never see another battle. I don't know that. But I do know that I don't wish to be a king who expects my people to pay the price for problems that are my responsibility to solve."

Wren glanced at her father, who looked a little stunned by this speech.

Basil had obviously noticed the expression as well, because he gave a rueful smile. "My point is, there's been blame on both sides. And I didn't come to Myst to avenge my father. I came out of a belief that if two kings sit together in a room with a genuine desire to resolve their problems peacefully, they surely must be able to rise from the table with a mutually agreeable solution that doesn't involve their people in war, or any other terrible sacrifice."

"An admirable belief," said Wren's father. "I haven't given you much reason to think that I share it, but I do. And I will be glad to sit down with you and hear everything you have to say."

Basil nodded his thanks. "I look forward to that, Your Majesty. There is still much to discuss—we will, of course, need to reach agreement regarding the border, taking into account the location of the iron ore and the fire jasper. From what I observed in the mine, there is still plenty to be harvested."

He glanced down at Wren, his face softening into a smile which she responded to instinctively. Listening to his calm convictions filled her heart with such pride, it almost ached.

"But I was hoping to go beyond such agreements," Basil told

King Lloyd. "I wish to seek a more concrete alliance between our kingdoms."

"You do?" Wren's father seemed both surprised and gratified, no doubt thinking of his own treatment of the calm young king. "Well, there will be time enough to discuss the details of an alliance—"

"Actually," Basil once again cut him off, "I'm not, as you've gathered, very good at being patient. I was hoping to discuss those particular details now."

"Very well," said King Lloyd, sounding taken aback. "What do you propose?"

"Excellent choice of words," said Basil promptly. Again he smiled down at Wren, and she beamed back at him. "Your Majesty," said Basil, his eyes still on Wren, "it can come as no surprise to you that after two months in her company, I'm hopelessly in love with your daughter. Now that she's freed from the role of your heir, and my suggestion won't be misconstrued as an attempt to annex your kingdom to mine, I wish to marry her and carry her off to Tola with me."

"A marriage alliance?" King Lloyd repeated, a little stunned. "With Wren?"

"That's it in a nutshell, yes," said Basil, laughing a little.

"Wren?" prompted her father, his eyes searching her face. "This is what you want?"

She nodded, pressing closer to Basil's side. Her eyes passed to her mother's, laughter in their depths. "I'm sorry I was so difficult when you tried to train me to become queen. I should have listened to every word. It seems I'm going to be queen after all, and much younger than we anticipated. Just not Mistra's queen."

"No," Basil agreed, sending a shiver down Wren's spine with the whisper just for her. "*My* queen."

Pulling her gaze from her mother's brimming eyes, and disregarding the not entirely impressed expressions on her brothers' faces, Wren turned to face him. "I might not break the habit of silence all at once," she warned him, a touch anxiously.

"Why should you?" he replied promptly. "We don't need words as much as other people seem to, do we?"

She smiled, shaking her head. "And," she pressed, her eyes teasing him, "I'm very determined to knit clothes for waterfowl, whatever your populace thinks of the habit."

"Even better," Basil said solemnly. "I'll adopt an entire flock of geese especially for the purpose."

"Oi!" Conan's voice cut across their moment. "We were *not* geese!"

Wren's laugh was cut off by Basil's lips once again descending on hers, and the various protests of her brothers were drowned by the cheers of the watching crowd.

Her heart was so full she wondered how her body could contain it. After six years of war, six years of fear, and six years of silence, it was at last time for a new day. Peace for Mistra, freedom for its princes, and the happiest of new beginnings for its princess, who wanted nothing more than to spend her life with the one person who'd heard her when she didn't even have her voice.

Wren

"Are you ready?"

Wren turned at the sound of the familiar voice, her face lighting with a smile as she nodded. She'd be even more ready if it was tomorrow, and they were finally getting married. But she didn't complain. After a year of waiting, she could manage one more day. And the conference Basil had organized was important as well.

She took Basil's offered arm, a thrill going through her at the warmth of his skin on hers. In the three weeks since her arrival, she'd been enjoying the more casual fashion in the seaside capital. When Basil had been in Myst, he'd made more effort than she'd realized to adhere to their customs. It was something of a shock to see him in the short sleeved tunics favored by Entolian nobles, with laces at the front that were rarely pulled tight, so that she could actually see some of the skin of his chest.

A very pleasant shock, that was.

Princess Zinnia had personally assisted Wren in ordering her wardrobe, and her own gown had short sleeves as well. Not even sleeves, really. Just thick bands across her shoulders. The weather was getting warm, but windows stood open all along the corridor, providing a stunning view of the sea crashing against the cliffs below, and letting in the fresh salt air.

Wren was very well satisfied with her new home, and even more satisfied with the soon-to-be-husband whose hand squeezed hers where it rested on his arm.

When they entered the small meeting room where Basil had asked the others to gather, it was clear they were the last to arrive. The five men already in the room rose politely to their feet, and the five women inclined their heads respectfully to their host. There were only the ten of them, twelve now that Wren and Basil had entered. No servants were in attendance, and no guards were posted within the room. Basil had wanted to keep the matter private.

Some of Basil's advisors had caught wind of the planned meeting, just the day before. Over the last year, most of them had come to respect, if not fully appreciate, their king's preferred methods, and had made no attempt to interfere. A few, however, were still determined to be difficult, clearly believing they could mold him to be more like his father—or more like their view of a satisfactory king—if they pushed hard enough. Accordingly, they had tried their utmost to convince Basil to include them in the conference.

Satisfaction spread through Wren at the memory of that interaction. Having heard about the lack of support and respect these particular nobles had shown their young king—recounted in more detail by Zinnia than by Basil himself—it had brought her great satisfaction to hear her betrothed's calm response. He had told the outraged lords that since the results of his efforts in Myst had proven their advice in the matter of negotiating a ceasefire with Mistra to be egregiously—one might even say dangerously—incompetent, he would not be requiring their services for liaising with neighboring kingdoms on this occasion. He'd then informed them amicably that with time and faithful service, they may yet earn back his trust.

Still smiling at her mental image of the looks on their faces, Wren returned her attention to the meeting before her. Although she knew all of those present by name, only three were genuinely familiar. She sent a quick smile at Zinnia, whom she'd gotten to know well over the past year, then seated herself beside Anneliese and Caleb.

Letting her eyes wander over the distinguished group, Wren tried to read the silent messages she knew were always to be found on any face if you were paying attention. She was encouraged to see no sign of discontent or impatience. Every eye was turned expectantly to Basil, and to all appearances, they had all come ready for genuine discussion.

"Your Majesties, Your Highnesses, thank you all for attending." In his usual manner, Basil got straight to the point. "We've asked you here to speak about magic."

Wren noticed the golden-haired princess from Bansford exchange a startled look with her husband, but she said nothing. Zinnia, on the other hand, shifted her chair back and gave her brother a long-suffering look.

"Basil," she said reproachfully. "I'm as curious as everyone else to know why you've called this secret council of royals, but our guests have all come for your wedding, remember."

For a moment Basil blinked at her in confusion, and Zinnia let out small sigh.

"Half of them haven't even met Wren yet!"

"Oh," said Basil. "Of course." He glanced apologetically at Wren, but she shook her head with a smile. Zinnia was right, that the formalities should be observed. But Wren was with Basil—she'd rather get right to the heart of the matter.

"Wren has no need of an introduction to Prince Caleb and Princess Anneliese, of course," said Basil, inclining his head to the Mistran couple and using their titles for the benefit of others who may not have met them. "Or my sister, Princess Zinnia." He turned to the couple next to them. "Allow me also to introduce King Justin and Queen Felicity of Albury."

The pair, who looked to be in their early twenties, nodded in acknowledgment. The dark-haired king—whom Wren privately thought still looked as intimidating as ever, in spite of how his marriage had apparently softened him—contented himself with a polite smile. But his wife leaned forward so that her hair fell over her shoulder in copper waves, cupping one hand to her bulging belly as she examined Wren.

"I'm so glad to meet you, Princess Wren," she said cheerfully. "We were delighted to receive an invitation to your wedding."

"We're delighted you're here," said Wren softly, and sincerely. She'd been agog with curiosity to meet the girl who'd tamed the beast. Wren hadn't forgotten that Lord Kinley had once petitioned her parents to send her to Albury in an attempt to marry her to Justin and form an alliance between the kingdoms.

Her supposed status as heir had been no barrier then, she thought wryly. And yet, when the same idea had been suggested in relation to her and Basil, whom she actually wanted to marry, it had been described as treason. But then, no one in the Mistran court had ever seen clearly when it came to Entolia. At least until Basil came and shook up all their preconceptions about the neighboring kingdom.

"And this is Prince Bentleigh and Crown Princess Azalea of Listernia," Basil went on, and Wren's gaze shifted to the next royals. She'd noticed that Prince Bentleigh was chatting cheerfully with Albury's queen when she and Basil had entered. Evidently they were on good terms. It was heartening, given that

Wren remembered a time when the Alburian royals had wanted nothing to do with the rest of the kingdoms.

"Welcome," said Wren, smiling at Solstice's only female heir to a crown. Princess Azalea smiled brightly in return, her arm entwined unashamedly with her husband's, her warm brown skin contrasted strongly against his paler tone. She didn't seem like someone who'd be as daunted as Wren had once been about becoming queen. Probably because she wasn't trying to keep multiple older brothers alive by not accidentally revealing their presence.

"Crown Prince Rian and Princess Penny of Bansford," said Basil. Prince Rian sat next to the Listernian couple, his features clearly showing him to be Prince Bentleigh's brother. His golden-haired wife beside him was the one who'd had such a visible reaction when Basil mentioned magic.

"And finally," Basil said, "Crown Prince Amell of Fernedell."

The young prince gave a cheery wave. "Just me, I'm afraid," he said brightly. He glanced around the table. "Quite a couple fest, isn't it?" His grin grew cheeky as his gaze rested on Zinnia. "We should be sitting next to each other, shouldn't we, Zinnia? Just to even things out."

"Not in a hundred centuries, Amell," said Zinnia, without heat. "I don't think I could handle you, and I'm sure you couldn't handle me."

Prince Amell laughed, apparently unfazed. "I said we should sit together. I wasn't proposing a marriage alliance."

"For those who haven't yet had the pleasure," Basil cut in quickly, clearly seeing that Zinnia was ready to wage battle, "I'm delighted to introduce you to Princess Wren of Mistra, who tomorrow will become Queen Wren of Entolia." His eyes were warm as they rested on Wren, and a thrill shot through her, all the way down to her toes. Finally, after a year of waiting, tomorrow was the day.

Princess Azalea broke the moment with a little cheer, and Basil's gaze moved back to the rest of the group with an easy smile.

"And," he added as an afterthought, "since I'm making a marriage alliance myself, I'm happy to be able to guarantee that I will not be requiring any of my sisters to do so."

"I'm not sure if I'm being rescued, or Zinnia is," Prince Amell piped up, still grinning at the unimpressed Entolian princess.

"Both, by the sounds of it," Prince Bentleigh cut in dryly. "Now quiet in the back, Amell. I want to hear what King Basil called us here to say. What about magic?"

"Yes, thank you," said Basil, as Prince Amell subsided with a good-natured grin in Prince Bentleigh's direction. "It's come to our attention that a number of the crowns of Solstice have now been targeted by curses which have seemed too strong for the enchanters or enchantresses who cast them. Wren and I have wondered if it's possible there's a connection between these attacks. We hope that by discussing the matter openly, we can not only share information, but find strength in unity."

The pronouncement was met with utter silence, and Wren made a point of studying every face. To her surprise, Zinnia looked the most shocked of anyone. Wren already knew that Basil hadn't confided in his sister the purpose of the meeting, and knew that he had his reasons. But Zinnia's reaction was more than surprise. It was almost horror.

Locking that information away for later exploration, Wren looked around the group. King Justin was frowning, but as if in thought rather than in displeasure. The Listernian couple exchanged a quick look, and the Bansfordians appeared a little confused. Prince Amell looked like he was finding it difficult to sit still in his chair. But Wren was fairly certain that was normal for him.

"What do you mean when you say the curses are too strong for those who cast them?" King Justin asked cautiously.

Basil sat down at last, settling into his chair as if ready for an extensive discussion. "That was certainly the case for the curse on Wren's brothers," he said simply, nodding in Caleb's direction. "It's true that the enchantress who cast it was, quite frankly, out of her mind, but while that explains the bizarre nature of the curse, it doesn't explain its strength. The power that enchantress was born with was middling at best, and certainly not strong enough either to kill seven people on the spot, as she intended, or to turn six of them into swans with human intelligence, and trap them in that state for six years."

"When you say it like that," Prince Amell commented, "it does sound like some pretty potent magic."

"King Basil is right," said Caleb in his steady, deep voice. "The enchantress herself told us she had been offered extra power by someone. And she certainly didn't have proper control over the power she'd been given, like she would if it had been her own native magic."

"But Basil," Zinnia protested, frowning. "I thought you said you'd uncovered a conspiracy of Mistrans and Entolians collaborating to turn the kingdoms against each other so they could secretly mine the contested land. Isn't that where the extra power came from?"

Basil shook his head. "We thought so at first. But that whole operation was uncovered, and there were very few enchanters among them. Some had barely even been involved, like the Entolian farmer who simply gave Sir Gelding some power to work with, apparently not even knowing what the baronet planned to use it for."

"So this Sir Gelding collected power from other enchanters, and gave it to the woman who attacked the princes?" Prince Rian asked, frowning. He glanced at his wife. "I didn't even know that was possible."

She shrugged, looking apologetic. "Neither did I. But I still know very little about how magic can be used."

Wren cleared her throat, leaning forward slightly in her seat. "Sir Gelding didn't give power to that enchantress. She went rogue when she attacked us, without the approval of the wider group of conspirators."

Caleb nodded his support. "Wren is right. He was questioned extensively, with the assistance of an enchanter who can identify deception. He didn't give her extra power. And he clearly received additional power of his own from some source beyond the magic-users directly involved in his operation."

"What source?" demanded Princess Azalea.

Caleb shrugged. "We don't know. Sir Gelding couldn't say."

"You mean wouldn't say?" King Justin pressed.

"No." Caleb shook his head. "We think he wanted to, but something prevented him. Some kind of latent magic around him, according to the magic-users assisting us."

The Listernian couple exchanged a look. "I've experienced something like that," said Prince Bentleigh. "When I tried to tell Azalea's parents what I knew about her curse, and just...couldn't. The words wouldn't come."

His wife nodded, sitting up straighter. "It's not unlike what was happening to me, as well. I couldn't communicate by word or action. The curse wouldn't let me."

Basil nodded. "That's why you're here," he told them seriously. "Because of the curse you've experienced."

Prince Bentleigh's expression was thoughtful. "And we never found a satisfactory answer for how Montgomery's magic became so powerful, did we?"

Basil's eyes passed to the Alburian monarchs. "I invited you, Your Majesties, because I believe you also have experienced a curse where even the one who cast it was unable to explain its potency."

Queen Felicity nodded, her expression troubled. "We never did solve that mystery."

"The Mistran princes," said Basil, nodding at Caleb, "Albury's ruler," to Justin, "Listernia's heir," a nod toward Princess Azalea, "and even Bansford's troubles, unless I'm mistaken."

Prince Rian took a moment before answering, his brown eyes serious as they rested on Basil's face. "It's not quite the same as Ben and Azalea's situation," he said at last. "Or King Justin's. But it is true that there are some holes in our investigation into the magical attack we faced two years ago. Some of the things achieved by our enemies couldn't be explained by the sources of power that we're aware of."

"I must say, Fernedell is feeling left out at this point," chimed in Prince Amell cheerfully. "Why am I here, Basil? Because you thought I'd be upset to be left out?"

"Precisely," said Basil evenly. Wren hid her smile, but there was no need. Prince Amell clearly wasn't one to take offense.

"You were right," he assured his host. He rubbed his hands together as he looked around at the gathered royals. "So what do we think? That there's some kind of secret organization of powerful enchanters working against all the crowns?"

"It's a possibility," Basil acknowledged.

"What's the plan, then?" Prince Amell asked flippantly. "Shall we hunt down all the magic-users? No offense, Princess Penny."

"None taken," said the Bansfordian princess absently. Wren was aware that Princess Penny happened to be the only magic-user at the table—in fact, the only royal magic-user in Solstice. "Is it possible that one or more of the Enchanters' Guilds has turned against us?"

"Possible, of course," assented Basil. He glanced at Caleb. "King Lloyd and I have conducted our own investigations in the last year, and we're fairly confident that the leadership of the Mistran and Entolian Enchanters' Guilds remains solid."

"We conducted a similar investigation after our troubles," said King Justin of Albury, "but that was three years ago. We will do so again."

"I'll speak to my father about it," promised Princess Azalea.

"We're still establishing an Enchanters' Guild in Bansford," said Prince Rian. "And I doubt I need to tell you that my father is building in every safeguard imaginable to ensure that only those magic-users whose integrity is unquestionable have any position of influence within it."

"I'll leave it up to each of you what you choose to say or leave unsaid to your monarchs in relation to this matter," said Basil. "I know that most of you don't hold the reins in your kingdoms. This isn't intended to be a formal negotiation so much as a friendly opportunity to share information. And to be blunt, I thought we would deal better together than I might with counterparts not of my generation."

No one seemed to be either surprised or offended by Basil's plain speaking. Wren saw nods around the table, and was gratified by how seriously they were all taking her and Basil's theory.

"We can discuss the matter further once we've all had a chance to conduct our own inquiries closer to home," said King Justin, his piercing blue eyes scanning the group. "But I would certainly like to hear more of your theories, King Basil."

"Absolutely," agreed Basil. A smile suddenly broke through his habitually serious expression. "But give me a few months. I'm going to be a little distracted come tomorrow."

There were some chuckles from around the table, and Wren felt her neck heat in the most pleasant way. Her hand sought Basil's under the table, and he returned the pressure warmly.

The group began to break up, Prince Amell stopping to chat animatedly to Prince Bentleigh, and Zinnia wandering up to her brother and almost-sister-in-law. Wren noted that the princess still looked pale.

"Look at you, commanding a room full of royalty," she teased her brother, so lightly that Wren wondered if she'd imagined the strain on the other girl's face. Zinnia turned to Wren, quirking an eyebrow. "Don't let him get too big for his horse, Wren. You're allowed to get a word in occasionally, you know." She shuddered. "If I'd had to be silent for six years, I'd spend the next six talking constantly just to catch up."

"I don't doubt it," said Basil, smiling ruefully. She elbowed him gently in the ribs.

Wren just smiled, saying nothing. Her own brothers had also been surprised at her failure to revert to the chatterbox she'd been as a child. But as frustrating as her years of restraint had been, they hadn't left Wren with a burning desire to fill every silence with words. On the contrary, they'd taught her to appreciate the value of silence, and of all the ways of communicating that didn't involve speech. She hadn't felt the smallest need to jump in on Basil's speech to their gathered guests, convinced she'd been more useful as a quiet observer. She'd learned a lot from watching the reactions of the various royals while their focus was on her betrothed.

Princess Azalea claimed Zinnia's attention at that moment, and Queen Felicity moved to Wren's side.

"I was hoping I would get the chance to properly meet you before the wedding," she smiled. "We're so delighted for you and King Basil, and eager to celebrate the anniversary of the declaration of peace between our neighbors."

Wren returned the smile. "It seemed a fitting date for the wedding," she said. "Even if it's felt like a long wait at times."

She threw a glance at Caleb, standing nearby with his beautiful wife and leaning on his cane without a shadow of self-consciousness on his face. Anneliese glanced over at Wren and smiled, the expression softening into something secret and delightful as her gaze passed to Queen Felicity's bulging stomach. Wren couldn't help smiling herself. Anneliese wasn't far enough along to show like Queen Felicity, but she and Caleb had shared their news with the family already, and Wren couldn't be more delighted at the prospect of becoming an aunt.

Yes, she reflected, as difficult as the time apart from Basil had been, she wouldn't have traded the last year with her reunited family for anything. She could come to Entolia now with a light heart, knowing that each of her brothers was reestablished in the human world, and her parents had been given time to not only understand the mysteries behind Wren's behavior, but to move past them to a more genuine relationship with their daughter.

As slowly as the months had seemed to pass, it was still a little hard to believe it had been a year since the preliminary armistice was signed. The full negotiations about the new border had taken a little longer, of course, but the agreement reached seemed to have so far satisfied everyone. Certainly each kingdom gained plenty of iron and fire jasper under the new alignment. A year had passed, and it was still being mined on both sides of the border.

Remembering her manners, Wren returned her attention to the guest before her, catching Queen Felicity in the act of rubbing her stomach.

"It was particularly kind of you to come given your situation," Wren said, gesturing at the bulge hidden beneath the other woman's flowing gown.

Queen Felicity smiled. "It was well worth the trip. Although my family scolded me something fierce about making the journey this late in my pregnancy."

"They should have come with you," Wren said. "They would have been very welcome."

The young queen laughed. "No, thank you. The last thing they or I would want would be them fussing around me. My father and brother mean well, but the nurturing role doesn't come naturally to either of them."

Wren paused, not quite game to ask the obvious question. But Queen Felicity seemed to read her mind.

"My mother passed away when I was a small child," she explained softly. Her eyes grew a little distant, and her hand once again passed rhythmically over her extended belly. "I've been thinking about her a lot lately. It's a strange feeling, to be entering motherhood without my own mother at my back."

Wren felt a surge of sympathy for the other woman. She'd been thinking she would miss her mother once her family returned to Mistra, but that distance was nothing to the separation Queen Felicity faced.

"Do you have a picture of her?" Wren asked.

Queen Felicity returned to the present with a sigh. "I'm afraid not," she said, her voice cheerful again. "I didn't come from the nobility, you know. I don't believe her portrait was ever taken. She was very beautiful, though. I wish there was some way to—" She broke off mid-sentence, and Wren saw a sudden thought spark into life behind her eyes. Turning quickly, Queen Felicity addressed her husband, who was deep in conversation with Prince Rian.

"Justin! Can I borrow you for a minute?"

He made his way to them at once, concern lurking behind his regal expression as his eyes flicked to his wife's stomach. "Is everything all right?"

"Oh yes, it's fine," she said blithely. "I was just wondering if you have the mirror on you. I want to show it to Princess Wren."

"Felicity," muttered King Justin.

"Everyone knows about the mirror, Justin," said his wife patiently. "The rumor's been flying around Solstice for years."

"It's true," chimed in Prince Amell, as he sauntered past on his way to the door. King Justin sent a dark look after the carefree young prince, but with a sigh, he withdrew a hand mirror from an inner pocket of his cloak.

"He brings it when we're away from Albury, to allow us to keep up with what's going on at home," Felicity told Wren brightly.

"What do you want to show Princess Wren?" her husband demanded.

"I was saying I wish I had a picture of my mother," Felicity told him. "I don't know why I've never thought to use the mirror for that before." She turned to Wren. "I've never actually tried it, but from what Justin's told me, if you ask to see someone who's passed away, it just shows an image of their face at the age they last were, shrouded in a sort of fog."

It sounded a little disturbing to Wren, but the young queen was clearly excited, so she smiled encouragingly.

"Show me my mother," Felicity said to the mirror.

Its glassy surface shifted before Wren's fascinated gaze, but no shrouded face appeared. Instead it went suddenly blank, as if the reflective surface had been turned to stone. The solid gray faded away, and the mirror once again showed Queen Felicity's face. Except that face was now white and shocked.

The queen looked up slowly, her gaze locking with her husband's. Wren could only watch in bemusement as something silent and intense passed between them. Then King Justin's eyes widened suddenly in an incomprehensible realization of his own, and he bent over the mirror.

"Show me Aurelia." His voice came out even more gruff than usual.

Again, the mirror went oddly blank before returning to its

normal reflective state. Queen Felicity was actually shaking now, and the look on King Justin's face was beyond even Wren's skill to read.

"Excuse us," he said, looking at her with unfocused eyes.

And without another word, the two Alburians all but fled from the room.

"What was that about?" Basil asked, stepping up behind Wren and following the monarchs' exit with startled eyes.

"I'm not sure," Wren said. "That magic mirror of theirs wasn't working properly, and they sort of lost their calm over it."

"Strange," said Basil. "Maybe there's something important they need to follow at home that they're worried they'll miss now."

"Maybe," Wren mused, unconvinced.

"I don't much care to be honest," Basil said, a smile in his voice. "I have other things on my mind."

"Do you just?" Wren turned toward him, realizing everyone else had left while she was distracted, and they were alone in the room. It was a rare moment of privacy, free even from the hovering presence of Basil's guards. She snuck her arms up around his neck, pushing up on her toes to reach him as his hazel eyes burned into hers. "And what, do tell, could those other things be?"

Those same eyes drew Wren like a beacon the following day, as she finally began the long walk toward her future. She barely even noticed the crowd gathered on the grassy clifftop, her eyes fixed unwaveringly on Basil. He stood with his feet slightly apart and his hands clasped behind his back, a tall and steady figure against the backdrop of the surging ocean below and the cloudless sky above.

Her brothers stood to one side of Basil, lined up in a row, and Basil's twelve sisters stretched out from his other side. Her family was certainly growing.

No music attended her walk toward her groom, only the clear call of many conch shells, raised above the wind. There was something unearthly about the sound, but it was no less beautiful for it. Even the slightly unnerving presence of the two dragons, Rekavidur and Dannsair, didn't make Wren feel self-conscious. She knew royal weddings usually attracted the interest of at least a few dragons. There had been five at Caleb and Anneliese's. She was just grateful these particular ones no longer seemed to feel any need to smell her over.

Her gown flowed out behind her, simple and elegant rather than elaborate. There was a strong breeze on the clifftop, and the billowing folds of silk rose around Wren like white wings. Her rebellious hair had been tamed into a braided knot that she knew perfectly well wouldn't last the day. She no longer wore Caleb's ring around her neck, but at her throat gleamed another pendant of the same dull red, one golden thread woven across its surface. She'd insisted upon wearing a piece of fire jasper. Not out of any desire to benefit from the wealth that had led to so much greed and suffering. But as a reminder to all that her marriage to Basil wasn't just a sign of their devotion, but of an alliance that lifted their two kingdoms from a time of pain, deception, and bloodshed, a time to which they never wanted to return.

But even such weighty considerations fell away as she reached her groom, and he enveloped her hands in his warm ones. The only thing that mattered was Basil, and the future she would build with him, here in the land of her enemies, which had now become her home.

Basil squeezed her hands as the formal ceremony began, and her eyes traveled up to his. As their gazes held, Wren felt her mouth curve into a smile at the silent declaration in Basil's eyes. She returned the pressure, and marveled again at how much could be said without a single word.

But then, their love had never needed words to be understood.

NOTE FROM THE AUTHOR

Thank you for reading *Kingdom of Feathers*. I hope you enjoyed returning to the continent of Solstice! I would be so grateful if you would consider leaving a review on Amazon—it would really make a difference!

If you're wondering why Felicity and Justin were so rattled by what they saw in the mirror, or whether Amell will get his adventure at last, check out *Kingdom of Locks*, the next installment of the series. As always, more adventure, fantasy, mystery, and romance await.

Join up to my mailing list at deborahgracewhite.com to be kept up to date on new releases, specials, and giveaways, such as bonus chapters. You will also receive *Dragon's Sight*, an 8,000 word prequel to my first series *The Kyona Chronicles*, told from the perspective of the dragon Elddreki (who just happens to be Rekavidur's father).

Again, thanks for entering the world of *The Kingdom Tales*! I hope to see you back again.

Captive's Return (novella)
Legacy of the Curse
Downfall of the Curse
Downfall's Echo

The Kingdom Tales

Kingdom of Beauty: A Retelling of Beauty and the Beast
Kingdom of Slumber: A Retelling of Sleeping Beauty
Kingdom of Cinders: A Retelling of Cinderella
Kingdom of Feathers: A Retelling of The Wild Swans
Kingdom of Locks: A Retelling of Rapunzel
Kingdom of Dance: A Retelling of The Twelve Dancing
Princesses (coming 2022)

The Vazula Chronicles (coming 2022)

A Kingdom Submerged
A Kingdom Discovered
A Kingdom Threatened
A Kingdom Restored

ACKNOWLEDGMENTS

I'm so very grateful to all the people who helped make *Kingdom of Feathers* happen. Ray, you are the best husband and the best alpha listener, and I couldn't do this without you.

To my invaluable betas: Adrian, Mel W, Tamara, Mum, and Steph. Thanks for improving the story so much.

And the usual huge thanks to Dad for developmental and copy editing.

Thanks to Karri for the stunning cover, and to Becca for the beautifully drawn map.

To you, the reader, thank you for giving me the privilege of being an author.

And most importantly, to God, who bled to make His enemies His friends.

ABOUT THE AUTHOR

I've been a reader since I can remember, growing up on a wide range of books, from classic literature to light-hearted romps. The love of reading has traveled with me unchanged across multiple continents, and carried me from my own childhood all the way to having children of my own.

But if reading is like looking through a window into a magical and beautiful world, beginning to write my own stories was like discovering that I could open that window and climb right out into fantasyland.

I cannot believe how privileged I am to actually be living that childhood dream and publishing my own novels. I do so from my hometown of Adelaide, Australia, where I live with my husband and our three little ones.

I've never outgrown my love of young adult stories, so the genre of young adult fantasy was always going to be my niche. If you enjoy *The Kingdom Tales*, don't miss my finished YA fantasy series *The Kyona Chronicles*.

Feel free to email me at deborah@deborahgracewhite.com and introduce yourself! Or subscribe to my mailing list at deborahgracewhite.com for free giveaways, sales, and updates.